THE KNOWING

SARAH ELMORE

ISBN: 978-1-729-19843-8

Dedicated to my dad, Alfred David Williams...a true rebel, writer, and border-line genius. You always aspired to have your name published in a novel, and because of your lifelong dream and my own, I stopped at nothing to make this possible. The visual of you reading chapters of my book to Mom on your date nights will forever be embedded within my heart. Cancer took you from us too soon. R.I.P, Daddy. I hope I've made you proud.

Acknowledgments

My husband, Jared. My life would be empty, nonexistent, and completely boring without you. You are my hero in so many ways, love. I could not have accomplished this without your support or the daily homemade subs you made me when I'd forget to eat. The BEST husband EVER!

My mom, Nancy. Literally an angel on Earth. Your precious heart has helped me find the beauty in all things, both good and bad. I thank God every day for choosing you to be mine.

My kids, Aiden and Tyler. You are both my world. I love you infinity...squared.

Gene for being my brother, the quiet Leo in the family. I'm so incredibly proud of the man you are.

Crystal for being my muse, playmate, partner in crime, and for challenging me to write you a single chapter of a book for your Christmas present, because you believed that I could. Also for not stopping Jackson and Jayme from driving Jeff's rider lawnmower for four hours outside my writing window!

Paula, we've cried, laughed, suffered loss, and celebrated all aspects of our lives together. Our friendship is the true definition of fate. I couldn't imagine my world without you in it.

Liz (devoted soul sister), Baylie, Madison, and Regina, for hanging in there with me after I was diagnosed with Trigeminal Neuralgia and had to put the completion of my book on hold for several years. Your love and encouragement gave me the strength to push through to the finish.

Box, Fugus, Heidi, Ashley, Renee, and Heather, thank you all for your stellar mixology skills, and most importantly for your beautiful smiles and much needed laughs.

Rosemi Mederos, America's Editor, for your boundless patience, priceless direction, most stellar editing skills, and literally, your *words* of wisdom.

To Margery Walshaw. I believe we are subconsciously drawn to those we share similar souls with and knew from the moment we spoke, we shared an unspoken connection. I am grateful for your expertise in the publishing world, and more importantly, for your genuine desire to teach and help others succeed.

Ariel Perez for your amazing talent and assistance with *The Knowing* cover design.

Basker Dhandapani and Johannes Plenio for providing beautiful photos.

Special Thanks

I have always been a firm believer in that, "It takes a village." I am extremely blessed and grateful for the beautiful souls that have come into my life, who've not only supported my mission to help others, but also my own personal endeavors. Their belief in me has kept me moving towards my dreams at full speed ahead, and if accomplished, will allow me to continue paying it forward to those in need. I want to thank each one of you for possessing such enormous hearts. Without you, my audiobook wouldn't be possible. May each of your lives be rich with love and your worlds as beautiful as you are. Thank you!

Gene & Leslie Williams
Christel Tellbuescher
Dale Hall
Art Osborn
Loren and Brian Smith
Karen & Jeff Desfosse
Ann & Chris Banting
Jessica Sharp
Joyce Johnson-Bendowski
Rebecca James
Epris Blankenship

Ashley Clark
Erin Childers
Michelle K.
Mary Ann Mulligan
Melanie A. DeRossett
Cheryl Osborn Van Fleet
Brandi Lee
McCall Bennett-Lawrence

CONTENTS

PART ONE

PART TWO

PART ONE

Chapter One

S unday, February 2, 1997

CHARLES SCRAMBLED into the house to escape the thrashing rain. He removed his soaked black trench coat and placed it in the hall closet along with his briefcase. He moved toward the living room, combing his fingers through his thick black hair to shake the water from his drenched locks.

"Meredi—" He began to call out to his wife to let her know he was home but was distracted by the flickering oil lamp on the coffee table.

Charles had never come close to exhibiting a single trace of clairvoyance, but an abrupt and sickening intuition settled within his chest. His face, still damp from the rain, became hard and knowing as he approached the table where he saw an envelope addressed "Charles" resting against the lamp. Flashes of accelerated memories of his perfect life with Meredith and his son, Derek, played within his mind to the rhythm of every radical thump of his breaking heart. He ripped open the envelope.

SARAH ELMORE

My Dearest Charles,

Please know I love you and would never bring harm to you or our son. I warned you the unspoken law would force me to keep secrets from you, and I have done so to protect those I love.

When we opened Vista six years ago, I began keeping vision journals of all I saw to help organize the mangled riddles within my mind. The boy from my visions holding my father's antique dagger found them. He became privy to all I saw to come. Because I was careless, written paths began to shift. The boy and evil shadow are one in the same. I know that now. Find the dagger, reveal the monster.

I saw the outcome of every possible scenario to try and realign the natural order. Going to Lyle alone was the only way to prevent his wrath upon future victims and save those who'd be lost if he drowned the little girl.

She'll reveal his identity and his hideous inflictions upon my parents and his other innocent victims. She'll unknowingly become their voice. Unfortunately, his identity and truth weren't meant to be disclosed within mine or the woman from Baker's lifetime.

The woman from Baker's showed me a glimpse into his victims' and the little girl's future. Her existence plays a critical role in helping her family protect the chosen one. Millions will be saved.

My heart aches knowing we can't adopt the beautifully spirited little girl from Lyle Mountain 5.3.13 like we'd planned. We could've protected and loved her, shown her how to change the world through art.

Derek will also possess his own gifts one day. They'll lead him to my father and the woman at Baker's. It's then and only then you must stop him. My letter will guide him, but it's imperative he follow his own destined path to the little girl.

I've always known I'd go to Lyle without you. My time to save her has come. Shifting natural patterns was my mistake, so I alone will suffer the consequences. Please, Charles, heed my warning. Don't come for me. There's <u>nothing</u> you can do to bring me home. There never was.

Within our safe you'll find a new ID, passport, information on the bank account I transferred ten million dollars to, and a plane ticket.

There's also a sealed letter I've written to Derek. Give the letter to Quentin for safekeeping. However, he's only to give it to Derek when he's ready. You'll both be tempted to read it but cannot.

I won't be there to help you sift through the labyrinth of my own written words. You must find patience and allow yourself to follow your own path and Derek his, no matter how long it takes.

Tell Derek we love him, will always be with him, and that Vista is an important part of his life. Tell Fisher and those you trust I said thank you, then run!

I love you,
Meredith

P.S. In the end, they'll follow her tranquil path to the harrowing bloodstone.

THE LETTER FELL from his once strong hands until it settled upon the hardwood floor at his feet. His body began to tremble. He fell to his knees and placed his hands over his face in an attempt to not see what he knew was right in front of him. He began screaming, "Goddammit, Meredith. Why did you do this? No...please...God.... Why, Meredith?"

Charles was able to evade the scorching fire that tore through his mind long enough to know that Meredith was right. There would be nothing he could do to save her or change the natural pattern of what was meant to be. She was gone. Charles knew he was to follow Meredith's lead and mediocrity wasn't an option. His heart overpowered any logical thinking and told him to try and find his wife and save her.

Charles' rage for the monster who threatened to steal his life from him consumed every limb of his body. His violent roar shook the walls of the desolate home he knew he'd never share with his beautiful wife and son again.

Chapter Two

The lush green pines of Lyle Mountain swayed in the pale gray sky. Dusk was approaching, and Hank was already well on his way to becoming obliterated. Hank seemed to be more annoyed with Sheridan today than usual. Sheridan guessed it was because it was her birthday. She knew Hank could not stand the idea of her mother paying her even the slightest bit more attention than him. Hank's rampage tonight was fueled when Rhonda placed a home-made chocolate cake that held six candles onto the kitchen table in front of Sheridan.

Rhonda leaned down to her daughter's ear and whispered, "Happy Birthday, Sheridan."

Hank, in his drunken stupor, crawled out of his recliner and staggered over to where Sheridan was sitting. "Whoop-de-do, so it's your birthday. Somebody sound the goddamn alarms, it's Sheridan's birthday." He tilted his beer can above Sheridan's cake and poured intimidating droplets on each of the six lit candles to extinguish them.

Hank created what he thought were logical reasons to slap Sheridan around or demean her before executing his actual assault. He always warned Rhonda and Sheridan it was coming. The control Hank gained from Rhonda's and Sheridan's fear and their anticipation of the attack made him feel high, and mixed with alcohol, he felt invincible.

Today there was no warning. He drew his right arm above his head and thrust it down, backhanding Sheridan so forcefully she flew three feet away.

"Jesus, no! Hank, it's her birthday. Please, leave her be," Rhonda begged. "I'll take her to live with my sister in Kensington Manor, like you wanted, Hank. Please," Rhonda pleaded again, feeling defeated.

Hank, who towered over Sheridan, shifted his attention to Rhonda. "You're damn right you will, and you better not be lyin' to me this time, you stupid bitch. I don't want that bastard child in this house anymore," he said, pointing to Sheridan who was still lying limp on the floor but never taking his glare off of Rhonda. "This is your fault, you know? If you hadn't been such a whore, none of this would have happened," he growled.

Sheridan saw her mother's eyes glance to her and then to the back door. She took advantage of her mother's gift of distracting Hank, pulled her sluggish body up off the kitchen floor, and scurried out the back door.

SINCE SHERIDAN WAS FOUR, because of Hank's repetitious wrath upon her and her mom, she understood the need to be always prepared to leave the house if she had to. Next to the rusty shed in the backyard was an equally rusted old milk barrel in which she kept supplies hidden. It contained a jacket, galoshes, and a bag of unshelled peanuts.

The most precious item in the barrel, however, was Sheridan's doll, Becca. Sheridan could not remember who had given Becca to her, but she did know the fancy doll had been with her since she was born. Sheridan considered Becca to be her only true friend.

Becca's face was pale porcelain with rose-colored cheeks faded from the many kisses Sheridan had given her over the years. A golden necklace that held a tarnished skeleton key was sewn into the deep lavender velvet dress, layered with beautiful strands of antique white Victorian lace. Sheridan thought Becca's curly fiery red hair complemented the dress she wore. She kept Becca on top of the pile of supplies. If there were ever a time she could only grab one thing, she knew it would be her dearest friend. Sheridan was relentless in her efforts to keep Becca hidden from Hank. He had only gotten a hold of Becca once, and like he had done so many times to Sheridan, he hit Becca and left the doll with fractured porcelain lips.

Becca was the only thing Sheridan grabbed before she sprinted into the forest to hide from Hank. "C'mon, Becca, we have to hurry, Hank's really mad at me this time, but I promise I won't let him hurt cha."

ॐ

BECCA DANGLED from Sheridan's right hand as she dashed through the brush to escape Hank. She cringed with pain from the slicing sharp twigs that layered the earthy floor of the forest, now biting at her tiny bare feet.

A tree branch caught one of the straps of her dark blue overalls, slamming Sheridan to the ground and knocking the breath out of her. Becca was thrown into the foliage a few feet away from where Sheridan lay in a crippled fetal position.

Sheridan's head began to spin from the crack it had taken on a loose piece of solid mountain rock. Within seconds, a trickling stream of blood flowed out from under her hair. Her eyes fought to stay open as she reached out for her doll and whispered, "Becca." The moon's light vanished into darkness.

ॐ

SHERIDAN'S BODY lay limp and quiet in the stranger's arms. Her limbs swayed back and forth to the motion of his heavy steps. She was groggy and her head ached intensely, but she was aware she was being carried. She felt a hard sticky material over her eyes. The odd blindfold prevented her from opening her eyes, as if her lashes were glued shut. Sheridan knew something was not right and that the stranger carrying her was up to no good. Pure terror took over her reflexes. She was paralyzed with fear and couldn't attempt to struggle or make a single sound.

He felt the rippling movement of shock settle in Sheridan's bones then looked down at her and said, "Ah, there she is. I'm so glad you have decided to wake up and join me, Sheridan. Killing you would have been quite boring without your knowledge of it happening."

Tangled thoughts raced in her head, and she tried to understand who this bad man was. It wasn't Hank. She was sure of this because she'd felt Hank's wrath many times, heard his drunken slurred voice, and smelled the stench of beer or liquor that always occupied his breath.

This man smelled clean, spoke with an eloquent English accent, and felt much larger than Hank. She'd never known or met anyone who possessed this type of stylish mannerism.

His stride came to a sudden stop. He knelt down and rolled his little victim from his arms onto the damp ground next to the river's edge. "Sheridan, I want you to feel free to fight for your life. Of course, we both know that won't happen though, will it? You're not strong at all, are you, Sheridan? You've always been afraid to fight back, haven't you? What is it the kids say to you? Sheridan's scared again?" He inhaled through his nose, took a deep breath, closed his eyes for a long moment to remember, exhaled, and then confirmed, "Yes, that's it, and it is quite appropriate given your meager disposition.

"It would appear as though I will be doing you a huge favor by putting you out of your pathetic little misery, my dear. And speaking of pathetic, your stepfather Hank is quite the amateur, isn't he? He can't seriously think he could gain any real power or control from your fickle small mind, could he?"

His voice changed from steady and sophisticated to a low and rigid tone. "I'm not in the business of doing anyone any favors, you know? Especially you. Why shouldn't you have to endure a life of pain and suffering like the rest of us? However, under the circumstances, your death plays a significant role in protecting my secrets. I guess you can consider this your birthday present...from me...to you."

Sheridan listened to him talk in circles, not understanding the meaning behind his dark words. She laid on the river's edge still and silent, wishing Becca was with her. Sheridan hoped this stranger would be distracted by his own ramblings and forget she was even there.

"Your tardy savior couldn't have been right about you. Her visions are usually spot on, but your mental and physical appearance boggles me to no end. For her to see that you were ever worthy of being loved by anyone, let alone by someone who'll be gifted, is comical to me, quite hysterical, in fact. Well, that is neither here nor there. I'm not taking any chances." Without pause, the bad man took a handful of Sheridan's hair, dragged her into the river, and plunged her head under water several times until there was no breath left within her lungs.

He looked down at her lifeless little body and snickered with satisfying self-approval for accomplishing his mission to destroy her. He then took the heel of his shoe and shoved her into the river. Sheridan's motionless body floated in the water and drifted downriver.

"The clock is ticking...tick-tock, tick-tock, one down and one more clueless fortune teller to go." He walked away knowing that there would be no consequences for ending the defenseless child's life.

Chapter Three

A gasp of gurgled air escaped Sheridan's lungs. She began choking while trying to focus on her surroundings. The night air was sharp, and a haze of fog moved across the river, playing with Sheridan's obscured vision. The moon's reflection shimmered across the water like staggering pieces of gold, providing enough light to make out the familiar profile of the oaks that lined the river's edge.

"Sheridan, can you hear me? Honey, you have to look at me and listen to what I am saying. We don't have much time." Sheridan's eyes opened wide and were filled with terror. She began to wriggle to break free from what she thought were her predator's violent hands. She began wailing, "No! No! Let me go!"

Sheridan heard the voice of the person controlling her rabid movements say, "I am not going to hurt you, Sheridan. Please listen to me. I'm here to help you."

Sheridan's delicate little body became peaceful and relaxed when her eyes met the angel's. Her bewildered eyes stared at the illuminating glow projected from the outline of the angel's body. Even after the horrific encounter she'd been through, she couldn't resist the calm that draped over every inch of her being.

Once Sheridan relaxed, the angel brushed the soaked clumps of muddy hair from her face. "Sheridan, can you hear me?"

Sheridan answered in silence by blinking her long dark lashes and nodding.

"I know you're scared, but it's important that you listen to what I am saying so the bad man won't hurt you again."

Sheridan's body stiffened from the horrific memory of not being able to catch her breath under the dark water.

The angel whispered, "Shhh...shhh...it's okay. He won't be able to hurt you anymore if you do what I tell you. I am so sorry, Sheridan, but you can never tell anyone about me or what happened to you tonight. If you do, the bad man will come back and hurt you. Do you understand what I am saying? Can you keep these secrets?"

Sheridan, now shivering from the cold, provided the angel with another accepting nod. "I don't want him to hurt me anymore."

The angel's eyes became laced with tears as she cradled Sheridan's weak body and rocked her close. She pressed her cheek against Sheridan's and whispered, "I won't let him hurt you anymore, honey."

Sheridan lay mesmerized in the angel's arms for what seemed like an eternity but what had only been a matter of minutes. She had never seen her angel's face before but felt they had always been connected somehow. Sheridan reached up to the beautiful angel's face to touch it, to be sure she was real. Her skin was soft and warm but damp with tears. Sheridan caressed them away from the angel's cheek and said, "Don't cry, angel lady, I'm okay."

"I want to give you a present for your birthday, Sheridan." The angel pulled a gold necklace that held a small rugged amethyst stone from around her head and placed it around Sheridan's neck. "Happy birthday."

Sheridan lifted the stone dangling from the chain and placed it in the palm of her hand. "For me? I can keep it? It's pretty."

"Yes, you can keep it, but you must promise to keep it near you always. It will help you recognize the bad man before he can hurt you." Meredith's eyes grew serious. "You must always remember these words, Sheridan, always." She paused before speaking again to ensure she had

Sheridan's full attention. "Find the dagger, reveal the monster. Now, repeat what I said," she challenged.

"Find the da-dagger, reveal the monster."

"That's good, sweetie, that's good. You have to keep these words and the necklace a secret too. Can you do that?"

Sheridan didn't understand how the stone or scary words could help her see the bad man before he hurt her, but she agreed. "Uh-huh. I promise."

They rocked in silence for a while longer, both trying to embrace what little time they had left with one another.

"I don't want to leave you, but it is important that I do. I know you're hurt, but you have to be strong and find your way back home. You have to leave now, Sheridan. I promise I'll always be with you, right here." She placed her finger on Sheridan's heart.

Sheridan clenched her arms around the angel and refused to let her go. The angel pulled Sheridan away from her, met her eyes, and in a more stern voice demanded, "Go now, Sheridan, and don't look back."

Sheridan pushed herself away from the angel's arms and ran like wildfire through the forest. Against the angel's wishes, Sheridan paused to turn around one last time to see the beautiful angel who had saved her life, but she had already vanished. Her lips formed a slanted little smile, knowing her angel had and would always be with her.

MEREDITH'S black cotton knit newsboy hat mirrored the color of her attire, camouflaging her well within the blackness of the night. This was her intent. She held a solid gold dagger with an amethyst embedded within the hilt at her side. She positioned herself to hide behind a large Spanish oak only a few feet away from the blood-stained mountain rock Sheridan had slammed her head on earlier that night.

She knew her prey would be joining her any second now, and it was imperative she maintain her composure. She indulged in thoughts of how her son Derek and Sheridan would benefit from her death. She pictured how hurt Charles would be when he read the letter she'd left for him. Thinking about the emptiness and suffering her husband and son would endure was almost more than she could handle.

The pain on Meredith's face was now replaced with pure resentment for the man responsible for inflicting such dark destruction upon those she loved and those she never knew. She whispered to herself, "Come on, you son of a bitch, what the hell are you waiting for?"

"Well now, that's not nice to say about my mother, but you're right, she was a bitch," a dark voice said from behind her.

Meredith spun around and faced the masked man in the dark shadows. She lunged toward the sound of his voice and tried to drive the dagger into her prey's heart. He grabbed her wrist in midair, the dagger inches away from his chest.

"Trying to take my life before we're even properly introduced? That's not very polite now, is it? Didn't your mommy and daddy teach you any better?" he asked dryly.

She tried to jerk away from his hold to regain her position. He released her. "I must say, you are indeed much feistier than my last little victim."

Meredith charged at him again. "You bastard!"

He dodged her second attempt at killing him. "Ah...is somebody having a bad day? Well, it's only going to get worse, Meredith, I promise. Come on now, you can do it, come and get me," he taunted her.

She rushed him again. He stopped her cold with his fist crashing into her face. She yelped and her body smacked onto the ground. He jumped on top of her, straddled her legs, and held her wrists against the ground above her head.

"Really, Meredith? How stupid are you? Did you really think I wouldn't find out about her or that you would come after her once you realized I intended to kill her? I'm not even psychic and was still able to climb into your head through your own written words...so pathetic.

"You couldn't stop until you figured it all out, could you? Oh but that's right, you're a fucking saint, aren't you, Meredith? Always trying to save the world. What a joke.

"If you hadn't kept digging, I never would've found out she was a threat to me, and she'd still be alive. You're as much to blame as I am for Sheridan's death and the women I've punished, you know."

He began laughing. "You don't have a clue who I am, do you?" he asked, surprised she still hadn't figured out their connection in her visions.

"Well, let me enlighten you," he insisted, using his free hand to twist her face to meet his evil stare.

"Why don't you take the mask off, you coward, and let me see your disgusting face?" Meredith hissed.

"Now, do you think I'm that stupid? Oh no, Meredith, I'm not a coward. I know there are others like you who have visions. Like the poor sentient who led me to you. At least she tried to save my soul. I'll give her that," he mocked.

"Revealing my face would be my own death wish, and quite frankly, your death is the only one I'm concerned with at the moment. Look into my eyes, Meredith, you can do it," he taunted. "You wanted to know everything, didn't you?" She fought and resisted his grip. "I said, look into my eyes, bitch!" he roared now, leaving her no choice.

He took pleasure in the stream of tears rolling down her face. Meredith's head thrashed from side to side. "No...God...no!" she screamed in horror as she saw images of his brutal childhood and deranged past flash within her mind.

Convinced she'd seen everything, he released her face. "Ah...there it is. You see it now, don't you? Where was she when I needed saving, Meredith? Do you know that bitch looked right at me and smiled before I was left there...again?" he rambled.

"I-I didn't know," she wailed.

"And no one else will ever know now either. You thought killing me before I could destroy Sheridan would put what you call 'the natural pattern' back where it was meant to be, didn't you, you greedy bitch?" he growled.

"While I admit it took years to put the pieces of the puzzle from your journals and mind together, in the end, I discovered your morbid plan to slaughter me. All I had to do was show up a little earlier than I'd originally planned to kill Sheridan.

"Your elaborate plan to annihilate me failed you, and my secrets will now die with me. Sheridan is dead, your son Derek will never meet his true love, you will die, and your husband will take the fall for your murder and then take his own life."

Meredith began screaming beneath him while she tried to buck him off of her.

He taunted Meredith again, "Now that's the spirit I was looking for. Well, if nothing else, you must have some gratification knowing Derek will go on living. Although, he will suffer from the loss of his mommy and daddy," he implied, knowing she could sense her son's future emptiness. "I put one child out of their misery tonight, so it's only fair that one remain to carry on the pain and suffering, don't you think?"

Meredith was rattled by what she'd seen through his eyes but was able to find the strength to compose herself. *Nothing has changed. It's time*, she thought. She lifted her head up off the ground and spit into his hard, sarcastic face.

Her calm confidence threw him off guard. "Now, was that necessary?" he seethed.

She now taunted him, "Too bad you're not psychic. You would've seen it coming."

He crashed his forehead into hers and closed his lethal hands tight around her neck. Her legs kicked beneath him and she pulled at his arms to break free, but he was too strong. Her eyes grew wide with terror as she felt her lungs burning and her heart slowing. Her raw fear excited him, inspiring him to squeeze harder until she took her last breath.

Chapter Four

M

SHERIDAN YAWNED and rubbed her dark brown eyes as the early morning light began to spill into her bedroom. She cringed from pain when she grazed across the bruise Hank had stained her face with the day before. The throbbing wound on the back of Sheridan's head snapped her out of her haze. She heard footsteps approaching her door and panicked. She slid off her bed and scampered underneath it. She closed her eyes, scared the bad man was coming to get her again.

The door opened and within seconds her ankles were captured, and she was being dragged out from underneath the bed. "No! Don't hurt me! Don't hurt me!"

Rhonda knelt down on the floor to her daughter's level and tried to shake her daughter back into reality. "Sheridan!"

When Sheridan saw her mom, she leaped into her arms. Rhonda felt a flush of overwhelming guilt rise within her throat. "I'm so sorry Hank hurts you. I try so hard to protect you, but he's too strong, and he's never going to stop," Rhonda sobbed.

Rhonda held her daughter's chin in her hand and forced Sheridan to look into her eyes. "Do you know how much I love you?"

"Yes, mamma. I love you too."

"Do you trust me?"

"Yes, Ma'am."

"I can't protect you anymore, Sheridan. God knows I've tried. When I save enough money, I'm going to take you to live with Maggie. I don't know what else to do." Rhonda looked down at the floor, ashamed she had allowed Hank to physically and mentally abuse her child all these years. She knew she could not go back in time and change the past, but she could give Sheridan a better future.

"Who is Maggie, mamma?"

"She is your aunt. I haven't spoken to her since you were born," Rhonda confessed.

"Why not?"

"It's not important, darlin'."

"Are you gonna live there with me?"

"Yes, I'll live there too," Rhonda lied.

Rhonda brushed her fingers across the bruise Hank had left on Sheridan's face the night before. "It's all going to be okay, Sheridan. I promise."

Rhonda rose from the floor and wiped the tears from her face with the apron of her waitress uniform. "I have to go to work. Promise you'll do your best to stay clear of Hank."

"Okay, mamma."

Rhonda kissed Sheridan on the forehead and left for work. Sheridan pulled the necklace the angel had given her out from underneath her shirt and stared at the purple stone. "You have to keep my mamma safe too," she said out loud, as though the necklace could hear her wish.

Sheridan's moment of peace was interrupted when a new memory flooded her thoughts. "Becca! I left Becca." Sheridan bolted out of the house to find her friend.

SHERIDAN ALWAYS CAME to life when she entered the secret path that led her into the lush wilderness. She was fascinated by the endless and breathtaking colors that stained the bountiful trees and lavish wild-flowers throughout her wooded fortress. There was also the undying melody of tranquil sounds coming from the rippling creeks, petite waterfalls, and birds singing to their chicks.

Her entrance into the forest today, however, felt wrong and uneasy. Sheridan would try and pretend she wasn't scared long enough to find Becca and would then take her straight home. When Sheridan arrived where she last remembered having Becca, she weeded through several bushes that scratched her small hands in their hasty attempts to find Becca. She was not going to stop until she found her.

"Becca!" Sheridan screamed as she spotted the doll lying on the ground next to a patch of wild dwarf irises. "I knew I'd find you. I'm so sorry I left you," she said in a guilty voice as she smothered the doll in her arms and kissed her porcelain cheeks.

Sheridan's happy reunion with the doll ended when something caught her eye about twenty feet away from where she stood. She focused her eyes on a suspicious object lying just outside of a thick patch of tall cheatgrass. It was a fancy black boot. Sheridan gasped when she discovered it was attached to the foot of a woman lying within the patch of grass. Petrified, Sheridan turned and began running away.

She ran only a short distance then stopped. She stood still, almost frozen, and closed her eyes to balance her thoughts as the forest began spinning in circles around her. Something was beckoning her to see that the woman lying in the grass was her angel. After a few moments, Sheridan turned around and ran back.

Sheridan fell to the woman's side and began shaking her. "Angel lady, wake up, wake up. What's the matter? Please wake up." The purple glow that surrounded her beautiful angel last night was no longer there.

After many failed attempts to wake her angel, Sheridan curled up close to her cold body to keep it warm. She caressed her angel's face. She thought she heard someone whisper in her ear, "I love you."

"I love you too," she whispered back before her exhausted little body surrendered to the sleep she'd been fighting.

SHERIDAN WAS AWAKENED by the roaring blast of a gun. Following the blast, she heard faint voices coming towards her. She was startled by rustling leaves and twigs snapping only a few feet away from her behind three enormous loblolly pine trees. She stared at the trees, expecting someone to jump out from behind them. When she saw two pine cones fall to the ground from the trees, she dismissed the noise. The voices were still coming closer, and she knew she was running out of time to make a run for it. She looked down at her cold angel. A veil of sadness ripped through her heart at the thought of leaving her alone.

She gave her doll instructions, "Becca, I have to leave you here to protect our angel. I need you to stay with her and keep her warm for me. Okay? I'm sorr—" Sheridan was interrupted by another gun blast. She tucked Becca underneath one of her cold angel's arms and fled.

"I THINK I saw it run over there," Billy said as he ran to search for the deer he had shot at. Billy's rifle flew from his grip as he tripped over Meredith's corpse. When he looked over his shoulder to see what brought him to the ground, he started yelling, "Tommy, come quick, holy shit...there's a dead body over here!"

When Tommy saw Meredith's discolored body and the creepy doll in her arms, he began vomiting.

"What the fu—" Billy yelled when a tall man with a black trench coat draped over his arm darted out from behind the trees.

"Hey...you...stop!" Billy scrambled to find his rifle. He found the gun, pulled the scope to his eye, aimed at his target, who was running towards the thicket of the woods, and pulled the trigger.

"I got 'im!" Billy saw the man cringe and clutch the back of his left arm to hold it in place, still running deeper into the woods. Before Billy could take another shot, the man was gone.

"Wh-wh-who was that?" Tommy asked.

"How in the hell am I supposed to know who he was? I'm guessin' he's the son of a bitch who killed her." Billy pointed in Meredith's direction.

"We need to go get the Sheriff." Billy was shaking from the adrenaline running through him after shooting another human being.

"They're gonna know we was out here huntin' on the preservation."

"Jesus Christ, Tommy, who gives a shit? We can't leave her. We gotta go for help."

❦

DEPUTY FRANK LLOYD, the first responding officer on scene, met Sheriff Reed and Tennessee Bureau of Investigations Agent Richard Kelly just outside the perimeter of the taped off crime scene.

"What do you got for us, Frank?" Sheriff Reed asked.

Deputy Lloyd studied the polished agent and took a protective step in front of the crime scene entrance, waiting for Agent Kelly to present his credentials before he answered the Sheriff.

"It's all right, Frank. Agent Kelly and his team are from the TBI office and are here to assist us."

Agent Kelly raised a cocky brow and dangled his badge in front of the deputy. Deputy Lloyd shoved the crime scene log journal into Agent Kelly's hands for him to sign and turned his full attention back to the Sheriff.

"I was dispatched to the scene this mornin' after the Clemons boys called in via CB to report they'd found a dead body on Lyle. They waved me down on Cider Creek Road and led me to the victim's location. I checked the victim for vitals and didn't find any. I radioed dispatch to send backup, emergency medical personnel, the coroner, and you. After securin' and tapin' off the crime scene perimeter, I allowed our Medic JD on scene to assess the victim and confirm she didn't have any vitals. That's it, no one else has stepped foot onto the scene."

"Any word back from dispatch about the owner of the abandoned Jaguar Deputy Dyer found on Cider Creek Road?"

"All we know so far is the car is registered to a Charles and Meredith Young, and it wasn't reported stolen. Dyer's headed this way now with the driver's license they found in the car to see if it's our victim."

"Good work, Frank. Let me know when dispatch completes the background check and if they're able to find out the owner's current location. Be sure to send Dyer my way when he gets here. No one else gets through without my or Agent Kelly's authorization."

"Yes, sir."

"Who are these Clemons boys? Do they have first names?" Agent Kelly asked.

"Billy and Tommy Clemons are a couple of locals," the Sheriff answered. "I've known them since they was knee high to a grasshopper. They're decent boys who've never caused any kinda real trouble, with the exception of gettin' their hands smacked from time to time for huntin' on the preservation."

"I'll still need to question them," Agent Kelly insisted.

"I agree. Have at them. I'll catch up with them myself shortly." He then yelled over to Lloyd. "Make sure Billy and Tommy don't leave until I get a chance to talk to them," he ordered before walking to Meredith's body.

Sheriff Reed was serving his second term as Sheriff in Carter County, which had a total population of 2,597 and a department that had only been involved in one homicide in his eight years as Sheriff. He hovered over Meredith and studied her for a while.

"WHAT WERE you two boys doing up here on Lyle?" the Sheriff asked Billy and Tommy, eyeing them suspiciously.

Tommy looked up at the sky to avoid Sheriff Reed's stare. "We was fishin', Sheriff."

"I don't see any fishin' poles, boys, wanna try again?"

"Okay, okay. Tommy and I was huntin' deer. That's all though. I swear we didn't kill her. We just found her. We saw a man maybe six two, with short black hair, holdin' a black coat, runnin' away. That's the guy you need to be lookin' for."

"Which one of you boys shot him?"

"I did," Billy confirmed. "I'da killed that son of bitch too if I coulda got a second shot at him."

"I was gonna tackle him myself, but he took off too quick," Tommy offered.

"Bullshit, Tommy! You was too busy losin' your lunch and pissin' your panties to do anything," Billy bellowed.

"The truth's gonna set y'all free today, boys, but only because we have bigger fish to fry. Consider yourselves damn lucky. I swear by the good graces of God, though, if I so much as catch a single whiff of you back on this mountain, I'll throw both your asses in jail and lose the key. In fact, maybe I'll call your daddy. I'm sure ol' Clay would be more than happy to beat some sense into y'all—"

Deputy Dyer approached Sheriff Reed and handed him the wallet he found in the abandoned Jaguar. "Looks like we got a match on our victim."

"I reckon we do." Sheriff Reed stared at the woman's driver's license. He pulled a family picture out from the wallet and turned it around to show Billy and Tommy. "Do you boys recognize this man?"

"Holy shit, Sheriff, that's him, that's the asshole we saw runnin' into the woods," Billy confirmed.

"That's definitely him," Tommy followed.

"Looks like we have a prime suspect," the Sheriff announced. "You boys need to head on home. Don't wander off too far. We may need to ask you a few more questions over the next few days."

"Yes, sir," they agreed and left, passing Agent Kelly as he approached Sheriff Reed again.

Sheriff Reed pulled his two-way radio from his belt and put it to his mouth. "Dispatch, do we have the background check back on Charles and Meredith Young yet?"

"Hey there, Sheriff. It just came in. Meredith Hope Young, born in '65, age thirty-two, no criminal history. Her residence is located at 2145

Hill Crest Ave in West Village, New York. She is the founder of Vista House, a foster home for special needs children."

"And her husband?"

"Dr. Charles Young, born in '59, age thirty-eight. He's an obstetrician in Manhattan. He also has no criminal history."

"Do we know the husband's current location?"

"We called their home, but there was no answer. We also called Dr. Young's office, and his receptionist said he was at a physician's seminar in Chicago all week but was due to arrive back home on Sunday afternoon. He was supposed to be on call at the hospital for his partner Dr. Riley last night, but he never showed up or answered any pages.

"We called the airline, and they were able to confirm that the husband flew into Manhattan from Chicago yesterday afternoon and got right back on another flight later in the day and flew from Manhattan to Knoxville. He rented a 1996 Ford Bronco near the airport last night at 7:45 p.m. and has not been seen or heard from since."

"I'll need someone to book me a flight to New York." Agent Kelly pulled a business card from his wallet and handed it to Deputy Dyer. "Barney," he mocked, "I need you to call the New York Bureau of Investigations and tell Agent Dave Cabott I need a warrant to search the suspect's home in West Village. I used to work with him at the NBI before I was transferred to lovely Hicksville Tennessee, so getting a warrant should be fairly easy."

Deputy Dyer took a bold step toward Agent Kelly. "The name's Deputy Dwayne Dyer, asshole."

Sheriff Reed placed his hand on Deputy Dyer's chest to hold him back. "Now looky here, Agent Kelly. My deputies aren't secretaries. They're here to work with you, not for you. They've done most of the legwork up to this point, so I think it's best you make your own travel arrangements."

Agent Kelly shook his head, rolled his eyes, and strolled over to where one of the CSI agents was working.

Deputy Lloyd walked up to Sheriff Reed. "Sheriff, why can't one of us go to New York with Agent Kelly to investigate? It couldn't be any more obvious he can't stand small town cases. He admitted he was transferred from the NBI to TBI. I'm willin' to bet he didn't transfer willingly, which means he must have screwed up somewhere along the way. I don't trust him."

"Frank, we only have four deputies and myself coverin' Carter County. We don't have the manpower or the resources to do this alone. At least the TBI agreed to allow us to stay involved instead of takin' over the case altogether. We need to be patient and see what Agent Kelly comes back with from New York."

Deputy Lloyd shook his head with disgust and walked away. Even though the Sheriff was convinced it was Meredith's husband who killed her, he was even more puzzled now, staring at the family photo in Meredith's wallet, than he was when he first arrived at the scene. The family he saw looked happy and normal. *Why were they on Lyle Mountain of all places? And, what is the doll's sick role in all of this?*

The removal team zipped up the body bag and lifted Meredith into the hearse, closed the double black doors, and drove her away.

Chapter Five

C harles crushed his right fist into the dashboard of the Bronco, cracking the surface. "I'm so sorry, Meredith. I should have been with you. Jesus, I never got to say goodbye. Why didn't you tell me? I could've helped you. God, please forgive me," he wailed, as heartbreaking pictures of his wife holding the little girl and the doll in her arms flickered before his eyes.

Charles, who'd last slept on the flight to Knoxville the evening before, had been driving for more than nine hours to get back to New York after fleeing Carter County. He'd only stopped once to fill up the Bronco rental with gas and to control the bleeding from the gunshot wound in his arm. His gut twisted as random memories of Meredith rushed his tenuous thoughts.

He was twenty-seven and barely out of medical school. She was twenty-one and the VP of marketing for her parents' toy company. The first time his eyes found hers, she was carrying a box of donated toys for the children at Providence House, a women's abuse and rape crisis shelter. He'd been looking down at a patient's chart and ran into her. The box tumbled to the floor and he'd knelt down to help her pick it up. When their eyes met, it was like time stood still. In that moment he swore heaven had dropped an angel before him. He'd been so dumbfounded by her presence he let her walk away without saying a single word.

The following day he'd looked for her on every floor and department at Providence but to no avail. A few days later he was doing rounds and saw her in the nursery rocking a newborn. Anderson, a fellow volunteer at Providence, caught him staring at her from a distance. He told Charles Meredith was single, the newest member on the Board, and that she and her parents helped fund the project to reopen Providence. He found the courage to ask her out for a cup of coffee. She'd accepted, and from that moment on they were inseparable.

She'd known her purpose in life was to try and make a difference in the world. Her passion to give back opened his and so many others's eyes to what was important. Like her adoptive father, she'd been a ward of the state at Providence when it was an orphanage but was adopted at six. She donated her time and money to women and children all over New York. Paying forward the kindness and generosity her adoptive parents had shown her became her life mission.

And then ungodly tragedy fell upon her family. Meredith's adoptive mother was murdered and her father institutionalized after both he and Meredith witnessed her murder. The loss had been too much for Meredith, and she lost her way. She became withdrawn from those who loved her. Charles remembered how mortified Meredith was the first and last time she visited her father at Baker's. She'd found out her father had signed a durable power of attorney prior to being attacked, leaving all medical and financial decisions to be made on his behalf by their family attorney. Her father revoking her visiting privileges, however, was what broke her heart. He remembered her fleeing her father's room after the administrator informed her. Charles had run after her but lost her.

When he found her, she was in an unoccupied room sobbing. Her eyes were closed and it appeared as though she were comforting someone who wasn't there. The windows were shut, but a heavy breeze rolled in around her. Chills crawled up the back of his neck when her body rose from the floor and she slowly started spinning.

She'd screamed, "*Allumer la lumièire. Je vais les protéger*," which he'd later found out was French for "Ignite the light. I will protect them." A surge of energy burst through the air, breaking the fluorescent bulbs in the room. The combustion had been so powerful, Meredith was thrown back into him and they had fallen to the floor.

Charles hadn't understood what happened in the room that day but suspected Meredith had. That was the first night she'd had her first ferocious nightmare. For weeks, Charles was woken by her bloodcurdling screams. She'd been prescribed heavy doses of anti-anxiety medication to help her function and sleep, but they only masked her pain and panic, so he found himself cradling her in his arms until she would fall back asleep.

She became physically ill. He tried making her see a doctor and continue counseling, but she'd refused. After she fainted in the shower one morning, he didn't give her a choice and rushed her to the hospital. That's when they found out Meredith was expecting. Meredith finding out she was with child brought her back to Charles almost immediately. She agreed to continue counseling and wean off the anti-anxiety medication. She also began confiding in him about her obscure nightmares being more than dreams. She'd told him she was having premonitions of the man who'd attacked her family and could see and feel him torturing future victims but couldn't see his face.

She told him it started after seeing an apparition of a young woman at Baker's the day she visited her father. The woman showed her a glimpse of the future and gave her a choice to embrace or forsake the gifts of those called The Knowing. When she accepted, a light ignited within her. She was to guide and protect those born with spiritual gifts.

There were unspoken laws that forbid her to intentionally or unintentionally change one's written path based on what she was permitted to see. If she did, she risked triggering catastrophic consequences. Her visions were only to be used to guide and protect those gifted into the direction of their own righteous paths. She was no exception.

She'd warned him she'd be forced to keep secrets. If he couldn't love her unconditionally or accept her for who she'd become, he should leave and never look back. He remembered making her smile when he proposed to her during her tense confession. He told her if she was so special, she should've already known he loved her unconditionally and had from the first moment their eyes met. The memory of her accepting his proposal faded, and he was pulled back into the present.

Words from her letter now began dancing through his mind. He'd made several critical mistakes by going after his wife before giving the letter the attention it demanded. Because of the unspoken law, she'd planted hidden messages within the letter. Meredith must have seen he'd come after her even though she warned him, *"There's nothing you can do to bring me home. There never was."* She also must have known the hunters would see him at the scene and falsely identify him as her killer. He remembered her words, *"a new ID, passport, information on the bank I transferred ten million dollars to, and a plane ticket."*

There was much more within her letter he still couldn't see, but he knew the paths he chose moving forward would only be made when he understood what she intended him to see. Meredith was gone. Charles had to force himself to accept that because Derek was still alive and needed him. He passed a sign that read: 'Manhattan 26 miles'. Charles caught a second wind when he felt how close he was to seeing his son. It was time to call his brother.

❧

"COME ON, QUENTIN, CALL ME BACK," Charles mumbled under his breath as he paced back and forth in front of a payphone at a small gas station outside of Manhattan.

Charles lifted the receiver on the first ring and pulled it to his ear. "Quentin?" he answered guarded.

"Jesus, Charles, is that you? Why in the hell haven't you answered any of my calls or pages? Where have you and Meredith been? We've been trying to track both of you down since last night," he demanded.

"You have to listen to me. I don't have much time. Where is Derek?"

"Charles," Quentin now spoke tenderly, "as I said, we've been trying to track you and Meredith down to tell you that...Derek had some type of seizure last night and was admitted into St. Vincent's."

"Wh-What do you mean he's in the hospital? What caused the seizure?"

"He's going to be fine, Charles. Dr. Riley was able to rule out epilepsy from the negative results from the EEG tests and video monitoring this morning. After reviewing the first round of video footage, Derek showed signs of having psychogenic non-epileptic seizures. He said because PNES results from psychological trauma, he wanted to continue monitoring him until he could speak with you and Meredith."

Charles relaxed knowing Derek was being treated by Dr. Riley, his best friend and partner. He was confused by his diagnosis of PNES. Derek was a healthy and happy ten-year-old boy who had lived a sheltered life. The most traumatic thing that had ever happened to him was when his twelve-year-old cousin Brody accidentally shot him in his toe with a BB gun a few months back.

"Speaking of Riley," Quentin remembered, "I covered for you when he came to the hospital pissed last night and asked where you were. He said you were supposed to be on call for him. I told him that you got held over in Chicago, and he bought it."

"Thanks. Tell me what happened before and after you took him to the hospital," Charles commanded.

Quentin searched to find the words to describe what really happened without his brother thinking he was insane.

"Quentin? Answer me, goddamn it."

"Brody and Derek were running through the house last night playing cops and robbers. Around 8:50 p.m. Brody ran into my den screaming that something was wrong with Derek. I-I've seen the kids at Vista's psychic abilities but never anything like this."

"What did you see?"

"When I found him, he was out cold and..." Quentin paused, "he was...levitating above the floor."

"What?"

"I know it sounds crazy, believe me. I've tried a million times to convince myself it was my eyes playing tricks on me, but I can't. He was floating in midair. Brody saw it, too."

There was dead air on the line for a few seconds before Quentin began speaking again. "It was like he was dreaming while he hovered.

It sounded like he moaned, 'Sheridan's scared again.' When I went to grab him, he dropped into my arms. Lexus and I raced him to the hospital.

"Lexus drove while I held him in the backseat. He stopped breathing on the way there. After a few minutes of giving him CPR, he started gasping for air and spit up a mouthful of water, like he'd been... drowning. He whispered, 'Mamma' and then went under again. The boys were nowhere near water, Charles, I swear. I...I can't explain any of it."

"What else?"

"Lexus and the nurse said Derek woke up this morning for a few seconds, and as soon as his eyes closed again, they both heard him mumble 'I love you.' A short time later, he woke up again and began jerking around in his bed and screaming for you. Dr. Riley sedated him, but he's still monitoring his movements."

Charles knew everything Derek had experienced was connected to Meredith and her murder.

"Where are you, Charles? Where's Meredith?"

"I'm only half an hour away from the hospital," Charles struggled. "I can't explain it right now, but I need you to do something for me."

"Okay."

"I need you to page me and warn me if the authorities show up at the hospital or Derek's condition changes; use code 911. If they ask you where I am, tell them you haven't seen me since I dropped Derek off to you and Lexus last Friday," he said, then placed the phone on the receiver to avoid any further questions.

Chapter Six

"Dr. Young...Dr. Young...Charles!" Dr. Riley panted as he pushed a gurney and caught up to Charles, who was entering the ER. "I know you want to see Derek, but I assure you he's stable and resting. He's sedated, so he won't be awake until morning. We have multiple burn victims coming in from a fire that broke out at Providence House, and we don't have enough staff to treat them. We need your help. And by the way, you look like shit."

Dr. Riley nudged the gurney into Charles and gestured his head toward the entrance. Charles looked down at the burn victim laying on the gurney he and Dr. Riley were pushing. The man's face and body were disfigured from the fire that had melted his flesh, making him unrecognizable. The man's eyes were familiar to him. He knew without question it was his friend Fisher. Fisher was an old cook who volunteered regularly at Providence House with Meredith and Charles before Charles opened his own practice. Charles had played cards with him during their breaks, and had looked into those devilish card-playing eyes before.

Charles was determined to see Derek, but because he knew his son was stable, he couldn't justifiably turn his back on these victims or his colleagues. Charles pushed his own mental and physical pain aside and jumped into the middle of the chaos to try and help save as many lives as he could. He knew this was what Meredith would've wanted him to do.

☙

THE MOOD of St. Vincent Memorial Hospital was both triumphant and tragic. The hospital's staff worked diligently into the night trying to save who they could and comfort those who were not going to survive.

Dr. Riley walked toward the recovery room, pulled back the privacy curtain, and found Charles checking Fisher's vitals. "How's the patient doing?"

"Not good. Chapel Hill sent over one of their vascular surgeons to assist us. Said the blood flow to his right arm and leg were little to none, so he had to amputate. Said he did what he could, but he isn't hopeful he'll make it. He came out of surgery about an hour ago, and his anesthesia is starting to wear off. He keeps trying to tell me something, but I'm having a hard time making out what he's saying."

"All the victims have either been stabilized, gone to surgery, or were sent to the morgue. I think the ER staff can handle it from here. Why don't you go to the on-call room and get some rest before you go up and see Derek?"

"Meredith and I know him, you know," Charles said, still looking down at Fisher. "He doesn't have any family, so I am going to stay with him for a while and try to keep him comfortable."

"Suit yourself. Make sure you get some rest. I'm heading home. I'll see you in the morning," he said, then left them alone.

Charles couldn't understand how it was possible for Fisher to still be alive. Meredith had told him to tell Fisher thank you in the letter. *Why say thank you to Fisher? Why is he trying so hard to hold on? What's he trying to tell me?*

Fisher possessed psychic abilities, and it had been obvious when he'd first met him. Charles remembered Fisher teaching Meredith to speak to him without words. She would playfully help him cheat at Texas hold'em by revealing what cards Charles was holding in his hands. The memory of the sneaky pair brought a slight smile to his face.

Fisher began trying to speak to him again. "I...know...Meredith... my friend...help...you...me...chalet...hustle them," Fisher strained to say through his dry charred lips.

"Our chalet?" Charles whispered, shaking his head confused. *Is Meredith speaking through Fisher? Is she trying to tell me to go to our chalet to hide from the law?* He knew it was important to Fisher that he understood, so Charles tried to comfort him by acting as though he did. "Okay, Fish, okay, I got it. I understand," Charles lied. "Thank you, my friend."

Fisher's searching eyes instantly became calm and the tension in his remaining limbs relaxed when he felt his message was understood by Charles. "Hu-st-le...em..." were the last words Fisher whispered before the EKG machine flatlined.

Chapter Seven

I t was approaching 10:45 p.m. when Charles finally arrived to the pediatric ward. When he walked into Derek's room, he saw Quentin and his sister-in-law, Lexus, sleeping in chairs opposite each other at Derek's bedside. Charles laid his trench coat at the foot of Derek's bed as he rested his loving eyes on Derek, who was asleep. The picture before him sent a chill up his spine. Two more of Meredith's messages were now clear to him. *'Tell Fisher and those you trust I said thank you, then run!'* One ID, one passport, and one plane ticket. Derek was to be left behind and cared for by Quentin and Lexus.

Meredith was right. How could he possibly put Derek through the trauma of always being on the run? Meredith died fighting to protect Derek and Sheridan from the wickedness of the world, so if he did not let Derek go, her death would have been in vain. He became overwhelmed with the feeling of yet another loss in his life. A moan escaped his lips, waking Quentin and Lexus.

"Charles?" Quentin tried to focus his tired eyes on the tall figure at the foot of the bed.

Lexus rose from the chair and made her way to Charles and wrapped her arms around him, "Thank God you're okay," Lexus whispered. "Where's Meredith?"

Charles didn't have enough strength to answer her. "Charles, you look exhausted," Quentin said, then addressed Lexus. "Honey, would you mind getting Charles some coffee from the cafeteria?"

"The cafeteria's closed and has been for several hours, Quentin."

"They have snack and coffee machines." He reached in his pocket, pulled out a handful of change, and handed it to her.

Lexus turned to Charles. "How do you want your coffee?"

"Black is fine."

Lexus stood on the tip of her toes and kissed his forehead. "I'm glad you're home, Charles," she whispered and left the room.

❦

CHARLES WALKED to the window and opened it, allowing the cool night air to touch his face, hoping it would revive him.

"Are you okay?" Quentin asked.

"Yeah, I'm fine," Charles lied.

"Why did you want me to warn you with a 911 pager code if the authorities came here looking for you?"

"Meredith was murdered, Quentin, and they think I killed her." He fought the physical and mental exhaustion taking over his body.

"Murdered? What the hell are you talking about?"

"I'm saying she's gone, and she's not coming back."

"H-how?" Charles stood before his brother in a half-conscious state. Quentin grabbed Charles by the arms and shook him. "Answer me."

Charles growled and came to life when Quentin squeezed his wounded arm. Quentin pushed Charles' sleeve up revealing a bloody bandage wrapped around his brother's left arm. "What the hell happened to you?"

"I was shot."

"By who?"

It would be too dangerous to tell Quentin everything. "I didn't kill Meredith. When I came home from the conference in Chicago, Meredith wasn't there. She'd left a letter that indicated she might be in trouble, so I went after her to try and help her. I didn't know the exact location of where she was but knew she'd gone to Lyle Mountain. When I found her, she'd already been killed."

"By who?"

"I-I don't know."

"Was it the same person who shot you?"

"No. When I found Meredith, there were hunters in the woods. They saw me near her body and assumed I'd killed her. One of them took a shot at me."

"So why are you running from the law? Tell the authorities what happened."

"It is not that simple."

Charles knew there was no way the authorities would believe Meredith saw a vision of an evil shadow drowning a little girl and that, in an attempt to save the child, she was murdered. Meredith had gone to the NBI before the first victim in her visions was murdered and was labeled a crazy fortune teller.

"We can work this out. We can hire the best attorneys to prove your innocence. Mom and dad left us millions when they passed, God rest their souls. You've refused to spend a dime of it on anything other than humanitarian causes, but given the circumstances, I think your dilemma qualifies as a good cause, don't you?"

"Quentin, I need you and Lexus to do something for me."

"Yes. Anything."

"I need you to take care of Derek for me. He deserves to live a normal life, and he can't do that if he is running with me."

"Of course we'll take care of Derek. You know how much we adore him, and Brody already thinks of him as a brother. But I'm telling you, Charles, we can clear your name."

Charles pulled the letter Meredith had written for Derek from his back pocket and handed it to his brother. "She wrote this for Derek and told me to make you vow to never open it. Said you'd know when the right time was to give it to him. She also said Derek would possess psychic gifts of his own one day, and I think it's starting to happen. He'll need your guidance, Quentin, like the kids at Vista needed Meredith's."

"Jesus, are you crazy? Open the letter. It could be what clears your name for Christ's sake!"

"No. Promise me you'll never open this letter," he demanded.

"I promise," Quentin surrendered, overwhelmed. He paused before speaking again. "Where will you go?"

"Our chalet first to get this damn bullet out of my arm. After that, I don't know," he lied.

"Have Riley remove it. Jesus, he's your best friend and partner. He's probably still here." Quentin walked over to the phone to call Riley.

"No. I can't trust anyone."

"I'm trying to help you."

"I know, but I'm fine. The wound isn't fatal, and I've got the bleeding under control. Trust me, this is the least of my worries." He pulled his sleeve back over the bandage.

Quentin saw his brother was falling into a dark place, so he didn't push him anymore.

"I need to talk to my son alone," Charles insisted.

Quentin walked over to Charles and hugged him.

"I love you," Charles said, realizing it would likely be the last time he'd see his brother again. He looked at Quentin one last time, and whispered, "Thank you," as Quentin walked out the door.

CHARLES SAT on the bed and took one of his son's hands in his. He knew Derek was still under sedation, but this would be his last chance to tell his precious son how much he and Meredith loved him.

He sat silent for several minutes before he found the courage to say goodbye.

"Your mom and I love you, buddy," Charles began. "We'll always be with you, right here," he said, as he placed his free hand over Derek's heart.

"I have to leave you with your Uncle Quentin and Aunt Lexus. Your mom saw it was the right thing to do. They're going to take really good care of you, I promise," Charles said, finally allowing the tears he'd been holding back to freely roll down his face.

"You may be sad that Mom and I aren't here, and that's okay, but someday, the sadness will go away, and you'll find happiness, buddy. Your mom saw you'd have gifts. Don't be afraid of them, son. You were chosen to possess them, like your mom and the kids at Vista. One day, they'll allow you to help guide others within their own journeys, like she did."

Charles looked at his son one last time and tried to imprint the picture he saw of his peaceful son sleeping in his head. "I will always be with you, son. I love you." He leaned down and pressed his lips to Derek's cheek, closed his eyes tight, and said, "Goodbye."

Chapter Eight

T uesday, February 4, 1997

IT WAS JUST past 12:30 a.m., and I-87 was brutally dark and quiet, the traffic was close to nil. Charles' pager broke the silence in the Bronco. When he looked at it, he saw the numbers 911. Either the authorities had showed up at the hospital or Derek's condition had changed for the worse.

He was an hour and fifty minutes north of the hospital, going on thirty-one hours without sleep and a bullet still in his arm. He tried desperately to stay conscious long enough to reach the chalet, which was ten minutes away. He flipped the lid off a prescription bottle and popped another amphetamine he had taken from the narcotics room at the hospital to help him stay awake.

He pressed the gas pedal of the Bronco to the floor.

AGENT KELLY AND CATSKILL OFFICER MEDEROS drove down the

long dusty driveway to the chalet, the last lead they'd be working for the day. As they came around the last hidden corner, Agent Kelly spotted the Bronco Charles had rented in Knoxville.

"Gotcha," Agent Kelly mumbled under his breath, a smirk appearing on his face. He was about to get his suspect. When Agent Kelly heard sirens in the distance, he got out of the unit. He wanted Charles all to himself. He pulled his gun from its holster, placed it protectively in front of him, and crept toward the front door.

"Agent Kelly, backup is almost here. Hold tight."

Agent Kelly ignored Officer Mederos and was only fifteen feet away from the front entrance. Before he knew what hit him, Agent Kelly was being thrown back through the air. The explosion's sound was thunderous, and shards of glass and splintered wood flew from the chalet. Heavy smoke and raging fire seeped out of the empty window frames.

WHEN AGENT KELLY CAME TO, he couldn't hear and his vision was blurred. He tried making out what the paramedic above him was saying. He saw the forensics' team bagging evidence. *Case closed,* he thought, knowing Charles Young could have never survived the explosion. He hung his head over the side of the gurney and spit on the ground in disgust. "Good riddance," he rumbled beneath his breath, as the medics lifted him into the ambulance.

Chapter Nine

Carter County, TN and Greene County, NY Murder/Suicide Case Updates VOL. 54 – NO. 765 Carter, TN Wednesday, March 12, 1997 25 Cents

Murder/Suicide Cases—One Case Closed and One to Go
By Kathy Pritchett

O*n Monday, February 3, West Village New York resident and humanitarian Meredith Hope Young's lifeless body was discovered on Lyle Mountain by locals Billy and Tommy Clemons. Shortly after finding her body, they witnessed a man, identified as the victim's husband, Dr. Charles Young, fleeing the scene of the crime. Billy Clemons attempted to stop Young by shooting him with his .22 rifle, but the Carter County Sheriff's Office's prime suspect got away.*

Richard Kelly, the TBI agent assigned to assist Carter County Sheriff's Office in the murder investigation, tracked the prime suspect to a chalet owned by the Youngs in Catskill, NY. Within minutes of Agent Kelly's arrival, the chalet exploded, leaving him with minor injuries.

Catskill fire investigator reported the fire and explosion was caused by a

pilot light that filled the chalet with gas and ignited from inside the chalet. Greene County Fire Chief, Ronald Fuller, first engine on scene, confirmed Monday that based on his assessment and investigation, the fire was started deliberately.

Several pieces of human bone fragments were recovered and later confirmed to have come from inside the chalet where it was suspected Dr. Charles Young was hiding from authorities. Greene County Chief Medical Examiner, Greg Mills, couldn't determine cause or time of death due to extensive mutilation of the body during the explosion.

It was confirmed Friday by the Greene County DA's office that the bullet recovered from the Catskill scene was the bullet from Billy Clemons' rifle. The evidence placed Dr. Charles Young in the chalet, as well as the murder scene on Lyle Mountain where his wife was found murdered.

The Greene County DA's office ruled Dr. Charles Young's death a suicide and closed the case. DA Ronald Perkins had this to say, "The loss of both Meredith and Dr. Charles Young is considered a true tragedy. They were well known and loved throughout the state of New York for their humanitarian work and dedication to several charities. Our prayers and thoughts go out to their family and friends. We'll continue to offer any assistance we can to the Carter County DA's office in their ongoing murder investigation of Meredith Young."

Carter County DA's office has been slow to close their murder investigation due to lack of motive from Dr. Young and physical evidence collected from their murder scene. During a press conference yesterday, they released information confirming Meredith Young had transferred $10,000,000 from her and her husband's joint bank account in New York to a Swiss bank account two days before she was murdered.

Carter County DA's Office stated they feel confident their prime suspect, Dr. Young, is Meredith Young's murderer based on newly discovered motive and conclusive forensic evidence. During a press conference, Kelly stated they're tying up loose ends in their investigation, but based on definitive evidence, he expects they'll be closing Meredith Young's case by Friday.

"It's hard for people to wrap their minds around how someone could take another person's life, let alone their own. I still struggle with that same question every day in my career, but at the end of the day, residences of Carter County

and Catskills should rest a little easier knowing our prime suspect no longer poses a threat to society," Kelly said.

TBI Agent Richard Kelly is being honored by Greene County for his role and assistance in helping officials locate Dr. Young....

ॐ

WEDNESDAY, March 12, 1997

Sheriff Reed couldn't stomach reading the rest of the newspaper column. He crumbled it into a ball and threw it against the wall as Deputy Lloyd was walking into his office.

"What's eatin' you?"

Sheriff Reed picked up Meredith Young's case file from his desk and shoved it in front of Deputy Lloyd. "This case. Somethin' ain't right. We went after the wrong man. I'm tellin' you, I can feel it in my bones."

"Charles Young was the only suspect who made any sense. We dug into Meredith's past, and what happened to her parents ten years ago was crazy, but we all agreed her mamma's murder and her daddy being admitted to a nuthouse wasn't related. Too much time's past."

"Have a little respect, boy. What happened to Meredith and her parents back then doesn't give you the right to fun them folks."

Deputy Lloyd's brows came together. "I shouldn't have said nuthouse. I meant no disrespect. Christ, if anything, I feel awful about what happened at their toy factory. Losin' your parents at twenty-two is one thing, but Meredith saw her mamma brutally murdered. Not to mention seein' her mamma's killer cut her daddy's tongue and eyes out. Hell, she lost him too after he lost his mind."

"Can't imagine how she felt findin' out her daddy had given their family attorney durable power of attorney even before the attack. There wasn't a damn thing she could do about it either. I know it ain't possible, but it's almost like he knew what was gonna happen somehow and made arrangements to be sure she could get on with her life.

"At least he had the right mind to refuse her visitin' privileges after he was admitted to Baker's. No one should have to be reminded of that kinda brutality. And believe you me, I know exactly what it feels like to lose a parent that way," he said, remembering his own mother dying in a mental institution when he was thirteen.

Sheriff Reed shifted uncomfortably in his chair. He regretted their conversation had resurfaced such a bad time in Deputy Lloyd's life. It hadn't been his intention, so he redirected the conversation back to the case. "Can't say I wouldn't have gone crazy myself if I witnessed my own wife's murder. To be honest, I'm surprised Meredith didn't lose her mind too. Reckon that's why she sold her parents' toy company right after buryin' her mamma. Her daddy signed it over to her free and clear, but the records show she sold it for ten times less than it was worth.

"Anyway, the only thing the detective workin' her mamma's case told us that struck me odd was their twins disappearin' from the hospital right after they were born in '57. Said they were never found. They tried, but Mrs. Chancellor couldn't bear any more children after that. Reckon that's why they adopted Meredith fourteen years later.

"Beyond that, everything the detective found showed her parents were honest people who got dealt a tragic hand. It's a disgrace their case went cold and them folks didn't get the justice they deserved. Reckon that's why I owe it to Meredith to be sure we got the right man in her case."

Deputy Lloyd pulled his fingers through his hair. "The only possible suspect besides Charles Young who made any sense in Meredith's case was her mamma's killer."

"Yeah, but Meredith was there when her mamma was killed. If he wanted her dead, why wouldn't he have killed her that night too? Hell, even Meredith's statement said he never touched a hair on her head."

"Exactly, so what changed your mind about Charles Young?"

When Sheriff Reed didn't answer him right away, Deputy Lloyd picked up the file and began riffling through it to find something to help justify the Sheriff's instinct but couldn't. "It's all right here. You've got a ten million dollar motive for murder, two eyewitnesses who saw Charles Young fleeing the scene of the crime, the 1996 Ford Bronco Young rented in Knoxville found at the chalet in New York, and a bullet from Billy Clemons' rifle found at the Catskills crime scene. I don't think it could be any more obvious."

Sheriff Reed slammed his fist on his desk. "I thought Young was our guy too. I was sure of it. But, what about the key pieces of information Kelly and the DA's office chose to ignore? Like the millions of dollars and time they both donated to women's and children's shelters throughout the state of New York, all the folks they helped get approved to adopt their foster kids at Vista, which they themselves built and funded.

"And they were loaded well beyond the money she transferred to another bank, yet they both chose to live modest lives. Not to mention what we didn't find in our investigation. There were no enemies, no bad debt, no history of domestic violence, and no affairs. There was nothin'.

"Please help me understand, Frank, how the hell two upstandin' citizens who built their lives around helpin' people, who had no previous connection to Carter County, wind up on Lyle Mountain of all places? Why would Charles Young hang around the crime scene for almost ten hours after he murdered his wife? And finally, why in God's name would he make it a point to leave a creepy ass doll in her arms? It doesn't add up."

Sheriff Reed was planting the same doubt in Deputy Lloyd's head that had haunted him since realizing he'd named Charles Young as their prime suspect too quickly. He couldn't let it go because he was the one who had originally ordered the manhunt. If wrong, he'd be the one ultimately responsible for Charles taking his own life. Deputy Lloyd was a young rookie but had played a key role in Meredith's investigation. Sheriff Reed knew Frank didn't deserve to share the same questions suffocating his own thoughts, so he freed him of any doubt.

"You know, Frank, you're right," he offered, picking up the loose reports and placing them back into the file. "We have good evidence here. Forget what I said. It's been a really tough case for all of us, and I let the stress of it get to me. We'll tie up all the loose ends and eventually be able to close this case," he said as genuinely as he could manage.

After Deputy Lloyd left his office, he shut the door, leaned back in his chair, and tried to ignore the nagging thoughts that warned the case was far from being over.

SARAH ELMORE

Chapter Ten

Sheridan rested her chin upon her fist and laid her bruised cheek against the cool window of the beat up 1982 Plymouth Horizon. Thirteen hours had passed since fleeing Carter County, and Rhonda, still in shock and white-knuckling the steering wheel, had not spoken a single word. Sheridan wanted to take her mom's hand in hers to comfort her but feared the slightest sound or movement would make her snap.

For years, Hank had physically and mentally abused both Sheridan and Rhonda. They had become so conditioned to his habitual cruelty that they accepted it as a part of their lives. Hank's last rampage, however, was reckless. He had lost his mind. The horrific images of Hank trying to kill Sheridan held Rhonda's mind hostage.

The roaring sound of an oncoming semi's horn yanked Rhonda from her thoughts, and she lost control of the car. She tried to avoid smashing into the massive truck head-on, so she jerked the steering wheel hard to the right and crushed the brakes with both feet. The car flipped into the air, bounced hard on the ground, and rolled a second time. The roof's heavy metal scraped and slid across the asphalt before finally settling, leaving Rhonda and Sheridan dangling upside down. Rhonda's breath was knocked out of her from the impact of the steering wheel crashing into her chest. She looked over to her daughter to be sure she was alive. She saw small droplets of blood from a cut on Sheridan's forehead dripping onto the headliner of the car.

"Sheridan...Sheridan!" Rhonda pleaded as she fought with her seatbelt.

"Mamma," Sheridan cried out softly. The sound of her daughter's cracked voice calling out to her drove Rhonda to the edge of insanity. She stared at Sheridan as the horrid events from the previous day pulled her back in time.

WHEN RHONDA RETURNED home from work and pulled into the driveway, she heard Sheridan screaming inside the house. She rushed into the house and followed Sheridan's cries for help. When Rhonda entered the living room, she stopped cold in her tracks. The mortified gasp that slipped from her mouth went unnoticed by Hank and Sheridan. Hank was straddling Sheridan on the floor with a pillow over her face trying to suffocate her. Hank lifted the pillow from Sheridan's face long enough to crash his fist into her cheekbone to silence her.

"I told you to shut the hell up," Hank snarled.

It was the sight of Hank placing the pillow back over Sheridan's face that snapped Rhonda out of her shock. Crazed with adrenaline, she spotted Hank's baseball bat leaning against his recliner. She picked it up, drew it back as far as her arms would allow, and swung it into the back of Hank's head. The impact knocked Hank off of Sheridan and impaired him long enough for Rhonda to scoop Sheridan up in her arms before he pulled himself up off the floor.

Hank lunged at Rhonda and tackled her and Sheridan into a mirror on the wall, shattering it. Rhonda punched Hank twice in the mouth and stunned him, but within seconds, he threw her onto her back, placed his lethal hands around her throat, and began squeezing the life out of her. Her face was red and turning purple as she struggled for air.

Sheridan, who was coming out of a deep mental state, stood behind Hank and looked down into her mom's bulging eyes. Hank was not going to stop until he killed her. Sheridan jumped onto Hank's back, found his eyes, and gouged them with her sharp nails, refusing to loosen her hold. Hank had no other choice but to remove his hands from around Rhonda's neck.

Hank became even more enraged, drew his head back, threw his fists up in the air, and began roaring like a rabid animal. When he spun his head around to find Sheridan, she saw his disheveled hair, bleeding eyes and lip and swore she was looking into the eyes of Satan himself.

He jumped off of Rhonda and stormed back toward Sheridan, but the floor started shaking beneath his feet. Every light in the house began flickering on and off creating a strobe light effect in the darkness that was filling each room. Hanging pictures shook and made loud hammering noises. Knickknacks vibrated off their shelves and broke into pieces on the hardwood floor.

While Hank stood stupefied by the commotion, Rhonda grabbed onto the windowsill and pulled herself up. When she glanced out of a small slit in the curtain, she expected to see a tornado brewing outside. The sky was clear, pale blue, and laced with calm soft white clouds. The trees were hushed; not even a slight breeze blew through them.

Rhonda caught a glimpse of her car and remembered she'd left the keys in the ignition. In that moment, Rhonda decided she and Sheridan were going to have to make a run for it. She looked at Sheridan through the flickering lights and gestured her toward the door. Sheridan swallowed her fear, balanced herself, and began moving toward Rhonda, who was waiting for her at the door.

Rhonda saw Hank closing in on Sheridan and screamed, "Run, Sheridan, hurry, he's right behind you!"

The floor in front of Sheridan became stable, as though it was not connected to the rest of the house, and provided her a clear path to the door. In his last attempt to stop Sheridan, Hank dove into the air and landed only inches away from her. As Hank grabbed her foot, the solid oak couch accelerated across the floor. It slammed into him on its way to the other side of the room and pinned him against the wall. He was completely still in the vice that was crushing him.

"Mamma, do you hear him?" Sheridan asked, as she gazed up at the ceiling.

"Who?" Rhonda screamed.

"The boy, mamma. He is telling me to run."

"Yes, Sheridan, I hear him," Rhonda lied. "Do what he says. Run!"

Rhonda turned the doorknob, pulled the door open, and guided Sheridan in the direction of the car. "Hurry, Sheridan, get in the car."

"Yes, Ma'am," Sheridan said out of habit and rushed to the car and got in.

The old clunker started on the first try. Rhonda slammed on the gas pedal and screeched out of the driveway.

"MA'AM...MA'AM, CAN YOU HEAR ME?" the truck driver called out to Rhonda, who was still dangling upside down in the car.

Rhonda could hear sirens coming toward them. She began blinking as she returned to the present. She looked over to the passenger seat to find Sheridan, but she was gone. "Sheridan! Where's my daughter, Sheridan?"

"Ma'am, she's okay. She's right here," the truck driver assured her.

"Here I am, mamma." Sheridan dropped to her knees and bent down next to the driver's side window so that Rhonda could see her.

Rhonda began babbling. "I'm...I'm so sorry, Sheridan. I should've never let him hurt you. I should've left a long time ago. I...I didn't know how to leave. I was so scared. I'm so sorry, Sheridan, please forgive me." Rhonda wept uncontrollably.

"You busted his lip twice, mamma. I betcha that felt real good, huh?"

"Ye-yeah, it did feel good," Rhonda admitted, smiling between sobs at her daughter's amusement. "And what about you, little girl? I thought you were going to blind him for life."

Sheridan placed her fingertips over her mouth and giggled. Rhonda smiled at Sheridan. After everything they had been through, it was her six-year-old daughter who understood what they had accomplished. For the first time in their lives, they defended themselves from Hank. They had done it; they had escaped.

Chapter Eleven

T he rich tradition and history of Kensington Manor, Connecticut could be felt upon entering the prominent town. Elegant colonial homes sat on generous proportions of lush green land that spread six to ten acres between them. The landscaping was picturesque, and the gardens, sprinkled with an array of beautiful colors, were impeccable.

Sheridan, who was released from the emergency room with four stitches in her forehead, stepped out of the taxi in front of her aunt's colossal home and took in a breath of fresh air. She absorbed the beauty around her and thought of her secret fortress back on Lyle Mountain. The difference was that Kensington Manor's tranquility wasn't hidden and could be seen and felt by all who resided there.

Rhonda had no other choice but to ask her older sister for help. Maggie was the only family she had left. She prayed her sister would not turn them away again. She'd have to answer to Maggie for all of the lost years between them, but she was ready. Rhonda fussed over the outfit she'd bought for Sheridan. It was imperative that Sheridan be presentable to Maggie. She tried to brush the remaining wrinkles out of the flowing white cotton sundress she was wearing, and then stood back to view her. Still not happy, she pulled Sheridan's thick chestnut brown hair up into a long ponytail to reveal her amber brown almond-shaped eyes. Rhonda hesitantly reached for the doorbell and rang it.

They were greeted by Maggie's doorman, Jeffery. "Good afternoon, Mrs. Hayes." Maggie's ten-year-old son, Rodney, came bolting through the doorway.

"Mom, they're here!" He pulled Sheridan to him and hugged her. "You're my cousin Sheridan, huh?"

Sheridan smiled at her cousin Rodney's boisterous mood. The boys she knew were mean-spirited and rougher in appearance. Rhonda stared down at her nephew. *How did Rodney and Maggie know we'd be coming?* she wondered.

Jeffery saw her confusion. "We received a call from Dr. Moore after you were released from the hospital. Mrs. Thurston has been expecting you."

"I see," Rhonda said, relieved for a brief moment, until her sister Maggie stepped outside to greet them.

"Rhonda, is that you?" Maggie strained to recognize her little sister, whose tragic life had aged her over the last six years. "Dr. Moore told us you were in a car accident. Are you both okay?" Maggie looked them over, genuinely concerned for their well-being. She glanced at the bruises around Rhonda's neck and Sheridan's eye and guessed they were not a result of the car accident but did not vocalize her suspicion out loud.

"Ye-yes, we're fine Maggie, just a few scrapes and bruises," Rhonda said rushed, noticing her sister's observation of their war wounds from Hank. "Maggie, is there a place we can talk...in private?"

"Yes, of course, please, come in," she offered.

Sheridan was in awe of the extraordinary decor and towering structure of the contemporary home. As they stood in front of the sweeping circular stairway, Sheridan's head tilted all the way back to take in the full view of the two additional floors above her. Maggie saw Sheridan's fascination and used it as a ploy to buy some time to speak to Rhonda alone.

"Rodney, darling, why don't you take Sheridan on a tour of the house then to the kitchen and have Maria prepare her something to eat?"

Rodney grabbed Sheridan's hand and pulled her down the long hallway. When their voices could no longer be heard, Maggie gestured Rhonda into the library. Rhonda took in a deep breath to calm herself before she entered, knowing the moment she'd been dreading had arrived.

&.

AS THEY WALKED into the library, Rhonda's eyes were immediately drawn to the portrait of Maggie's late husband, James Wesley Thurston III. He was only forty-three when he lost his battle with lung cancer three years prior. James was a wealthy art broker who had carried on his family's business, as generations before him had. He'd never acted as though he were better than anyone else because of his wealth or prestigious status in the art world. He was a good man and had always shown Rhonda sincere kindness, even during his battle with cancer, she remembered, regretting not going to his funeral.

"She's beautiful," Maggie said, pulling Rhonda from her thoughts.

"What?"

"Sheridan is beautiful."

"Thank you."

Maggie sat behind the solid cherry oak desk that occupied the massive library and poured herself a glass of bourbon from a crystal decanter. She offered Rhonda to join her for a cocktail, but Rhonda declined.

"So, it's been over six years, Rhonda. What made you decide to talk to me after all this time? Wouldn't have anything to do with Hank, would it?" she accused.

"You must be thrilled to know you're right," Rhonda snapped. "How dare you sit behind that pretty little desk of yours and judge me?"

"Rhonda, I'm sorry, please forgive me for makin—"

"No, Maggie! Damn it, for once in your life, you are going to listen to me. I don't want to hear your psycho-babble bullshit or listen to your self-righteous advice about what's best for me or my daughter."

Maggie, an established psychologist, regretted the way she'd started the conversation. Her sister had every right to be angry.

"Have you really forgotten what happened, Maggie, or what led up to you forcing me to decide between you or my daughter?" Rhonda walked to an oversized window and turned her back to her sister. She closed her eyes and allowed herself to go back in time.

"Hank was my high school sweetheart. He used to always tell me we'd get married, have tons of kids, and even promised me a house with a white picket fence. Then I fell in love with William and broke Hank's heart. I'd fought my urge to give myself to William until I'd broken up with Hank. I wanted our first time together to be special because I knew our love was real and not some high-school romance.

"We snuck out and met by the river. William had a quilt laid out for us, wine, candles, and a bouquet of wild flowers he'd picked. It was perfect. It was his first time too, so we drank several glasses of wine to calm our nerves. We were tipsy, but he was still so gentle. Afterward, we drank more wine and lay under the stars holding each other without a care in the world.

"That was the last time my world was ever perfect," she said, trying hard to swallow the anger and shame rising to her throat. "We heard someone coming, and I got spooked. I didn't want anyone to catch us together because no one knew about William and me yet. I begged him to run in the opposite direction. He argued at first, because I was so drunk, but he finally did.

"I started running back to the house but could barely see anything in front of me and tripped. Everything was spinning. I saw a blurry figure standing over me. He threw some kind of cloth over my face and never said a word. He tore my clothes off and started groping at me. I heard him pulling his zipper down then felt something hard touching my inner thigh. When I realized what it was, I panicked, but I was so drunk I couldn't move. The last thing I remembered before passing out was feeling his heavy breath on my face while he took what he wanted.

"I was so ashamed," Rhonda confessed, placing both her hands over her face to mask her pain and silent tears. "I couldn't face William. The thought of him looking at me any other way than the last moments we shared together killed me. I managed to avoid him and everyone else for a couple weeks. I lied and told everyone I'd been sick. After a while, William became suspicious and came to the house. He let himself in when I didn't answer the door and found me in the bathroom getting sick, so he took me to see Doc.

"William was holding my hand when Doc came in the room and told me I was pregnant. I'll never forget how excited William looked when he thought the baby was his. Because we'd used a condom, I knew the baby wasn't his and panicked. With a cold straight face, I lied and told him I hadn't really been a virgin and that I'd been sleeping around with other boys. My God, I'll never forget the hurt in his eyes.

"Word traveled fast that I was pregnant when Doc let it slip one night after a few drinks at Dottie's. That's when Hank started coming around again. He told me he still loved me, said he'd marry me, and offered to take care of me and the baby. I couldn't believe he was willing to give everything up for me, especially after I'd hurt him.

"I knew it was a mistake the minute I agreed. I knew I didn't love him, but Mamma was gone and you were in Kensington, so I accepted Hank's offer. Not long after he moved in, I started showing. I could tell the sight of my stomach upset him. He started coming home drunk, calling me names, and pushing me around. Over time his pushing and name calling turned into hitting. Two weeks before Sheridan was born, I finally found the courage to leave him and came to you for help. I was barely eighteen, scared, beaten, and eight and a half months pregnant. I'd swallowed my pride and trusted you with my secret. You were my sister...I needed you."

Rhonda swiftly turned to face her sister and began pacing back and forth in front of the desk where Maggie was sitting. "It was you, Maggie, who drove me to that shelter in New York to deliver Sheridan so James and your precious reputations wouldn't be damaged by your young hillbilly sister. It was you who told me to leave her at Providence House after she was born, and I listened to you.

"For five days, my heart was torn to pieces over leaving her there, and I had a change of heart. It was you who threatened to never speak to me again or help me if I went back for her. Yes, Maggie, I chose my daughter over you, because even though she was created from rape, my blood still ran through her, and she was mine. You act like a victim because I haven't spoken to you in six years, but it was your ultimatum that tore us apart.

"After you turned me away, I didn't have a choice but to go back to Lyle Mountain. I was all alone with a new baby. Hank begged me for another chance and swore he'd never hit me again. I made a horrible mistake by trusting him and have always regretted that decision."

Rhonda placed her palms on the desk and glared into her sister's eyes. "I want the chance to make up for all the years of pain Sheridan had to endure because of my own fear and stupidity," she said embarrassed. "I'm swallowing my pride again for the sake of my daughter's future. This is why I'm here."

"May I speak now?" Maggie asked cautiously.

"I've said my piece."

"When you came to me for help and told me what happened, I was mortified. I'd gone to school for my art psychology degree to help people who had been through exactly what you had suffered. But you weren't just anyone, Rhonda, you were my sister. I thought if you gave up your baby, you would have a much better chance of starting a new life. I was only trying to help you."

"Help me?" Rhonda huffed.

"Please, hear me out," Maggie pleaded. "I was wrong, and I'm sorry. I never should have told you to give up your baby, regardless of the circumstances." She rose from her chair and walked over to her sister.

"What did you say?"

"I was wrong, Rhonda. You did the right thing by going back for Sheridan. Every unopened letter I sent to you over the years said that. Every time I called, I was trying to tell you I was sorry, but you would never stay on the phone long enough to listen to me. Just like you want to make up for your mistakes with Sheridan, I want to make up for my lost time and mistakes with you...and Sheridan."

Rhonda looked down at the floor ashamed. "When I went back for her, I had every intention of giving her a good life, you know? Instead, I allowed Hank to break her...break me," she said defeated.

"I will do everything I absolutely can to help you both," Maggie stressed.

"Before you agree to help her, it's only fair you know what your niece has been through. Helping her isn't going to be as easy as you might think. She's been through a lot. When Sheridan was four, I finally told Hank the truth about how she was conceived. He told me I deserved to be raped because I was nothing more than a two-bit whore with a bastard child. That's when he started abusing Sheridan too. I should have left right then, but after years of abuse and how he'd responded to me being raped, I believed it was my fault.

"Because I wasn't strong enough for the both of us, Sheridan found her own ways to cope. When she turned four, she started spending most of her time playing in the woods with Becca."

"Becca?"

"Becca was her doll and Sheridan's only friend."

"Besides her doll, what else does she like?"

"Since her birthday she's become obsessed with drawing angels. She draws them in the dirt, on windows, scrap paper...on everything." Rhonda riffled through her purse to find one of the pictures Sheridan had given her. When she found one, she handed it to Maggie.

Maggie studied the drawing. "This is beautiful, Rhonda. And I truly mean that," Maggie emphasized, flabbergasted by her niece's talent and detail. "Art was James' life on so many levels and what connected us. He taught me how to interpret art to better help me understand the psychological depth and emotion within my own patients' art, no matter what artistic method they use."

"What do you see in Sheridan's drawing?"

"Sheridan's angel is the face of love and hope. She has an exceptional gift, and we can use her raw talent and passion for drawing to help her heal."

Rhonda wanted so much to hold on to the calmness in that moment but knew she had to tell her sister everything. "She's been hearing voices too, or should I say, a little boy's voice." Rhonda placed the palms of her hands over her face. "My God, what have I done?"

"Children who are quiet or uncomfortable sharing their feelings often use imaginary friends as an outlet to express their own fears, which in return helps them build a sense of security and comfort. The fact that Sheridan is using her imaginary friend and drawings to express herself is healthy. I can help you both," Maggie stressed again.

"I can't stay, Maggie. I have to go back to Lyle Mountain."

"You can't go back. If you do, Hank will wind up beating you to death."

"Hank tried to...he tried to kill her, and it's my fault. I have to make this right by her," Rhonda said, plagued with guilt.

"This is not your fault. The blame needs to lie where it belongs, which is on Hank and the man who raped you. Don't let them continue to control you. You did the right thing by coming here and asking for help. The strength and courage it took for you to do that can never be taken away from you."

Rhonda wiped her tear-laced eyes and became rigid. "As God is my witness, that son of a bitch will never hurt Sheridan again," Rhonda hissed.

"You're going back to kill him, aren't you?"

Rhonda's eerie silence provided Maggie with the answer.

"As much as I would like to kill Hank myself, neither of us can take the law into our own hands, Rhonda. You will go to prison and Sheridan needs you. I know you don't believe that right now, but it is true...she needs you."

"If I don't, he will come after us and won't stop until he destroys us. I am so tired of being scared all of the time."

Maggie walked over to her sister and cupped Rhonda's chin in her hands. "Look at me. We'll make sure that son of a bitch pays for everything he has done to you and Sheridan, but we have to do it the right way. You don't have to do this alone."

"Could it really be that simple?"

"If you give me the chance, I promise I'll never allow him to hurt you or Sheridan again. Please, let me help you."

"Okay...okay...we'll do it your way," she agreed, allowing her faith and the love for her daughter to guide her decision to stay.

PART TWO

Chapter One

W*ednesday, April 24, 2013*

DEREK'S BREATHS became shallow and hard as he saw the same images that had haunted his dreams for the last sixteen years. The visions were painful and had come to him in the same sequence each time.

First was his mother rocking him as a baby and a mangled red-haired doll within the safety of her arms. He could hear his mother's heartbeat as she protectively held him to her chest.

Second was a little girl floating in a moonlit river face down, as a beautiful red rose drifted alongside her.

Third was a gold dagger with a chipped amethyst embedded within the hilt resting upon a large brown leather journal, showcased and locked within an opulent crystalline box.

Fourth was a blurry image of a heavenly angel. She was protecting several infants within the embrace of her wings, with a single child just outside her reach. He knew without question the angel was his mother.

Derek always became restless as the final visions in his dream surfaced. While he couldn't see her, he felt the little girl's paralyzed fear when the shadowy man placed a pillow over her face in an attempt to take the last breath from her lungs. An isolated door slowly revealed itself within the darkness of his mind. A rush of light spilled in around the silhouette of the little girl as she walked through an earthquake and into the warm embrace of freedom. Derek felt himself pulling back from his dream as he'd always done when he felt the little girl was safe.

From a distance, an echoed voice began calling his name over and over again. *Derek...Derek...* He was on the verge of waking when he was sucked back into a tunnel of heavy darkness. Beads of sweat formed on his forehead and a searing heat spread through his limbs. Unfamiliar strobe-like flashes and new visions of the little girl he'd not seen before began vibrating in and out of a silvery light.

Heavy rain fell from the unlit sky, making it difficult for him to see her. She was petrified and running for her life through clusters of trees that only revealed themselves when lightning filled the pitch black sky. When she reached what appeared to be a river's edge, she began screaming madly; she was terrified. A golden light began peeking through the clouds, and he felt her mind slipping away somehow. She was in a shallow puddle balled up in a fetal position. *Get up. Run!* Derek roared within his mind. *Stay with me.*

Derek saw the shadow of her predator approaching from behind her. He kneeled to the ground, grabbed her lifeless arm, and pulled her over onto her back to face him. Lightning bolts cracked through the sky as her predator thrust the back of his hand into her cheek. The man hastily crawled on top of the little girl and straddled her. She closed her eyes and lay still beneath him. He lifted the white drenched sundress she was wearing and slowly began to slide it up her thigh. Derek felt her suffering; he was losing her. His eyes rolled behind his closed lids, and his back arched as though someone had just sliced into him with a jagged knife. "God, no!" Derek roared out into the darkness.

Derek tried hard to focus through the madness he felt for the man who was hurting her. He intended to take her innocence. *I have to stop him. Why can't you hear me? Run,* he roared. Lightning cracked again, providing enough light for Derek to make out a sign in the river that read *Lyle Mountain Preservation NO TRESPASSING*. Everything within Derek's mind came to an abrupt halt. He could no longer feel or see her. The little girl he'd seen walk into a euphoric light a million times before within his dreams was pulled back into the darkness. She was no longer free; he'd lost her.

❧

DEREK COULD HEAR his name being called again. His eyes flew open, but his focus was blurry. He saw a large shadowy figure standing over him. He thrust himself up from his bed, grabbed the figure's throat, and began squeezing.

"Derek, it's me. Stop! Derek!"

Derek focused in on his prey and released his victim when he realized it was his cousin Brody.

"What the fuck is wrong with you, man?" Brody shouted.

"Shit...Brody, I'm sorry."

"Are you okay?"

Derek sat slumped on the edge of his bed. He pulled his thick, brown, disheveled hair through his fingers in an attempt to pull himself back into reality. "Yeah, I am fine," Derek lied.

"That one seemed pretty intense. It was about the little girl, wasn't it?"

"Yeah, it was."

Derek walked over to the window and pulled up the shades. He squinted as the sun rolled into his room, stinging his hazel green eyes.

"What time is it?"

"Nine fifteen," Brody answered.

"I was supposed to meet Anderson for breakfast to talk about staffing house parents for Vista and funding plans for more houses." Derek found a pair of faded blue jeans on the hardwood floor and pulled them over his black boxer briefs. He placed his hands on each side of the window frame in front of him and stared out at the view of the Hudson River from his twelfth floor New York condo. The water reminded him of the little girl again.

Derek was six feet tall with a solid masculine build and looks that had already melted and broken the hearts of many women. He was a philanthropist and had started profiling crimes for his cousin. He was admired by many; some even envied him. At twenty-six, Derek appeared to have it all. Brody knew better. He knew Derek would give it all up if he could bring his parents back or find a single glimpse of closure to the mystery behind the events that led to their deaths.

Brody was twelve when he witnessed all hell break loose in his ten-year-old cousin's life. It was his aunt's and uncle's tragic deaths and his cousin's childhood pain that influenced Brody's career at the New York Bureau of Investigations. He wanted to give Derek closure about his parents. But every lead turned cold.

"Cut that shit out, Brody," Derek demanded, breaking the silence.

"Cut what out?"

"Seriously, Brody? Feeling sorry for me isn't going to help either one of us."

"It's frustrating for me not to understand all of this psychic shit, your dreams, or be able to jump inside your head, instead of you always being in mine."

Derek turned to face his cousin. "You're frustrated? I've spent the last two and a half months trying to help you solve cold cases. I reopened Vista House and am building and staffing more foster homes for kids with special abilities. Yet for some reason, I can't even solve the mysteries of my own fucking life. What's the point of my gifts resurfacing after all these years if I can't even use them for my own benefit?"

With the exception of the recurring dreams of his mother and the mysterious little girl, he hadn't had a single vision of anyone or anything since his parents' deaths until two and a half months ago. Not knowing why they died consumed him, and he refused to stop until he found the truth.

Derek locked in on the picture of his parents framed in black marble sitting on the stone mantel of the bedroom's gas fireplace. "I've tried so many times to see what really happened the night my mother was murdered, but I see nothing. I can't prove it, but I can feel it within my entire core; my father didn't kill my mother. Why can't I see them or what really happened?" Derek lashed out, focusing on the picture. The frame began to vibrate and clatter. It lifted and levitated above the dresser. Brody ducked as the frame took flight across the room. The frame cracked when it hit the wall on the opposite side of the room.

"Well, that's new," Brody said, shaken.

"Fuck you."

"What about the little girl? What did you see this time?"

"She was so...scared."

"What did you see?" Brody asked again.

"He was trying to rape her," Derek struggled to get out. "I saw a sign in the river that said Lyle Mountain Preservation, No Trespassing. The little girl was on Lyle Mountain. The sign was at the river where she was being attacked and where my mother was killed. They have to be connected somehow," Derek insisted.

"I know it makes no sense. After all these years she's never aged, and I can't see her face. I can't explain why her and my mother haunted me in the same dream, but this new vision tells me they're connected. There were times I questioned if she was real, but I can feel her. She's in trouble."

Brody had made a vow to Derek years ago to help him find the little girl, or at the very least, help him understand her entity. But, because of so many dead-end leads, Brody had also doubted the little girl was real and had given up. Illusion or not, her existence affected every part of his cousin's being. He'd claimed the role of her protector since the first time she'd entered his eccentric universe all those years ago, and nothing was going to change that. "We'll find her, Derek," Brody assured.

The sound of Brody's cell phone ringing broke the tension in the room. Brody didn't answer at first. "Answer it," Derek insisted.

"Agent Young," he answered. "Yeah, I'm on my way," Brody informed, then hung up. "Just got a lead on the Midtown Butcher cold case you've been helping me with. That's actually why I'd stopped by to see you."

"We're done here." He walked over to the dresser and pulled a plain white T-shirt out of the drawer and pulled it over his head. He sat back on the edge of his bed and pulled his black boots on. "Which victim and where are we going?" Derek asked.

"Clara Ramsey, Manhattan. What about your meeting with Anderson?"

"I can hook up with him later. He's psychic. He knew I wouldn't make it anyway," Derek said, trying to lighten the heaviness in the room.

"You cool?"

"I'm good. The sooner we follow up on the Ramsey lead, the sooner I can plan a trip to Lyle Mountain."

"You read my mind," Brody confessed.

Chapter Two

Rhonda stood outside the doorway of Sheridan's art studio not wanting to disturb her daughter as she watched her paint with intensity. An illuminating soft glow fell around Sheridan. Rhonda visualized her as one of the breathtaking angels she painted. Each stroke she made bled into the canvas and was done with passion and precision. The casual tank top she wore was stained with exquisite colors from her current work in progress and complemented her delicate, curvy figure. Her thick chestnut hair was pulled back with a purple bandana, exposing her flawless porcelain face. Her cheeks were a natural blush pink, as were her full lips.

As she continued to watch Sheridan, she thought about how Maggie had been right about so many things. She would've missed out on seeing Sheridan blossom into a beautiful young woman if she'd gone back to Lyle Mountain to kill Hank. It would be her serving a prison sentence instead of Hank, who'd received fifteen years for attempted murder. Hank's prosecution had been a grueling and painful process, but in the end, he was convicted. A cold shiver climbed Rhonda's spine as she remembered the call they'd gotten last year informing them Hank was being released from prison.

She placed her right palm over her heart and felt a twinge of guilt rising in her chest. The first six years of her daughter's life had been hell on earth, and Rhonda still blamed herself. At twenty-two, Sheridan was a struggling artist and worked part-time at her mom's diner. Her passion, however, was volunteering her time teaching art to children at Maggie's counseling center. Sheridan had perfected veiling her past, but Rhonda wasn't naive. There was so much missing from her daughter's life—love, trust, and any kind of life outside her immediate world in Kensington.

Rhonda understood why Sheridan had built protective walls around her world. Rhonda had played a huge role in Hank's conviction, but she herself had refused to face or address being raped all those years ago. It was easier to pretend it never happened rather than have to feel the horrific shame or be forced to face evil. Like Sheridan, Rhonda had chosen to embrace what happiness they did have and thanked God every day for their second chance in life. They may not have been perfect, but they were alive and Rhonda was grateful.

Rhonda jumped when a figure from behind her placed his palm on her shoulder and whispered her name.

"YOU SCARED ME, RODNEY," Rhonda hissed.

Rodney giggled. "Sorry, Auntie Rhonda," he whispered.

"You know I can hear you two, right?" Sheridan asked, not taking her eyes off the canvas in front of her.

"Sorry, Mona Lisa, but I've got news, big news." Rodney walked over to his cousin with pep in his step. Before he could reach her, Sheridan hastily covered the painting she'd been working on with a tarp.

"What do we have here?" Rodney asked as he lifted the corner of the sheet to steal a peek.

Sheridan laughed and smacked his hand. "Oh no you don't, Rodney Allen! You'll have to wait until it's finished like everyone else. You know the rules, mister."

She'd been intrigued by Rodney from the first day they'd arrived in Kensington Manor, knew he was special, and always felt alive when she was with him. His young handsome face hadn't changed, nor had his buoyant personality. He was the only person she'd ever confided in or trusted when they were growing up. When she was eleven, she transitioned from sketch drawings to canvas paintings. He'd been the only person ever allowed to see her first canvas painting, which was of her childhood doll, Becca.

Rodney turned to face Sheridan. "Well...you did it. You got your first art exhibition at the Museum of Modern Art in New York."

"I-I don't understand. MoMA? Why would they host an exhibition for me?"

"Every year MoMA's Board members submit work from emerging artists in the tri-state area to the museum's art director. The director chooses one emerging artist to feature and reveal on the night of the event. It's five hundred dollars a head. The proceeds go to the museum's non-profit art foundation and an elected charity. It's a modern-day ball, attire is formal and by invitation only."

"Okay..." she probed.

"It's called the Unmasked Charity Ball. You're the emerging artist they chose to reveal and feature this year. There will be a silent auction held for your work. One hundred percent of the proceeds from your work will go to your own elected charity, which is a small price to pay for having your work exposed in this type of medium. Only the most prestigious art collectors and critics will be attending. They've been marketing this event for two months. It's a really big deal."

"I love that you're my art agent and you know I'm all about giving back, and I will, but you promised to allow my work to be discovered on its own," she reprimanded.

When Rodney took over his father's art brokerage business last year, he and Maggie insisted she allow them to help her become discovered through their strong connections in the art world, but she'd refused. She wanted to build her own career, just as her mother had. Rhonda had agreed to live with Maggie and Rodney all those years ago, but she'd also insisted on paying her own way. She had taken out a second mortgage on their house on Lyle and saved enough money to open her own small diner. Sheridan was moved and inspired by her mother's work ethic and perseverance and wanted to follow her lead.

She refused to have her career in art handed to her, so she made her aunt and cousin promise to respect her wishes and allow her work to be discovered on its own.

"I promise, my mother and I didn't call in any favors."

"Then how did they get my work?"

"You can actually thank your mom for her famous key lime pie."

"My pie?" Rhonda asked.

Sheridan looked at her mother. "Mamma?"

"A private art collector and Board member at MoMA frequently passes through Kensington. He always stops at your mom's diner for pie and has purchased a few of your paintings over the years. Anyway, your mom gave him my business card, and he submitted your work to the art director at MoMA. They called me about three months ago and asked for more examples of your work. I sent them your portfolio. Your talent is what got you this opportunity, not me."

Sheridan addressed Rhonda. "Why didn't you tell me, Mamma?"

"A lot of people buy your paintings from the diner, honey. I give every last one of them Rodney's card in case they want to buy more. I bet it was the man who stops in two or three times a year," Rhonda guessed. "Always buys one of your paintings when he comes through. In fact, he bought four about three and a half months ago. Always goes on and on about his love for my key lime pie too," Rhonda said, allowing a tinge of pride to form on her face.

"Oh, he's buying more than four, Auntie Rhonda. After he saw Sheridan's portfolio, he said he wants to purchase her five-piece angel collection too."

Sheridan became suspicious. "But, my angel collection wasn't in my portfolio."

"I mentioned it to him. He said after seeing and purchasing your other work over the years, he wanted first dibs. I told him I'd have to talk to you first, but he was more than welcome to put down a deposit, and he did." Rodney pointed his thumbs backward at himself. "Who's the best art agent ever? This guy."

"What's his name?" Sheridan asked.

"Oh, I know his name, honey, because it's on the big fat check he signed." He pulled out a check from the inner pocket of his designer suit and handed it to Sheridan. "His name is Dr. Duncan Riley."

"This is...this is for two hundred and fifty thousand dollars, Rodney," Sheridan stuttered and became faint.

"Yes, lovey, it is. And remember, it's only a deposit," Rodney squealed. "I did insist he let us reveal the angel collection as the main attraction at the ball though, and he agreed."

Sheridan struggled to not black out where she stood. She'd waited so long for this day to come.

"Wh-When is the show?" Sheridan asked.

"Nine days. How freaking excited are you, Mona Lisa, or should I say, Cinder–freaking–rella?" Rodney teased.

"Nine days? I-I'm lost," Sheridan confessed.

"There's no need for you to worry. This is my specialty. They chose twenty-five pieces from your portfolio to exhibit and auction, not including the five-piece angel collection. We'll fly in to New York a few days before the ball to be sure the paintings are received.

"The art director is meeting with us next Tuesday to go over the details, so you know what to expect. Food, music, lighting, art staging, ambiance, press, et cetera. Your schedule is going to be tight. We'll have to shop for your gown and get you ready for your big night."

Sheridan became uneasy. "What do you mean, get me ready?" Since they'd been kids, Rodney had taken every opportunity he could to doll her up, and she wasn't having it.

"This is the big break you've been waiting for, and it's a formal event. You're going to have to bite the damn bullet and set your blue jeans and T-shirts aside for one night. I kept my end of the bargain and let your art be discovered on its own, and as your agent, I refuse to let you show up at your first exhibition looking like Pippy Longstocking. Consider me your fairy godmother."

"Fine."

"I'm so proud of you, honey," Rhonda said, choked with emotion. She embraced Sheridan and whispered in her ear, "You did it, darlin'."

"No, mamma, we did it," Sheridan whispered.

Chapter Three

rody and Derek tried to find their way down the dimly lit and narrow hallway. They both cupped their faces to avoid the stench coming from rotten garbage and bums sprawled out on the floors around every turn. Brody wiped his right hand on his pants after knocking three times on the grungy apartment door, but no one answered. They could hear a loud television inside, so Derek rapped on the door again.

The door finally cracked open as much as the latched chain lock would allow. Peeking through the opening was a little girl with long red curly hair and a filthy face.

"Is your mommy home?" Brody asked softly. She said nothing. "How about your daddy?" The little girl stared up at Brody and Derek.

"Who the hell is it?" a voice screamed from inside.

"NBI, ma'am. I'm here to ask you a few questions about your mother."

They both heard angry footsteps approaching the door. "Jesus... move!" the woman yelled, shoving the little girl out of her way.

"Oh, we've got a real winner on our hands here," Brody mumbled under his breath. He revealed his badge through the open space of the door to identify himself. The woman removed the chain from the door and jerked it open all the way.

"What do you mean, my mother? You're joking, right?"

"Abigail?" Brody asked.

"Yeah, I'm Abigail, but I ain't got no mamma, asshole."

Brody guessed from the bruises on the woman's forearm and her long unkempt greasy blond hair that she was a heroin addict. Her teeth showed no signs of long-term use, so he figured she'd just started using. The uncontrolled twitching in her face was a telltale sign she was having withdrawals, so he used it to his advantage. "I'll throw you a twenty if you let us in and answer a few questions."

"Hell, I've done a lot more for less than that. Knock yourself out, badge boy, come on in." She stumbled across the room and covered a bag of heroin and a deck of tarot cards on the coffee table with a magazine, then plopped herself on the couch.

Derek had funded, built, and volunteered at women's and children's shelters, so he was no stranger to seeing the repercussions of addiction or abuse. Seeing it repeatedly never made it any easier. He felt his blood rising from the horrible conditions of the rat-infested apartment and the neglected little girl.

Derek squatted down to the little girl's level, who was now drawing a picture with her crayons. "What's your name, sweetheart?"

"You're not going to get anything out of that little weirdo. She's mute."

"Mute?" Brody asked.

"Yeah, a mute, you know, she can't talk. All she does is lay around drawing creepy ass pictures all day," Abigail said, pointing to a pile of papers in the corner of the room.

"What's her name?" Derek asked.

"Rebecca. Should've called her ass Bacardi though, cause one of the drunk bastards I slept with on my sixteenth birthday decided to get me knocked up. Some sweet sixteen present, huh?"

Brody saw Derek getting ready to blow and put the focus of the conversation back on questioning Abigail. "Your mom's name was Clara, Clara Ramsey."

"Well, you can tell that bitch I don't want to meet her. If she wanted to know me, she shouldn't have left my ass at that shelter after she had me."

"Your mother was kidnapped then murdered after she gave birth to you in 1991, Abigail." Brody left out the gory details of her mother's butchered body being found in an alley in Midtown New York.

Abigail paused and looked down at the floor in disbelief, almost ashamed. She'd always believed her mother had thrown her away. She looked back up at them through wet eyes and steadied her tone. "Murdered, huh? Well, I guess she got to take the easy way out then. Unlike me, who was molested, beaten, and treated like a fucking slave until I finally ran away from my last foster home when I was twelve," she hissed.

"I'm sorry that happened to you, Abigail," Brody said, with sincerity in his voice. He spread out three other Midtown Butcher victim pictures on the coffee table. "Do any of these women look familiar to you?"

"No, and why do you think this Clara is my mother anyway?"

Brody cleared his throat. "Because you're in our criminal database, we were able to match you to your mother's DNA collected from the crime scene."

"Well, aren't I lucky?"

"Has your father or maybe another relative reached out or found you over the years?" Brody asked.

"Nope, didn't know daddy either, badge boy."

Rebecca walked over to comfort her mother. She caressed the side of her mother's face with her little hand.

Abigail turned to her daughter. "You're a bastard too, little girl." She pushed her away.

Derek grabbed Abigail's wrist. The minute he touched Abigail, his eyes closed tight and complete darkness filled his mind. He couldn't see the woman he heard screaming or her attacker but could hear her begging for her life. The sound of a baby wailing in the background distracted him until he heard the woman's ear-piercing pleas for her child's life. *'Please, don't hurt my baby, please.'*

81

"What's he doing? Let me go, you fucking freak." Abigail tried to pull her wrist from Derek's hold.

Brody pried Derek's grip off of Abigail. "Back off, Derek. I got this," Brody whispered. He pulled Abigail up off the couch and placed her arms behind her back. "You have the right to remain silent."

"What the hell are you doing? Why are you arresting me?" She resisted as Brody placed the handcuffs around her wrists.

Derek picked up the heroin from under the magazine and held it in front of her. He leaned into her ear and whispered, "If you ever touch her again, I'll kill you."

⟨⟩

RAIN FELL from the dreary Manhattan sky outside the slum apartment building. Derek and Brody sat in the Escalade and watched through the windshield wipers as the NYPD pulled away with Abigail contained in the back of the unit. Shelby, a local Manhattan social worker, was helping Rebecca into the backseat of a government-issued car.

"What the fuck happened in there?" Brody asked.

"You were there. You saw what happened. The girl was clearly neglected, and her mom's a junkie."

"The little girl is going to be fine, Derek. Shelby's taking her to Vista House as soon as she's done processing the paperwork. Vista's meant for kids with special abilities. Why Rebecca at Vista? Did you sense she has some kind of gift?"

Derek handed Brody the picture Rebecca was drawing while they were there. "Tell me what you see."

"Purple hands cupping a tree with purple leav—holy shit...it's the Vista logo."

"Yeah, it is. She's five, maybe six, so it's not likely she's seen it before. I also saw Abigail cover up a deck of tarot cards when we got there. She could have the gift to read cards, or she uses them to scam people. Either way, what I do know is that the little girl knew she was going to Vista, Brody."

"Do you think she can help us with the Midtown Butcher's cold case?"

"I don't know, but I'll have Anderson work with her to see if there's anything there. We need to give her some time to adjust before we go digging around in her head."

"It's obvious the kid's been through hell. Clara is Rebecca's grandmother, so if she does have visions, she might be able to tell us something about Clara or his other victims."

"Did you forget she can't talk?"

"Yeah, but maybe she can draw something that will help."

Derek understood why Brody was pressing the issue about using Rebecca to help them with the case. Bringing Clara Ramsey and the other three victims connected to the case justice was important to Brody, just like finding out what really happened to his parents was to him. Derek had visions and Brody had a badge, each came with heavy expectations and responsibility. He knew how frustrating it was to have several pieces of a puzzle but not have them all. If the missing pieces weren't found fast enough, someone could die or murderers would walk away, free to kill again.

"You saw something when you had Abigail's wrist in a death grip didn't you?" Brody asked.

"I heard a baby screaming. I could hear a woman. She sounded desperate. She was begging for her child's life. That's it. That's all I saw before you pulled me out of it. I don't understand what it means. Sorry, I wish I had more."

"It's not your fault, you know. You can't save the world."

"Yeah, I know."

"Give yourself some credit, man. You've kept your parents' legacy alive by continuing their humanitarian work. They'd be proud of you."

Derek looked over at Brody. "Wow, Brody, do you want to hug it out now, perhaps a little kiss too?"

"You're such an asshole, Derek," he said, with a slanted smile on his face. "My point is, Clara Ramsey's murder has been cold for over twenty years. I'm not saying I'm giving up on her or the other women, because I won't, but we also have to start recognizing the good shit we do too, or we'll both go insane. We need a break. Abigail was my last lead on Clara, so I'm free to go to Lyle Mountain if you're game. I'll bring the case files with me in case something else pops up."

"Of course I'm game." Derek felt a heaviness settling in his chest, not knowing what they would or wouldn't find on Lyle Mountain. *It's time*, he thought.

Chapter Four

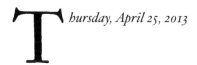hursday, April 25, 2013

"SAL DE MI COCINA!" Maria scolded Rodney as she tapped his forehead for picking at the food she was preparing.

"Rodney, really, do you always have to upset Maria first thing in the morning? I swear you're going to give that woman a heart attack," Maggie said, as she walked past him and entered the breakfast nook.

Maggie walked over to where Sheridan was already seated at the table and kissed her forehead. "Good morning, love."

"Good morning, Aunt Maggie."

"Where's your mom?"

"Carol called out, so she went in early to open the diner."

Rodney sat down next to Sheridan, still chewing on the piece of bacon he'd just swiped from the kitchen. Maggie placed her hands over Sheridan's and looked into her niece's eyes with pride. "Rodney told me about the fabulous news. We are so, so proud of you."

"You'll be there, right?" Sheridan asked.

"Of course I'll be there. We'll all be there."

Maria entered the nook with breakfast plates. "Maria, just coffee for me this morning. I have a patient at eight-thirty," Maggie said.

When Rodney reached across the table to grab his mother's untouched plate of food, Maria grabbed his ear firm with one hand and took the extra plate of food with the other. Maria mumbled to herself under her breath as she left the nook.

Maggie glanced at her watch. "Sorry to run, but I'm late. I'll see you two at dinner tonight?"

"Probably not. We're going shopping later today to get Sheridan ready for her trip to Manhattan, so we'll just grab something while we're out."

Maggie knew how much her niece hated it when Rodney tried to play dress up with her, so she couldn't help but chuckle. "Well, you two have fun," Maggie said, then left Rodney and Sheridan alone in the nook.

SHERIDAN SAT at the table picking at her breakfast. Rodney was rambling, but Sheridan wasn't paying attention. "I have a few appointments this morning myself, but I thought I could swing back by here and pick you up at two. Will that work for you?" Sheridan didn't respond. "Will two be okay?" Rodney asked again. He tapped his fingers on her forearm to get her attention. "Earth to Sheridan. Hey, you okay?"

"What? Um, yeah, two is fine."

"Okay, what's going on in that pretty little head of yours?"

"Nothing. There's a lot going on, but I'll be fine."

"I know it's more than just 'a lot going on.' You should know by now you can talk to me."

"I do, but—"

"No buts. Talk to me."

"I-I'm going back to Lyle Mountain."

Sheridan had confided in Rodney about Hank abusing her and her mom when she was little. But Rodney always felt there was something or someone out there much darker than she'd ever revealed to him.

"My mom's worked so hard to provide a better life for me here and only left Lyle Mountain to save my life. Saving her childhood home was her life before I came into the picture. She's sacrificed so much and I'm grateful, but I know Lyle Mountain is really where her heart is, even with Hank out of prison.

"I'm using the money Dr. Riley paid for the angel collection to pay off both mortgages on her house. I don't want the deed sent in the mail. I want to have it physically put in my hands. I've already called to have the lights and gas turned on at the house. I also talked to Carter County Mortgage, Title and Loans and they're expecting me Saturday morning."

"Saturday? Whoa, that soon?"

"My flight's tomorrow. I want to take care of it before we go to Manhattan next week, so I can give her the deed as a surprise when she drives to New York for the exhibition. I-I just want her to feel what I am experiencing right now."

"And what's that?"

"Hope."

"Is that the only reason you want to go back to Lyle Mountain?"

"I have to face my fears and my past. It's time for a new chapter, and that will never happen if I keep hiding from things I don't understand, like how I was conceived," she slipped.

"What do you mean, how you were conceived? Are you going back to Lyle to find out who your real father is?"

"No. I'll never know who my biological father is. And believe me, I have no desire to meet him," she confessed.

"People make mistakes. Your mom was young and wild when she was experimenting. Maybe your real father's a good man who regrets not taking responsibility for you, or hell, maybe he doesn't even know about you," he offered.

"My mom lied. She was never experimenting with boys. She was raped. My father's a rapist."

"What are you talking about? You told me when you were sixteen you asked your mom who your real father was, and she confessed she'd had a few one-night stands."

"She lied to protect me. I checked my birth certificate and it states

I was born at Providence House, which is a women's abuse and rape crisis shelter in New York."

"But how do you know she was raped? Did she tell you?"

Sheridan stared down into her plate of food, ashamed by how she'd found out the truth. "No. I...I read it in her chart."

"What chart? What the hell are you talking about?"

"A couple of weeks ago, your mom asked me to pull Shelly Hayes' chart and bring it home so she could work on her case. I went to pull the file, and I saw my mom's right in front of Shelly's...Rhonda May Hayes. I swear I wasn't looking for it, it was just there," she said defensively. "Allen was her counselor."

"Oh, wow. Allen was the one who got through to me after my dad died from cancer. If it weren't for him, I'd still be lost."

"I am sure she only agreed to even try counseling because it was Allen. She started going seven years ago and only went for six months. On the last session she had with him, he noted she refused to continue counseling after he'd advised her to tell me the truth about how and where I was conceived. I feel horrible about violating her privacy. You can't tell anyone you know, not even your mom, even though she knows."

"She told my mom?"

"Yes, she did. My mom could've had an abortion after she was raped. She could've left me at Providence House but came back for me five days after I was born. She could've left me with you and your mom sixteen years ago, but she stayed with me. She's been holding so much guilt inside because of my childhood with Hank. She blames herself for being raped and for the way I isolate myself from the world.

"I'm going back to face my own fears and secrets, so I can make peace with my past and move on with my life. I want my mom to be proud of me and to be guilt free."

"Oh, honey, she is proud of you. You know that, right?"

"I know she is, but my mom's not an idiot. She can sense I don't trust anyone. What she doesn't know is that Hank is not the only person from my past that I am scared of," she confessed, regretting she let her last words slip from her lips.

"Who else are you scared of?"

She wanted more than anything to tell Rodney about the monster who tried to drown her, her angel, and everything else that happened that night. But she just couldn't find the courage to do it. As a grown woman, she still feared he would come back for her if she broke her promise not to tell.

"Do you remember when you were in the closet, and even though I knew you were gay, you couldn't bring yourself to tell me or anyone else? You had to do it your own way and in your own time. Isn't that what you'd said?" she asked.

"Yes, but—"

"No buts. I have to do this my way."

"Touché. I won't pressure you to tell me the other motives for your trip back to Lyle if you let me go with you. We can head straight to New York from there."

Sheridan started laughing.

"What the hell is so funny?"

"I'm imagining you of all people prancing around in Carter County. Talk about sticking out like a sore thumb."

"What? I can be Woodchuck Fabulous, right?"

"Do you really think I would've gone without you? We'll tell my mom we're going to Manhattan earlier than planned, so I can look at a few apartments and get ready for the exhibition. If she knows we're going to Lyle, she'll worry."

"You sneaky little shit," he accused. "We're grown adults, you know. You're allowed to go anywhere you want without your mom's permission."

"Fine, so there's no problem telling your mom you're going too, right?"

"Touché again. Manhattan it is. When did you become such a smart ass? What happened to my sweet and shy little cousin?"

"I learned from the best," she teased. "We leave Friday to Lyle, then we'll fly into New York on Monday to start getting ready for the exhibition. My mom had to let the property management company in Lyle go a few years back because she couldn't afford to keep them on, so I'll need a few days to get it cleaned up before she sees it again."

"Well, I guess we'll need to shop for our trip to Carter County now too then, huh? I just thought of the perfect outfit for you to wear when you go to get the deed to your mom's house. It would so represent a full circle moment for you."

"I like my jeans and T-shirts just fine."

"Just hear me out," he asked. "When you first came to Kensington Manor, you were wearing a simple white sundress. It was the first and last time I've ever seen you wear a dress. How liberating would it be for you to go back, head held high, with the same look you had when you took that first step toward your new life?"

Sheridan didn't share the same belief as Rodney in that one should have an outfit for every single milestone in life. But, she also didn't have the heart to rain on the perfect vision he had of her taking the next steps toward reclaiming her life.

"A white sundress sounds perfect," she humored.

Chapter Five

Vista House was quiet at eleven-thirty in the afternoon. Derek entered the four-story nineteenth century brownstone town-house in the West Village.

"Hello? Anyone here?" Derek called out. He'd grown accustomed to being jumped on by at least one of the children who currently resided there. Anderson Allan, the house counselor, peeked his head out from behind a door and motioned Derek to join him in his office.

Derek took a seat across from Anderson, who sat behind his desk. "Sorry I missed you yesterday morning for breakfast. Brody came by, so I got a little sidetracked."

"No worries," Anderson replied, as he placed his phone in his laptop bag.

"Going somewhere?"

"Yes. I thought your aunt told you. A friend of mine in Florida passed away unexpectedly, so I'm taking a couple of days off to attend the funeral. Thomas should be here any minute to take me to the airport. I'll still be available via email and phone if the kids need anything, though."

"No, she didn't mention it when I talked to her last night. Sorry for your loss."

Anderson stopped packing his bag and stared at Derek with a crooked salt and pepper brow. "She told me you were going out of town yourself, but don't worry, I hired permanent house parents this morning. They start tomorrow. Thomas and your aunt are going to stay with the kids while I'm gone and help get the new house parents settled in, so you're free to get on the road."

"You did what?" Derek asked, angry. "We were supposed to make all staffing decisions together," Derek reminded him.

"I understand you're upset, Derek, but you left me no choice. Your aunt and I can't do this on our own, and thank God Thomas has been here to help out or we would have really been screwed. Vista has been reopened for a month and a half, and you've let every decision and issue fall into our laps. The kids needed someone here permanently, so I took care of it, just like everything else."

Derek's mother built Vista when he was four. Her dream was to build foster havens for children who possessed special psychic abilities because it was nearly impossible to find families to foster, let alone adopt, children they didn't understand. Vista had been the first haven built, but it closed its doors after she was killed. Reopening Vista House and building additional foster homes seemed like the easiest way to bring his mother's dream back to life. Once he'd done it, he began doubting himself and questioned whether he was qualified to help these children, even with his own gifts resurfacing.

Derek knew Anderson was right. Even Anderson's adopted son, Thomas, had given more to Vista's reopening than Derek had. "I had a lot on my mind lately," Derek confessed. "But I'm dealing with it. I'm going to Carter County for a few days to try and find some closure about my parents' deaths. When I come back, my head will be in the right place, and we can start making plans for the construction and staffing of more Vistas."

Anderson had volunteered as a psychic counselor to the children at the first Vista House before it closed, so he knew Derek well. His Aunt Lexus had asked Anderson to work with him after his parents' deaths to help him cope, but Anderson had never been able to get through to him. Derek learned early on how to manipulate him and everyone else in his life into thinking he was fine. He'd perfected appearing normal and unfazed by anything or anyone, so he'd thought.

"With or without my gifts, I can see right through your bullshit." Anderson paused before he spoke again to avoid saying something he'd regret. "Listen, I've known you your entire life and have done everything I can to help you heal. It's up to you now to accept the fact that the closure you seek about your parents may never come. You have to move on and live your life. You've built bulletproof walls around yourself, and it makes it impossible for anyone to help you."

Derek looked down at the floor embarrassed, attempting to avoid Anderson's uncomfortable stare. Derek had seen firsthand how Anderson had turned his own adopted son around all those years ago and regretted not allowing Anderson in. Maybe if he had, his life would have turned out different.

"Go to Carter County and find your closure. When you come back, I want you to promise you'll leave your ghosts behind. Otherwise, I can't promise I'll continue on as the counselor at Vista."

"I hear you," Derek confirmed. "So, where is everyone?"

"Your aunt drove all the kids to Dr. Riley's office this morning for their physicals and then over to Dr. William to get their teeth cleaned."

"Did you get a chance to meet Rebecca?"

"I spent a little time with her this morning before they all left, but she refuses to let anyone near her."

"Were you able to pick anything up on her at all?"

"Unfortunately, no. You know as well as I do that these kids come from horrific circumstances. Because of the neglect and abuse they've suffered, they subconsciously build walls around their emotions and thoughts. Sound familiar?"

When Derek didn't respond, Anderson continued. "They repress memories and create unreliable make-believe worlds. It takes time to weed out what's real and what's not. We can't even try hypnotherapy on her because she's physically incapable of telling us anything."

"Did you see her drawings?"

"Yes, but I'm not a miracle worker nor do I understand what her drawings mean yet. Rebecca has serious communication limitations, not to mention the fact that she can't read or write."

"But we can work with her, right? I mean, she did know she was coming to Vista. She drew it," he said, then pulled from his pocket the drawing Rebecca had drawn the day before.

"It's the Vista logo. Interesting. There's a chance we can help her, but my instinct tells me she'll need special care we're not equipped to provide her here."

"The whole point of building Vista Houses was to take in kids just like her, who'd otherwise be placed in institutions or thrown around from foster home to foster home. So she's got some communication issues. We can find someone who can work with her and interpret what her drawings mean."

"I'll have Thomas try and work with her while I'm out of town. Just don't get your hopes up, okay?"

"Listen, I know I should've been more involved and admit that I haven't been, but I sense somehow that I'm supposed to help her, and I can't ignore it."

"We're back," Derek and Anderson heard Lexus call out.

A car honked from the street. "Sounds like Thomas is here. They're all yours," he jested. Anderson rose from his desk and threw his laptop bag over his shoulder. "Be sure to tell your aunt to call if she needs anything."

As Anderson reached the office doorway, Derek stopped him. "I appreciate all the sacrifices you've made to make Vista a reality again, Anderson. Really."

"Just remember what I said. When you get back, be sure to leave those ghosts behind."

"DEREK!" four-year-old Charlie yelled out when he spotted Derek in the hallway.

"Hey, buddy. I heard you went to see Dr. Riley. How'd it go?"

"He gave me a big ol' shot, and I didn't even cry at all."

"Well, aren't you brave a little man?"

"Yep."

"Derek, Derek!" four other children screamed with excitement when they realized he was there. They ran to him, all pulling at and talking to him at the same time.

"Okay. Okay. One at a time," Derek laughed at the motley crew begging for his undivided attention.

He may not have been as involved in the administrative decisions at Vista as he should've been, but he'd grown to care for each of the five children who had come into his life. He understood them.

Each possessed different psychic abilities. Ashley was the oldest at fifteen, and Charlie was the youngest at four. Adam and Luke, who were twins, were nine, and Tamika was six. And then there was Vista's newest addition, Rebecca, who was also six.

"Okay, everyone, upstairs to wash up for lunch," Lexus ordered. "Ashley, would you be a dear and help them?"

"Yes, ma'am," Ashley agreed. "Okay, guys, let's go. March."

Lexus stood on the tips of her toes, reached for Derek's forehead, and planted a loving kiss upon it. "I thought you and Brody had already left for Carter County."

"I'm meeting him in half an hour to take off. I wanted to stop by to check on Rebecca before I left."

"Oh, that poor child. She won't let anyone near her, Derek."

"Yeah, that's what Anderson said."

Derek was puzzled by Rebecca's newfound fear of people. The child he'd seen the day before was not scared at all. Quiet, but not scared. She'd even tried to show her mother affection before Abigail had shoved her away. Maybe the shock of being taken away from her mother was to blame. Lexus could sense Derek's concern, so she took his hand in hers and led him to the front entryway. "Do you remember them?" she asked, pointing to one of the pictures hanging on the wall of his mom and four of the kids from the first Vista House.

"Of course I do. Thomas, Sarah, Vanessa, and Ian," he said pointing to each of the kids in the picture.

"And do you remember how scared they all were when your mom first brought them to Vista?"

"Yeah."

"Rebecca needs time to adjust. Just like your mom helped them, you'll help her. I promise, she'll come around," Lexus assured.

Derek smiled. "Well, I'm glad you believe in me. Let's just hope she does too."

"Speaking of people who believe in you, your Uncle Quentin called this morning and said he needed to see you before you left. Did he ever call you?"

Derek pulled his cell phone from his pocket and checked for any missed calls. "No. Did he say what he needed?"

"No, but he seemed pretty adamant about talking to you after I told him you and Brody were going to Carter County. He said he needed to give you something before you left."

Quentin always became uneasy whenever Derek talked about looking further into his parents' deaths. He assumed Quentin wanted to try and talk him out of going to Carter County.

"Derek, he loves you, you know? He worries about you; we both do."

"I know, but I have to see if anything was missed in their investigation. Every part of me says something doesn't add up."

"I don't believe your father killed your mother either. I never have. I've learned to accept what I know in my heart to be true and remember your parents for the wonderful people they were."

"Are you sure you don't need me to stay with the kids until the new house parents get here tomorrow? You and Thomas haven't left the kids or had a break since we reopened."

"I love these children and I love you. I'm not here because I have to be. I'm here because I want to be. I loved your mother and everything she was trying to accomplish. It's just as important to me as it is to you that we bring her dream back to life."

"What would I have ever done without you, Aunt Lexus?"

"I know Quentin and I will never take the place of your parents, but I hope we've shown you how much we love you. In my heart, you will always be my son, just as much as Brody is."

Derek pulled his aunt into his arms, closed his eyes, and whispered, "I may have never called you mom, but you've always been a mother to me. I would've been lost without you and Uncle Quentin. I appreciate everything you've done and continue to do for me. You know that, right?"

When Derek opened his eyes, he saw Rebecca standing about six feet away staring at him and his aunt. "Hey there, Rebecca," he said softly.

Rebecca walked straight to Derek and raised her arms up to him. Derek followed her lead and picked her up. Rebecca started caressing the side of Derek's face then kissed him on his forehead. Derek's heart began to thump as staggered images of the mental abuse Abigail had inflicted upon Rebecca entered his mind. Normally Derek had to concentrate to see or feel anything from a person he was trying to read. He saw Abigail trying to shoot heroin into her bruised arm and collapsed veins. He felt how she used it to mask her own pain and suffering.

Rebecca tapped Derek's chest and pulled him out of his visions. When she had his attention, she motioned to the floor with her finger for Derek to put her down, and he did. She reached into the front pocket of her overalls and pulled out a picture she'd drawn and handed it to him. The Vista logo sat on top of a mountain with a river drawn around it. Just outside the water were two stick figures. One was of a girl in a dress lying in a puddle, and the second was an angry man with horns standing over her. Rebecca had drawn a picture of the little girl from his dream. Derek was sure of it.

"Rebecca, do you know who this little girl is?" Derek asked. Rebecca didn't answer. "Rebecca," he asked again, bending down to her level and pulling her to him. "Sweetie, it's important I know who she is. Do you know her?" She stared through him.

"Derek, let her go," Lexus demanded, seeing Derek was becoming anxious.

"Please, Rebecca, tell me who she is." Rebecca pulled away from his grip and ran upstairs. Derek stood dumbfounded and watched Rebecca run from him.

"What was that about?" Lexus asked.

Besides Brody, Derek had not told anyone about the dreams he'd had about the little girl and his mother. "Nothing. It's nothing. I have to go or I'm going to be late meeting Brody. We'll see you next week." He kissed the top of his aunt's head before leaving.

Chapter Six

F*riday, April 26, 2013*

THE AFTERNOON DRIVE from Knoxville International Airport to Lyle Mountain was quiet and relaxing. Sheridan allowed the cool spring air to dance against her palm and through her delicate long fingers, which were dangling outside the rented Jeep Wrangler's window. The scenic route from Knoxville was exactly what she needed to try and calm herself before arriving to Lyle Mountain.

Rodney sensed Sheridan was a bundle of nerves, so he turned the radio to a station playing "Mountain Music" and began trying to sing along as he drove.

"Please stop," Sheridan laughed. "You should never, ever sing... ever," she teased. Sheridan's mood shifted when they passed a sign that read Lyle Mountain Exit 15 miles.

"Breathe, you're okay."

"I'll tell you how to get there," she said, shaky. Even though sixteen years had passed, she still remembered every single inch of Lyle Mountain. She had hoped she wouldn't.

§.

RODNEY DROVE up the dirt driveway, which was congested with majestic oaks and an array of vibrant wildflowers. The entrance to Sheridan's home was beautiful.

"Just a little farther up," Sheridan instructed with a cracked voice.

When the house came into view, Rodney was stunned by the house's condition. As a child, he'd always imagined his cousin's home to be a creepy old and broken-down shack, haunted with memories of a wicked and hideous stepfather. What he saw was a charming white two-story Victorian cottage with a porch that wrapped around. Two mossy oaks towered over the roof. Evergreen ivy clung to each side of the house's solid wood foundation.

"It's beautiful, Sheridan."

"Our great grandfather built it with his bare hands in the early 1900s. That's why this house is so precious to my mom. She told Allen in one of their sessions she missed her childhood home and wanted to go back one day."

Rodney pulled in front of the house and turned the ignition off. Sheridan took a deep breath, opened the Jeep's door, and walked over to the porch steps. When she got to the front door, she paused.

"You're in control, Sheridan," Rodney encouraged. "He can't hurt you. You can do this."

Sheridan unlocked the door and flung it open. She walked confidently to the front window and yanked the drapes open to allow the sun's light to pour in. Spider webs filled the empty spaces between the furniture, which had been covered with sheets. Sheridan began ripping the sheets off the furniture then moved the pieces to their assigned places within the room.

Rodney stood in the doorway and watched his cousin. He wanted to soothe her and tell her she was going to be okay, but he didn't move. He knew she needed to feel every ounce of anger she'd been holding in her whole life.

"I have a lot of work to do to get this place ready. I want my mom to walk in and have nothing to do except reclaim her life," Sheridan said as she moved things around.

"I'll help you, honey," Rodney offered. "I'll need to buy a new do-rag and apron though."

Rodney's comment brought Sheridan back from the dark place she'd begun to fall into. She allowed a slanted smile to form on her lips and chuckled.

"You scared me there for a second. I thought you were going to bring those sheets to their brutal deaths."

Sheridan rolled her eyes. "Thanks for coming with me, and for...you know...always being my gorgeous rock."

"Gorgeous is right, honey, and don't you forget it. Now show me the rest of the house."

❦

RODNEY HAD Sheridan's suitcase in his right hand and in his left he held her garment bag with the white sundress they'd bought the day before leaving Kensington. "Okay, this suitcase is getting heavy, and those stairs killed me, toots. Let's see this room of yours."

When they entered, Sheridan reached inside her blouse and cupped the amethyst stone that hanged from its chain. She walked over to the oil lamp sitting on the nightstand next to her bed and began tracing within the outline of an angel she'd drawn in dust sixteen years ago. Her knees became weak and the color drained from her face.

Rodney dropped the suitcase and garment bag and ran over to her to prevent Sheridan from falling. "What's wrong?" he asked, maneuvering her over to the bed so she could sit down. "Hey, look at me," he said, softly patting the side of her face.

Sheridan met his gaze and tried to focus. "I'm okay." She tried getting up from the bed.

"Okay? I don't think so. Humor me and sit here for a minute." Sheridan sat still for what seemed like an eternity to Rodney. His gut told him that whatever had just happened to her had nothing to do with Hank.

Sheridan remembered what her angel had said to her. *'You can never tell anyone about me or what happened to you tonight. If you do, the bad man will come back and hurt you.'*

"It hurts that you don't trust me, but I understand," he offered.

"I do trust you, and I will tell you everything one day."

"Fine. Just don't go blacking out on me; my delicate little heart can't take that, okay?"

"I won't. We need to get the dry food and cooler out of the Jeep. We can make do for dinner tonight, but we'll need to pick up more groceries tomorrow while we're in town. We also need to pick up cleaning supplies, and your do-rag and apron, sir."

"Ah, she's back. There's my little smart ass," he teased.

Chapter Seven

The late afternoon sun glared off of Derek's sunglasses. He felt judging eyes from the two elderly men who occupied handcrafted rocking chairs outside the barbershop. The paved streets were lined with locally owned businesses. The main attractions were the grocery store, a historic movie theatre directly across the street from the Sheriff's Office, and a malt shop that looked like it had come right out of the 1950s.

"I'd say we're not in Kansas anymore, but it looks like we've just arrived," Brody said.

"Yeah, you're not kidding, but it's nice to know that places like this still exist. I kind of like it here," he confessed.

When they walked into the Sheriff's Office, they were greeted at the front desk by Deputy Dyer. "Can I help you boys?"

Brody flashed his badge to identify himself. "We're here investigating the murder of Meredith Hope Young. I'd like to speak to Sheriff Frank Lloyd if he's available."

"That case has been cold for sixteen years, and aren't you boys a little out of your jurisdiction?"

"We're following up on a few loose ends from the case," Brody said.

"Stay here, I'll see if the Sheriff's available," he instructed, not taking his eyes off them until he rounded the corner.

Sheriff Lloyd walked out from the back and over to where Derek and Brody were waiting. He offered them a friendly smile and extended his hand out to Brody first and introduced himself. When he gripped Derek's hand and shook it, Derek instantly saw an image of his mother lying lifeless and pale in a patch of overgrown grass. Just as quickly as the image surfaced, it disappeared, allowing him to maintain his cool.

"So, what can I do for y'all?"

"I spoke to you on the phone a few months ago about Meredith Young's case and was hoping to ask you a few more questions about the investigation," Brody said.

"Yeah, I remember. Her nephew, right? And how about you?" he addressed Derek. "You any relation to Mrs. Young?"

"She was my mother and Charles Young was my father," he disclosed in a ridged tone.

Sheriff Lloyd's demeanor became guarded. "I'm sorry for your loss. I can't imagine how hard your parents' deaths must have been on you."

"No, you can't." Derek regretted coming off hard. "I'm sorry. I'm trying to understand what happened the night my mom was murdered."

"I understand," Sheriff Lloyd offered. "Come on back to my office so we can talk in private." He addressed Deputy Dyer. "Dwayne, be sure we don't get interrupted."

SHERIFF LLOYD BROUGHT Brody and Derek into his office and asked them to have a seat. He offered them coffee, but they declined, so he left them alone to get himself a cup.

"You think he's going to give us anything?" Derek asked.

"I don't think he's a bad guy. Let's just feel him out and give him a chance."

"Yeah, he was real helpful last time you talked to him," Derek said sarcastically.

"It's not like he could just mail me your mom's file or FedEx me the physical evidence. It's still classified as an open investigation, so we can't force him to talk or the DA to release the case files."

"Open investigation, my ass. The Sheriff and the DA think my mom's killer is dead, and they haven't had an investigator assigned to her case in over a decade."

Sheriff Lloyd reentered his office with a cup of coffee in his right hand and two files in his left, one much thicker than the other. He dropped them on top of his desk and sat down.

"Because the TBI allowed us to maintain jurisdiction, we took the hit when your mamma's case turned cold. Carter County had and continues to have the authority to deny or approve the release of those records. I'm sorry the DA's office denied your cousin's request, but that's out of my hands."

"So why talk to us if you can't help?"

"That's funny, I don't recall sayin' I wasn't gonna help you. I only said that releasin' official records was out of my hands."

Sheriff Lloyd slid the thicker of the two files sitting in front of him over to Derek. The file had sloppy handwritten notes all over the front cover. Derek was able to make out the name Walter Reed. "Reed... wasn't he the Sheriff in Carter County when my mom was murdered?"

"He was. Walt was also a mentor and friend of mine."

Derek began flipping through the file. "What is all of this?"

"Walt's sixteen-year private investigation," Sheriff Lloyd answered. "Shortly after your mamma was murdered, he started ruffling a bunch of feathers in the DA's office by insistin' we'd gone after the wrong man. People started thinkin' he was losin' his mind, so he was given two options: step down as Sheriff voluntarily or a recall election would be formed to remove him from his position. He knew the locals would support the recall because everybody believed your daddy was guilty, including me.

"He agreed to resign but only if the DA's office agreed to leave your mamma's case open. They were confident our prime suspect was the murderer, so they didn't see any harm in leaving the case open to make him happy and avoid bad media."

"Where's Reed now?" Brody chimed in.

"Oh, he's still around. In fact, you can find Walt every Saturday night holdin' up the bar at Dottie's Lounge next door to the inn. Walt's the only reason I even agreed to sit down and talk to you two."

"Why's that?" Derek asked.

"After Walt resigned, he spent the next sixteen years of his life investigatin' your parents on his own. He became obsessed and refused to stop until he found proof we'd accused the wrong man. Because of his obsession, he lost his life savings, his wife, the locals' respect, and a few months back, his mind.

"That file you're holdin' is filled with the blood and sweat he poured into tryin' to find out the truth about your parents. Everything he found is in there, right down to where they were born, what schools they went to, their hobbies, every doctor they'd seen, and well...even you."

"So why show us this file if you think my father was guilty too?" Derek asked.

"The bottle and the case finally got the best of old Walt a few months back, so he came to me and asked me to hold onto it. I just thought on top of losin' his mind, he was becomin' paranoid. To appease him, I put the file in my safe.

"After the DA denied your request for your mamma's file, my own curiosity got the best of me, and I started goin' through Walt's records myself. It took me some time, but I came across one of your mamma's medical records and started questionin' a few things about our original ten million dollar motive," he confessed.

"Medical records?" Derek interrupted.

"Your mamma had a malignant brain tumor. According to her records, she had less than three months to live before she was murdered. Your daddy would've only had to wait three months for her to pass to get forty million dollars from her life insurance policy. That was four times the amount taken from their joint account, so for me, that shot the DA's original motive for murder."

"So my dad knew about her cancer?" Derek asked, swallowing hard.

"Yeah, he did. Accordin' to Walt's notes, the nurse who gave him a copy of her medical records said your daddy and a woman named Lexus held your mamma's hand for six years through radiation and chemo treatments. Outside of the staff who treated her, they were the only ones who ever knew. She'd insisted on hidin' it. They drove fifty miles outside of Manhattan to Norwalk for her treatments. Even used a different name at the treatment center to hide her identity."

"How did Sheriff Reed get my aunt's medical records?" Brody asked.

"Like I said, Walt lost his life savings. It's amazin' how unethical people become for the right amount of money."

"So why hasn't this new information been released?" Derek asked.

"Well, after I confirmed the amount of money from your mamma's life insurance policy, I took the information to Clay Clemons, who was the Assistant DA at the time."

"Wait a second...Clay Clemons, is he any relation to Billy Clemons, the boy who shot my dad?"

"Yep, they're related," Sheriff Lloyd confirmed. "Billy is Clay's son and was labeled a town hero after he shot your dad to stop him from fleein' the scene of the crime. Made me about sick every time Clay reminded everyone about his son's courageous act, especially durin' election time. I hate to say it, but that's likely what helped him become the new District Attorney in Carter County a couple months ago."

"Son of a bitch," Brody said. "Carter County locals have always been convinced my aunt's murderer was dead. So, reassigning the case based on new evidence wouldn't be too smart or look good during election time if someone could prove my aunt's real killer was still out there alive and well, right? That also explains the DAs office's resistance in giving me my aunt's case file."

"Now you're gettin it'," Sheriff Lloyd said.

"What did this Clay Clemons do with the information you gave him?" Derek asked.

"He told me Walt's records would be inadmissible due to the way he'd obtained most of them. Unfortunately, he was right. My hands are tied unless I can get my hands on some solid evidence or records obtained legally.

"For now, the case is still open, so the sooner y'all find somethin', the better. If the TBI agent assigned to the case back then had his way, your mamma's case would've been closed on the ten million dollar motive alone."

"Agent Kelly, right?" Brody asked. "That guy's a real asshole."

"You know him?" Sheriff Lloyd asked.

"Oh, yeah. I had the unfortunate pleasure of talking to that jackass twice so far in my career. The first time was a few months ago when I'd called to talk to him about my aunt's case and his findings. He was the uncooperative prick who advised me to call the DA's office. The second was last month about another cold case I'm currently working he'd initially helped investigate back when he was with the NBI. There are other cases he dropped the ball on too. Some of my colleagues from the NBI worked with Kelly back then and said he's always been a real asshole. Apparently, our first murder victim's case, Gale Broderick, was the one that got him transferred out of the NBI due to his lack of follow-up on leads. I don't know all the details but was told he didn't leave quietly."

"Seems like he has a real knack for turning things cold, doesn't he?"

"Small world," Sheriff Lloyd said. "He wasn't liked around these parts either. I didn't trust his intentions from the moment I set my eyes on him. When he showed up in Carter County to assist with the investigation, he made it real clear he couldn't stand small town cases. When he realized how prominent your parents were and they came from New York, it lit a fire under his ass and he started takin' the case more serious."

"I guess he proved himself to be as useless with the TBI as he was with the NBI," Derek said.

"Yeah, I reckon so." Sheriff Lloyd looked at his watch. He shifted in his chair and addressed Brody. "I noticed you have the latest iPhone. I was thinkin' about upgrading myself cause of the new camera features." He tapped the file in front of him. "You never know when you might need to take a good quality picture or two."

Brody allowed a cunning smile to form on his lips.

"Well, boys, I need another cup of coffee. I figure it's gonna take me at least fifteen minutes to brew another pot," Sheriff Lloyd said, slapping the file in front of him before rising from his chair to leave. "You can go ahead and take Walt's file with you, cause those records ain't official and all. But again, I can't release these here case files, so they'd better be sittin' here when I come back. If you boys ain't here when I get back from gettin' my coffee, I'd understand, cause I believe we're all done, right?"

"Yeah, I guess we are," Brody agreed.

Before Sheriff Lloyd exited his office, he turned and addressed Derek one last time. "Can I give you one piece of advice, son?"

"Sure," Derek said.

"My mamma claimed to have the gift to see like you. Mamma had a real hard time distinguishin' what was real and what wasn't though. She got herself locked up in a padded room, and that's where she spent her last days. She was only twenty-nine when she died. Anyway, what I know is real is that none of the local folks around here committed your mamma's murder, and the one man cold enough to do somethin' like that had a solid alibi. Life's too short to go wastin' it on people or things that don't mean anything or get you what you really need."

With the exception of Brody, no one in Derek's life knew Derek's visions had resurfaced, so he was taken aback when Sheriff Lloyd picked up on them. "How'd you know?"

"When I was a youngin', I remember my mamma havin' the same look you had when you shook my hand. It was only a suspicion, but I reckon you just confirmed it. Anyway, hope you find that closure you're searchin' for, son." He then turned his back and left the room.

"I'll be damned," Derek said.

"Yeah, no shit, I could probably learn a few interrogation skills from that guy," Brody joked.

Derek reached for the other file occupying the desk. Brody pulled his cell from his belt clip and started taking pictures of the official records.

"I guess there are a few good guys left after all," Brody said.

"Yeah, he shared a lot, but there's something he's not telling us."

"Why do you say that?"

"I sensed he was an honest man but was holding something back to protect someone."

"Who?"

"That, I don't know."

❧

AN OLD COPPER cowbell hanging from the glass door of Nancy's Diner rang as Brody and Derek entered. They were the only patrons in the place at four in the afternoon. The decor of the quaint diner offered a warm and inviting southern feel. Rustic farmhouse rooster paintings and antique farm tools hung from the walls, which were covered in a country floral print. A solid oak counter lined with ten russet swivel stools sat in front of the kitchen's pickup window, nestled into the far back wall of the diner.

There were twelve empty tables covered with beige and olive-green checkerboard tablecloths. In the center of each were thick iron condiment holders and vases filled with fresh-cut wildflowers. When Brody picked up the worn menu, a handwritten dinner special insert slipped out. "Nancy's famous fried chicken and award-winning baked beans and coleslaw," he said, trying to mimic a heavy southern accent.

Derek shook his head in amusement. "You're an idiot."

A petite woman in her mid-twenties with jade-green eyes and long red hair approached their table, immediately catching Brody's attention.

"Afternoon, gentlemen. What can I get for ya?" She pulled a pen from behind her ear and order pad from the back pocket of her fitted jeans.

"Just coffee for me," Derek replied.

"Yeah, um...m-me too," Brody stuttered as he admired the freckles sprinkled across the curvy waitress' cheeks.

"Y'all are obviously from out of town or you'd know that in about an hour, there'll be a line outside that door with people waitin' to get in for tonight's dinner special. My advice to you is to get it while the gettin's good," she said, offering them both a flirtatious smile.

Brody bit. "We certainly wouldn't want to pass up on old Nancy's chicken, beans, and slaw now, would we?"

"No, you wouldn't. It would be right silly to pass up my cookin'."

"You're Nancy?" Brody asked.

She allowed a slight chuckle to escape, inspired by the dumbfounded look on Brody's face. "It's all right, darlin'. I get that response from every stranger who passes through town. Guess everyone assumes I'm a little old lady who doesn't have anything better to do but run a small diner and cook homemade food all day."

"You're far from being a little old lady," Brody complimented.

"All right now, don't push it," she teased. "I'll put your orders in and be back shortly with your coffee." She walked away, leaving them alone again.

"Oh no, you let it fall on the floor," Derek said.

"What?"

"Don't worry. I got it."

"Got what?"

Derek cupped his hands and pushed them toward Brody's mouth. "Your tongue, dumb ass. Could you be any more obvious?"

"Screw you. I mean, Jesus, are you blind? She's gorgeous."

"Stay focused on why we're here."

"I'll try, but she's making it real hard," Brody joked.

"What's your take on our meeting with Sheriff Lloyd?"

"I think we hit the jackpot with Walt's file. It's going to take us weeks, possibly months, to review sixteen years of his research, but there has to be something there."

"We'll get through it."

"What did you see when you shook Sheriff Lloyd's hand anyway?"

"Nothing really," Derek lied. The vision of his mother lying dead in the grass was too painful. He was exhausted and in no mood to talk about it. "There are a few people the Sheriff mentioned I want to follow up on while we're here."

"Like who?"

"He mentioned an attempted murder about a month after my mom was murdered. I think we should look into that some more."

"Actually, I'm familiar with the case he's talking about. When I started investigating your parents on my own, I researched Carter County's newspaper archives to find some kind of connection as to why your mom was even on Lyle Mountain."

"Did you find one?"

"No, but that's when I came across the attempted murder case the Sheriff mentioned. Apparently, a man name Hank Sheldon tried killing his wife and daughter. He was found guilty and sentenced to fifteen years in prison but got out last year."

"Yeah, we need to take a closer look at that son of a bitch," Derek reiterated.

"The authorities questioned him about where he was the night your mom was murdered, and he had a solid alibi. His wife confirmed he was knocked out in his recliner all night, sleeping one off."

"Yeah, well, I still think we need to talk to both of them again."

"Hank moved back to Carter County after he was released, so he'll be easy enough to find, but we'll have to locate the ex-wife. She and her daughter moved out of state."

"I also want to talk to Walter."

Nancy brought a pot of coffee to the table and filled the mugs sitting in front of them. "Y'all need anything else before your order comes up?" she asked, directing the question more toward Brody.

"No, I think we're good," Derek answered.

"Just holler if you need anything."

Brody stared at her backside as she walked away. Derek snapped his fingers in front of Derek's face. "Hey, over here," he said.

"Sorry. What were you saying?"

"You're a lost cause. I was saying I want to talk to Walt before we leave Carter County."

Brody's face turned serious. "From what Sheriff Lloyd said, Walt's been carrying around some heavy guilt for sixteen years. I don't know how he's going to react if the son of the man he wrongly accused confronts him. He said Walt's at Dottie's every Saturday night, so I'll go talk to him myself and feel him out first."

"You're probably right. I'm torn on how I feel about the guy anyway."

"I say we put it to bed for tonight."

Nancy arrived at their table holding a tray of food. "All right, boys, get ready for the best meal you're ever gonna eat."

Brody patted his stomach. "Wow, that's a lot of food. I don't know if I can handle all this."

She offered him a sweet smile. "Yeah, this ain't New York where you get a spoon full of this and a spoon full of that. We try to make our men nice and plump around here."

Derek glanced up at Nancy. "How'd you know we were from New York?"

"Nothin's sacred in this town. It's a real shame what happened to that poor woman on the mountain though." Nancy seemed unaware Brody and Derek were related to Meredith. They didn't inform her otherwise and shot each other a knowing glance to allow her to continue. "It was like someone put a curse on that mountain back then. I was barely ten myself, but I'll never forget how that woman's murder and Rhonda and her little girl almost gettin' killed shook the town locals up."

"Who's Rhonda?" Derek asked, already knowing the answer but prodding to get more information.

"Rhonda's a woman my sister Emma used to go to high school with. She used to be so jealous of Rhonda 'cause she was so popular back then and was datin' the high school quarterback, Hank. They were inseparable, accordin' to Emma.

"There was a bunch of them hangin' out at the Dyer's Malt Shop one night, and those two got in a fight. It must have been pretty serious 'cause Rhonda broke up with him."

"So, you don't know what the fight was about?" Brody asked.

"No one knew, but people said Hank became a different person after that."

"Different how?" Brody asked.

"She said Hank used to be a social butterfly in school. But after Rhonda broke up with him, he started drinkin' real heavy and isolated himself from everyone, even his parents. There was also gossip that Rhonda was sleepin' around with other boys and got herself pregnant. Everyone felt sorry for Hank and couldn't believe he'd offered to marry her and help take care of her baby. After the baby was born, Rhonda only came in to town for work, and when she did, she was usually bruised up pretty bad."

"So he abused her?" Derek asked.

"Oh, yeah. Emma tried to help her, but she told Emma to mind her own damn business. Anyway, I reckon Hank just snapped one day and tried to kill both her and her little girl. He just got out of prison not too long ago and comes into the diner every now and then. That man gives me the heebie-jeebies. If you ask me, he ain't right in the head."

"Interesting," Derek said.

"I'd say it's more sad than interestin'," she said.

"And what about the woman who was murdered on the mountain?" Derek asked.

"Like I said, I was barely ten when it happened. I don't know all the details, so I don't have much of an opinion to give. Right after she was murdered, a couple teenagers were on Lyle makin' out by the river, and they swore they'd seen her spirit. Said she was wearin' a sheer white gown, glowin' and floatin' above the river weepin'. Anyway, before long, other folks around here said they'd seen her too. They call her the Lady of Lyle."

"Have you ever seen her?" Derek asked, trying to stay cool as his chest tightened at the thought of his mom being part of a ridiculous myth.

"Heavens no," she admitted. "I've never gone wanderin' around that mountain just for that reason."

"I see," Derek replied.

Nancy hadn't caught the chill in Derek's voice. "Well, I reckon I better get back to the kitchen. I need to get ready for the rush. You boys enjoy now."

"Nancy," Brody called out to her. She turned around and walked back to the table. He pulled out one of his business cards and handed it to her. "If there's anything else you can think of that might help our investigation, please don't hesitate to call."

"What if I don't have anything else to offer? Can I still call ya?"

"Uh, yeah, absolutely," Brody replied, taken aback by her forwardness.

"All right then," she said, then turned and walked away.

"That's just fucking great," Derek whispered. "My mom's pegged as the Lady of Lyle? Seriously?"

"I know you're upset, and you have every right to be. You're going to have to stay cool if we are going to get anything else out of these people. We got a lot done today, so let's just try to stay focused on the progress we've made."

Derek squeezed his forehead between his thumb and index finger. "My head's a little messed up right now. Not to mention I'm starting to get a migraine. After we eat I'm going to head back over to the inn and try to get some sleep."

"Great idea. The drive here last night kicked my ass, and we have our work cut out for us tomorrow."

Chapter Eight

S aturday, April 27, 2013

SHERIDAN'S SCARED AGAIN, a man's voice taunted diabolically over and over again as he plunged Sheridan's face into the chilled murky water. *You're not worthy of love...you're pathetic,* she heard muffled from beneath the water each time her face was submerged. She felt the reality and terror of her last breath escaping her and began to succumb to the darkness closing in around her mind. Sheridan's eyes flew open. She tried to gain control of her breathing. Rodney opened Sheridan's bedroom door holding a cup of coffee he'd prepared for her. When he realized what was happening, he ran to her.

"Okay, honey, look at me and follow my breathing," he instructed. "That's it...just breathe." Sheridan struggled to stay focused at first, but after five minutes, her breathing was normal again. "Listen, I don't think you should sleep in this room anymore."

"I don't know what happened," she said, feeling lightheaded. She'd had nightmares her whole life, but this was different.

"I'm no doctor, but I'd say you were just introduced to your first panic attack."

"I'm just tired," she said.

His face turned serious. "You're tired, beyond stressed, and have barely eaten a thing in the last few days. You need to start taking better care of yourself. In fact, why don't you let me go into town today and get the deed to your mom's house? You can take one of my Valiums and stay here and relax today."

Sheridan's cheeks turned red and she bolted up out of the bed. "I'm not a child, Rodney. I can take care of myself, and I'm fine," she hissed. "I don't need you watching over me all the time."

Rodney's brows lifted in disbelief. "Really?" he snapped back. "Well, who the hell else is going to take care of you? You don't allow anyone else to get close to you. Jesus, why can't you just get over your past and be normal?" he blurted out.

Sheridan's face turned numb and hurt. She swallowed hard to clear her throat before she spoke. "I'm sorry I'm not normal and my life isn't everything you and my mom think it should be and that you think I'm too weak to get over my past. I'm doing the best I can."

"I'm sorry, Sheridan. I didn't mean it like that."

Sheridan looked down at the floor. "It's fine. I have to get ready for my appointment with the mortgage company."

"Sheridan, please, can we just talk about this?"

"I said it's fine, Rodney. Please, just leave me be."

Rodney knew she wanted to cry, and it would only add insult to injury if she were forced to weep in front of him because that was something she'd never done. His face was apologetic, but he remained silent as he left her room and shut the door behind him. When she was certain he was gone, she cupped her quivering lips with her left palm to muffle the uncontrollable sobs escaping her.

NEITHER SHERIDAN nor Rodney said a word to each other on the morning drive into town. They pulled into the parking lot of Carter County Mortgage, Title and Loans. Rodney's face was still covered in shame from the harsh words he'd said to Sheridan earlier that morning. They were twenty minutes early, and the silence between them was killing him. "You look beautiful. The sundress was the perfect choice, and your hair looks great pulled up off your face."

"Thank you." Sheridan offered him a slight, forced smile.

"I'm so sorry I hurt you. I'm an asshole. I was wrong and didn't mean—"

"No, you're right. My past has held me back. There's so much I want to tell you but can't. If you promise not to push me, I'll tell you what I can."

"I promise."

Sheridan began fidgeting with the material of her sundress. "On my sixth birthday, Hank was in a drunken stupor, and like always, I ran into the woods to hide. I fell, hit my head on a rock, and passed out. When I came to, my eyes were taped shut and I was being carried by a strange man. There were certain details he knew about me, like the fact that it was my birthday. He told me I was pathetic, not worthy of being loved by anyone, and that he was doing me a favor by putting me out of my pathetic misery," she confessed painfully.

Sheridan pulled her stare from her lap and looked out the Jeep's window. Rodney took Sheridan's left hand into his right and held it as he waited for her to start speaking again.

"After he was done tormenting me with his humiliating words, he dragged me into the water by my hair and started drowning me. The last thing I remember was walking, almost floating really, toward a breathtaking light. It's hard to explain, but I felt like I was in a state of pure tranquility, where no one could or would ever want to hurt me," she explained.

"If he drowned you, how'd you come back?"

"That is where my story ends."

An undeniable anger began to rise within Rodney toward the man who'd hurt her, and he wanted to seek out the justice she deserved.

"Does your mom know?"

She jerked her hand from his. "No, and she never will."

"I won't say a word. I promise."

"What I will tell you is this. There have been two men in my life, one I know and one I don't, who've tried to kill me. They both agree I'm not worthy of being loved or even being alive."

"That's not true, goddamn it."

"If you're told enough that you're no good or have it literally beaten into you, eventually, you start believing it. I'm still alive, and I have always thought it was because God had a bigger purpose for me. That's why I pour my entire heart into teaching art to displaced kids. They've become my purpose. Does that make sense?" she asked.

"I'm trying to understand. I don't get where you fit into all of this. I mean, it is one thing to have a purpose and help the kids, but what about your own happiness?"

Sheridan threw him a defeated look and her voice rose. "This is precisely why I came back to Lyle. How in the hell am I ever going to get over my past unless I face what has held me back?"

"I'm an asshole," he blurted out, trying to distract her from the fire he'd ignited within her again. "What I should've been telling you this whole time is how proud of you I am. It's hard for me to wrap my brain around everything that's happened to you. No one, let alone a child, should ever have to experience what you have."

Sheridan saw his eyes welling up and grabbed his hand again to comfort him. "It's okay. I'm going to get through this."

"They hurt you, and that will never be okay," he stressed. "I've seen how their malicious actions have affected you. I've seen it in the depth of your paintings and within the cozy shelter you've built around your-self. Beyond my father dying of cancer, I've never experienced the kind of pain or fear you have. And...I'm sorry for treating you like a child. I just want you to be happy."

Sheridan reached over from her seat and embraced him. "I'm working on it. I promise," she whispered.

Sheridan pulled away from him and grabbed her purse from the backseat. "Are you okay?" she asked.

"Of course, silly. I'm a man, honey, we're always okay," he tried to tease then turned the Jeep's rearview mirror into his view so he could straighten himself up.

She took in a deep breath, smiled, and allowed herself to switch gears and embrace the moment.

Chapter Nine

Derek stood over twenty-two piles of Walter Reed's reports he'd sprawled out on the royal blue carpet of his motel room. His eyes were heavy and burned from lack of sleep. He began pacing the empty space of the floor. He concentrated on each stack he passed, hoping something about his parents' deaths would come to him in a vision. His concentration was broken by Brody kicking the bottom of his motel room door. When he opened the door, he found Brody holding two large sodas, one in each hand, and a greasy paper bag was hanging from his mouth.

"Hey, morning," Derek took one of the sodas from Brody.

"Morning? It's nearly two o'clock in the afternoon. I called you around eight this morning to see if you wanted to grab some breakfast at Nancy's, but you didn't answer. I figured you were probably wiped out, so I let you sleep."

Derek walked over to the nightstand where he'd plugged in his phone the night before to charge it. "Shit, the outlet must not work. My phone's completely dead," he said, then plugged it into another outlet.

"Yeah, when I called, it kept going straight to voicemail. My dad was blowing up my phone last night, asking me why you weren't answering or returning his calls either."

"Did he say what he wanted?"

"No, but you can ask him yourself when he gets here."

"What do you mean when he gets here?"

"Oh yeah, he's definitely coming. You must be in some pretty deep shit for him to be coming all the way here to talk to you," Brody said, amused and relieved that Derek would be feeling Quentin's wrath rather than himself.

"Shit." Derek brushed his tired fingers through his disheveled hair and yawned.

"You look like shit. Did you sleep at all last night?"

"No. I was trying to weed through Walt's notes and reports. I organized them by date and relevance, but it took all night. You'd think this guy was a doctor from his sloppy ass handwriting."

"Did you find anything?"

"I haven't been able to go over everything, but from what I've researched so far, I think Sheriff Lloyd was right about my mom's killer not being from Carter County. I still want to follow up on Hank Sheldon and his ex-wife while we're here."

"I agree. I'll call my office and have someone run the ex-wife's name so we can find out where she lives now."

"Sheriff Lloyd was also right about Walt researching my parents' pasts pretty thoroughly. There's a lot in here I wasn't aware of."

"Like what?"

"My mom was adopted when she was six by a couple who owned Chancellor Toys. Walt's files said her adoptive mom was murdered, and her dad's face butchered in one of their toy molding factories in New York. I remember seeing pictures of them around the house when I was a kid and asking my mom who they were. She'd said they were my grandparents but had both passed away. She never told me how they died. I was only four, so I never put anymore thought into it."

"You were young. I'm sure she just didn't want to fill your head with the gory details."

"That would make sense, except her adoptive dad is still alive. He was institutionalized at Baker's Mental Institution after witnessing his wife's murder. According to Walt's records, after her dad refused my mom visitation privileges, she decided to sell their factory. Her dad's still a patient there, or at least he was a few months ago according to Walt's records."

"You don't think he has anything to do with your mom's murder, do you?"

"He's been locked up at Baker's for twenty-six years, so no, it's not likely. He was a part of my mom's life, so I would like to...you know... talk to him."

"If she was adopted when she was six, she was likely in foster care for a while. That would explain why she donated so much time and money to Providence House and built Vista."

"It would. I read a lot of newspaper articles about my parents' work at different shelters and charities. I knew they were into humanitarian work, but they were also responsible for recruiting a lot of prominent people to help with their causes around New York. There were doctors, lawyers, government officials, fire chiefs. The list goes on and on."

"Well, they got my mom and dad in on their mission. I can't remember a time when my mom wasn't volunteering her time somewhere or my dad pulling out his checkbook to contribute."

Brody saw anger forming on Derek's face. He suspected it was because Derek's parents didn't deserve the ending they were given in life after they'd given so much of themselves to others.

"All right," Brody said, "I guess I'll head over to Dottie's tonight to see if I can get anything out of Walt."

Derek walked over to the desk in the corner of the room and picked up a stack of papers and handed it to Brody. "These are some of the notes Walt jotted down during his investigation, but again, I can't make out all his entries. Maybe he can tell you what they say, because I sure as hell don't have a clue."

"I'm on it. Last night, I went through some of the pictures we took of the DA's case files. Looks like Carter County Sheriff's Office was thorough in documenting their investigation and findings as far as questioning locals, evidence, et cetera...but, I want to talk to Agent

Kelly again. He was real light on documenting his own findings from Carter County and Catskills."

"Yeah, from what you and Sheriff Lloyd said, that guy sounds like a real prick. I read a lot of newspaper articles written about my parents' cases, and it was pretty obvious this Kelly was a media junkie."

"Yeah, no shit," Brody agreed. "Well, it's after two o'clock now, so I have a while before heading over to Dottie's." Brody threw the greasy bag he'd brought with him over to Derek. "I brought you a hamburger and fries from Nancy's, and holy shit, her burgers are banging too."

"Oh, I bet they are," Derek said with a slanted smile.

"Anyway...why don't you eat and get a few hours of sleep? When I get back tonight, I'll wake you up so we can go over what I got from Walt."

"I'm going to look over some more of Walt's records a little longer, but, yeah, I'll try to get some shuteye for sure." Derek walked to the nightstand and picked up a large, thick piece of paper that was rolled up.

"What's that?"

"It's the map of my mom's crime scene location. I'm going to Lyle tomorrow when there's more daylight to look around."

"Do you think that's a good idea? I mean, it's been sixteen years, so I doubt you'll find anything now."

"It's going to be uncomfortable, but I want to see if I'm able to sense anything."

"You haven't had any visions about that night in all these years. Do you really think you'll see anything now?"

"Maybe being there, you know, closer to where it happened, will help me see something. I'd be okay with anything at this point."

"It's your call." Brody grabbed Derek's spare motel room key off the dresser. "I'm going to take this just in case you're sleeping when I come back tonight."

"Good idea."

"See ya in a bit."

"Call me if shit gets weird with Walt."

"Will do."

Chapter Ten

Sheridan's and Rodney's moods had changed for the better after leaving the mortgage company. They'd had lunch at Nancy's Diner then walked over to the Piggly Wiggly to purchase cleaning supplies. The minute they arrived back to the house, Sheridan changed out of her sundress and into cleaning clothes. Rodney held true to his word and wore a pink do-rag and frilly apron while he helped clean. They'd been going strong all day.

Sheridan put away the last of the clean dishes and walked over to the pile of cleaning products on the floor in the corner of the kitchen. "We bought bleach, right?" she asked.

"I don't think we did."

"I wanted to tackle the bathroom and porch next."

"It's almost dinnertime, so why don't we call it a day, and I'll drive to town first thing in the morning and pick some up?"

"I'll go back into town now to get it. We're leaving for New York Monday, and there's still a lot left to do, so I don't want to stop."

"Well, if you're on such a roll, I wouldn't want to be rude and stop you, so I'll go into town and get the bleach," Rodney offered, wanting to escape the dust and dirt for a while.

Sheridan liked the idea of having some time to herself. "You should grab some dinner while you're out too, so we don't have to cook tonight and mess the kitchen up again."

"I'll need a shower before I go. Do you need me to do anything else before I leave?"

"Nope, I think I'm all set."

"Sweet." Rodney bolted up the stairs to take a shower before she changed her mind. When he was ready to go, Sheridan walked him out to the Jeep.

"I plugged in your cell to charge it. It's sitting on the nightstand next to your bed, so if I call to check in on you, you better answer, young lady," Rodney scolded.

"Yes, Dad," Sheridan mocked. She leaned against one of the posts on the front porch with her arms crossed and watched Rodney drive away before going back inside the house and locking the front door.

﹩

HIS CHEST BURNED from raw adrenaline pumping through his searing blood. His thoughts were scattered as he peered at Sheridan through the bushes. *She's alive...How's that possible? I fucking drowned her and I don't make mistakes.* His eyes bulged with fury when he finally understood that Meredith had manipulated him.

You fucking bitch, he thought, disgusted by his own misgivings. *Your journal entries were bullshit, weren't they? You figured out I was reading them and planted what you wanted me to see. You wanted me to think you didn't know about my plan to go earlier to kill her, and then showed up earlier yourself. You were there when I drowned her. You saved her.* He imagined Meredith was there with him in his dark psychotic world.

He placed his palms on his forehead to try and control the unbalanced thoughts. He was positive Meredith hadn't figured out his identity or their connection until right before he'd killed her, which meant she couldn't have told anyone who he was. Knowing this helped him step off the ledge of doubt he was balancing on. *You may have bought her sixteen years, but that ends tonight.*

﹩

Chapter Eleven

Deputy Dyer, who was off duty, followed Brody with suspicious eyes as he walked up to the enormous horseshoe-shaped bar at Dottie's. Small clouds of cigarette smoke rolled slowly through the air, and the crack of billiard balls could be heard from the pool tables being played to the left of the bar. On the opposite side of the dimly lit room, the dance floor was crowded with line dancers moving in sync to music being played by Tall Order, the town's local country band. Brody was thrown off guard when he approached the bar and was greeted by Nancy tending bar.

"Dinner at the diner yesterday, lunch today, and now you're at Dottie's. Are you stalking me, Brody?" Nancy flirted.

"Is there anything in this town you don't do?"

Nancy smiled. "A girl's got to make a livin', doesn't she? So, what's your poison?"

"I'm here on business," he confessed, now wishing he wasn't.

Nancy saw the file Brody was holding in his right hand. "I know you're looking to find some answers about that poor woman's murder, but you'd best be careful. The locals around here get jumpy when strangers are in town."

"Yeah, I gathered that. I'm not here to talk to the locals though. I'm only here to talk to one man."

"And who might that be?"

"Walter Reed."

"Old Walt? Good luck with that one."

"Why would I need luck?"

"Every Saturday night for months he comes in, sits on the same bar stool, has more than his fill of whiskey, and keeps to himself for the most part."

"For the most part?"

"When he does talk, it's usually to himself, and he goes on and on about how the doll is the key or how sorry he is for killing Charles Young. You rarely know what you're going to get. I reckon it just depends on how much he's had to drink, which demons are in his head, or how early he passes out on the bar."

"I'd like to talk to him anyway."

"Listen, I know there's a lot of folks around here who think old Walt's crazy, and maybe he is, but he's paid his dues, Brody. And I—"

Brody gently placed his hand over Nancy's. "I just want to talk to him. I'm actually on his side."

She paused for a moment then nodded her head towards the last stool at the back of the solid oak bar being occupied by an elderly man.

"Maybe when you're done talkin' to old Walt, you'll find time for that drink."

"Mind if I sit down?" Brody asked in a friendly tone.

Walter ignored Brody, never moving his bloodshot eyes from the shot of Jim Beam he attempted to hold securely within his shaky hands. Brody took a seat next to Walter, pulled his wallet from the back pocket of his jeans, and slid his badge in front of Walter. "Name's Brody. I work for the NBI. I'm here investigating the murder of Meredith Hope Young. I was hoping to ask you a few questions about your investigation."

Walter slammed back his shot and gestured to Nancy for a refill.

He glared at Brody with disdain in his eyes. "I've had more than my fill of you arrogant bureau boys. Y'all think you know somethin' about the truth, but I'm here to tell ya, you don't know shit," Walter slurred, his drunken breath lingering toward Brody. He turned his attention back to the shot glass Nancy was refilling.

Brody slid the file he'd brought with him in front of Walter and opened it. "I'm not here to ask you about the DA's investigation. I'm here to ask you about your investigation."

Walter's demeanor turned from rigid and cold to suspicious and accusing. "Where the hell did you get them files, boy?" he demanded.

Brody turned his stool to face Walter. "Sheriff Lloyd. Charles Young is my uncle. I'm here looking for the truth, just like you tried to do after you realized you pegged the wrong man."

A flush of guilt covered Walter's face. His eyes searched Brody's to determine if he was there for the truth or revenge.

"I'm not here to start trouble, Mr. Reed. I believe they were chasing the wrong man. I need your help finding the real murderer, so I can bring my aunt and uncle the justice they deserve." He paused before he spoke again. "They also left a son behind whose looking for closure about his parents' deaths, and I think you're just the man to help him find that closure."

"Derek?"

"Yes."

Walter's head began to bobble as he tried to lift his head again and focus on his empty shot glass. Brody gestured for Nancy to pour Walter another.

"Is he in town with you?"

"Yes, he is. We're staying at the Carter County Inn next door."

"Why didn't he come here with ya?"

"He—"

"Never mind. No need to explain. I already know why he didn't come, and I'm grateful for his mercy on me. I'd give my own life if I had the chance to bring that boy's daddy back, ya know?"

"Mr. Reed, Derek knows the sacrifices you made to try and clear his dad's name. Like me, his only intention for being here is to find out the truth about what happened that night. Helping us would be the first step in showing him that you're a good man."

"There's no good in me, boy, only the wicked darkness that I've been tryin' my damnedest to kill with my ol' friend Jim." He slammed back another shot. "But yeah, I'll help."

Nancy slid a glass in front of Brody and poured him a shot of whiskey. "That's enough," Nancy warned Brody beneath her breath. "Just, let him be 'til he's sober tomorrow."

Brody lifted his shot glass to thank Nancy for the shot. Before he could pull the drink to his lips, someone bumped into his right shoulder. When Brody looked to see who the culprit was, he was surprised to see a well-groomed man in his mid-twenties wearing a pink flannel shirt, Ralph Lauren jeans, and a pair of new gray snakeskin cowboy boots.

❧

"OH MY GOD, I'm so sorry, honey. These boots are new, and I'm having a hard time breaking them in. Let me buy you another drink."

"It's fine," Brody said, using a napkin to absorb the drink, which had splattered on his shirt.

"I insist."

"Yeah, sure, why not?"

Rodney called Nancy over to where they were sitting. "I'd like to buy my friend here another shot, please. Hey, aren't you the waitress from Nancy's?"

"I am," she replied with a friendly smile.

"Well, aren't you a busy little bee?" Rodney observed.

"That's what I said," Brody chuckled.

"I was heartbroken when I went to the diner tonight and it was already closed. I saw Dottie's sign on the diner door that said chicken wings and line dancing, so I couldn't resist walking over here."

"Do you want me to put in an order of wings for ya, sugar?" Nancy asked.

"Yes. I'll take thirty medium wings and a side of fries, but I need them to go."

"Thirty wings? Goodness gracious, you must have a pretty hefty appetite," Nancy said.

"Oh no, they're not all for me. Trust me, honey, my thighs couldn't handle that much food," Rodney joked in a low whisper.

"That's right, I saw you with Sheridan this afternoon for lunch at the diner. How is she?" Nancy asked.

"You know her?" Rodney asked.

"We went to elementary school together for a bit, but I was a few grades ahead of her, so we really didn't talk too much. My sister Emma went to high school and worked at the diner with her mamma, Rhonda, though." She shot Brody a quick glance to see if he'd caught the connection. Brody did and sat patiently waiting for his opportunity to include himself in their conversation.

"Okay...okay. Rhonda's my aunt. So, you must know my mom Maggie too then?"

"Maggie May's your mamma? What a small world. I heard she did really well for herself after she left Lyle."

"Yeah, she's done pretty well. Aunt Rhonda and Sheridan have also done well. Aunt Rhonda opened up her own diner, and Sheridan's the emerging artist MoMA chose to feature this year," Rodney bragged.

"That's really great," Nancy said.

"MoMA, huh? That's impressive. I live in New York, too. It must have been a culture shock for them moving from Lyle to New York," Brody said, trying to engage Rodney.

"Oh, we don't live in New York, at least not yet. We live in Kensington Manor, Connecticut, but we're leaving for New York Monday to start hunting for an apartment in Manhattan for Sheridan. You know, so she can be closer to the art scene and all."

"I see," Brody said.

Rodney extended his hand out to Brody. "I'm Rodney. And you are?"

"Brody," he replied, then shook Rodney's hand.

"So what do you do in New York, and what the hell are you doing here in Carter County of all places?" Rodney said.

"I work for the NBI. I'm here on business."

"The NBI, huh? That sounds like dangerous work. Did you come to Carter County alone?"

"I came here with my cousin."

"Does he work for the NBI too?" Rodney asked.

"No, he tagged along to look into some investment real estate," he lied.

"Can I get you a drink while you wait for your food, hon?" Nancy asked Rodney.

"Absolutely. Let's see...I'll take a mudslide with extra whipped cream and extra cherries."

Brody was grateful for the lighter mood Rodney's presence had created compared to the dark one they'd been deep in only moments before with Walter. Unfortunately, the lighter mood was short lived the minute Tommy Clemons, who was half-lit, and a group of his obnoxious friends walked in.

"Who's that?" Brody asked, noticing Nancy had become uneasy the minute she saw the men.

"Tommy Clemons and his entourage."

"Clemons? Billy Clemons' brother, right?" Brody was ready to pounce on the brother of the man who'd shot his uncle.

"Please, Brody," she whispered, "now's not the time or place to confront him."

Rodney looked over his right shoulder to see what had caught Brody's undivided attention. He saw five burly men walking toward the bar. Tommy staggered over to the bar and stood behind Walter, who was passed out. "Looks like all the freaks came out to play tonight," Tommy bellowed out.

Deputy Dyer, who'd had his eyes on Brody and Rodney from the moment they'd each walked in, made his way through the crowd of people on the dance floor. His gut told him all hell was getting ready to break loose, and he wanted to stop it before it started.

"Let's see, you got your washed up old Sheriff who's the crazy town drunk, an agent snooping around town where he ain't got no business, and a gay fairy princess in pink flannel," Tommy taunted.

"All right, Tommy, you've had your fun. Now, I reckon you'd better be gettin' on home," Nancy encouraged.

"Wait a minute, fellas, looks like we're missing the biggest freak of them all. Where's she at, fairy boy? She hiding in the bathroom? What's a matter? Is Sheridan scared again?" Tommy mocked.

"I will scratch your fucking eyes out, you hillbilly piece of shit!" Rodney threatened.

"Come on, queer boy, give me your best shot." Tommy threw both arms up in the air and invited Rodney to jump.

"Fuck this asshole," Brody said and darted up from his stool and cold-cocked Tommy in the jaw.

Tommy fell hard, leaving Brody standing over him. Tommy didn't move, but the four men he'd come with started moving towards Brody. Before the men reached Brody, Rodney cracked one of the men in the side of the head with his fist. Brody shot Rodney a grateful look for having his back. Rodney dodged a punch from one of Tommy's friends, swung back to defend himself, and hit Deputy Dyer square in the jaw.

"Shit," Brody said, knowing full well what was coming next.

⁊

"I TOLD you not to do it," Nancy scolded Brody, who was standing in front of her now in handcuffs.

"Clocking that jackass was worth spending a couple nights in jail."

"A couple nights?"

"Oh yeah, Sheriff Lloyd said the judge is out of town until Monday, so bail can't be set."

"A little too convenient," Nancy said.

"I don't mind doing a little hard time in Carter County Jail," Brody joked, forcing a smile on Nancy's face.

"What about him?" Nancy looked over at Rodney who was also in handcuffs and leaning against one of the pool tables.

"He'll be fine. He's worried about his cousin, though. He drove their only vehicle into town, so she's stuck up on the mountain with no transportation. Sheriff Lloyd let him try to call her, but she didn't answer. He left her a few voicemails, but she hasn't called back. I told Rodney I'd have you call Derek and have him go check on her to let her know what's going on."

"I can do that." She pulled the pen that was tucked in behind her ear and wrote 'Derek' on the palm of her hand. "All right, shoot."

"His number is 217-555-0312. Tell him what happened and that I'm not getting out of jail until Monday. Let him know Rodney had my back in the fight, and that I need him to do me a favor and drive out to Lyle tonight to check in on Rhonda's daughter. Rodney left her a few messages, so she'd know to expect him. Be sure to stress that she's Rhonda's daughter, and if it comes up about why we're in Carter County, he's here looking at investment property."

"All right, boys, time to go," Sheriff Lloyd instructed. "I need to ask Nancy a few more questions, but I'll head back over to the station after," he informed his deputies.

§.

SHERIFF LLOYD WALKED over to Nancy and rested his right hand on her shoulder. "Sorry to close ya down so early, but I thought it was best for everybody to just go on home and call it a night. My gut told me there'd be trouble when they pulled into town."

"Now wait a second, Frank, you've got it all wrong. Brody and the other guy were mindin' their own damn business before Tommy and his boys came in here like bulls in a china shop. This ain't the first time Tommy's started trouble at Dottie's, and you know it."

"Slow down there, missy," he warned. "First of all, your friend Brody works for the NBI and knew better than to go throwin' punches, especially the first one. And his friend hittin' a deputy, accident or not, didn't help matters much either, now did it?"

"Tommy would've thrown the first punch if Brody hadn't beat him to it, and you know it, Sheriff."

"Listen, I know you think I'm takin' sides here, but I'm not. Those boys started the fight and left me no choice but to haul their asses in. If I was takin' sides, why the hell would I be makin' Tommy spend the weekend in jail too? I have no problem with Brody and his cousin being in town. Believe me, I'd love nothin' more than to see those boys bring ol' Walt a little redemption."

"So then you know why they're here?"

"Yeah I do, and so does the DA's office, which is why I can't go showin' those boys any favoritism."

"The DA's office? What the hell do they have to do with anything?"

Sheriff Lloyd scoped the room to ensure they were alone before he spoke. "The DA's office doesn't want them here. They're afraid they'll find out about the missing evidence from Meredith Young's crime scene."

"Missing evidence? What are you talkin' about, Frank?"

"There was a doll and a few pictures of Meredith Young holdin' it in her arms taken at the crime scene that turned up missin'. The DA's office had the few of us who had access to the evidence picked up for questionin'. When they went to pick up Walt, he was found in his backyard burnin' the pictures in a fire pit. A half-charred picture was all that was recovered, and it was definitely of Meredith Young."

"And the doll?"

"It was never recovered. Even though Walt was caught red handed, to this day he swears he didn't take the evidence. Says he was set up. Our participation in the initial investigation had already been considered a joke. The TBI agent assistin' us with the case made sure of that by labelin' us as a bunch of pencil pushers. The DA's office wanted to avoid any bad press that was sure to come if the media found out one of our own lost his mind, so they covered it up like the evidence never even existed."

"And you never told anyone about the cover-up?"

"All the evidence was there provin' we had the right man, even without the doll or pictures. I may not have agreed with Walt back then about his suspicions, but he was my mentor and friend. If it got out, he would've been prosecuted for tampering with evidence, so I left it alone."

"So what changed your mind?"

"Let's just say I found somethin' that made me scratch my head about Charles Young's suspected motive to kill his wife. I went to the DA's office with what I found, but they immediately shut me down. I was afraid they'd drum up another cover-up or close the case if they thought I was strayin' from our original motive. I had to backpedal my ass real quick to make them think I still believed we had the right guy.

If I hadn't arrested those boys tonight, the DA's office would have become suspicious."

"So why are you telling me all of this?"

"You're the only person in this town Walt trusts besides me. I've been trying to get him to shoot me straight about the doll and pictures for years, but he ain't talkin'."

"What does that have to do with me?"

"I need you to get Walt to admit he took the evidence and see if he destroyed the doll. I'm still not convinced the doll is even relevant, but at this point, I need to be sure."

"Let's say the doll is still around. What then?"

"If it is and it's relevant to the case, I turn it over to Brody and Derek, I won't have a choice."

"And if it's not?"

"We leave well enough alone. Listen, you don't have to do this. I'm just runnin' out of options here."

"I'll see what I can get out of him. It's not going to be easy though. I'll need to sober him up."

"Guess I should head over to the jail and be sure everyone's playin' nice, but I'll check in with ya at the diner in the mornin'."

"All right," she replied, as he walked toward the door. "You're a good man, Sheriff."

He didn't stop walking but turned his head to the side, tilted his hat down, and bid her good night.

Chapter Twelve

Derek's peaceful slumber ended when a loud rapping on his door woke him. He got up, pulled his jeans on, and opened the door. He was surprised to see his uncle standing in the doorway. "I'm sorry I haven't returned your calls. We've had a lot of distractions since we left and my phone was dead—" Derek explained before Quentin cut him off.

"It's fine, Derek. I needed to see you in person. Where's Brody?"

"I'm not sure, I just woke up, but I can call him."

"No, it's fine. I wanted to talk to you in private."

"What's going on? Is Aunt Lexus okay?"

"She's fine. I have something to give you and it couldn't wait. I need you to understand I was given specific instructions by your father not to give this to you until I thought you were ready to read it." He then pulled Meredith's letter from the inner pocket of his trench coat.

Derek took a step back. "My father?"

"Before your father fled to the chalet in New York, he came to the hospital to see you. He asked me to give you this letter and made me vow to never read it. It's from your mother, Derek. I was told to give it to you when I thought you were ready, and when I heard you were going to Lyle Mountain, my gut told me it was time." Quentin handed the letter over. Derek stared down at it and walked over to the chair by the desk and sat down.

"I'm sorr—" Quentin began saying before Derek put his left hand in the air as a warning to Quentin to not approach him. His fingers moved along the seal of the envelope and opened it.

☙

MY DEAREST DEREK,

BY THE TIME you receive my letter, you will have learned so much about life. You will have also discovered your ability to see pieces of the past and future. But, there will still be much for you to learn and recognize, my love.

Blessed with the use of his own third eye, my adopted father saw the light of The Knowing within me. Unlike you and the children from Vista, The Knowing's abilities are not predestined at birth. They're bestowed later on in life to those who possess the light of The Knowing within. The gift is a choice. It's either embraced or forsaken.

If forsaken, the light dims, and one simply continues on their prewritten journey. If embraced, the light of The Knowing ignites, and our prewritten courses shift to foster the evolution of mankind.

The role of The Knowing is to protect and guide those born with spiritual gifts. Although we're permitted to see well beyond what the normal mind will allow, an unspoken law forbids us to see all or manipulate one's fate. The triggering of catastrophic events is the consequence of altering anyone's pure state of being. Only God is omniscient, which is why we're only given small pieces of much larger puzzles. Acceptance of your own purpose will lead you to the answers you seek.

I struggled with my gifts in the beginning. My first visions came to me at twenty-two within my dreams. They were of a deranged boy clutching my father's antique Masonic dagger within his hands as though it were his trophy. He began coming to me in the form of an evil shadow who inflicted unspeakable acts upon innocent and unsuspecting victims. What I saw were his malicious acts of violence before they came to full fruition.

I was warned by another like me not to go to the authorities with my visions. Days before you were born, I became desperate to help the evil shadow's future victims and foolishly ignored the warning. I confessed what I'd seen with hopes I could prevent another victim from suffering at the hands of this dark monster.

Because we're only given small pieces of any given puzzle, I was unable to give an accurate description of the assailant, his victims, or when the attacks would take place. I was discredited and dismissed as being a crazy, unbalanced fortuneteller. I was threatened to be institutionalized just as the woman before me had who'd also claimed to have visions.

I couldn't risk losing you. When I left that day, I never spoke about my visions out loud to anyone again. I accepted my new path in life, which was to protect and guide those who came into the world with special gifts. Thus, the creation of Vista House.

Shortly after we opened Vista, I was diagnosed with brain cancer. While the tumor was in its early stages, it immediately began affecting the clarity of my visions. I began journaling what I saw to ensure I could continue protecting those who played a significant role in the future of mankind.

To this day, I'm not sure how, but the evil shadow from my visions discovered my journals. When he became privy to all I saw to come, including his own capture, natural patterns began to shift.

For six years, he's used his knowledge from my own written words to hide his identity, even from me. He's plotted his own path of destruction and plans to prevent the future I predicted from occurring.

What he didn't know is I discovered he found my journals, and that I too have been plotting all these years to fix what I myself have broken. I've continued writing in my journals but have written only what I've intended for him to see. I was able to make him believe he would be caught if he continued his wrath upon the innocent, and so his violence stopped.

Once I lose my battle with cancer, I'll no longer be able to protect you or those who have the ability to put the natural pattern back on its destined path.

This is why it's imperative he believes everyone and everything that could reveal his past has been destroyed. The only way to accomplish this is by my own death occurring before its natural course. Please know, my love, that my death will be of my own free will and not by the hands of your father who loved us both more than his own life.

If my visions are right, the monster will discover I've deceived him in sixteen years' time. Because he's ruthless, he'll stop at nothing to protect his identity and the crimes he's committed.

Once I'm gone, it will be up to you to finish what I've started. My letter is meant to guide those you trust when the time comes. Your true journey will begin when the secrets of the stars are revealed and you accept the blessings of five thousand, two hundred, and thirteen angels.

Please take comfort in knowing your father and I are always watching over you, and that everything we've done, has been for the evolution of mankind and our undying love for you.

FOREVER AND ALWAYS,
   Mom

❧

THE REVELATION of his mother's self-sacrifice for him and the greater good of mankind ripped through Derek's heart. For the first time since his mother's death, Derek felt her presence with him. He sat, eyes closed, and played each word she'd written over and over again until they burned within his mind.

There was so much she'd disclosed to him, and so much she hadn't, and he knew this was her intent. She could only guide him, but he was to discover and follow his own written path. She had confirmed what he'd always known; his father hadn't killed her. *I wish he was here to help me finish what you started, Mom, but Dad is gone. Even without him, your death won't be in vain.*

"I'll find you, you son of a bitch. You'll pay for what you've done," he said under his breath.

❧

"YOU OKAY?" Quentin asked.

Derek's eyes opened, and he became guarded when he realized Quentin was still in the room.

"I'm fine," Derek lied.

Quentin had fought the burning temptation to open the letter more than once but had managed to keep his word to Charles. However, the anticipation of finally knowing what Meredith had written began strangling his cool composure. He took in a deep breath and tried to be mindful of Derek's current state. "What did it say?"

"My father didn't ki—" he started then paused, remembering his mother's words. *The evil shadow from my visions discovered my journals. When he became privy to all I saw to come, including his own capture, natural patterns began to shift.*

Derek understood Quentin's desire to know what the letter said, but his mother had sacrificed her own life to put the natural pattern back on its destined path. If anyone found his mother's letter, prewritten paths would be at risk of changing again. He refused to allow his parents' deaths to be without purpose.

Derek took the pack of matches from the clean ashtray sitting on the desk, lit one, and began burning his mother's letter. Once the first page fully ignited, he threw the remaining pages and matches in the metal garbage can next to the desk.

"What have you done? That letter could've proven your father's innocence!" Quentin roared.

"More death is all that would come if anyone ever found her letter. You have to trust me."

"Then why, Derek? Why would she write you a letter?"

"Tell me, Uncle Quentin, how did you know that my trip to Lyle was the right time to give me the letter? Why didn't you open it years ago, or why not just give it to me much sooner than you did?"

"I-I just knew."

"Exactly. You just knew. Just like my parents knew they could trust you. Just like I knew the letter had to be destroyed. Have you ever once believed for a second that my father killed my mom?"

"No, of course not."

"Why?"

"Because I just know—" he started and then stopped, understanding what Derek was trying to explain.

Derek offered him a warm smile. "Sometimes, with or without a gift, we just know."

"I guess we do."

"You've been like a father to me and have always referred to me as one of your sons. Because you love me, I need you to believe I will not stop until I bring them each justice. Can you do that?"

Quentin placed his hands over Derek's cheeks and patted the left. "I can do that," he said, remembering the lost child Derek once was but seeing the man he'd now become.

Both Derek and Quentin became distracted by the sudden blaring of Derek's cell phone ringing. Derek walked over to the nightstand and picked up his cell.

❧

"HELLO?" Derek answered. "Yeah, this is Derek. Who's this?...Nancy. From the diner, right? Brody's not here, but I'll have him call you when he gets back. Is everything okay?" Derek put the phone on speaker so Quentin could hear the conversation too.

"He's fine...but...he's in jail and will be until the judge comes in on Monday to set bail," Nancy said.

"What the hell happened?"

"Brody and another guy from out of town got into a fight with a few of the locals."

"A few?"

"You're sure he's okay?" Quentin chimed in.

"Sorry, his dad's here, and I have you on speaker," Derek confessed.

"Oh, hi. Yes. He's fine."

"I appreciate you calling to let us know what's going on. I'll head over to the jail."

"Derek?" Nancy called out.

"I'm here."

"Brody also wanted me to ask you if you could do a favor for the man who helped him during the fight."

"Absolutely."

"The guy's visiting from out of town and came here with his cousin. They're leaving Lyle on Monday to fly to New York, but he drove their only vehicle into town, so she's stuck up on Lyle without a car. He tried to call her, but she didn't answer, so he's pretty worried. Anyway, Brody told him you wouldn't mind driving up to Lyle to check in on her tonight, but if you can't, I can do it."

Derek looked down at his watch and saw that it was a little after nine-thirty. "You don't think she'll get spooked by a strange man coming out this late, do you?" he asked.

"Brody said Rodney left her a message lettin' her know you'd be comin' out, but again, I can go if you think a woman showin' up would be better."

"No, if she knows I'm coming, it'll be fine. What's the address?" Derek asked, scrambling to find a piece of paper and a pen. Quentin pulled both from the desk drawer and handed them to him.

"You ready?" Nancy asked

"Yep."

"It's 261 Cider Creek Road."

Derek was blinded by a bright picture that flashed before his eyes of a white two-story house, sitting in the darkness behind two enormous trees.

"Derek?" Nancy called out again.

Derek forced himself to shake the vision off and answered her. "Yeah, I'm still here."

"Brody wanted me to make sure I told you the woman you're going to check in on is Rhonda's daughter, and if it comes up, you're in Carter County looking at investment property."

"Does Rhonda's daughter have a name?"

"Sheridan Hayes."

"Got it. I'll head that way in a few minutes."

"Let me know if I can do anything else."

"Will do. Thanks again for calling." Derek said then hung up.

Derek walked over to the dresser and pulled a pair of socks and a clean white T-shirt from the dresser drawer. "Looks like our badass lost his temper and got his ass thrown in jail," Derek said as he pulled the T-shirt over his head and half tucked it into his jeans.

"What the hell was he thinking? If you're going up to Lyle to check on that girl, I'll head over to the jail and find out what's going on with his bail being set."

Derek sat on the bed and started putting his socks and boots on. "By the time I get up to Lyle Mountain and back, it'll be too late for me to do anything, so just call and let me know what's going on."

"Will do. So who is Rhonda's daughter?"

"Sheridan Hayes is the daughter of a woman we wanted to follow up with about the case."

"Do you think Rhonda has anything to do with your mom's murder?"

"Not likely. Rhonda gave her ex-husband an alibi the night my mom was murdered. We want to be sure the alibi was solid so we can rule her ex-husband out. The daughter was pretty young back then, but she might remember something that will help us."

"Okay. Well, I guess I'll head over to the jail, do you know the addre—" Quentin started to say before a loud crack of thunder distracted both of them.

Heavy rain started thrashing against the motel room door. "Great, nothing like driving up a steep dark mountain in the pouring rain," Derek said then turned to Quentin. "The Sheriff's Office is three blocks up the road. You can't miss it." He grabbed his leather jacket and the map of Meredith's crime scene.

"I'll call you when I find out what's going on with Brody's bail."

"All right." Derek opened the door and lifted his jacket above his head to shelter himself and the map from getting soaked.

Chapter Thirteen

Sheridan climbed a step stool sitting under the dusty ceiling fan in the living room. When she stood on the tip of her toes to reach the upper blades of the fan, she lost her balance and crashed hard onto the large bucket of cleaning fluid sitting next to the stool.

"Son of a bitch," she screeched out from the stinging pain wrapping itself around her right ankle and ribs. She used the arm of the leather recliner to pull herself up off the floor. She was relieved when she was able to apply pressure on the injured foot, which meant it was a minor sprain. However, her ribs felt like they were jabbing into her side making it difficult for her to breathe. "You've got to be kidding me."

Sheridan stopped several times on the stairs to give her ankle a rest, attempting to not make it worse. When she reached the top, she focused on two doors. *Bedroom or bathroom? Get my cell and call Rodney to pick up an elastic bandage and listen to him scold me, or a hot bath? I'm so taking the hot bath.* She limped into the bathroom.

Sheridan undressed while the tub filled. When she turned to throw her clothes next to the hamper, she caught her reflection in the oblong mirror hanging on the back of the door. She cringed in pain as she traced around the red mark forming around her injured ribs. She turned from the mirror to step into the tub and saw Rodney's grooming bag on the back of the toilet. There were two prescription bottles peeking out from the top. *Valium 10mg TAKE 1 TABLET BY MOUTH ONCE A DAY.* "And what do we have here?" she whispered, then read the next bottle. *Hydrocodone 7.5mg TAKE 1 TABLET BY MOUTH EVERY 8 HOURS AS NEEDED FOR PAIN.*

After another sharp pain twisted in her side, the decision to give in to the relief the pills would offer came easy. Sheridan popped off the caps, placed one pill from each bottle on her tongue, then swallowed them both back with water she sipped from under the faucet. Sheridan stepped into the hot bath, and a sigh of pleasure escaped her lips as the events of the day began to melt away.

A SERENE SMILE formed on Sheridan's lips, and she allowed herself to indulge in the tranquil sensation the pills were providing. Her pain was nil, and her mind relaxed as she twirled the amethyst stone necklace between her lazy fingers.

A hard but casual knocking on the downstairs door pulled her away from the slumber she'd only been seconds from slipping into. She turned her head toward the bathroom door, as if doing so would help her hear. The knocking stopped momentarily, but then resumed, and started becoming more persistent. Sheridan guessed Rodney forgot the spare key was under the mat, so he thought he was locked out. She placed her hands on each side of the tub and pushed herself up to get out. When she reached for the thin white towel hanging from the rack, she became unsteady.

She placed her right hand on the bathroom wall to brace herself and stepped out of the tub. She patted her groggy eyes and body dry with the towel, then searched the bathroom for her robe, but to no avail. She opened the lid of the hamper, pulled her sundress out, and began pulling it over her head just as the knocking downstairs became more obnoxious. "Hold on, Rodney, I'm coming," she slurred.

Sheridan walked down the stairs, taking each step one at a time to prevent making her ankle any worse. When Sheridan got to the front door, she saw it was opened and looked outside. A flash of lightning lit up the driveway. The rental car wasn't anywhere in sight.

She tiptoed in the dark toward the kitchen in an effort to make a run for it out the back door. As she reached the entrance of the kitchen, she saw a dark hooded silhouette move within the shadows of the living room to the right of her. Pure adrenaline took over when the hooded shadow stepped toward her. She scurried through the kitchen, pulling a chair between them to slow him down. She bolted out the back door and into the downpour of rain.

When she saw the rusty old milk barrel next to the equally rusty shed in the backyard, she paused to grab supplies. Still drugged, Sheridan had stepped back into the role of the six-year-old child who'd always planned her escapes from Hank. She lifted the lid and saw the empty barrel. She made herself keep moving, running deep into the forest. His relentless footsteps were close behind.

DEREK'S GPS had gotten him right up to the last turn that should've taken him to Rhonda's house before it lost its signal. There had been no signs of a house for the last three quarters of a mile, so he questioned whether the GPS had turned him down the wrong driveway. He knew if he were lost, there would be no way to find the house in the pitch darkness and pouring rain. Brody had arranged for him to talk to Sheridan without intimidation because he was just a guy doing her cousin a favor. However, if he couldn't find the place on his own, he'd have no choice but to call the Sheriff and have him drive out to Lyle and make sure she was okay.

"Shit," Derek barked and slammed his right palm hard on the steering wheel when the gas light came on. Just as he started to pull his cell phone from his back pocket to call Quentin for help, he saw the lights from the porch on the familiar two-story house. He pulled the Escalade up as close as possible to the porch to avoid getting soaked, then jumped out, and ran up the steps. Without question, he knew this was the same house that had crept into his mind back at the motel while talking to Nancy. He became uneasy when he saw the front door was ajar. He knocked with the knuckle of his index finger and pushed the door open further.

"Sheridan? Hello? Anybody here?" He cautiously walked inside the dimly lit entrance and scanned the house. There was a chair on its side in the middle of the kitchen floor and uneven muddy footprints leading to the backyard. The screen door was hanging by one hinge and slamming against the back of the house. He caught it before it slammed again. Bolts of lightning lit up the sky, and he heard a woman's bloodcurdling screams. Each scream faded and was lost within the rolling crashes of thunder.

Without pause, Derek jumped off the back porch and flew into the woods.

PURE TERROR BEGAN OPPRESSING Sheridan's mind when she sensed the ferocious madman was closing in on her heels. The familiar path she'd taken in the past to escape Hank was all she had to rely on. Long soaked layers of hair obscured her vision as she ran wild through the tangled woods. Agonizing moans slipped from her trembling lips each time the sharp earthy floor sliced into her bare feet. Her breathing was labored and tremors of fear shook her.

An exposed tree root on the river's edge caught Sheridan's right foot and brought her down hard on her injured ribs. The distraction of the fall permitted the cool wet air to settle into her bones and her teeth began chattering. She tried pushing herself up but kept losing her footing in the slippery puddle of mud beneath her. Deranged panic set in when she saw her necklace had fallen off and was laying just out of her reach. On her last failed attempt to reach it, she began screaming.

When the moon removed itself from behind a bank of ominous dark clouds, her screams hushed, and she became silent and still. She laid in a fetal position, staring blankly at the staggering pieces of gold illuminating off the crashes of water in the rapid running river. His slow approaching footsteps snapped the twigs and foliage behind her, mocking the unbalanced emotions that were now holding her own mind hostage. Sheridan's will to fight him was lost. She was now accepting the death she'd escaped by his hands sixteen years earlier.

He knelt down behind her and whispered in her ear. "Aw, what's the matter, little girl? Are you not happy to see me?"

When Sheridan didn't respond, he became enraged and rolled her onto her back. He thrust the back of his hand across her cheek as a bolt of lightning lit up the sky. He crawled on top of her and snatched a handful of hair from the back of her head and pulled her face closer to meet his eyes. "I can assure you, bitch, the feeling is mutual."

Malicious intent veiled his face as he stared down at his comatose victim, and he began laughing. "You're making this way too easy for me, Sheridan." He slid the sheer sundress clinging to her soaked body halfway up her left thigh.

"It's been a long time since I've felt the gratification of tormenting and shredding a woman of her innocence. Your savior's manipulated journals made sure of it. But, she's dead, and her written words mean nothing to me now." He paused, distracted by his revelation of coincidence between time passed and the mandated age of all his victims.

"Well, it appears as though I'm having a full circle moment, my dear. Twenty-two years have passed, twenty-two years they were, and twenty-two years you are. Don't you see, Sheridan? You're exactly where you're supposed to be, which is right here, right now, with me. You'll receive the same stimulating ritual as the other selfish whores, with only one exception. I won't wait nine months to bring you to your death and rip out your fucking uterus."

He jerked her head back and began ravishing her exposed neck with his greedy mouth and shoved her sundress up the remainder of her thigh. He paused to look deep into her soulless eyes with heinous satisfaction and taunted her before executing his plan to take her. "Who's going to save you now, Sheridan?" he seethed.

"That would be me, asshole!" Derek crashed his right shoulder into the baleful silhouette straddling Sheridan, knocking him off her. The impact of Derek's blow threw them both tumbling into the angry river. The depth of water met Derek's waist. He fought to stand up, never letting go of the back of his adversary's neck. The current was unforgiving, and they began drifting downstream.

Derek was being pulled farther away from Sheridan, and his mind began racing. He knew saving himself would be the only way he could go back to help her, so he focused in on his surroundings. Ahead, there was a metal sign to the right and dangling branches to the left of him that provided two opportunities.

He saw the dangling branches to the left were his best option, so he squeezed the back of his deadweight's neck one last time before letting him go. Derek's thunderous frustration echoed throughout the mountains as he watched the man's shadow flow downstream to freedom. Exhausted and gasping for air, Derek managed to pull himself up onto the riverbank. He struggled with his footing on the wet earthy ground, but his raw determination to get back to Sheridan helped him prevail.

THE RAIN HAD SLOWED to a light drizzle. Derek tore his way through clusters of branches along the river's edge to find Sheridan. When he broke through the last of the wild foliage, he found her in the small clearing next to the river, lying cold and still, just as he'd left her. Derek fell hard to his knees beside her and placed his ear to her chest to listen for a heartbeat. When his face touched her shivering flesh, a scorching ache rushed his blood, rendering him blind, yet filling his soul with sublime completion. He knew with certainty she'd been the faceless child who haunted his dreams within the locked chambers of his mind. The enchanted creature that lay before him, however, was without question a woman.

A soft moan escaped her lips and pulled him from the enigmatic euphoria he'd fallen in. Thick dark strands of soaked muddy hair veiled her delicate pale face. He brushed them away with the tip of his index finger, exposing her closed lids. He blinked away wet drops of rain from his lashes to see her better. "Sheridan, can you hear me?" he whispered. When she didn't respond, he cupped her chin within his right palm and caressed her cheek with his thumb. "Sheridan, can you hear me?" he whispered again.

Her long black lashes lifted and when her gaze met his familiar eyes, she whispered, "I love you, angel." She lifted her hand and tenderly touched his face, making his heart ache. Her arm fell limply to the ground, and her eyes fell back into the depth of her mind.

"Sheridan? No, please stay with me. I just found you. I can't lose you now, please," Derek pleaded. He heard a turbulent roll of thunder exploding behind them. Heavy rain began falling from the unlit sky again. Without hesitation, he scooped her body up into his arms and began moving swiftly back through the woods. Intrusive snippets of Sheridan's life began playing in reverse within his mind. The visuals and raw emotion of Sheridan's past were cutting into his own shaken soul. He felt her memories were significant and tried to embrace each one as they imprinted within his mind.

All were of her and coming to him hard and fast, flashing in sync with the pounding of his own rapid heartbeat: *a necklace holding a rugged amethyst stone laying outside a shallow muddy puddle; the attacker ravishing her body as she lay numb in the mud on the river's edge; the mile marker sign to Lyle Mountain; a pillow placed forcefully over her face as a child; her gasping for air before being submerged into dark murky water as a child; her little body covered in bruises curled up in a dark corner; her first cry upon entering the world; her name written next to his in a weathered brown journal by Meredith's hand with a beautiful red rose sitting just above her alluring penmanship...*

THE SILHOUETTE of the back porch pulled Derek from his subconscious state. He hooked his foot around the bottom of the broken screen door and flung it off its last hinge to remove it from his path. He realized the power must have gone out from the storm because the only light seeping into small corners of the house was from the moon.

Sheridan's dangling arm brushed the sides of his hip as he climbed the unlit stairs to find a warm place to lay her down. With his right shoulder, he pushed open the door of her bedroom and laid her on the bed. A glare coming off the glass oil lamp next to the bed caught his attention. He riffled through the nightstand's drawer, hoping to find something to ignite the wick. He found a small box of wooden matches and lit the lamp.

The room filled with a soft warm glow, and he saw Sheridan was now shaking from the cold air trapped in the small space. The mud from her hair and skin had been washed away by the downpour of rain. Her sundress was soaked and her supple breasts were exposed through the wet, sheer material.

Out of respect and to warm her, he pulled her long terry cloth robe from the bedpost and laid it over the length of her dainty body. He walked over to the cherry oak dresser and rummaged through the drawers until he found a loose pair of black cotton pajamas. A small chair in the right corner of the room held a handmade quilt, which he added to the stack in his arms then walked back over to her. He covered her with the quilt, removed the robe from underneath, and slid her sundress up over her head. Maneuvering his way blindly under the quilt to re-dress her was a challenge. Just as he'd pulled the last of the black camisole down to her sides, Sheridan cringed in pain.

He lifted the quilt and pulled back the bottom corner of her camisole to see what had made her jerk. "Jesus," he softly whispered, empathetic and worried from the sight of the welt and bruises that stained her right lower ribs.

Discovering the bruises encouraged a more thorough examination. He pulled the quilt down below her feet and held the lamp just above her head so he could see her better. After brushing away long pieces of damp hair from her face, he saw a large red mark on her cheek just below her right eye. When he pulled the light down the remainder of her body, he saw thin scratches along her legs, her swollen right ankle, and small cuts layering the bottoms of her feet.

Sheridan's pulse was steady, but she wasn't waking up, so he worried there might be internal injuries. Not being able to get her back into town without running out of gas concerned him. He reached in the back pocket of his jeans for his cell to call an ambulance, but when he didn't find it, he assumed it had fallen out by the river. He walked over to Sheridan's purse on the dresser and began looking through it for a cell, but there wasn't one to be found.

Kitchen, he remembered, and with the oil lamp in hand, he bolted downstairs to where he'd seen a tan wall phone hanging by the back door. When he pulled the receiver to his ear and heard the line was dead, he slammed it back onto its cradle. He grabbed a kitchen towel and filled it with ice. He found the upstairs bathroom, located an old roll of gauze, a bottle of rubbing alcohol, and cotton balls.

Derek walked back into the bedroom and sat the supplies he'd gathered on the nightstand. He slid the chair over to the right side of the bed and cleaned the cuts on her feet first. Sheridan moaned after he'd cleaned the first, so he blew softly on each one to try and cool the burning sting from the alcohol. He rolled up the extra pillow from the bed and placed it under her right calf and wrapped the gauze tightly around her ankle.

"I'm sorry, Sheridan," he warned in advance, as he placed the towel of ice on her right side. Sheridan's back arched, and she let out a cry from the pain. "Shh, it's okay, Sheridan, I've got you." Based on his visions of her, he knew she'd been through hell, and it was killing him to be another person causing her pain. A semblance of calm entered the room after Sheridan adjusted to the ice and settled back down to the bed again. Derek's protective eyes were tired, but he couldn't pull them from the warm flickering light dancing on her soft porcelain face.

"Who are you, Sheridan Hayes?" He wondered why he'd seen her in his dream as a little girl and not the stunning woman she clearly was. What was shaking him beyond his own comprehension was what he was feeling for her. From the first moment he'd touched her to listen for her heartbeat, he felt his vexed world changing. Protecting her was no longer a complicated desire within his mind but a mission within the reality of their immediate world.

Ambiguous questions about his unexpected emotions for Sheridan and her impalpable connection with his mother swam in circles around his thoughts. His eyes became heavy and his jaded body was overtaking his ability to fight the sleep he'd deprived himself of for two days. The last words that drifted through Derek's mind before his world became silent were from his mother's letter. *Only God is omniscient, which is why we're only given small pieces of much larger puzzles. Acceptance of your own purpose will lead you to the answers you seek.*

Chapter Fourteen

S*unday, April 28, 2013*

SHERIDAN'S EYES fluttered as the sun's early morning light flooded into the room. The fragrant aroma of breakfast being cooked downstairs seeped in under the door, stirring her empty stomach. She turned to reach the nightstand to check the time on her cell. A soft moan escaped her lips from the sharp stabbing pains in her right side and ankle. Her pulse was throbbing hard in her temples, making it difficult to adjust to her surroundings.

She tried to focus in on the nightstand again for her cell then peeled off the quilt tucked in tight around her and attempted to get out of bed. As soon as her right foot made contact with the floor, her ankle gave out, and she fell to the side of the bed onto her hands and knees. She maneuvered her body so she was sitting up on the floor with her back rested against the nightstand and saw her ankle was bandaged. Sheridan scanned the room to find something, anything, out of place that would jog her memory.

The chair from the corner of the room had been moved to the

right side of the bed and the nightstand next to the chair held a bottle of rubbing alcohol and cotton balls. *Jesus, Sheridan, what the hell did you do to yourself?* She assumed Rodney had come home and taken care of her. Three slight vibrations came from under the bed. "Ah, there you are," she sighed then reached under the bed and grabbed her phone. Her home screen indicated she had three voicemails and sixteen missed calls.

She heard footsteps coming up the stairs and didn't want Rodney to find her on the floor, so she used the chair next to the bed to pull herself up. When she did, the chair slid into the nightstand and knocked the oil lamp onto the floor. The door swung open and Derek rushed into the room. When their eyes met, he saw how petrified she was by his unexpected presence. He placed the plate of food he was holding onto the dresser. Her adrenaline kicked in, triggering her last memory from the night before. She reached up to her throat to feel for her necklace, and panic crept into her chest when it wasn't there. She began planning her next escape.

"I'm not going to hurt you. Your cousin Rodney asked me to come check on you last night and—" was all Derek could get out before Sheridan panicked and flung her cell phone hard at his head. "Fuck!" he barked, when the cell phone made contact and nicked his right brow.

Two light droplets of blood slid down Derek's face. "Who are you? Where is my cousin?" Sheridan wailed.

"Damn it, listen to me." He took a step toward her to stop her from moving like a wild animal backed in a corner. Moving closer made her more scared, so he stopped. "I-I think your ribs are fractured, so you've got to stop moving around like that." Derek put both palms up gesturing a truce. "If you just stop and listen to me, I promise I won't take another step near you."

There was no way for her to get around him. Her chest was rising and falling hard from heavy breathing, but she cooperated. Derek put his hands down. "My cousin Brody and Rodney got into a fight last night at Dottie's and were arrested. Rodney tried to call you, but you didn't answer, so he got worried and asked if I'd come out here to check on you and let you know what's going on."

She didn't know if Derek was telling her the truth. Derek picked up on her doubt. "I was told Rodney left you a voicemail to warn you that I was coming, but clearly you never got it," he said, then wiped a drop of blood away from his brow.

"No, I didn't," she answered accusing, then looked at the cell phone that fell just outside of the room after it had made contact with Derek's brow. Derek walked backward to the phone and picked it up.

"If he did leave a message, it should still be on my phone, right?" She gestured for him to give her the phone, hoping he'd be gullible enough to, so she could call 911 or use it as a weapon again.

"Not a chance, lady," Derek informed dryly, knowing exactly what she was thinking. Derek knew Sheridan hearing Rodney's message would be the only way she'd believe him, so he pressed the voicemail button on the phone and put it on speaker.

Sheridan became fully engaged when she heard Rodney's voice.

Message one: Hey, Mona Lisa...I, um, got myself into a little trouble in town, and need you to call me right back. It's an emergency, so call me right back.

Message two: Sheridan, it's me again. Why the hell aren't you answering your phone? I know it's charged. I really need you to call me right back.

Message three: Okay, now I'm worried. Why aren't you answering your damn phone? Just give me a second, please. Sorry, they're rushing me. Listen, I don't want you to worry about me because I'm fine, but I got into a bar fight and they're taking me to jail. My bail won't be set until Monday, which is bull-shit, but there's nothing I can do about it. I don't know why you're not answering your phone, and I'm freaking out. The guy I was helping said his cousin....What's his name?...Derek is going to come out to the house and check in on you. I'm just letting you know, so you don't freak out when he gets there. And, honey, if he looks anything like his cousin, you'll be thanking me later....All right, all right...I have to go. I love y—

When the message cut off, Sheridan's embarrassed eyes searched Derek's to try and sort out the night's events in her head. After a few moments, he saw her face settle with clarity but decided to wait for her to speak first.

"I-I'm so sorry. I-I don't even know what to say," she said. "When I saw you standing in the living room last night, it was dark. I'd taken a painkiller after I fell off the stool, and I couldn't see your face, so I thought you were the ba—" she paused. "I mean, I thought you were a burglar and that's the only reason I ran. The last thing I remember was losing my necklace by the river," she explained, placing her palm on her bare neck.

"So, you don't remember—" he said then cut his sentence off short. Derek had seen her past, felt her pain, and knew how much she'd suffered. "It's okay. Really, I'm just glad you're okay," he said then offered her a warm smile. "Now, may I please help you up off the floor?" he asked.

"Thank you, but no, I can—oh...okay," she said when Derek didn't wait for permission and lifted her into his arms with ease. He swung her around and began walking her to the other side of the bed. Sheridan felt faint as a symphony of overwhelming emotions danced throughout her entire body, settling within her surrendering heart. She looked into his bewitching green eyes and expelled a single soft breath as he returned her stare.

The room spun fast and reckless around them. In the center of the illuminating whirlwind, their bodies moved in slow motion, almost as though time were trying to stop. Sheridan closed her eyes to balance her thoughts and find reason for the convulsion of paralyzing emotions running fiercely through her blood. *This can't be real. I'm dreaming.*

"There," Derek said, satisfied she was lying back down. Sheridan looked up at him and didn't say a word; she couldn't. There was a long silence between them, and Derek tried to fill it. "So, after I figured out how to use your gas stove, I made you some breakfast. The power went out last night, but there was some thawed bacon in the freezer and the eggs were still good. I hope you're hungry." He handed her the plate of food.

Sheridan accepted the plate. She smiled and shifted in the bed. She knew it was irrational, but she trusted this magnificent stranger and sensed they had somehow shared an inexplicable connection.

"Are you okay?" he asked.

"Um, y-yeah, I-I'm just worried about Rodney."

Derek smiled down at her. "I doubt Carter County Jail sees many hard-core criminals, so I'm sure your cousin and Brody are just fine. You, however, need to be seen by a doctor." Derek held her cell phone up and slightly shook it in his right hand. "This would have come in real handy last night, but I didn't see it or have enough gas to get you back into town. May I use it to call a tow truck and see about getting us some gas out here?"

"Yes, of course."

"I'll give it back to you when I'm done as long as you promise not to chuck it at my good eye," he teased, then walked out of the room and downstairs to make the call.

❧

"Two six one Cedar Creek Road. Twenty minutes? All right, thanks," Derek said before he walked back into the room and saw Sheridan dressed and sitting in the chair next to the bed. He cleared his throat and tried to ignore the arousing sensation he felt from the vision of her. She was wearing a pair of old ripped Levi's that fit snug around her delicate curves, and a plain white tank top that revealed the shapeli-ness of her full breasts. Her hair was pulled back from her face in a long ponytail exposing her enticing neck.

"Everything okay?" Sheridan asked.

"What? I mean, yeah, everything's fine. I just made a few calls."

"A few?"

"Yeah, I got a status on the power outage, and the electric company said you should have power back by noon."

"Thank you."

"I also called the jail and talked to the Sheriff. Looks like Brody and Rodney are definitely not getting out until tomorrow."

"Why?"

"The judge can't be reached, and he's not scheduled to be in until tomorrow morning, so they're just going to have to wait it out." Derek suspected the real reason the judge couldn't be reached was because the DA caught wind of Brody being arrested. His lack of cooperation and support in Brody digging around in his mom's case likely inspired a call to the judge to ensure he wouldn't be available.

"Sheriff said the doctor's office in town was closed, but he'd have the doctor open up and meet us there so we can get you checked out."

What Derek didn't tell her was that he also asked Sheriff Lloyd to meet him there.

"And a tow truck?"

"Apparently Skeeter's Tow and Tire is in the area and should be here in about twenty minutes with gas."

"Sounds like you've taken care of everything." She patted the side of the bed in front of her. "Come sit." She doused a cotton ball with alcohol and offered him a friendly smile when he sat in front of her. "Your turn to be taken care of," she said, then dabbed the cotton ball on the small cut.

Derek followed her lips each time she blew on his eye to lessen the sting. "You're a pro at this."

"I've been around a few feisty children before is all."

"Are you saying I'm feisty or I'm a child?"

"Now how could I assume either? I don't even know you," she replied with a slanted smile and doused another clean cotton ball.

"I'm Derek, Sheridan," he said in a low, soft tone then searched her eyes for the same hungry desire slaying every rational reason he had not to kiss her.

Sheridan's heart fluttered from the intensity of his stare and how he'd spoken her name. She swallowed hard before trying to respond. "I-I know. Rodney said so in his message." Sheridan returned his fervid stare and felt a throbbing heat rush to her cheeks. She closed her eyes, consumed by the rapturous moment and leaned into his inviting lips. Derek saw a sudden flash of her permitting him to take her well beyond the kiss and felt her ravenous desire. He feared he'd be incapable of denying her what they both craved if he tasted even the slightest serving of her mouth. He bolted up from the bed before their lips met and walked to the window with his back to her to cool off.

Derek sensed she'd felt the same euphoria while in his arms that he had upon listening to the beating of her beautiful heart. He understood her awkward forwardness and undying need to consummate their undeniable connection but sensed that she questioned it. Until she fully accepted they were destined to be, he wouldn't touch her and would court her as though he'd never seen her in his dreams. He sensed she'd never loved let alone given herself to a man. Surrendering now would leave Sheridan with irreversible regrets, and he refused to be another disappointment in her life. His gifts gave him the advantage of seeing pieces of who she was and what she feared, but Sheridan didn't have the same luxury, so he needed her to discover and accept who he was and their connection in her own time.

Why Sheridan had haunted his dreams, why she was now in his life, and her connection to his mother, was still a mystery to him. Taking things at a slow and natural pace would be necessary to reveal the larger portion of the disconcerting puzzle. "I'm so sorry. I don't know why I did that. I've never even kissed anyone—I just meant that I don't even know you," Sheridan confessed, stung by his rejection.

Derek heard the shame in her voice and turned from the window and walked back over to her. "Hey, look at me," he said, then sat back down on the bed in front of her again. Derek cupped her chin in his palm and pulled her face up to meet his. "Do you know how beautiful you are?"

Sheridan jerked her face from his hold. "Don't talk to me like I'm some kind of unsophisticated bimbo who needs to hear meaningless compliments just to feel better about herself," she snapped, regretting she had and wishing she could take it back.

Derek was amused by her quick and unexpected temper, so he decided to play with it to change the heavy mood. Animated, he threw his hands up in front of his face. "Take cover and hide your cell phones, folks; I just gave the ugly bimbo a compliment and she's gone mad."

Sheridan bit her bottom lip to keep from laughing. "So, you think you're a funny guy, huh? How about giving my cell phone back so I can show your left eye just how funny you really are?" she threatened playfully.

"You jest, but you may need that cell phone to defend yourself once I come for that kiss...because I will eventually come for it, Sheridan."

"That was a once-in-a-lifetime opportunity, buddy, and you missed it. Sorry, no redos."

"Is that a challenge, because I will win, you know?"

Sheridan's lashes fluttered. "Not likely."

"So, you mentioned you lost your necklace."

Sheridan's eyes grew wide. "Yes, by the river. You didn't find it, did you?" Even as an adult Sheridan believed the necklace protected her from her attacker, and without it now, she felt lost and exposed.

"No, I didn't, but when we get back from getting you checked out in town, I'll go back to where I found you last night and look for it."

"I appreciate your offer, but there's no reason you should have to come all the way back up here. I'll drive our Jeep back and have Rodney look for my necklace tomorrow."

"Is the Jeep a stick shift?"

"Yes."

"So, how exactly do you plan on driving all the way back here and then back into town tomorrow to bail your cousin out of jail with a messed up ankle and ribs?" He'd set her up and she knew it but didn't care because she wanted him to stay.

Sheridan stared at him playfully through agitated eyes. "You know, Derek, I know I don't know you, but you remind me an awful lot of my cousin Rodney."

"Why's that?"

"Because, like you, he's a real smart ass."

"Well, that may be true, but at least I'm not an ugly bimbo." Sheridan laughed. They turned their heads toward the window when the tow truck driver honked his horn in the driveway. "Ha, saved by Skeeter's," Derek said.

For the first time in her life, she felt alive, out of control, but alive.

Chapter Fifteen

othing's changed, Sheridan thought as she sat alone in the exam room looking around at the familiar decor waiting for Doc to come back in with her X-rays. She smiled at the nostalgic Norman Rockwell prints still hanging on the earthy beige and brown striped wallpaper. As a child, she'd imagined her and Becca being the little girl and baby doll in Rockwell's *Doctor and the Doll* painting. Sheridan's smile faded when a slight musty smell snuck into the room from the dated wood flooring and took her back to her childhood visits with Doc. With every bruise or fractured bone had come an excuse or lie about how she or her mom had obtained them. She remembered her mom trying to tell Doc the truth about Hank's abuse early on, and how he'd reminded her how lucky she was that Hank was taking care of them. The memory of her mom's defeated face when he'd dismissed her cry for help settled heavy in Sheridan's chest. *Why did I even come here?* she thought as Doc walked back in.

He walked to the far wall and slipped two X-rays into the old light box then patted the pockets of his white lab coat to find his glasses. Sheridan cleared her throat to get his attention and pointed to his balding head. "Oh yes, thank you, dear," he said, pulling the glasses from the top of his head then putting them on to review the films.

Doc sat on a rolling metal stool. "Do you want the good news or the bad news first?"

"How long will this take? I have someone waiting on me," she snipped, now heated from how he'd treated her mom all those years ago.

"Well, nothin's broken, but you've got a pretty bad sprain in your ankle and some nasty bruised ribs that are gonna take some time to heal."

"How long?"

"Four to six weeks to heal completely, but you're gonna need to stay off that ankle for a couple days, so I wouldn't count on doing too much. I'll give ya a brace for your ribs and a boot for your ankle, but no crutches cause of those ribs."

"That's just great," Sheridan said, upset she wouldn't be able to finish her mom's house before leaving Lyle.

"I'll prescribe you somethin' for the pain, but you can't be overdoin' anything just cause ya think ya feel better."

"I don't need painkillers," she said, remembering her experience the night before.

"I'll write you a script just in case you change your mind. So, how's your mamma doin' anyway?" he asked as he wrote Sheridan's prescription.

"She's been great since we got away from Hank."

Doc looked to the ceiling deep in thought. "Why, I don't reckon I've seen your mamma in over sixteen years," he said then looked back to her again. "Your mamma used to be my patient when she was growing up too, ya know?"

"Listen Doc, I'm not trying to be rude, but like I said, I have someone waiting for me, so if you don't mind, I'd like to wrap this up so we can be on our way."

"Don't worry your pretty little head, your friend's just fine. In fact, the Sheriff just got here, and they're outside talkin', so a few more minutes won't kill either one of ya."

"The Sheriff? Why's he here?"

"Don't know. I reckon you'll need to ask your friend," he answered, then got up and started walking toward the door. "I'll be back, I've got to get a boot and rib brace from the supply closet. Try and make yourself comfortable."

૱

DEREK PUT his sunglasses on to shade his eyes from the late morning sun as he and Sheriff Lloyd stepped outside the doctor's office to talk. "I appreciate you agreeing to bring me Brody's phone," Derek offered.

Sheriff Lloyd reached in his front pocket, pulled out Brody's cell, and handed it to Derek. "I figured you'd have one of your own."

"I do but lost it somewhere up on Lyle last night. That's the reason I asked you to meet me here."

"To talk to me about your lost phone?"

"No, about how I lost it. As a favor to Rodney, Brody asked me to go out to Lyle and check on Sheridan last night. When I got there, I heard her screaming in the woods. When I found her, she was being attacked."

"By who?" Sheriff Lloyd asked with a hard scowl on his face.

"I don't know. Between it being dark and the rain, I couldn't see him, but I was able to knock him off of her. If I hadn't found her, Sheriff, there's no question in my mind she would've been violated."

"Why in Sam Hill didn't you call the station?"

"Like I said, I lost my phone and didn't know about Sheridan's cell until just before I called you this morning."

Sheriff Lloyd started to reach for the radio hanging on his belt to call dispatch. "I need to get my boys out there and find out where the hell Hank is."

"Sheridan doesn't know, Sheriff."

"What do you mean she doesn't know?"

"She doesn't remember being attacked."

"Jesus Christ, Derek, how in the hell am I supposed to bring Hank or anyone else for that matter if she doesn't even know it happened?"

"I don't know."

Sheriff Lloyd took his Stetson off and pulled his stressed fingers through his hair. "Maybe if I sit down and talk with her, it'll jog her memory."

"You know the hell she went through as a kid on Lyle. Telling her she was almost violated is cruel."

"I can't not check this out. You know that, right?"

"Yeah, I know, which is exactly why I told you. I'm just asking you not to tell her anything until we figure out who it was."

Sheriff Lloyd shook his head disapprovingly. "Whether I agree with you or not, I can't just let her go back up to Lyle alone."

"I agree, which is why I offered to stay with her until we bail Brody and Rodney out in the morning. Nancy told me Sheridan and Rodney are leaving for New York tomorrow. Even though I'd planned on staying in Carter County a few more days, I'll head back to New York tomorrow myself, so I can keep an eye on her until we figure out who attacked her."

"Now that's a mighty generous offer for someone you just met. Wouldn't have anything to do with your gift, would it?"

"As long as I keep her safe, does it really matter what reasons I have to protect her?"

"No, I reckon it doesn't, but I'm not sure what to do here, Derek." Sheriff Lloyd knew of Sheridan's past and didn't want to cause her any unnecessary stress either. From a legal standpoint, there wasn't much he could do but knew she needed protection in both Lyle and New York until they found her attacker.

"I won't let anything happen to her, Sheriff. You have my word."

"All right, we'll do it your way, but I'm sendin' one of my deputies out to Lyle to keep an eye on the house until mornin'. I can't touch Hank if she's not able to press charges, but I'll at least try to find out where he was last night."

Derek held up Brody's phone. "I'll call you on my end if there's any trouble."

"You better make damn sure nothin' happens to her or I'll—" he started to say as Sheridan came limping out of the office.

Derek helped her off the step outside the door. "So, what's the damage?"

"A sprain and some bruised ribs. I'll be fine."

Sheriff Lloyd cooled his composure before he spoke. "Well, look at you all grown up. You sure know how to make a man feel old. How's your mamma?"

"She's fine, Sheriff. How's Rodney doing?"

"Oh, well now, he's doing just fine. I can't say the same about the other two he's locked up with though. He's been singing the same song all mornin' and said he wasn't gonna stop either until I checked up on ya."

Sheridan assumed Rodney was the reason for Sheriff Lloyd's visit and felt a little more relaxed. "Let me guess, 'It's Raining Men'?"

"Yep, that would be the one."

"Am I able to see him today?"

"Visitin' hours are tomorrow between one and two, and he'll be out well before then. I'll be sure to let him call you today though, so we can all get a break from his vocal cords."

"Thank you."

Sheriff Lloyd put his hat back on. "Well, I reckon I'd better head back over to the station, but I'll see you both in the mornin'." He gave Derek a glance that suggested he'd better take care of her and left them alone.

"You okay?" Derek asked.

"I'm fine. I just paid off my mom's house and planned on surprising her with the deed and a clean house. I've barely touched what needs to be done."

"You need to stay off that foot and rest those ribs, but I'm perfectly capable of helping out. You just have to tell me what needs to be done. I need to stop at the motel before we head back to Lyle, though. My uncle's flying back to New York, so I wanted to see him off and grab a change of clothes."

"Your uncle? I didn't realize someone else was in town with you. I'm so sorry. I didn't mean to keep you from your family."

"No worries. He was just passing through between business trips and got caught up in trying to get Brody out of jail," he lied. "I called him this morning and told him there wasn't any reason for him to stay and that I'd take care of it tomorrow."

"Are you sure? I mean, the boot and rib brace are helping, so I can just drive the Jeep back. And besides, there's way too much to get done at my mom's house to even try at this point," she insisted.

"Listen, your cousin helped Brody out last night, so the least I can do is make sure you're in one piece when he sees you tomorrow," he teased.

"I just feel bad."

"Feel bad? Why? The motel room doesn't have a stove, so you're actually doing me a favor. I'm craving pasta and Nancy's doesn't have a big pasta selection. We can stop at the store, and I'll grab a few things to make us a couple of my famous subs for lunch and pasta for dinner."

"I guess after everything you've done for me, the least I can do is let you use my stove."

Chapter Sixteen

Sheridan had been quiet on the afternoon drive back from town. She'd let her hair down and stared out the window at passing trees for most of the ride. When they arrived at the house, Derek helped her walk in, settled her at the kitchen table, and propped her ankle up on one of the extra chairs. When he went back out to the Escalade to get the groceries, he spotted Deputy Dyer's patrol car slowly pulling up the driveway just out of the house's view. As he carried the bags up the front steps, he looked back over his shoulder to ensure Sheridan wouldn't be able to see the patrol car.

"Hope you're ready for one of my famous Italian subs," he bragged, then pulled the ingredients out of the bags and placed them on the kitchen table.

"I bet they're great, but I'm not hungry."

"Do you honestly think I didn't notice you took less than half a bite of the breakfast I slaved over a hot stove for you?"

Sheridan smiled at his exaggerated animation. "Sorry, I was hoping you didn't catch that."

Derek grabbed a knife and cutting board then walked over to where Sheridan was sitting and stood next to her. "Yeah, I did catch it, and now you're rejecting my cooking again. I'm a sensitive guy, you know?"

Sheridan couldn't help but laugh. She had to tilt her head all the way back to look up at him. "Fine, I'll have a sandwich. God forbid I hurt your feelings, you big baby."

Derek sat down in the chair to the right of her and opened up the bag of fresh Italian rolls. "One Italian sub, coming right up."

"So besides being a sensitive chef, what else do you do?"

"You mean for a living?"

"Yeah."

"I'm a philanthropist, but I also dabble in strategic stock and property investments from time to time to keep a healthy cash flow running through the organizations I work with. What about you?"

"Back up. You're a philanthropist?"

"Yeah."

"What's your favorite cause?"

"Vista House is my most recent project and probably the one closest to my heart. Our plan is to eventually build and fund other Vista Houses around the world. To be honest, I haven't given the reopening or the kids the attention they deserve. My plan is to dive in head first when I get back to New York."

"What type of work does Vista House do exactly?"

"We take in kids with special needs who are institutionalized or come from abusive homes. Unfortunately, the special care they require is overlooked, and they get lost in the system."

"Special needs. Do you mean like physical handicaps, intellectual disabilities...?" Sheridan probed.

"Currently, we have six kids at Vista, which are unique in that they all have psychic abilities. Before we found them, they'd all been misdiagnosed, misunderstood, and dismissed. Unfortunately, these types of children's families and doctors, if they've been lucky enough to be seen by one, don't understand or accept the children's gifts. So ultimately, they're placed in institutions or given up for adoption. In some cases, their parents' misguided frustrations turn into abuse. By the time we find them, they've been filtered through several unfit foster homes or have been admitted into psych wards."

"I can't imagine. That's horrible."

"Yeah, it is. Our goal is to treat the physical and psychological trauma they've suffered first and then focus on their gifts. Because of what they've been through, most of the children are afraid to talk to us about what they're experiencing on a psychic level. I'd say earning their trust is the biggest challenge, but once we do, the real work can begin."

"How do you earn their trust?"

"We use traditional counseling, role-playing activities, group sessions. The norm. We also use hypnotherapy to reveal their repressed memories. Once we can understand what they fear, we're able to use the information to develop individual rehabilitative plans both socially and psychically."

"Sorry for so many questions. It's fascinating that you've found such a unique cause."

Derek offered her a warm smile. "Please, don't apologize. In fact, I'm surprised I'm not boring you. Most people's skepticism about psychics shut them down the minute I explain what we do at Vista, or they get freaked out about things they don't understand."

"I'm not sure what my own beliefs are one way or the other, but at the end of the day, you're helping children, and that's all that matters. So tell me, how do you find these unique children?"

"My family's been bringing awareness to the cause for over twenty-two years. They've recruited physicians, psychologists, social workers, attorneys—anyone who frequently comes in contact with these types of kids."

"You mentioned the reopening of Vista. I'm assuming there was another?"

Derek knew this question would thread back to his mother, so he turned the conversation over to her. "Okay, enough about me. Besides being an ugly bimbo, what do you do for a living?"

Sheridan squinted through playful eyes. "You're hysterical."

"Seriously, what do you do?"

"Let's see...I work at my mom's diner part-time, I'm an artist, and I volunteer at my aunt's counseling center. That's it. So, tell me more about Vista."

"You think you're pretty sly, huh? I believe it's your turn to back it up. You're an artist?"

"It's not a big deal. Painting has always been my own personal therapy."

"What do you paint?"

"Anything. Like I said, painting is my therapy. My real passion is teaching art to the children at my aunt's counseling center."

"So, you volunteer. Looks like we have something in common then, huh?"

"I'd hardly say my volunteer work even comes close to being on the same level as a philanthropist, but yeah, I guess we do."

"Is your specialty art therapy?"

"I guess you could say that. We use art to pull out children's subconscious feelings. My students are amazing. It's rewarding to see them go from not being able to speak about their feelings to stroking out their puzzles on a canvas. It's beautiful."

Derek stopped cutting into the tomato he was slicing. *Rebecca...son of a bitch, that's it*, he thought.

Sheridan saw he was distracted. "You okay?"

Derek's lips formed a knowing smile and found her curious eyes. "I need you."

A heated blush settled into Sheridan's cheeks. "Wh-What?"

"I believe everything happens for a reason and that we're all connected."

Chills crawled up Sheridan's spine as she remembered the connection she'd felt to Derek when he'd lifted her in his arms. Her heart began racing and she wanted to confess what she'd felt the first moment he'd touched her, but her words fell silent.

"On the way to Carter County, I was trying to figure out a way I could help one of the little girls who just came to Vista. And you just gave me the answer I was searching for."

"How?"

"Our house counselor, Anderson, can't use hypnotherapy or any of our other traditional therapies with her because she's mute, so she literally can't tell him anything. She draws pictures to try and communicate now. I can't explain it, but I sense there's more she needs me to understand. Art therapy is the answer."

"I can give you the names of several prestigious art therapists who practice in New York."

"I don't want their names. I want you."

"I'm flying to New York tomorrow, but I don't know that I'm experienced enough for the type of therapy she needs."

"Is it about money? Name your price and consider it done."

"Jesus, Derek, it's not about money. I have money. I-I just don't want to screw up. You said the kids at Vista need special care, and I'm not confident I'm capable of giving her what she needs...what she deserves."

"I'm sorry. It wasn't my intention to offend you. It's important to me that you're the one who helps her."

Sheridan felt the depth of his sincerity and offered him a forgiving smile. "Why me, Derek?"

When Sheridan had mentioned the children not being able to speak at all, he'd thought of Rebecca and her drawing. Rebecca had been trying to tell him to save the girl from the angry man and bring her back to Vista.

"My gut tells me you're the one who can help her. She needs you. I need you."

"I can try. I'll only have Wednesday free to work with her, and I need at least a week with her. I guess I could extend my stay in New York and work with her after my exhibition, but..." she paused.

"But?"

"But, if I can't get through to her, you have to promise to call one of my contacts who I'm confident can."

"You have my word."

"I'm not sure how I feel about you pulling at my heartstrings to get your way."

"I don't know what you're talking about," he teased. He started cutting into the tomato again. "Did I hear you say you had an art exhibition in New York?"

"Yes, my work is being featured at MoMA's Unmasked Charity Ball this Friday."

"So, you just paint for therapy, huh? I'd say having a gig at the MoMA is a little more than personal therapy. I'm impressed."

Sheridan laughed. "Yeah, well, I have a man's love for my mamma's key lime pie to thank for my big break, so don't be too impressed."

Derek caught a hint of Sheridan's well-hidden southern accent and grinned. "I know some of the members on the MoMA Board, and trust me, they don't host exhibitions for just anyone. I don't care how good your mamma's pie is," he said, mocking the southern drawl she'd let slip.

"Well, I reckon Dr. Duncan Riley likes it just fine," she shot back playfully.

Derek's smile faded by the mention of the familiar name. He knew Dr. Duncan Riley all too well. He was a family friend, his father's best friend and partner, his childhood doctor, and Vista House's new volunteer pediatrician.

"Dr. Duncan Ril—" was all he got out before he saw a vision of Dr. Riley standing over him as a child in a hospital bed. The knife Derek was holding dropped to the floor. He grabbed the top of his head with both hands when an unforgiving burn seeped into his mind, and he saw a vision of his father weeping at the same bedside he'd seen Dr. Riley.

"Derek, what's wrong?" She held both sides of his face and turned it to meet hers. Sheridan felt the kitchen table vibrating faintly, but she didn't release his face. "Derek, please, tell me what's happening." Derek began pulling himself back to her. The table stopped vibrating when his eyes opened and fixated on Sheridan's terrified face.

"Are you okay? Jesus, what the hell just happened?"

Since his parents' death, he'd seen repetitive visions of his mother within his dreams and now within his newest visions. However, he'd not seen a single vision of his father after he'd died until now. His head throbbed from erratic pictures and memories that began filling his head, and he was struggling with what was real and what wasn't. The only thing he knew with absolute certainty was that he needed Sheridan in his life, and he was now at risk of losing her. How could he tell her what he himself still didn't understand? He shot up from the chair and started walking toward the front door. "Sorry, I need some air. I'll be back."

"Where are you going?"

"For a walk. I'll be back. I need you to lock the door."

"Th-There's a spare key under the welcome mat. You'll need it to get back in."

He walked out the door, shut it behind him, and then locked the deadbolt from the outside with the spare key, leaving Sheridan inside sitting dumfounded and alone. Derek walked down the driveway to the patrol car and tapped on the driver's side window. Deputy Dyer glared at him and rolled the window halfway down.

"I'm going for a walk and need you to watch her."

"I don't reckon I take orders from you, boy."

"Didn't the Sheriff order you to come up here and keep an eye on her?"

"Yeah."

He slammed his fist on top of the patrol car. "Then I suggest you do your fucking job," Derek snapped then walked away.

Chapter Seventeen

Derek had been gone for a little less than an hour and had left Sheridan rattled by what happened. She'd convinced herself the table vibrating had only been her imagination and that she'd somehow been the cause of Derek's abrupt need to leave. She tried to keep herself busy to pass the time and settle her nerves, so she finished the sandwiches and cleaned the kitchen. Just as she started cleaning the living room, her cell rang. She hobbled over to the coat hook by the front door and pulled her cell from her purse.

"Hello?"

"What happened and why the hell didn't you answer my calls?" Rodney screeched. "The Sheriff said you banged yourself up. Are you okay?"

"I'm fine, Rodney. My cell was on vibrate and fell behind the bed, so I didn't hear your calls, but that's neither here nor there. The question is, how are you holding up and what happened?"

"A few local hillbillies started trouble with me and another guy from out of town," he said, leaving out the fact that one of them had disrespected her.

"A few? My God, are you okay?"

"Oh yeah, but you should see the other guys," he bragged.

"All right, Chuck Norris, well, I'll be there first thing in the morning to get you out."

"How? They said the Jeep is still here."

"Derek."

"Oh yeah, Brody's cousin, right? Our flight leaves at one o'clock. The Sheriff said the judge wouldn't be setting our bail until around nine, and we still have to drive all the way to Knoxville International."

"Don't worry, I'll pack our bags tonight so we can leave right from the jail in the morning. Derek's staying here with me tonight, so we'll be there well before your bail is set."

"Whoa...staying the ni—? Okay, toots, I've only got a few minutes left. Start spilling, and I want every lusty detail."

"There are no lusty details. I'm pretty sure he thinks I'm a complete and utter nutjob."

"And why would he think that?"

"Let's see, where do I begin?"

"From the start but make it quick, I don't have much time."

"When he came to check on me last night, I ran into the woods like a madwoman, and he found me passed out lying by the river."

"What's that?"

"Oh, yeah, it gets better. He actually carried me back to the house in the rain, took care of my injuries, and served me breakfast in bed."

"Holy shit, he stayed the night? Okay, who abducted my innocent cousin? Who knew you were such a brazen hussy, girl?"

"That's not all. After everything he did for me, I-I cut his eye open with my cell phone this morning after I flung it at his head. And then I tried kissing him half an hour after meeting him."

Rodney started choking on his own laughter. "You what?"

"Oh, God, I know. What the hell's wrong with me? I mean, it's like he has this...spell over me or something. My hormones are completely out of control and I can't explain it, but I feel like I've known him my whole life."

"Please tell me you didn't tell him that?"

"I might be crazy, but I'm not an idiot."

"Oh, thank God. Listen, if he offered to stay with you again after you tried to kill him, there's a good chance he doesn't think you're crazy. And who gives a shit if he does anyway?"

"I do."

"You said yourself one of the reasons you came back to Lyle was to face your fears and learn to start taking more risks, right?"

"Yeah, but I don't even know him."

"Don't fight it, honey, just go with it."

"There's nothing to go with. He rejected my kiss."

"Well, that only means one of two things, honey. He's either gay or he's actually a respectable guy who really wants to get to know you before he pounces on you. I'm thinking number two is the winner. Hold on a sec....If you don't let me wrap this call up, I have plenty of Liza Minnelli songs in my back pocket I'd be glad to sing for you....Yeah, that's what I thought....Sorry about that. I have to go. Be yourself, Sheridan. You're beautiful, intelligent, and you're a woman. You may have a shaky past, but don't we all? If you like him as much as it sounds like you do, you're going to have to let your walls down."

"Did you hear me, Rodney? I don't even know him."

"Then get to know him."

Sheridan heard footsteps on the back porch. "Hey, I think he's back," she whispered.

Rodney laughed. "Well, go get him, toots. I'll see you in the morning. Love you."

"Love you too." Sheridan placed her cell in her back pocket and limped back to the kitchen. Derek had fixed the screen door earlier that morning, but it still creaked as she opened it and stepped outside to greet Derek.

"Hey, I put the sandwiches in the fridge—" Sheridan got out before realizing the footsteps she'd heard on the back porch weren't Derek's.

SHERIDAN GASPED but then swallowed the fierce trepidation settling in her throat. She took a step back to create space between them, but the solid foundation of the house prevented her from going any further.

"Ha-Hank. Wh-What are you doing here?"

His eyes squinted as he crept upon her and filled the gap between them. "Reckon I'm here for a little family reunion."

Sheridan turned her face to escape the stench of whiskey exuding from his sweaty pores and lingering breath. "You're not welcome here."

"Y'all had me locked up for fifteen years, and this is the home-comin' I get?"

Sheridan didn't respond.

"Aren't ya happy to see your daddy?"

"You're not my dad."

He moved his face within an inch of hers. "You sure about that, little girl? Course, you ain't a little girl anymore now, are ya?" he slurred, caressing the length of her arm with the tip of his index finger.

She smacked his hand away. Her face turned rigid and met his culpable eyes. "My mom was raped."

Hank's lips formed a malicious smile. "Was she really raped, or did that prick tease whore get what was comin' to her?"

Sheridan's eyes grew wide from his impending confession. Her mind began racing and everything within her told her to scream, hit him, run, do something. Constraining the murderous rage building within her was agonizing, but she needed him to say it. It was no longer about her own fear or finding redemption for the childhood he'd made her suffer but about bringing her mom the justice she deserved. She slowed her breathing, steadied her thoughts, and found the strength to resist the compulsion she had to lash out at him. Rodney was the last person she called on her cell, so she inconspicuously, placed her right hand in her back pocket and felt her way around her phone to find the call button. When she felt the vibration of the button being pushed, she knew it was redialing. Rodney was in jail, so it would go to his voicemail and record every word Hank said. She'd have proof.

"Wh-What are you saying, Hank?"

"Oh, I think you know exactly what I'm sayin'."

"She would have known it was you and never agreed to marry you."

He chuckled. "Now that's where you're wrong, darlin'. If she hadn't gotten herself all drunk or spread her legs for another man right before I took what was mine, she might have figured it out. But she didn't."

Sheridan's body shook with debilitating hate. "Why? Why would you do that to her?" she growled.

"Didn't ya hear me, girl? She had it comin'. Your mamma's to blame, ya know? If she hadn't broken up with me, I wouldn't have had to take what she promised me. I waited an entire year for that bitch to give it up when we was datin', then she broke it off and slept with another guy," he defended, as though his actions were somehow justified. "Makin' that whore pay for six more years was just a bonus and was worth every day I spent in prison."

Sheridan felt physically ill. "So why tell me?"

Hank pressed his body hard up against hers and traced the outline of her bare collarbone with his finger. "I brought you into this world. Seems only fittin' I'm the one who takes you out."

Sheridan knew she had enough recorded to get him convicted, so she allowed herself to unleash her venomous fury. She pushed his chest with the palms of her hands, making him stagger back away from her. "You're nothing but a coward. I mean, really, beating up women and little girls? Do you think that makes you a man? You're not a real man. You're pathetic!" she hissed and pushed him again. "I bet your inmates smelled you coming a mile away, didn't they?" she taunted and shoved him again. "Tell me, Hank, how many times did someone in prison make you their bitch?"

He backed her up against the house and placed his right hand firmly around her neck. The porch began shaking violently beneath their feet, distracting Hank long enough for her to get her cell from her back pocket. She pulled her arm back and then thrust it into the side of his forehead.

He felt blood slide down the side of his face. Hank steadied his footing to ensure she couldn't escape and threw her down on the deck. "You're a fuckin' witch, ain't ya, girly?"

Just as he knelt down to recapture her neck, now with both hands, Derek flew up the steps, grabbed the back of his shirt and threw him off her and off the porch. Hank, pulled himself up from the ground to his hands and knees and tried scurrying away. Derek jumped off the porch and tackled him. He flipped him over and met his bloodshot eyes. Derek's turbulent fist connected with Hank's face several times, even after blood began pouring out from Hank's broken nose.

"Derek, stop! You'll kill him. He's not worth it. Please, Derek!"

Each time his fist met Hank's face, he saw visions of him raping Rhonda and beating Sheridan and felt their terror. The visions drove Derek into a lawless madness.

"Derek, you're killing him. Please!"

The sound of her desperate voice stopped Derek's fist in midair, and the trembling ground became still. Hank was breathing, but he wasn't moving. Derek pulled himself up and hovered just above Hank.

Sheridan turned Derek's face to hers. "Look at me," Sheridan said. "No more."

Deputy Dyer came from around the front of the house with his gun drawn. When he saw Hank lying beneath Derek, he placed his gun back in its holster and pulled out his handcuffs. "I-I've got it from here," he stuttered.

Derek looked Sheridan over to see if she was harmed. "I should've never left you. Did he hurt you?"

"No," she answered, numb and dazed. The familiar earthquake on the porch had saved her from Hank, just as it had when she and her mom fled Hank's wrath when she was six. Her knowing eyes looked into Derek's for confirmation of the irrefutable truth.

DEREK AND SHERIFF LLOYD stood in the distance talking while Sheridan sat solemn on the porch steps. She hadn't said a word since giving Sheriff Lloyd Rodney's voicemail passcode so he could hear for himself what transpired. Even the sound of the ambulance's sirens roaring as it pulled out of the driveway to transport Hank to the hospital hadn't fazed her. Sheriff Lloyd took his hat off and walked over to Sheridan. When he approached her, she was staring numbly into the woods.

"Sheridan?" When she didn't answer, he placed his left hand gently on her shoulder. "Sheridan, I need to talk to you. Can you look at me?"

"Yes," she answered detached but never took her eyes from the bulk of trees lined before her.

Sheriff Lloyd spoke softly. "Your mamma didn't report being raped back then, and in Tennessee, the offense of rape has to be prosecuted within eight years or within fifteen for aggravated rape. Even if she wanted to press charges now, I can't legally charge him."

"Of course you can't," she whispered, short and defeated.

"He can still be brought up on charges for breaking the no-contact order issued at his parole hearin', though, and for what he did here today."

He pulled a plastic baggie out of his pocket that contained a cotton swab within it. "I swear by the good graces of God, I hope it ain't true, but if we can prove he's your daddy, it could only help your case. If nothing else, you'd know one way or the other." He paused before he continued. "All I need is a swab of the inside of your cheek to have your DNA tested," he asked more than stated.

Sheridan didn't answer or acknowledge his request, so he continued trying to convince her. "We can use the blood on your phone to test his DNA, and I can—" he got out before she opened her mouth and allowed him to get what he needed.

He knelt down, pulled the swab from the bag, brushed the inside of her cheek, and placed it back into the bag. "I'm owed a few favors at the lab, so I'll put a rush on the testing," he assured then stood up.

Her desolate silence was tearing at his heart, but he understood it. "I know you want justice for your mamma and don't feel hopeful right now. I promise I won't stop until both you and your mamma get justice." He turned and walked back over to Derek.

"So she agreed to the swab?" Derek asked.

"Yeah. But I gotta warn ya, Derek, she's in a dark place."

"You didn't say anything to her about being attacked last night, did you?"

"As the Sheriff, I reckon I should have. But no, I just didn't have it in me to cause her anymore pain today."

"I saw everything that happened to them in a vision—what he did to her mom, to her as a little girl. I'm trying to understand why no one helped them back then."

Guilt rushed Sheriff Lloyd's face. "I can't speak for anyone else, but I sure as hell didn't know. I mean, Rhonda was a different person back in high school, ya know, popular, full of life, had the world in her hands. After she got pregnant with Sheridan, she changed. It was like she just fell off the face of the earth.

"Only time she came into town was for work or to buy food, and even then she didn't allow anyone to get close to her. Wasn't til we picked Hank up for attempted murder I found out, and I'd only had about six months under my belt as a deputy back then. I reckon it all makes sense now though."

Derek sensed Sheriff Lloyd was telling the truth and felt like a hypocrite for even questioning him. He'd worked with women like Rhonda and knew firsthand how battered women perfected hiding their abuse. And when they finally did reach out for help, it was usually because their lives literally depended on it.

Sheriff Lloyd and Derek watched Sheridan get up from the steps and walk into the house. "If I'd have known, I would've protected them."

"I know."

"I can't go back in time to change things, but I reckon I can try and help her now. Are y'all gonna be okay up here tonight?"

"Yeah, we're good."

"I've got a deputy heading over to the hospital now to stand watch in case Hank gets admitted. From the looks of what ya did to him, I expect he'll be in there a while."

Derek didn't respond.

"I reckon we'll see y'all in the morning, then," Sheriff Lloyd said and then got into his patrol car and pulled out of the driveway.

Derek walked back toward the house with heavy anticipation weighing on his chest. He knew Sheridan would be inside waiting for answers about the distraction he'd subconsciously composed on the back porch to distract Hank. She deserved to know the truth about his dreams of her, his abilities, and their destined connection, and would tell her everything he safely could. Continuing to conceal the visions he'd had of his mother's and Sheridan's connection was still necessary.

She was in danger, and he needed to understand who wanted to kill her and why so he could better protect her. Dr. Duncan Riley was the first person on Derek's list to visit upon his return to New York. He wanted to believe that Dr. Riley's business relationship with Sheridan was just a coincidence, but his gut told him different.

Chapter Eighteen

Derek walked back inside and pulled his blood-stained shirt from over his head and tossed it in the kitchen sink then cleaned his gashed knuckles under the cool stream of water from the faucet. As he shut the water off, he heard a sudden outbreak of boisterous crashes coming from the walls of Sheridan's bedroom and sprinted upstairs. When he rushed in, he ducked as Sheridan threw random objects within her reach around the room aimlessly.

Memories of her ill-fated childhood echoed rapidly within her tortured mind, releasing themselves from the depth of her subconscious where she had them tucked away. Every bruise, fractured bone, and humiliating word Hank had inflicted upon her and her mom ripped through her thoughts like shards of glass. Images of her mother being raped by the same monster who'd claimed to give her life sickened her. "Why, why did you hurt us? I should have let him kill you for what you did to her....No!" she wailed as unforgiving tears slid down her frail face.

Witnessing the uncontrived rawness of her harrowing pain cut into Derek's heart, and he regretted not finishing Hank off when he'd had the chance. Her mind was falling into a dark world, and he needed to pull her from her mental demise. He knew he'd be caught in the crossfire of her fury if he tried to touch her but couldn't watch her suffer alone, so he pulled her into his arms. Locked within his embrace, she began beating his chest with her fists to break free from his hold, but he refused to let her go. "He can't be my father!" she screamed.

Desperate to save her from her isolated world, he slid his fingers up the nape of her delicate neck and tilted her head back to face him, then leaned down to her quivering lips. "Come back to me, Sheridan. Please, I need you," he whispered huskily, searching her wandering eyes. Sheridan's erratic movements faded when she heard Derek's voice and found his tormented eyes. Never taking her stare from his, she placed one palm on his warm chest to be sure he was real.

When Derek sensed she was with him, he brushed a soft comforting kiss across her lips. "You're safe, Sheridan, I'll never let him hurt you again," he whispered. Sheridan's eyes closed, drawn in to his inviting lips, and she pressed her mouth against his. Her accepting gesture tore through Derek's blood, and he parted her lips with his hungry mouth. Their tongues danced in rhythm to the explosion of their unconditional hearts.

Sheridan began withdrawing from her mind again from Derek's amorous touch, taking him with her this time. Their world was filled with beautiful kaleidoscopic colors. Golds, purples, blues, and pale greens melted intimately into one another, leaving them both breathless and knowing. The prevailing energy flowing through their bodies was almost crippling. Derek struggled to stay on his feet from the vigorous collision of their souls intertwining. An enchanting moan escaped Sheridan's lips, and she became weak in Derek's arms. When he felt her go limp, he lifted her trembling body, placed one knee on the bed to balance them both, then lay down beside her, never releasing her from his hold.

SHERIDAN LAY still against Derek's body and hadn't spoken or moved for well over twenty minutes, so he thought she'd fallen asleep in his arms. He pulled his head back to see if her lids were closed. When their eyes met, Sheridan turned her face away from him.

"Are you okay?"

"You're like the kids from Vista House, aren't you?"

"Yes, I am."

"I know it was you."

"Me?"

"You were the little boy's voice telling me to run the day Hank tried killing my mom and me, weren't you? You shook the house, just like you did on the porch today, so we could escape. You...you saved our lives."

"I've dreamed of you and that day my entire life, Sheridan, but I can't take credit for saving your lives. I was only ten then and have no idea why or even how my energy reached you in that precise moment." The honesty in his words inspired her to turn and face him again.

"In every dream, you came to me as a frail and frightened child. Every emotion that consumed you rushed my veins. Your fears, your pain, your celestial love. Each time I saw Hank hurting you, I imagined you walking through a protective earthquake and into a heavenly light that spilled in around your beautiful essence, but I thought it was a dream.

"Your entity haunted me because I'd always sensed somehow I was supposed to find you and protect you." Derek paused. "When I finally found you and heard your heart beating by the river, it was like I'd felt my own for the first time in my life."

Sheridan's body quivered from his impassioned reality, because it was also her own. Nothing else mattered to her in their immediate world, and she allowed herself to revel in their unmasked moment. Impulsively, she moved closer into the safety of his arms to help soothe his own timorous thoughts. "I felt it when you first touched me. I thought I was crazy. I don't understand how it's even possible, but it's like something is beckoning me to accept how you make me feel, how I...how I feel about you."

Derek exhaled a constricted breath and closed his eyes, relieved by how naturally she'd accepted and felt their foretold truths.

"How did you find me?" she whispered.

Derek hadn't known the little girl from his dreams was the same woman he was asked to check on and was at a loss for lucid words to explain it, so he answered what his heart knew to be true. "Fate," he said as he caressed her shoulder with the tips of his fingers.

"Yo-you're not using your gifts to make me feel this way, right?"

Derek smiled. "No. I promise, charming beautiful women out of mystical wicker baskets isn't one of my talents."

"So what is then?"

"I'm still trying to figure that out myself."

"You mean you don't know?"

Derek tried to explain. "When I was ten, I had a few psychic experiences, and my family thought I might be an indigo child. After a few weeks, my gifts vanished, like they'd never existed. With the exception of recurring dreams, I went about my life just like any other normal kid," he offered, leaving out the pain he'd felt as a child from his parents' morbid deaths.

"And now?"

"A couple months ago, my cousin Brody was talking to me about a case he was working, and images of four victims started spilling into my head. I tried pretending they weren't real, but when he showed me pictures of the victims, I couldn't deny it. I've come to terms with my gifts resurfacing but am still trying to make sense of what I've been permitted to see."

"Permitted to see?"

"Unfortunately, there's a common misconception about what psychics see and how they see it. It would be great if our visions came to us with real-time clarity or in some kind of logical order that made sense, but they don't. The visions I've had are pieces of the past and, just recently, pieces of the future, but even then, what I've seen has been pretty subjective."

"Subjective how?"

"You, for example. I've always seen you as a little girl in my dreams, but here in my arms, you're a breathtakingly beautiful woman."

Sheridan blushed. "How were you able to make the porch shake?"

"I don't know. It has telekinesis features, but I've never known telekinesis to have the kind of intense energy it would take to shake the earth. I've noticed it surfaces when I'm upset but never to the extent it did today."

"I see." Sheridan got up from the bed and walked to the window.

Derek walked over to her. Standing behind her, he placed his hands on her shoulders. "What is it?"

Sheridan found the courage to ask what plagued her thoughts. "I-I want to know if you saw what happened to my mother?"

"Yes, I did."

"So it's true?"

Derek turned her around to look into her eyes. "Yes."

"This will crush her. How will she ever be able to look at me the same when she finds out I'm his biological daughter?"

"Your mom loves you, and I know this because I felt it."

"What do you mean, you felt it?"

"With my visions of people also come their emotions. Your mom has always known how you were conceived, yet she never gave you up. It doesn't matter whether Hank's your father or not. He'll never have the power to take away the love your mother holds in her heart for you, Sheridan.

"And besides, it just didn't feel like Hank's your—" Derek stopped himself short.

"What?" When Derek didn't respond right away, she knew he was trying to protect her from something. "I can take it, Derek. Please, just say it."

"I-I don't want to give you false hope or hurt you if I'm wrong."

"Please," she pressed.

"It felt like you were created from love."

Sheridan's eyes became laced with hopeful tears. "Are you saying there's a chance he's not my father?"

"Yes, but I could be wrong, Sheridan. Like I said, my visions and the attached feelings are subjective, which is why I encouraged Sheriff Lloyd to run a paternity test to be sure."

"So it was your idea to run the DNA test?"

"Yes," he confessed.

"Why didn't you just tell me? I'm not the little girl from your dreams. I can take it." Sheridan caught a glimpse of guilt settle on Derek's face. "There's more, isn't there? What else are you keeping from me, Derek?"

Derek felt himself being backed into a corner. There was still so much he didn't understand and couldn't explain, but he didn't want to lie to her either. His voice turned protective and firm. "Do you trust me?"

"Yes."

"Then believe me when I tell you that I'll never lie to you about things I can protect you from or about things I know are real. But in my world, there are images that crawl around in my head and haunt me, or that I don't understand, so I can't and won't inflict those things upon you or anyone else. Please tell me you can accept that."

Sheridan swallowed hard hearing the raw tribulation in his voice. Her heart ached, not because he refused to share the mangled visions that tormented his thoughts but because they were even allowed to exist at all. For sixteen years she'd kept her own secrets from those she loved to protect them. "Yes, I can accept that. I'm sorry."

Derek kissed the top of her head. "You're amazing," he whispered.

"No, not amazing. I just know what it feels like to be pushed into explaining things I don't understand. I'd be a hypocrite if I asked you to do the same."

"You've been through hell, and it's killing me not to be able to give you the answers you deserve. But, I can give you this." He pulled Sheridan's necklace from the front pocket of his jeans.

Sheridan's eyes grew wide, and a slight smile formed on her face. "You found it. How? I mean, when?" she laughed with nervous relief and excitement.

"When I left to get air earlier, I walked down to the river to look for it. I thought it would have washed away, but—" Sheridan threw her arms around his neck.

"You have no idea how important this necklace is to me."

Derek had seen the necklace in the montage of visions he'd had right after finding her by the river. "Was it a gift?"

Sheridan pulled herself slightly away from him to meet his stare. "Like you, there are things in my life I can't explain myself, and this is one of them," she cautioned with a warm smile.

"Fair enough."

"So, what now?"

Derek tucked a stray strand of hair behind Sheridan's ear and looked down at her concerned. "We have a busy morning in town tomorrow, so you need to eat and get some rest."

"No, I-I meant, what happens now, with us?"

Derek smiled. "Well, I guess at this point, I should probably ask you out on a date."

Sheridan returned his smile. "I'm being serious."

"So am I. I don't need my gift to see you're overwhelmed right now. I know you need time, and I'm prepared to give you all you need." He cupped her face. "I'm not going anywhere, but it's important to me that you have no regrets or doubts where we're concerned. The only way I can ensure you don't is by putting my own selfish needs aside and allowing us to take each other on at a natural pace."

Sheridan lifted herself by standing on the tip of her toes and kissed Derek's lips. She took his hand and looked deep into his eyes. "You're right, so that will be the last selfish kiss I steal from you. The next will be yours to take." She pulled her hand slowly from his and walked away from him.

Enchanted, Derek watched Sheridan leave the room, her body swaying in slow motion until he no longer saw her. He looked up to the ceiling. *God, give me the strength to protect her, and her the courage to accept and see what I already know.*

Chapter Nineteen

M*onday, April 29, 2013*

SHERIDAN TOOK a seat in the waiting area of the Sheriff's Office while Derek walked up to the front desk to get a status on when Brody and Rodney would be released. "Shocker," Derek said under his breath when he saw no one was manning the front desk. They'd already been to the courthouse, where Judge Hardy had set Brody and Rodney's bail, paid the Bondsman to get them out, and got the Jeep out of impoundment.

Sheridan and Derek heard what sounded like two men arguing in one of the back offices. The voices became louder when Sheriff Lloyd opened his door. "Get your arrogant ass out of my office," Sheriff Lloyd ordered.

"Send them on their way, Sheriff, or the DA will be getting my recommendation to officially close the case," the man warned then charged down the hall toward the exit.

Just as Derek rounded the corner to see if Sheriff Lloyd needed assistance, a tall graying man in his late forties brushed against Derek's right shoulder in passing. A swift vision of the man and a woman rushed his head. The vision was in black and white. He saw the man and woman sitting across from one another in rusted stained metal chairs in a small but well-lit white room. The woman was distressed. The vision faded as he had two men forcefully escort her out of the room.

Another swift vision of his mother and the man talking in the same room came to him. His mother's face was frightened. She tried to catch her breath as tears rolled down her frail cheeks as she spoke to him. It was cold and undisturbed. An image of the man looking down at her shaking his head was the last thing Derek saw before the vision faded and Sheridan walked around the corner.

"Everything okay?" she asked.

"Yeah, I just—" Derek started before Rodney's voice yelling out Sheridan's name interrupted him.

Rodney threw his arms around her, then pulled away to examine her physical state. He caught a glimpse of the bulky boot brace on her foot and sighed. "Oh, honey."

Sheridan shot him a look that warned him not to start lecturing or doting over her. "Derek, this is Rodney, Rodney, Derek."

A slight smile formed Rodney's lips, as he extended his hand out to him. "Ah, Derek," Rodney said, looking him over. "I can't thank you enough for watching over this one while I was in the slammer."

Derek shook Rodney's hand. "It wasn't a problem, with the exception of her lethal aim and use of cell phones, that is."

Rodney laughed. "Yeah, she gets a little feisty sometimes." Rodney turned to Sheridan. "Speaking of cell phones, Deputy Dyer said they couldn't release mine to me. What the hell is that about?" Sheridan glanced over at Derek.

"Any idea when Brody will be released?" Derek asked.

"He was being processed when Deputy Dyer was bringing me out, so he should be coming out any minute."

Derek turned his attention to Sheridan. "I need to talk to Sheriff Lloyd and wait for Brody, so why don't you two grab some breakfast at Nancy's, and we'll meet you over there."

"Sounds good."

"What was that all about?"

Sheridan grabbed Rodney's hand and guided him toward the front door. "We'll talk about it at Nancy's."

꒰꒱

DEREK STOOD in Sheriff Lloyd's doorway. "Got a minute?" Sheriff Lloyd gestured for Derek to take a seat. Derek walked in and shut the door behind him but didn't sit down. "Who's the man that just left your office?"

"Agent Kelly," Sheriff Lloyd replied with a stiff tone.

"The TBI agent who helped investigate my mom and dad's case?"

"Yep, and he ain't happy about you and your cousin bein' here either, as I'm sure you heard. Said, if I don't run you boys out of town, he's gonna make a recommendation to the DA's office to officially close your mamma's case." Derek didn't respond. "Did ya hear what I said?"

"It doesn't make any sense."

Sheriff Lloyd adjusted in his chair. "What doesn't make sense?"

"Agent Kelly brushed against me when he was leaving and I saw a vision of an unfamiliar woman and my mom talking to him in a small room. I think he talked to them separately, but it was him, and I'm sure it was the same room."

"I can't speak about the other woman, but your mamma was long gone when we found her, so it ain't possible Kelly talked to her." Sheriff Lloyd paused before he spoke again. "Listen to me, son. I warned you about knowin' the difference between what's real and what ain't. I told you, it's that kind of talk right there that got my mamma locked up in a crazy house, so you'd better be damn sure what you're sayin' means somethin' before you go tellin' anyone Kelly's talkin' to the dead."

"I know my visions are subjective, Sheriff, but what I saw has to mean something. I just don't know what yet." He pulled his fingers through his hair. "Everything and everyone is starting to blend in together. I need to get the hell out of this town so I can think straight."

"Now that's the first thing you've said since walkin' in here that makes any sense."

Derek's eyes slanted. "So you want us to leave?"

"You have some trust issues, don't ya, boy?" His voice turned to a low husky whisper. "Jesus, what more can I do to show you can trust me?"

"You're right. I have trust issues. Like I said, everyone and everything's just starting to blend in together, and I don't know who to trust."

"Well, I can assure you, I'm not the one you should be doubtin' right now," he said, then cut his sentence short when Brody knocked on his office door.

"How'd you know I was in the Sheriff's Office?"

"I didn't," Brody confessed. "The Sheriff asked me to come see him when I was released. Why? Aren't you happy to see me?"

"Of course I am. Sorry, a lot's happened since Saturday and I've been a little distracted," Derek admitted.

"So, I heard."

Derek shot Sheriff Lloyd a sharp look. "What do you mean, you heard?"

"He filled me in."

"On what, exactly?"

"Everything," Sheriff Lloyd admitted. "At least what I know for sure and what you've chosen to tell me."

"You know you would have told me anyway, so what difference does it make who told me first?" Brody asked then walked over to the empty seat across from Sheriff Lloyd's desk and sat down. "So, I'm guessing you haven't told him about the plan yet?" Brody asked Sheriff Lloyd.

"Was just about to before you walked in," he informed.

"What plan?" Derek asked.

"I got a call from Nancy last night givin' me a heads up that Agent Kelly was in town havin' a drink at Dottie's. He came to ensure ya'll wouldn't be stayin'. I brought Brody into my office last night after I got Nancy's call to figure out how we could get the scent off you two, so you can continue your investigation without raisin' any more red flags."

"And...?" Derek probed.

Brody adjusted in his chair. "We both think Walt's the key to revealing who killed your mom. Unfortunately, Walt's in no condition to help anyone right now, including himself. I mean, shit, he's going to need a few days off the bottle before we can even think about getting anything logical out of him."

"How in the hell are we going to make sure he stays dry if we're both expected to leave town, and how do you know he's even willing to help us at this point?" Derek asked.

"He wants to help, Derek," Brody said. "I know you don't want to hear this right now, but he feels a lot of deep-seated guilt for what happened to your Dad back then."

"Okay, so he wants to help, but that still doesn't explain how we help him stay off the bottle if we can't be here to babysit him twenty-four-seven."

"Nancy," Sheriff Lloyd chimed in.

"Why would she be willing to do that?" Derek asked.

"Besides me, Nancy's the only other person in the world who cares about Old Walt," Sheriff Lloyd said. "I talked to her early this mornin', and she's already made arrangements to have someone cover for her at the diner and Dottie's for the next week or so while she takes a much-needed vacation. Walt lives about fifteen minutes from town in the middle of the woods and doesn't get visitors, so no one will know she's there."

"So she gets Walt sober and stable. Then what? The minute we step foot back into Carter County to pick his brain, Agent Kelly and the DA's office will be all over our asses," Derek pointed out.

Sheriff Lloyd chimed in. "She's gonna need some time to get Walt right, but when she does, I'll be the one pickin' his brain. Anything I get out of him will be sent your way. Both the DA's and Kelly's eyes are on me right now. I have to stay low myself to avoid raising any suspicion, so we'll need to be discreet."

Brody looked down at his watch. "I called my dad last night. He's sending the jet back to Knoxville International to pick us up. In fact, it's probably there waiting on us now. Nancy picked my stuff up from the hotel this morning, so we have to stop at the diner to grab it before we head out."

"Looks like you two have figured it all out," Derek said then looked over to Sheriff Lloyd. "Sorry I doubted you."

"Apology accepted," Sheriff Lloyd returned.

Derek looked over to Brody. "I'm going to offer Sheridan and Rodney to fly back with us to New York."

"I'm one step ahead of you," Brody said. "I told Rodney they were welcome to fly back with us this morning."

"Did he accept?" Derek asked.

"Yeah, he was all for it."

Sheriff Lloyd stood up. "Listen, I don't mean to rush you boys, but it's gonna start lookin' suspicious if ya'll are in here too long."

Brody stood up and walked toward the door. "We need to get going anyway."

Sheriff Lloyd told Brody and Derek to follow his lead and not ask any questions. As they walked down the short hallway, Sheriff Lloyd made it a point to speak loudly. "You boys have more than overstayed your welcome here in Carter County, so I don't expect we'll be seein' you again anytime soon. Your business is done here. Do I make myself clear?"

Brody controlled the smile forming on his face and replied. "Loud and clear, Sheriff," he said as he and Derek walked out of the department.

Chapter Twenty

With the exception of one lingering local sitting at the counter finishing his breakfast, Sheridan and Rodney were the only other patrons at the diner. Nancy saw Sheridan and Rodney were deep in conversation, so she stood behind the counter and made small talk with the remaining customer to give them privacy. Rodney's face was mortified as Sheridan explained the tragic events that transpired with Hank the day before. She was still shaken by all that happened but buried her anger to avoid upsetting Rodney any more than he already was.

Rodney held her hand. "I'll be there with you when you tell your mom, honey," he offered.

"I'm not doing anything until the paternity test comes back, which probably won't be until after the ball."

"Why not just tell her now? I mean, you've pressed charges against Hank. She's going to find out, and doesn't she deserve to know Hank was the one who raped her back then, so she can seek justice?"

"Tennessee law dictates that too much time has passed for her to legally press charges."

"That doesn't make any sense. He can't just get away with it."

"But he will. I was up all night thinking about whether reopening her wounds would be fair."

"And what did you come up with?"

"I don't know. I need more time. My mom's gone to great lengths to keep her secret from me. She's managed to make peace with her past, and I'm hesitant to be the one who makes it resurface. Especially if I'm his daughter."

"My voicemail recorded his confession."

"It was a half-ass confession regarding the rape. But his threat to take my life again was clear. Because he broke the no-contact order issued when he was paroled, he'll do time regardless. I want to wait until the paternity test comes back. If I'm his daughter, I'll tell her. She'd have a right to know his blood runs through my veins."

"And if it comes back negative?"

"I don't know. I have plenty to keep me busy until we get the results back. Getting ready for the exhibition, giving my mom the deed to her house, Derek," she blurted out.

"Derek?"

"There's a little girl at Vista he thinks might benefit from art therapy. He asked if I'd be willing to work with her while we were in New York and I told him I would."

"You're not going to have any time to—"

"Don't worry. I told him I had Wednesday free and would extend my stay in New York to work with her for a week or so after the exhibition."

"Okay, I want to be sure you stay focused. Anyway, Brody mentioned the place in conversation. Vista House, right? They take care of foster kids with special needs or something like that."

"Yeah, something like that."

"This guy's making it really hard for me not to like him. I mean, he's gorgeous, has money, and a soft spot for kids? If only he were gay." Rodney looked down at his watch. "Speaking of smoking hot men who aren't gay, Brody offered to let us fly with them to New York on their jet. Glad I accepted, because there's no way we would've caught our flight."

"That was generous of him," Sheridan said, glad she'd have more time to spend with Derek.

Rodney picked up on the sparkle in Sheridan's eyes. "You've been through hell, and you have a lot to think about. I will support you no matter what you decide to do about Hank or telling your mom. All I ask is that while you explore love and all the perks that come with it, you don't forget why we're actually going to New York. Okay?"

Sheridan squeezed his hand. "I never said I was in love, but no, I haven't forgotten why we're going to New York," she said, as Brody and Derek walked into the diner and over to their table.

Sheridan stood up, smiled, and extended her hand out to Brody. "Hi. I'm Sheridan. You must be Brody. It's nice to meet you."

When Brody saw how attractive Sheridan was, he turned his head to Derek and smiled, then looked back to Sheridan and shook her hand. "It's nice to meet you too."

"Don't you have to get your things from Nancy?" Derek asked under his breath then slapped Brody on the shoulder to nudge him on his way.

"Yeah," Brody chuckled. "I'll just be a few minutes then we can head out."

Sheridan sat back down and Derek stood next to her at the table. "I heard you two are flying back to New York with us."

"Yes, and we really appreciate it," Sheridan answered.

"Where you two staying?" Derek asked.

"The Plaza," Rodney said.

"I see. While you're in town, I'll be sure you two have a car and driver available."

"I appreciate the offer, but we already hired a car service."

Derek needed a way to keep an eye on Sheridan when she wasn't with him without making it obvious. Hiring undercover security would be the best way to accomplish this, so he pushed. "I'm not sure if Sheridan's told you, but she's agreed to work with one of our foster kids at Vista, so making it easier for her to get around, especially in New York, is the least I can do," he insisted.

"Yeah, she mentioned it."

Sheridan looked up at Derek. "You don't have to do that."

"Please, I insist."

"I'll make a deal with you. If you agree to go to the Unmasked Charity Ball and give us a tour of the art district next week, we'll use your car and driver," Rodney said.

"Done." Derek quickly agreed. He then looked down at Sheridan. "I was wondering if I was ever going to get an invite," he teased.

⁂

THE CHILLED LATE afternoon air in New York inspired Sheridan to wrap her scarf snugly around her neck as Derek helped her walk down the jet's stairs and onto the private runway. Two limo drivers approached the group and began loading Derek's and Brody's luggage into one car and Sheridan's and Rodney's into the other. Derek had used the drive to Knoxville International to fill Brody in on everything he'd seen in Carter County and to make security arrangements for Sheridan to be guarded while in New York. Derek nodded at Sheridan's driver inconspicuously to be sure he understood his objective, which was to protect Sheridan at all costs. When the limo driver nodded in acceptance, Derek returned his attention back to Sheridan.

"So, I guess I won't see you until Wednesday?"

"I wish I could come sooner, but I have to meet the art director at the museum tomorrow."

Derek grabbed both her hands and placed them in his. "This is your big debut." Derek kissed the top of her head. "Go, I'll see you Wednesday."

Sheridan smiled then walked to the limo. The driver held the door open and assisted her into the car. When the car drove away, Derek felt his chest tighten with worry. Brody saw Derek's jaw tense. "I know Roger personally, Derek. She's going to be fine."

"How can you be so sure?"

"He was in the Marines and had twenty years in at the bureau before he started his own agency. I promise, Roger or anyone of his hand-selected men watching her will jump in front of a bullet for her."

"Marine or not, if anything happens to her, I'll kill him myself."

⁂

Chapter Twenty-One

T uesday, April 30, 2013

DEREK'S exhausted eyes brightened as he walked into Vista House and all the children who'd been standing in a perfect line broke free from it and ran up to him with rowdy excitement. As usual, Charlie was the first to reach him.

"Guess where we're going, Derek?" he asked.

"Where?"

Tamika, who was holding Rebecca's hand, screamed out before Charlie could answer, "To the park with Mr. and Mrs. Jenkins!"

"But I wanted to tell him, Tamika," Charlie pouted.

"Okay, ladies and gents, back in line. Chop chop," Vanessa ordered, clapping her hands, as she walked around the corner and down the hall.

Derek stared at her with disbelieving eyes. "Holy shit, Vanessa, is that you?"

"Derek said shit," Charlie tattled.

"Do I need to wash your mouth out with soap, Derek?" Vanessa teased.

"She'll do it too," Blake warned as he approached the group carrying two large picnic baskets.

Derek smiled. Vanessa and Blake were two of the original Vista House kids, and he'd only seen them a handful of times after the first Vista closed. "What the hell are you two doing here?" he asked then hugged Vanessa.

"Derek said H-E double hockey sticks," Charlie tattled again.

Derek looked down at Charlie. "Sorry, buddy."

Blake shook Derek's hand. "We're the new house parents."

Derek offered them an accepting smile. "Anderson told me but not that it was you two." He addressed Vanessa. "I just had a conversation with Lexus about you, Sarah, Ian, and Thomas. Brought back so many memories."

"Yeah, we were pretty inseparable back then," Vanessa reminisced.

Derek smiled. "I can't stress enough how grateful I am to have you both on board. So, Mr. and Mrs. Jenkins, huh?"

Vanessa raised her left ring finger and flashed her wedding band. "We eloped last year. Crazy, right?"

"So, what do you think of the new Vista?" Derek asked.

"Even though we've only been here a few days, we're both impressed. And my God, the kids are incredible. Your mom would be so proud of you," Vanessa replied.

"We were told you had a meeting with Anderson, Thomas, and Lexus this morning. We decided to take the kids to the park to give you all some privacy. They're waiting in the conference room for you," Blake informed.

"I'd better get in there then. You know how Anderson hates tardiness."

Vanessa laughed. "Oh, I remember. Let's make it a point to catch up though. In fact, Sarah's coming into town Thursday to work with Ashley on her healing techniques. She'll be here for a week or so. Maybe we can all get together for dinner this weekend."

Derek chuckled. "Ah, Sarah, the ornery artistic twin. Is she still painting?"

"Sarah paints here and there. And trust me, she's still as ornery as she ever was," Vanessa teased.

"I would expect nothing less. Anyway, yeah, let's do dinner," Derek agreed. "There's someone I'd like Sarah to meet."

"The untouchable Derek Young's found a lady? Who would've guessed?" Vanessa mocked.

"I never said it was a woman."

"Please, your smile gave it away."

"Busted. Anyway, you'll meet her tomorrow when she comes to work with Rebecca. She's an artist and doesn't really know anyone here, so I thought her and Sarah might have something in common to talk about."

"All right you little heathens, back in line if you want to go to the park," Blake shouted.

"Everybody, say goodbye to Derek," Vanessa instructed.

All the children, with the exception of Rebecca, spoke in unison, "Goodbye, Derek," as he walked down the hall to the conference room.

§♦

WHEN DEREK ENTERED the conference room, Anderson, Thomas, and Lexus were sitting at the small round cherry wood table talking about the climate differences between New York and Florida.

"There you are," Lexus said, as Derek took a seat. "How was your trip, sweetie?"

"Interesting." Derek looked over at Anderson. "I just ran into Vanessa and Blake. How'd that happen?"

Anderson scowled. "Why, do you disapprove?"

"Sorry. Didn't mean for that to sound offensive. Still trying to recover from my trip, I guess. I'm impressed you were able to convince them to join the team."

Anderson's brows relaxed. "It didn't take much convincing. Thomas and I ran into them a couple months ago at Union Square, and they invited us to join them for lunch. We were catching up, I told them about the reopening of Vista, they asked what they could do to help, I mentioned we were in need of house parents, and they jumped on the opportunity to give back. It was that simple," he said rushed.

"Don't be so modest, Anderson. You worked with Vanessa and Sarah after my mom saved them from their last foster home," Derek said. "I'm sure Vanessa wanted to pay forward what you and my mom did for them."

Anderson smiled. "I'd like to think we helped, but either way, I think Vanessa and Blake are going to be perfect for the kids."

"Yeah, me too," Derek agreed.

"I should have told you, but they called to accept the position the morning I left for my friend's funeral, so—" Anderson tried to apologize.

Derek held up a dismissing hand. "No explanation necessary, Anderson. Really, it was a smart decision. In fact, I'm the one who needs to apologize to all of you," he said, addressing everyone in the room. "I know I haven't been involved in a lot of the administrative decisions or spent enough time with the kids, but that's going to change."

"So does that mean you found the closure you were looking for in Carter County?"

Derek skirted around the truth. "Let's just say I met someone who's opened my eyes and is helping me see things a little differently."

Lexus became excited. "So, you've met someone?"

"Yeah, but we're taking things slow."

"Do we know her?" Thomas asked.

"No. Her name is Sheridan Hayes. I met her in Carter County, but she lives in Connecticut where she volunteers teaching art therapy to children at a counseling center. I talked to her about Rebecca, and she's agreed to come work with her tomorrow and then another week or so after her art debut at MoMA on Friday."

"MoMA? So, she's a professional artist as well?" Anderson asked.

Derek smiled. "Yeah, she is."

Lexus picked up her cup of coffee with both hands and took a cautious sip. "You know, art therapy might work with Rebecca. If Sheridan can help her translate her feelings and thoughts through art, we'd be better able to understand what she needs from a psychological standpoint."

Thomas pushed the file sitting in front of him over to Derek. "I've been working with her the last few days and haven't felt anything. Her mind's like Fort Knox. I mean, if Sheridan can open her up through art therapy, I'm all for it, but she's going to have her work cut out for her."

"Why is that?" Derek asked.

"She hasn't drawn a single picture since Friday," Thomas informed.

"This is what I was afraid of," Anderson said. "I'm not saying we should give up on her. I agree we should give Ms. Hayes a shot with her. But, if she can't break Rebecca's barrier, we'll need to accept we may not be equipped enough to help her here."

"We'll cross that bridge if and when we come to it," Derek said. "There's something I need to ask of each of you."

"What is it?" Lexus asked.

"While Sheridan is here, I need you to refrain from discussing my parents or how they died. I know it's going to be difficult because of their history with the first Vista, but it's necessary."

Lexus frowned. "Why?"

"I need some time to ease her into my complicated life. Does that make sense?"

Lexus' loyalty rested with Derek, so she agreed. "There are a few pictures hanging in the front entrance of your parents and the original Vista children. Should I take them down?"

"Just the ones my parents are in, but I promise we'll hang them back up as soon as I work this out," he assured. Derek addressed Thomas. "I meant to call and ask you to pick up a few art supplies she'll need, but with everything going on, it slipped my mind."

"We have some art supplies on hand, but I'll be sure to set everything out before she gets here."

"I'm taking the kids to get their pictures done at Stephan's Photography Studio early tomorrow morning. What time will Sheridan be here tomorrow?"

"Around nine-thirty."

"We probably won't be back until around ten-thirty. Should I cancel the shoot?" Lexus asked.

"I wanted her to meet Thomas and Anderson and give her a tour of Vista anyway, so that will work out perfect."

Thomas rose from his chair. "Well, unless there's anything else, I need to head out for another appointment."

"Nope, that was it."

Just as Anderson began to rise from his chair, Derek stopped him. "I wanted to discuss plans for future Vista Houses with you. Do you have a few minutes?"

Anderson sat back down. "Yes. Of course."

Lexus walked over to Derek and kissed the top of his head. "Welcome home," she said. She and Thomas left the conference room, shutting the door behind them.

"You don't want to talk about future Vista House plans, do you?" Anderson asked.

"You read me?" Derek asked.

Anderson chuckled. "Don't worry, Derek, your mind is still as closed off to me and everyone else as it was when you were little."

"How'd you know then?"

"Sometimes people don't need a gift to figure out when something's wrong with those they care about. Like Rebecca, for example."

"What about Rebecca?"

"I just found out myself, but the day you brought Rebecca here, her mom was bailed out of jail and tried to kill herself. She had to be put on life support. They pulled the plug this morning. She's gone. Maybe Rebecca sensed it. That would explain why she's been withdrawn and hasn't drawn anything."

Derek took in a frustrated breath before he spoke. "Are they sure Abigail didn't OD on meth?"

"She didn't OD. She was found in her bathtub with her wrists slit."

"Jesus. She was pretty messed up, but I wouldn't wish that on anyone."

"Remember, Derek, people aren't born horrible," he scolded. "According to the notes you left me, Clara Ramsey was murdered but not before abandoning Abigail. She was dealt a pretty hard hand. Like our kids, Abigail probably got lost in the system, was tossed around to different foster homes, and was likely neglected and abused. So, does that make her a horrible person? No. It simply makes her a product of the environment she was thrown into."

"I meant no disrespect. It's a vicious cycle. Unfortunately, Rebecca's the one left here to suffer."

"You're right, but Rebecca, unlike her mother, has us to guide her. We're in the beginning stages of that process though, so I think we should hold off on telling her about her mom."

"Agreed. If we can break through to her, it may help soften the blow when we do."

Anderson leaned back in his chair. "So moving on, what is it you wanted to talk to me about? Everything okay?"

"Not really. Sorry I lied, I just didn't want my aunt to worry."

"About what?"

"Sheridan. I need your help and have no idea where to even start."

"The beginning is usually good," he advised.

Derek searched for the right words to explain without giving away too much. "Sheridan was attacked on Lyle Mountain but doesn't remember it happening. I don't know why she doesn't, but it's frustrating trying to protect her when I don't have a clue who or what the hell it is I'm protecting her from."

"Okay, slow down. First of all, how do you know she was attacked if she doesn't remember?"

"Long story."

Anderson adjusted in his seat. "I'm not going anywhere."

"I was asked to check on her up on Lyle after her cousin and Brody got in a bar fight and were thrown in jail. When I got there, I heard her screaming in the woods. When I finally found her, she was being attacked. I threw the guy off her but couldn't see him. I carried her back to her house and watched over her through the night. When she woke up the next morning and we talked, I realized she hadn't remembered anything."

"Did you tell her?"

"No, I told the Sheriff the day after that she was assaulted."

"And did he tell her?"

"No. He didn't want to put her through any unnecessary trauma until he had more to go on. The same day I reported the incident, she was ambushed by her stepfather, who's currently on parole for trying to kill her when she was a little girl."

"Christ. Did they catch him?"

"Yeah. He's in the hospital being guarded."

"Why is he in the hospital?"

"Let's just say he's lucky I didn't finish him off."

"I see. So, it was the stepfather who attacked her the night you found her?"

"That's what the Sheriff thinks, but my gut tells me there's someone else out there who wants to hurt her."

Anderson looked at Derek through suspicious eyes. "Is it just your gut telling you that, or are you having visions again?"

"No. No visions, just my gut," he lied.

"Interesting."

"Don't get me wrong. Sheriff Lloyd could be right. It may have been her stepfather on both attacks. But, until he can find proof it was him, I'm not taking any chances, so I hired undercover security to watch and protect her."

"And Sheridan isn't suspicious as to why she's being guarded?"

"She doesn't know."

Anderson scratched his head. "Well, I'm not going to lie, Derek. I'm a little concerned about your newest distraction. My hope was that you'd come back from Carter County with a clear head, and it seems as though you've come back with more on your plate than you left with."

"I understand your concern," Derek snapped. "But, if my newest distraction is a problem for you, you're free to utilize your services somewhere other than Vista."

Anderson leaned forward in his chair and slammed his fist on the table. "Jesus, Derek, if you don't want my honesty, why bother telling me any of this?"

"Because, my hope was that you'd save your lectures for the children and help me figure out a way to help her remember without fucking her head up."

"I've devoted years of my life to help build both Vistas, counseled the children, picked up all the pieces along the way you've chosen to neglect, and this is how you talk to me?"

"I'm sorry." Derek looked down at the table, embarrassed by his own behavior. "I don't even know what to say."

"You can say what's on your mind, Derek," he encouraged. "Just don't get pissed off when I tell you what's on mine. Besides, I didn't say I wouldn't help you; I was just making an observation."

Derek looked up at Anderson through lost and weary eyes. "How do I help her?"

"I don't want to jump the gun here, but based on what little you've told me she went through as a child and just recently, it sounds like her memory loss could be a result of post-traumatic stress disorder. Of course, I can't make an accurate diagnosis or treat her until I can evaluate her. That isn't going to be easy without her knowledge of the attack."

"Should I have told her?"

"You did the right thing. Telling her could have made her symptoms worse. She's no different than the children we work with who repress their own tragic pasts or build protective walls around their subconscious thoughts. It's going to take time and patience to break through to her, if we even can."

"Time's something I don't have where her safety is concerned. I mean, shit, maybe you can try to read her, hypnotherapy, something, anything."

"Even if I can, it won't give us all the answers. Not to mention the fact that she'd have to be open to it and allow me in."

"What do you suggest we do then?"

"We use the time she's here at Vista to get through to her somehow. You said yourself her stepfather assaulted her, so maybe you try and convince her to talk to me about that isolated attack."

"I can try."

"You look exhausted, Derek. Go home and get some rest."

Derek rose from his chair. "Everything we discussed stays within this room."

"You have my word."

※

Chapter Twenty-Two

T uesday, April 30, 2013

RODNEY INSTRUCTED their driver to take the scenic route from The Plaza to The Museum of Modern Art. His goal was to give Sheridan a small glimpse of what New York City life had to offer. Sheridan's eyes beamed and her mouth fell in awe as they passed several historical landmarks like Central Park, Rockefeller Center, Carnegie Hall, and St. Patrick's Cathedral. When the driver pulled up to The Museum of Modern Art, Sheridan's admiration for the city turned into unsettled nerves.

To get to the art director's office, they had to walk through a large section of the museum. Sheridan became intimidated as they passed famous works of art by Pablo Picasso, Frida Kahlo, Salvador Dalí, and Henri Matisse. "I don't know if I can do this, Rodney," Sheridan admitted.

"I'll take care of everything," Rodney assured as they approached the receptionist's desk. "Ms. Hayes and I have an appointment with Mrs. Hershkowitz," he informed.

The receptionist, who was in her mid-sixties and wearing a modest turquoise suit rose from her chair. "Yes, of course. She's expecting you."

❦

MRS. HERSHKOWITZ REVIEWED the logistics of the Unmasked Charity Ball with Sheridan and Rodney. "We arranged a previewing of your silent auction pieces to our VIP guests. The main event starts at seven. The VIP viewing will begin at five-thirty. You won't be required to attend this portion of the event. Your auction pieces will also be displayed at the opening of the event, which will allow ample time for non-VIP guest bidding.

"Your angel collection will be unveiled after dinner. You and your angel collection will be introduced and unmasked simultaneously, which will intensify the theatrics of both reveals. We've built the hype around your hidden identity and talent being exposed, so it is imperative that you not remove your mask until after you make your stage entrance."

"The guests will assume you'll be making your grand entrance from the second floor down the imperial staircase to the center of the ballroom. Lighting, the stair's decor, and the announcer will help build that expectation."

"Where will I be making my entrance?" Sheridan asked.

Mrs. Hershkowitz looked down at Sheridan's ankle boot and then back up to Sheridan. She then pointed to the center of the ballroom. "There."

"So, she'll just be standing in the middle of the ballroom?" Rodney asked.

"No, of course not," Mrs. Hershkowitz said, then smiled and addressed Sheridan. "We received word about your injuries and decided making you walk the length of the staircase to center stage wouldn't be practical. We'll be utilizing the trap door in the center of the ballroom that leads down to the museum's basement. We're renting a hydraulic stage lift that will bring you up to the center of the custom stage. It will be quite dramatic and different.

"We're also building a custom revolving stage. This will allow the additional art you've chosen for the auction to be seen by all collectors attending. With your approval, of course."

Sheridan forced a smile. "Yes, that will be fine."

"Great. All that's left is your music selection and layout for the angel collection's reveal."

"I have both," Rodney said, then pulled the paperwork out from his briefcase and handed it to her.

Mrs. Hershkowitz smiled. "Perfect."

"May I see the layout please?" Sheridan asked.

Mrs. Hershkowitz handed her the papers to review.

Sheridan studied the draft then looked up at Rodney. "The layout needs to be changed."

Rodney's brows drew together. "Changed how?"

"How it's displayed. There were only five paintings within the original angel collection, but I finished another piece the day you told me Dr. Riley wanted to purchase the set. I decided it needs to be displayed with the others and given to him after the ball."

"I'm sure he'll want to purchase the other painting too, so that shouldn't be a problem."

"No. I won't accept another penny for a painting that belonged within the collection anyway."

Rodney smiled. "As you wish. We'll need to make arrangements to get the painting here."

"I'd be happy to take care of that for you, Ms. Hayes," Mrs. Hershkowitz offered.

"Please, call me Sheridan, and no, that won't be necessary. My mom and aunt are driving in tomorrow morning, so I'll have them bring it with them."

Rodney addressed Sheridan. "And the layout?"

"The new painting should be the centerpiece." She took the pen from Rodney's pocket and started drawing a new layout. "I'd also like to change the music to 'Tears of an Angel' by RyanDan to be played during the angel collection's reveal."

"Okay. Anything else?"

"No, we're good," Rodney replied.

Mrs. Hershkowitz handed them both her business card. "If either of you need anything, give me a call. It's going to be a hectic couple of days, so be sure to enjoy what free time you have tomorrow."

Rodney looked over at Sheridan with mischievous eyes and then back to Mrs. Hershkowitz. "Not to worry, our emerging star is on a tight leash after tomorrow."

Chapter Twenty-Three

Wednesday, May 1st, 2013

BRODY HANDED Derek a cup of coffee when he walked into the kitchen. "Here, thought you'd need this," he said, then sat on one of the stools at the kitchen's bar. Derek grabbed the metal canister of sugar sitting on the counter and began scooping several hefty spoonfuls into his cup.

"Jesus. Want any coffee with your sugar?"

"Sheridan's coming to Vista this morning to work with Rebecca. I need to wake up."

"You said she wasn't going to be there until nine-thirty." Brody looked at his watch. "It's only a little after seven. You've got plenty of time to get your shit together."

"Yeah, well, the sooner we talk about our game plan with the investigation, the sooner I can get out of here. Have you checked in with Nancy?"

Brody took a sip of his coffee before he answered. "Yeah, I called her last night. She said Walt's having withdrawals, but she was still trying to detox him, and..." he started to say then paused.

"And...?"

"The night I went to Dottie's to talk to Walt, Nancy told me how Walt always went on and on about 'the doll is key' when he was tying one on. I didn't really think anything of it until she mentioned it again last night on the phone. She said he'd screamed it out in his sleep. When I asked her to be more specific about what he'd said exactly, she clammed up on me."

"Why the fuck didn't you tell me? You know I've had the same recurring dream of my mom rocking me and a mangled haired doll since I was a kid."

"I forgot. We were just kids when you told me about the images you saw in your dreams. And shit, I'd just gotten out of jail and was driving to the airport when you brought me up to speed on everything that happened. It was a lot of information to digest. The doll comment slipped my mind, but I'm telling you now. Between these Midtown Butcher cold cases I'm working and your mom's investigation, my head is cluttered with a lot of shit that doesn't make any sense."

"We need to find an effective way to start sorting through my visions and all the other information we've collected so far."

"There's a lot to comb through, but using an evidence board might help us find plausible connections and leads a little easier."

"Speaking of leads, I stopped by Dr. Riley's office yesterday to talk to him about his possible connection to Sheridan. His office said he was out of town until Friday morning, so I'll be making an unannounced visit."

"You really think he's the one who bought Sheridan's paintings?"

"I know he is."

"How?"

"I did a state search for Duncan Riley. There were two listed in New York but only one was a doctor. I'm not saying there's any foul play behind his connection with Sheridan. He's on the MoMA Board, so it could be a coincidence."

"What about your mom's adoptive dad? Did you find out if he's still at Baker's Mental Institution?"

"Yeah. He's there. I'm going to visit him tomorrow."

"Want me to go with you? You know, for support?"

"I'm good. What about Sheriff Lloyd? Any updates?"

"No, not yet. I left him the scribbled notes from Walt's file. Maybe he can help shed some light on what they say." Brody got up from the stool. "I have a meeting at eight-thirty to go over my progress on the Midtown Butcher case. I still can't believe Abigail killed herself. She was the warmest lead we had. Anyway, I need to head out."

"Yeah, I need to shower and shave then head over to Vista." Derek walked Brody to the door. "Listen, I wouldn't push Nancy for more information about Walt's doll comment until we follow up with Sheriff Lloyd. I'm sure it's nothing, but if she's keeping something from you, we don't want to spook her."

"Got it," Brody agreed.

Chapter Twenty-Four

D erek saw Sheridan's limo pull up and park on the street in front of Vista House. There was a light drizzle outside, so he grabbed one of the umbrellas by the front door and walked out to the car to meet her. The driver, also holding an umbrella, walked around to the back of the limo and opened Sheridan's door.

She greeted Derek with a smile. "Good morning."

"Good morning," Derek returned then addressed the driver. "Thanks. I've got it from here." He placed the umbrella over Sheridan's head and escorted her up the wet steps leading to the four-story townhouse.

"Where's your boot brace?"

"It was digging into my ankle and making it hurt worse, so I left it at the hotel. Trust me, I walk just as good out of it as I do in it."

When they walked inside, Sheridan removed her damp trench coat and scarf and placed them on the coat rack hanging to the left of the entrance. When she realized he was staring at her attire, which consisted of faded pegged denim overalls, a simple white T-shirt, and a pair of white Keds, her cheeks became flushed.

"Oh God, I dressed way too casual, didn't I? Rodney told me I was underdressed this morning before I left The Plaza. I dressed like this because the kids are less likely to be intimidated by me, and painting gets messy if you're doing it right."

"I promise, you look fine. I was only staring at you because you look both adorable and sexy at the same time if that's even possible."

Sheridan blushed and started to take a bold step toward him before Anderson, Thomas, and Ashley walked into the front entryway.

෫෨

"So, you must be Sheridan. I'm Thomas." He shook Sheridan's hand.

"And I'm Anderson, Thomas' dad, and Vista's Psychic House Counselor. It's nice to meet you." He gave her his business card and also shook her hand.

"This is Ashley, our oldest child at Vista," Derek said.

"Geez, Derek, I'm not a child anymore, you know? Even your Aunt Lexus agrees I became a young lady last week when I turned sixteen."

"You don't think I forgot your birthday, do you?" he teased.

"Well, didn't you?"

Derek reached in his back jean pocket and pulled out a small envelope and handed it to her. "Enjoy, young lady."

Ashley opened the envelope and pulled out the tickets. When she realized they were tickets to see *The Phantom of the Opera*, she threw her arms around his waist and hugged him. "I can't believe it. Thank you!"

"Happy belated sixteenth," Sheridan offered.

Ashley let go of Derek, walked around him, then cupped Sheridan's right hand into both of hers. "Sorry, didn't mean to be rude. My name's Ashley."

"It's nice to meet you." Ashley's piercing green eyes closed, and she became withdrawn. "You okay?"

When Ashley spoke, her face turned sympathetic. "You're hurt. I can see blockage around your right ankle and also around your...your right side." Ashley's eyes shot open. She smiled then released Sheridan's hand.

"Ho-How did you know where I was hurt?"

Anderson walked up behind Ashley and placed his hands on top of her shoulders. "Our Ashley here is an energy healer. Her gift allows her to locate energy blockages within an individual's chakras or aura. Once she locates the blockage, she can eliminate them by using energy to heal emotional and physical ailments through her hands and, just recently, at a distance."

"That's amazing, Ashley," Sheridan complimented.

"I can take your pain away, you know," Ashley offered. "But, you'd have to be open to the process and permit me to do so, or it won't work."

Sheridan reached up and touched her side. "I am pretty sore. You can fix me up if you promise to paint with me while I'm here."

Ashley's eyes became enthusiastic. "You mean, like, real painting?"

Sheridan laughed. "Yes, real painting."

"Deal," Ashley accepted.

"So, how'd you manage to get out of going with the rest of the gang to get pictures taken this morning?" Derek asked.

Ashley snorted. "If you saw how your Aunt Lexus dressed everybody this morning, you'd totally get how I mysteriously came down with a twenty-four-hour bug. Seriously, they looked like a colorful collage of frilly lace dresses and bow ties."

Derek laughed. "Trust me, I get it. I grew up with her and suffered through many themed photo shoots."

A cluster of pictures hanging on the wall opposite the front door caught Sheridan's eye. "Are these pictures of the current Vista children?"

Derek was relieved when he saw Lexus remembered to take down the pictures with his parents in them. "The picture on the right is. The two to the left of it are of some of the kids who lived at the first Vista before they were adopted."

Sheridan began studying the picture of the first Vista House kids, then turned and looked at Thomas. "Is that you?"

Thomas smirked. "Yes, and it's a horrible picture," he said embarrassed, then pointed out the other three children within the picture. "That's Vanessa, her twin Sarah, and that's Ian. Because we were the first kids to come to Vista, we all became pretty close. The four of us, including Derek, were nearly inseparable back then."

"So how old were you in this picture, Thomas?"

Anderson spoke up. "Eight. His adoption was finalized the day before that picture was taken."

"We were all adopted before they closed Vista, even the twins and Ian, but I was the lucky one who got the house shrink," Thomas said.

"Hey, watch it, smart guy," Anderson teased.

"And what about you, Mr. Young? Where are you in all these pictures?" Sheridan teased.

Thomas was quick to point Derek out. "That's him there. It was taken in '96 at the Vista's annual barbecue we held at our home in Greystone. We held one every year to reunite with some of the other kids who lived at Vista but were eventually adopted and moved away." He pointed to a little girl standing next to Derek in the photo. "That's Jada. She was adopted in '92 and moved to Catskills, but the Fuller's were really great about bringing her to the barbecues."

"This is little Charlie," Derek said, redirecting her focus to the photo of the newest Vista kids. "You better watch out for this one, he's quite the charmer," he warned teasingly.

"He's a cutie," Sheridan observed. "So, what's little Charlie's gift?"

Anderson answered. "He's clairaudient, which basically means he's able to hear sounds or voices from spirits outside the range of normal spectrum hearing. Before he came to Vista, he'd been misdiagnosed with having Tourretes and autism, so we're working with him on filtering techniques."

Sheridan pointed to another child within the picture. "And who's this?"

"That's Tamika. She's telepathic but also starting to show signs of clairvoyance," Anderson answered.

"So, she can read or control someone's mind?" Sheridan asked.

Anderson chuckled. "No. Or should I say, it's not like what you see on the big screen. In the short time we've worked with Tamika, we've learned she's capable of sending and receiving thoughts, sensations, and visions. With time and guidance, she'll have the ability to see and communicate with any energy source. Her possibilities are limitless."

"And these two little guys. Twins, right?" Sheridan observed.

Thomas worked with the twins the most, so he felt inclined to answer. "Yes, and like Tamika, Andrew and Luke possess telepathy-like characteristics. The difference is they only communicate with each other, which isn't uncommon in twins. We discovered Andrew also possesses kinetic energy abilities, which in layman's terms means he's a walking force field that unintentionally moves objects without the use of physical means."

"Fascinating," Sheridan said. "I only see five children in the picture. Didn't you say there were six at Vista?" Sheridan paused. "You know, it just dawned on me. I don't even know the little girl's name I'll be working with."

Derek spoke up. "Her name is Rebecca."

They were interrupted by the phone ringing in Anderson's office down the hall. "Ashley, dear, would you mind grabbing that?" Anderson asked.

"Sure," she said then walked down the hall to answer it.

When Sheridan began speaking again she addressed Derek. "You told me Rebecca's mute but draws pictures to communicate. Was she brought to Vista because you feel she possesses psychic abilities herself?"

"I do. Based on a few of her drawings, I'm leaning toward her being clairvoyant. Because she can't speak, I think she's drawing what she's seeing and feeling in both our world and other dimensions."

Anderson looked at Sheridan, and his tone turned serious. "We're grateful you've come to work with Rebecca, but it's important you understand these children come from unthinkable and unique circumstances. They've been beaten down both physically and mentally, thrown away by those who were supposed to love them, and treated like freaks of nature. They need special care that requires experience and understanding about what they've been through."

"I understand your concern," Sheridan replied. *More than you know*, she thought to herself. "I know I'm not experienced or familiar with your unique counseling techniques, but I'm willing to learn if you're willing to teach."

"Well, I suppose we could start by having you participate in a hypnotherapy session with me," Anderson said. "It may help give you some insight on what we do here and what the kids go through. You never know, you may even learn something about yourself in the process."

"I'm not opposed to that," she lied, shaking inside at the thought of someone digging around in her head.

"I have some time available today," Anderson offered.

"Unfortunately, I won't have any spare time until next week."

"I see. Monday then?"

"I'll let you know."

Thomas picked up on Sheridan's nerves and tried to redirect the conversation. "To be honest, Dad, I think Sheridan's a natural. Didn't you pick up on how quickly she was able to bond with Ashley?"

"I noticed it too," Derek confirmed.

"Yes, that was impressive. You see, Ashley's older, so unfortunately, she's been in and out of the system a lot longer than the other children. You know, institutions, hospitals, foster homes. Needless to say, she has trust issues but did seem to connect with you right away."

Thomas chimed in. "Do you think it would be beneficial to have all the children participate in the session?"

"That's a great idea," Sheridan agreed. "Rebecca may be more comfortable and open to it if the other children are involved at first."

Ashley walked back into the front entryway. "That was Lexus on the phone. She said they finished early and they're on their way back."

"Before they get here, I want to give you a tour of the rest of the house."

Anderson addressed Derek. "I hope you don't mind if I don't join you on the tour. I need to catch up on a few things."

"We'll manage," Derek assured.

"I'll see you two in a bit then," Anderson said then started walking down the hall with Thomas to his office. Before he entered, he addressed Ashley. "If I were you, I'd get upstairs and in bed. You're sick, remember?"

Ashley's face turned worried. "Got to go."

Derek laughed. "We have an emergency elevator down the hall we can use," he told Sheridan.

"Whatever you want to do," Sheridan replied.

"Let's start in the kitchen," he said and led the way.

≈

WHEN DEREK and Sheridan reached the final room on the tour, Derek paused before he opened the door. "This is the room where you'll be working with the kids today. We're still in the process of finishing the art room, so I apologize for the strong paint smell," he said then opened the door.

Each wall was painted a different bright color. The sink on the back wall, an instruction easel, six chairs around a long table holding art supplies, and six table easels were the only things in the room.

"You could have fifteen to twenty people painting in here at once," Sheridan said.

"Lexus has been working on getting the room completed but hasn't had time to finish it with all the other tasks she's had to take on in my absence. She's been a saint in helping reopen Vista. I'd finish it myself to give her a much needed break but wouldn't have a clue where to start."

"Is your aunt psychic?"

Derek chuckled. "You'd think she was, but no, not at all."

"What about Anderson and Thomas? I wanted to ask them earlier downstairs but didn't want to get too personal."

"Yes. They're both clairsentience, which means they have the ability to receive silent thoughts, messages, or projected emotions. They absorb and feel the sensations of a person's actual emotional and physical pain, though."

"I can't imagine how hard that must be."

"When Thomas first came to Vista, he was four and wasn't in a good place at all. He was sick all the time and really depressed."

"He seems fine now."

"He has Anderson to thank for that. Before Anderson adopted Thomas, he'd counseled him at Vista and helped him learn how to use and live with his gift. He helped Vanessa and Blake too, which are the new house parents at Vista. You'll meet them when they get back with the kids."

"What are their gifts?"

"Blake was clairaudient like Charlie, but after he went to college, his ability to hear sounds and spirits vanished, which isn't uncommon. In fact, Jada lost her gifts right after she arrived to Vista House, which is probably why she got adopted before some of the others did."

"And Vanessa?"

"Vanessa is a medium. Her twin sister Sarah is a healer."

"So Vanessa talks to the dead?"

"In a nutshell, yes," he confirmed then walked over to where she was standing. Derek smiled. "All right, enough paranormal talk. Instead, let's talk about this empty space. So, if this were your room and you could do anything you wanted with it, what would you do?"

"Derek, I'm only staying until the end of next week."

"I just wanted to pick your brain about what this room needs for completion. If I can remove the project from my aunt's plate, it would help my guilty conscience."

Sheridan smiled. "Well, let's start with your budget. How much money will you have to work with?"

"A lot."

"So, the sky's the limit, huh? Well, the first thing I would do is not limit this room for just painting. If it were mine, I'd use it for all kinds of arts and crafts. You know, like porcelain painting, sculpting, weaving, drawing, and holiday crafts. I mean, there are so many things the kids could do in here."

"Good point. So, what would we need to accommodate both arts and crafts?"

"Well, you already have a sink, but I'd have several cabinets installed, top and bottom, on that back wall to store your supplies. I'd also buy at least four more long plastic multipurpose tables. That would allow you to have five different work stations for different art projects going on simultaneously."

She turned and looked at the left wall. "I'd have several bookshelves installed on this wall, so the children could put their more solid creations on display. You could use this entire right wall to hang and display the kid's drawings, colorings, and paintings. And for this front wall, I might install several colorful stacked cubbies to store the supplies the kids use the most for easy access. That's really about it."

"Really, that's it?" Derek asked, overwhelmed.

Sheridan laughed. "Well, you asked," she teased.

Small voices poured into the house from downstairs.

Derek grinned. "Sounds like they're back. Are you ready to meet them?"

"What if they don't like me?"

"They're going to love you." He took her hand and led her to the elevator.

Chapter Twenty-Five

As the elevator doors opened on the first floor, Sheridan and Derek saw Blake, Vanessa, and Anderson standing in the hallway.

"How'd the photo shoot go?" Derek asked Vanessa.

"Awesome. The kids look adorable."

"Yeah, Ashley told us they were dressed to the nines."

Vanessa smirked. "That's an understatement," she said then looked over at Sheridan. "Sheridan, right? I'm Vanessa, and this is my husband Blake."

Sheridan offered them both a warm smile and shook their hands. "Derek tells me you're the new house parents."

"Yes, and we love it. Anderson was telling us you're going to be doing art therapy with all the kids now instead of just Rebecca. They'll love that."

Sheridan smiled. "I hope so. I'm anxious to meet them."

"Well, your timing's perfect. Lexus took the kids in the family room to get a few more pictures in front of the fireplace before they change." She then addressed Derek. "In fact, I was just looking for you and Anderson. Lexus wants to get a few shots of you two with the children."

"Of course she does."

Blake laughed. "Well, we've done our time, so we'll catch up with you guys a little later."

Anderson looked over at Derek defeated. "You know she's going to get her way, so we might as well get it over with."

❧

LEXUS STOOD at the fireplace and fussed over the fidgety children. "Charlie, dear, I need you to stand next to Tamika. Andrew, hold Rebecca's hand and fix your bow tie, honey. Luke, you're perfect, sweetie, so don't move," Lexus instructed then pulled the camera's lens to her eye to snap a picture.

"Some things never change, do they, Aunt Lexus?" Derek teased as he, Sheridan, and Anderson walked into the family room.

Lexus guessed the kids would break free from the perfect pose she'd orchestrated when they saw Derek, so she tried to prevent it. "Kids, stay put," she warned but then felt unnerved by how quiet and motionless the children became.

Derek attempted to ignore the uncomfortable eeriness filling the room by way of introductions. He walked up to Rebecca and knelt down to her level. "Hey, Rebecca, I want you to meet—" he started then lost his wording when he turned around and saw how shaken Sheridan had become. Her face had drained of all color, and she stood paralyzed staring at Rebecca as though she'd seen a ghost.

Sheridan's tearing thoughts vanquished her ability to speak. She was both frightened and entranced by the little girl who looked exactly like her childhood doll. She had the same long curly flame red hair, pale cheeks, and was wearing the same quaint lavender velvet dress layered in lace. Four-year-old Charlie stood trance-like, then pulled his right arm up and pointed at Sheridan accusingly. His large, brown doe eyes dilated, and he began screaming where he stood. He repeated the same sentence over and over like an obsessed broken record continuously skipping. "Sheridan's scared again! Sheridan's scared again!"

"Make him stop," Andrew shouted and placed his hands over his ears to drown out Charlie's screams. The lights within the room began flickering, and the fireplace behind the children ignited on its own. Pictures and knickknacks within the room vibrated in their places as the walls and floor began shaking.

"Get the kids out of here, now," Derek ordered in the thickness of chaos.

Anderson scooped up little Charlie in his arms and carried him out of the room. Andrew, Luke, Tamika, and Lexus followed, but Rebecca did not. Instead, she walked up to Sheridan. Rebecca looked up at Sheridan's spooked face, giggled, and then spoke. "Hello, I've been waiting for you," she said in a small unearthly voice.

The room's tremulous calamities came to an alarming halt.

"Sheridan," Derek called out concerned when he saw her body begin to sway and her eyes flutter in disbelief.

Sheridan looked down at Rebecca before Derek reached her. Her mouth fell open in awe, "B-Becca?" were the last words she said before her eyes rolled to the back of her head and she collapsed into Derek's arms.

§

SHERIDAN'S EYELIDS fluttered as she regained consciousness. She tried to focus in on the familiar setting of the room she was in. She pulled herself up and sat on the chaise lounge sofa she'd been lying on.

"Sheridan," a woman's soft voice called out to her.

She turned toward a silhouette sitting in the therapist chair. "Aunt Maggie?"

"No, sweetie, I'm Lexus. You okay?" she asked as she turned on the floor lamp next to her.

"Wh-Where am I?"

"You're in Anderson's office. Derek carried you in here when you fainted."

Not a dream, she thought. Sheridan was embarrassed and felt a heavy anxiety rise to her throat. "Where's Derek?"

"He went to get a cool cloth for your face and to check in on the kids."

"The kids. Oh God, I-I'm so sorry. I didn't mean to frighten them."

Lexus smiled. "Oh, sweetie, you didn't frighten the children, they frightened you, and that's okay," Lexus assured.

"I don't understand."

"What you witnessed in that family room is exactly why Vista exists and, quite frankly, what these children have to live with every day of their lives."

"Are they okay?"

"Yes, they're fine. They're worried you're going to leave. They think they've upset you. And while he didn't say it himself, I suspect Derek's wondering the same thing."

"No, I'm not going to leave. I have to tell them," she said, rising from the chaise lounge. She stood up too quickly, became dizzy, and sat back down.

"It's okay, Sheridan. Just take it easy," Lexus advised.

They both turned to the door frame when they heard the floor creak and saw Tamika peeking in at them.

Sheridan pulled herself together and smiled at her. "Hi. You're Tamika, right?"

"Yes, ma'am." Tamika walked to where Sheridan was and sat down next to her. "I have to tell you a secret, but only you."

"Okay, tell me," she encouraged, light and playful.

Tamika leaned in to Sheridan's left ear and began whispering so faintly Sheridan could barely hear her. "They said you're the beautiful light that will help them all see."

Sheridan felt a chill crawl up the back of her neck. "Wh-who are they?" she asked in her own low whisper.

"I don't know them, but they said it's almost time."

"I see. Did they say anything else?"

Tamika tried hard to remember. "Uh-huh. They said your life has meaning, and you're both wor-worvy of love."

Sheridan's heart thumped hard within her chest. "You mean worthy?"

Tamika pulled away from Sheridan's ear and spoke in a normal tone. "Uh-huh. I don't know what that word means, but that's what they said." Tamika got up from the chaise and skipped over to the door to leave. She stopped and turned around. "Rebecca said you were really pretty like the Lady of Lyle, and you are."

Sheridan forced a smile. "Thank you."

Tamika giggled. "You're welcome," she said then skipped out the door.

"You okay?" Lexus asked.

"Yes. I'm fine," she lied.

"You get used to it."

"To what?"

"To the unknown. I remember how terrified I was years ago when I worked with the first Vista kids. There were so many times I thought I was going to crawl out of my own skin with fear."

"So, when did you stop being scared?"

"When I finally understood that the children were much more terrified than me. On the surface, their gifts seem glamorous, but I can assure you, they're not. The constant voices they hear or visions they see are like horrific nightmares. The only difference is, they're all happening while they're wide awake."

"Derek said what he receives is subjective too. I can't imagine how stressful and scary it must be for him and the children to not understand what they're seeing or hearing."

Lexus leaned forward in the chair and whispered, "Are you saying his visions have returned?"

It hadn't even dawned on Sheridan that Derek hadn't told anyone about his gifts resurfacing, so she tried to recant. "He said he had visions for a short time as a child."

Lexus leaned back in her chair. "That was such a difficult time in his life. All our lives. They say death comes in threes, but there were many more than that. Derek's parents, Fisher—" she stopped when she realized she'd slipped.

Sheridan's body ached with sorrow. "How'd they die?"

There was a long uncomfortable pause before Lexus answered her. "I shouldn't have said anything. When the time's right, Derek will open up to you about his parents. Pushing him to talk about them will only make him more guarded," she warned. "Unfortunately, I learned that the hard way."

Sheridan could hear the stress in Lexus' voice. "How so?"

"Derek came to live with my husband Quentin and me when he was ten. I wanted to take his pain away and help him understand his new gifts. So, I pushed him into counseling right away, which never gave him time to grieve. It was too much too soon, and he closed everyone out. He lost his gifts, and I blame myself for that. If you care about him, you'll give him time," she pleaded.

"I promise. I won't push him." Sheridan paused. "You said there were other deaths around that time. Who else died?"

"A family friend, Fisher, and many others died in a fire that nearly burned Providence House down to the ground."

"Providence House?" Sheridan probed. Sheridan knew that was where her Aunt Maggie had taken her mom to deliver her.

"Yes. Derek's mom was adopted from there back in the sixties. The orphanage was closed down a couple years after she was adopted due to an undercover investigation that confirmed reports of torture chambers and sexual and physical abuse. She'd always said she knew her purpose in life was to give back after being one of the lucky ones who was adopted and saved from that horrible place.

"Thirteen years after the orphanage closed, she and her parents helped fund the project that turned it into a woman's shelter and clinic. Derek's parents volunteered there, which is where they met. They just rebuilt and reopened Providence House a few months before we reopened Vista. For the first time in a long time, it feels like there's hope again.

"Jesus, I've done it again. It's just so hard not to talk about them, because they were such a big part of our lives and so many others. Even years after their deaths, they still have volunteers and influential contributors supporting all their causes."

"They sound like wonderful people," Sheridan said.

Derek walked in holding a damp cloth in his hand. "Everything okay?"

"Yes, dear, everything's fine. I was just talking to Sheridan about the children."

Derek addressed Sheridan. "How are you feeling?"

"I'm fine. I didn't eat breakfast this morning, which is probably why I got light-headed."

"Oh my," Lexus said, knowing Derek wasn't foolish enough to believe Sheridan's weak excuse for fainting. She got up from the chair to leave. "I'm going to go check in on the kids and give you two some privacy." She walked to the door and shut it behind her.

"You don't have to pretend you weren't overwhelmed. I'll understand if you don't want to stay or come back next week."

Sheridan shot up from the chaise lounge and looked up at him. "Fine. I'll admit it. I was frightened, but that doesn't mean I want to leave."

Derek caressed the side of her face lightly with the tips of his fingers. "Okay, Mona Lisa."

"Why did you call me that?"

"Nothing psychic related. I heard your cousin call you that. I get it. You're a beautiful and mysterious woman whose moods are ambiguous. Just when I think I understand how you're really feeling, you surprise me."

Sheridan blushed and dodged his compliment. "The only mood I'm in right now is an anxious one, because I'd really like to meet and start working with the kids."

"So then you want to work with all the kids in a group setting before working one on one with Rebecca?"

"You still want me to work with Rebecca one on one?"

"Yeah, of course I do. Why wouldn't I?"

"I assumed now that she's talking, you'd be able to communicate with her."

"Talking?"

"Yes, talking. You were standing right there when she told me she'd been waiting for me."

"Sheridan, she never said a word," he said in a concerned tone.

"But, I heard her."

"You were overwhelmed. There was a lot happening in that room. Maybe you just thought you heard her talk."

Sheridan pinched her forehead between her thumb and index finger. She tried to remember what happened and began questioning herself. *Did I imagine it?* She entertained the idea of telling Derek how Rebecca was almost an exact replica of her childhood doll and that Charlie had screamed the same cruel words her schoolmates had taunted her with as a little girl. She decided against it when she saw him looking at her like she'd lost her mind.

"You're right. I just imagined it."

Chapter Twenty-Six

Sheridan stared into the door's observation window and saw the children sitting quietly waiting for her. They wore basic white aprons, and each had their own table easel sitting in front of them holding new blank canvases. In front of the children's table was a large instruction easel.

"I'll be in there with you, and the others are right downstairs if we need them," Derek assured.

"Wh-what do I say to them? What if they become upset again?"

"Don't lie to them. Say what you're feeling. They'll be much more at ease with you if you're honest and don't tiptoe around them."

"Here we go," Sheridan said then opened the door and entered. She walked to the middle of the room, stood beside the floor easel, and faced the children with an apprehensive smile on her face. Derek observed from the door. Sheridan could still see the haunting resemblance between Rebecca and her childhood doll. When she felt Rebecca's stare and smile lock in on her, she turned her attention over to Ashley's familiar face.

"I'm surprised Lexus is letting you paint with us today even though you're sick," Sheridan attempted to tease.

Ashley looked irked. "The jig is up. I got popped and she's making me get my pictures done this weekend. Lexus doesn't even have any psychic abilities but still has the power to make you tell the truth."

Sheridan smiled. "Well, at least your conscience is clear now," she said. She was distracted by the sound of Charlie sniveling. Sheridan saw him sitting slumped in his chair and looking down at the table. "Charlie, you okay?" Sheridan asked. When he didn't acknowledge her, she walked up to the table and said his name again. "Charlie?"

He slowly lifted his head and looked up at her. His brown eyes were laced with worry, and his bottom lip was quivering. She reached over the table and placed his hands into hers. "Hey, what's the matter, buddy?"

It was obvious to Sheridan that Charlie was trying not to cry when she felt him inhale and hold a long breath. "It's okay, breathe." She felt him exhale. "I know you've just met me, but I promise, you can tell me what's wrong."

Charlie's mouth drew into a deep frown. His brows came together and he bit his bottom lip. "My heart hurts 'cause I scared you, and you don't want to be my friend now. I don't know how come I said what I was saying. I-I didn't mean to, I promise."

"Oh, sweetheart, I do want to be your friend."

Charlie's eyes beamed. "You do?"

"Yeah, I do."

Charlie wrapped his little arms around her neck and hugged it. He pulled back and smiled at her. "I'm glad you're my friend."

Sheridan returned his smile. "Me too, buddy."

She walked back around the table and faced all the children. "I want to explain why I was frightened earlier in the family room. It wasn't because the walls were shaking or because Charlie heard voices. I was only shaken by the words Charlie said and what I thought I saw. You see, when I was six, I got picked on at school a lot by some not nice kids. They used to chant 'Sheridan's scared again', over and over, and it hurt my feelings. And even though I'm an adult now, the memory of those words still hurt," she admitted.

"You have a special gift, Charlie. You repeated something you heard from my past, but you are not one of those mean kids. Make sense?"

Charlie nodded. Ashley raised her hand. "Yes, Ashley?"

"I wasn't in the room, so didn't, like, see anything. But, you said you thought you saw something. What was it?"

Sheridan looked for the right words to explain. "When I was a little girl, I had a beautiful doll I considered my best friend. I named her Becca. I had her since I was born, and she made me feel so safe." Sheridan looked over at Rebecca with loving eyes. "You see, Rebecca, when I first saw you, you reminded me so much of my beautiful doll. You have the same hair, eyes, and were even dressed like her. Because I loved my childhood friend so much, I became overwhelmed with emotion."

"Do you still have your doll?" Tamika asked.

"No, I lost her a long time ago."

Sheridan looked over at Derek who was holding up his phone to let her know he needed to step out and make a call. She nodded to let him know she'd be fine.

"Hey, are we going to paint or what?" Luke asked.

Sheridan laughed. "What do you think, guys? You ready to have a little fun?"

DEREK STOOD in the hallway for fifteen minutes trying to figure out the doll connection before calling Brody. Brody answered on the fourth ring.

"Agent Young."

"It's Derek."

Brody heard the urgency in Derek's tone. "Everything okay?"

"You alone?"

"Yeah, I'm driving. Why, what's up?"

"I figured out the doll connection."

"What is it?"

"In short, Sheridan had a childhood doll since she was born—" Saying the word 'born' triggered something within Derek, bringing him sudden clarity.

"Derek?" Brody called out. "Derek, you there?"

"Do you remember me telling you about seeing my mom rocking

me as a baby with a doll, or the little girl floating face down in the river in my dreams?"

"Yeah, we talked about it this morning, but what does that have to do with anything?"

"It wasn't me I saw my mom rocking in the chair. It was Sheridan. And, it was Sheridan's body I saw floating face down in the river on Lyle. I'd also seen a vision of her face being plunged in and out of murky water the night I was carrying her through the woods on Lyle. Someone drowned her. I'm sure of it."

"Yeah, except Sheridan's alive. It couldn't have been her."

"Just hear me out. Sheridan's mom was raped the night Sheridan was conceived, so it makes sense she could've wound up at Providence House to deliver her...where my mom and dad volunteered," he stressed. "My mom must have had a premonition when she held Sheridan as a baby and given the doll to her before she left Providence House."

"Okay, so you've figured out how your mom and Sheridan are connected, but what does it mean?"

"My mom knew she was going to die the night she was murdered and welcomed her own death to save other lives. If Sheridan was the little girl floating face down in the river, maybe she was one of the lives my mom saved. That would also explain why my mom was on Lyle Mountain of all places."

"Save her from who and why?"

"I don't know, but my guess is that it had something to do with Sheridan and Rebecca meeting. My mom was psychic, and her adoptive parents were the previous owners of Chancellor Toys. She could've seen a vision of what Rebecca looked like in the future and easily had a doll custom-made and molded to look like her. My mom needed Sheridan to recognize Rebecca."

"Again, why?"

"I can't explain it all yet, but I know I'm right. My dreams and visions may not have played out in order, but they all fit, Brody. Just this morning Sheridan heard Rebecca tell her she'd been waiting for her. There's a lot we still don't know, but we're getting close. I can feel it."

"You're right. There's a lot we don't understand, like the antique dagger and leather journal displayed together in a case, or your mom as an archangel protecting children within her wings." Brody paused. "There's something that's been bothering me since you found Sheridan on Lyle."

"What?"

"Why in your recurring dreams and even in the newest ones of Sheridan, has her image come to you as her being a child? Shit, even all the visions you had of her while you were carrying her through the woods on Lyle were of her as a baby or little girl."

"So you've been paying attention."

"Yeah, I pay attention and have since we were kids. I also know when you're keeping shit from me. Like exactly when and how you found out your mom knew she was going to die the night she was murdered. I'm going to need you to keep that in mind next time you hand my ass to me on a platter for missing something. It's really hard for me to see things clearly or help you when you don't tell me everything," Brody reprimanded.

Derek felt a sharp twinge of guilt rise into his chest for not apologizing to Brody earlier that morning because he'd initially missed the doll connection. "I thought the dreams of my mom and Sheridan were two separate entities, but they're not. Their connection was in front of me all along. I didn't see it either."

"Is your confession your way of admitting you were being a hypocritical dick this morning?"

"Yeah, something like that. Hold on a sec," he said when he saw Sheridan poke her head out the door.

"Sorry, didn't mean to interrupt, but, I think you should see something."

"I'll be right there."

"Okay," she replied then closed the door.

"Listen, I've got to go, but we need to talk later about how the hell Walt could've known about the doll connection. Don't get me wrong. He was thorough in his investigation, but he couldn't have possibly known about my or my mom's visions of Sheridan or the doll. We're missing something there for sure."

"I agree. I'm talking to Nancy again tonight. You still want me to hold off trying to probe her for more information about Walt's references to the doll?"

"I'd press her a little, but if you feel like she's still hiding something, back off. We'll call Sheriff Lloyd and have him go out to Walt's and talk to her in person."

"All right. I'll catch up with you later."

THE CHILDREN WERE INTENTLY PAINTING, so much so, they hadn't seen or heard Derek come in. Sheridan stood at the sink emptying and refilling paint cups with water. When she saw Derek, she gestured for him to walk over to her.

Derek smiled when he approached her. "I'm impressed. I don't know if I've ever seen them this focused or quiet before."

Sheridan held her index finger up to her lips then spoke in a low voice. "Did you see it?"

"See what?" he whispered.

"Rebecca and Tamika painting."

"Sorry, I wasn't paying attention."

"I don't know how they're doing it, but it's incredible."

Derek walked around the far side of the room then up behind them, so he saw their paintings without causing any distractions. He looked twice to be sure his eyes weren't playing tricks on him. He watched Rebecca and Tamika paint the same exact picture and do so while stroking their brushes in sync with one another. He looked at the other children's paintings to see if theirs were similar, but they weren't. The objects within their paintings were initially hard for Derek to make out.

Each canvas was divided to reflect day and night. The left side's background color was sky blue. A large yellow star sat center, just above several bright green patches of grass. Within the yellow star was a stick figure. Above the star was a purple eye with white effervescent strokes all around it. The only other objects within the day section of their paintings were puffy white clouds, an orange sun, and a few scattered black birds throughout.

The right side's background color was black. There was a large gold dagger stuck into what appeared to be earthy mountain rocks. Within the hilt of the dagger was a large purple circle that contained a smaller stick figure within it. The only other object within the night section of their paintings was a large pale moon with faint gray clouds hovering over the lower half.

Derek didn't speak until Rebecca and Tamika lay their brushes down. He took a picture of Tamika's painting with his phone then walked over to her and knelt to her level. "Wow, you're a really good painter, Tamika. Can you tell me about it?"

"It's the good man and the bad boy," she whispered.

"So this one's a boy?" He pointed to the stick figure within the purple circle.

"Uh-huh."

"What are their names?" he probed.

"We don't know their names, silly."

"So Rebecca doesn't know their names either?"

Tamika looked over at Rebecca. "Uh-uh, she said she doesn't know."

"Can you tell me what they look like?"

Tamika pointed to the stick figure within the star. "The daddy looks like this, and he's really nice."

"Whose daddy is he?"

"Sheridan's."

Derek paused before he spoke again to refrain from letting the emotions he felt rising within him scare or affect Tamika. "Can you tell me about the little boy?"

Tamika frowned then slowly pointed to the stick figure within the purple circle. "He looks like this, and he's really angry."

"Why's the little boy angry,?"

Her frown grew deeper. "Because his mommy and daddy threw him away, like mine did me."

Derek saw she was becoming upset, so he backed off. "You did a really good job."

"Rebecca helped," she confessed.

"I know she did, and she did a good job too," he said, then looked over at Rebecca and saw her grinning at him.

They both looked up when they heard Sheridan address all the children. "So when we started earlier, I asked each of you to paint anything that makes you happy. Now, we're going to say one sentence about why they do. I'll go first."

Sheridan turned her easel around to reveal her own simple painting of an angel. "Angels make me happy because I know they're watching over me and protecting me from things that sometimes scare me."

Sheridan addressed Ashley. "Okay, Ashley, your turn."

Ashley got up from her chair and held her painting up. "I painted a field of flowers and a sun whose rays are touching each petal, because it's the imaginary place I go to find inner peace."

"That's so beautiful, Ashley. Thank you. Okay, how about you now, Charlie?"

Charlie stood and held his painting up excitedly. "I painted dinosaurs 'cause they're really cool and stuff."

"Yes, Charlie, they certainly are. Okay, Luke, how about you?"

Both Luke and Andrew stood up together. Luke spoke first. "I painted Superman because he's a hero and his comic books make me happy. Plus, he's strong and can fly away from all the bad guys."

Andrew looked at his brother annoyed. "That was two sentences, Luke."

"So?"

Sheridan spoke up. "Okay, Andrew, now tell us about your painting."

Andrew glared at Luke. "I painted Spiderman because it makes me happy to know he's way better than Superman."

"No he's not," Luke shot back.

Derek jumped in. "Everybody knows that Superman and Spiderman are equally cool."

Sheridan chimed in. "He's right, boys, and you both did an awesome job. Okay, your turn Tamika."

Tamika stood. "Me and Rebecca painted the same thing. We didn't paint what would make us happy but what would make you happy."

"And what makes me happy, Tamika?"

"The man in the star."

"And what about the man in the pretty purple circle?" Sheridan asked.

"He's not a man. He's a little boy and he's—"

All the kids turned and looked at the door when they heard Vanessa come in. Her face was apologetic. "Sorry, it's just that the kids' lunch is ready downstairs."

Sheridan looked down at her watch, saw that it was twelve, then addressed the kids. "I guess time flies when you're having fun. Before you all go, be sure to leave your aprons on the back of your chairs."

"We get to paint tomorrow too, right?" Tamika asked.

Sheridan smiled. "We're going to take a little break until Monday, but then we'll be painting all next week."

"Good, because I want to paint my own painting."

Charlie walked up to Sheridan and wrapped his little arms around her left leg and hugged it. "Bye," he said then walked over to Vanessa.

"Bye, buddy." Sheridan was touched when the rest of the kids followed Charlie's lead and hugged her before leaving Derek and her alone in the room. Sheridan picked up the kids' paintings and began leaning them against the far right wall to dry. "I wish we had a peg board, so we could hang these."

"I'll add that to the list."

"Good idea."

"So, how do you think it went today?"

"Really well, actually. It usually takes more time for children who come from such horrible circumstances to fully cooperate, but they all jumped right in. Next week will be the real test though."

"Why's that?"

Sheridan washed the paint table as she spoke. "I'll be asking them to paint things that make them unhappy then talk about it afterward."

"What did you think about Tamika and Rebecca painting in sync with one another?"

"I wasn't scared if that's what you're asking."

"No, just curious about what you thought."

"Well, I'm no expert, but after your and Anderson's explanation of the girls' gifts this morning, I think Rebecca may be communicating through Tamika. Now as far as them being able to stroke their brushes in sync...not a clue."

"I think you're right. You catch on pretty quick. What do you think their paintings mean?"

"I don't know. I've seen some pretty disturbing paintings from my other students, but like your visions, a painting's meaning can be subjective. That's why having the children talk about what their work means to them is important."

"Tamika said the man in the gold star was someone who makes you happy. Who do you think he is?"

Sheridan grinned. "Why, are you jealous?"

Her playful response confirmed that Sheridan hadn't been overly fazed by the content within the girls' paintings. He grinned. "I don't know. What if I am?"

"Well then you'd better get around to asking me out on that date before somebody else comes along and sweeps me off my feet. Of course at this point, I may just say no anyway."

Derek laughed. "I haven't asked sooner because I know your schedule is hectic until after the exhibition. I was actually going to ask you to have lunch with me today though."

"Sorry, can't, I already have plans."

"Ouch, you weren't kidding about shooting me down, were you?"

Sheridan laughed. "I swear, I really do have plans. My mom and Aunt Maggie drove in to New York this morning. They brought a painting I'm including for the reveal at the exhibition, so we're meeting at MoMA for lunch at The Modern then shopping after. I'd cancel, but I'm giving my mom the deed to her house at lunch."

"Ah, you mean the deed to the house you shamefully never finished cleaning because of your injuries?" he teased.

Sheridan grinned. "You know, your sarcasm isn't going to help you get that date any quicker."

"Ouch again. I know you have a lot going on the next couple of days, but how about dinner tonight?"

"Only if you agree to take me to one of those street vendor hot dog stands. I've been craving one since we got here, but Rodney keeps talking me out of it. He's afraid I won't fit into my dress. Besides, I'm having dinner with the MoMA Board tomorrow, so I would love to do casual tonight."

"Done. Pick you up at six-thirty?"

"That's perfect. That'll give me some time to freshen up after lunch and shopping. My suite number is 507." Sheridan looked at her watch. "Speaking of which, I'm supposed to meet them at one-thirty."

"You're fine. If you leave now, your driver should be able to get you there on time. Come, I'll walk you to your car."

Chapter Twenty-Seven

"Welcome to The Modern. How many in your party?"

"I'm meeting two people for lunch. I'm not sure if the reservation's under Maggie Thurston or Rhonda Hayes. It's most likely under Thurston though," she said, fumbling to get her coat on to conceal her mellow attire.

"Yes, of course. You must be Sheridan, Mr. and Mrs. Thurston's niece. Your party is waiting for you. Please, follow me," she said.

Maggie and Rhonda stood, walked around the table and hugged Sheridan before sitting back down.

"We ordered you a Chardonnay and the roasted wild salmon. Is that okay, dear, or would you like something else?" Maggie asked.

"No, that's perfect." Sheridan said, and then addressed her mom. "So, how was the drive?"

Rhonda answered. "It wasn't bad at all. We got in around nine or so and met Rodney for breakfast at the hotel."

"Speaking of Rodney, is he joining us?" Sheridan asked.

Maggie sipped her Merlot then answered. "No. He drove us here and took your painting to Mrs. Hershkowitz. He said he had a few other errands to run but would meet us for shopping and dinner a little later."

"Oh, I um, already have plans for dinner," Sheridan confessed.

Rhonda smirked. "And who exactly do you have plans with? It wouldn't be with Derek, would it?"

"H-How did you know?" Their waiter approached the table with a tray holding three house salads and a crystal vase with two dozen white roses. "I've been asked to deliver these to," he paused to look at the name on the note card, "Ms. Sheridan Hayes?"

Rhonda spoke up when Sheridan didn't answer. "She's Sheridan."

The waiter placed the vase of roses in front of her and served them their salads. When the waiter left them alone again, Rhonda said, "Well now, what do we have here? White roses signify marriage or new beginnings, you know? So, which is it, Sheridan?"

"Neither...I mean, I don't know."

Maggie chortled. "Did you think Rodney would keep Derek a secret? We got an earful at breakfast."

"What else did he tell you?" Sheridan asked, fearing he'd told them about her encounter with Hank.

"Well, let's see. We know you went to Lyle before you flew to New York, about your ankle, ribs, something about a bar fight. Am I leaving anything out, Rhonda?"

"Oh why yes, Maggie, you are. What about the part where Derek, 'who's beyond baby daddy gorgeous', your cousin's words, not mine, spent the weekend taking care of you while Rodney was in jail?"

Sheridan could tell by her mom's and aunt's playfulness, Rodney hadn't told them about Hank or the deed and felt guilty for thinking he would. "I'm glad you two are having so much fun at my expense. And yes, it's all true, even the part about Derek staying with me, but nothing happened."

Maggie rose from her chair. "On that note, I'm excusing myself to the ladies room, be right back."

Rhonda placed a loving hand over Sheridan's. "The great thing about being an adult is that you don't have to answer to me anymore. I'll admit I was a little thrown off as to why you chose Lyle out of all the places you could've gone. With that said, I'm glad you did something spontaneous and even met someone along the way."

"So you're really not mad?"

"No, I'm not. All I've ever wanted is for you to experience life. We can't change the past. God knows I wish we could. But, what we can do is live in the moment and embrace all the possibilities life has to offer. Life's too short, and we've only got one shot at it." Rhonda squeezed Sheridan's hand. "Please, don't waste so much precious time like I did before you finally see that."

"I'm trying."

Rhonda smiled. "I know you are, hon, and so am I. Now, tell me about this Derek," she said, attempting to lighten the mood again.

"He's a philanthropist who works with several women's and children's shelters here in New York and just reopened Vista House, which is a foster home for special needs children."

Rhonda took a sip of her ice tea. "Rodney told us you were working with one of the little girls today. How'd it go?"

Sheridan's eyes beamed. "I worked with all of them. I know this is going to sound crazy, but in the short time I spent with them, it felt like I was right where I was supposed to be."

"And do you feel that way when you're with Derek?"

"Yes, I do. I've tried to talk myself out of it a thousand times or find the words to explain how he makes me feel, but there are none. My heart just knows...if that makes any sense."

Rhonda smiled. "Yes, it does. I felt that way about someone once, you know?"

"What happened?"

"I let my foolish pride get in the way and pushed him out of my life." Rhonda squeezed Sheridan's hand again. "Don't make the same mistake I did. Hold on tight if you feel that strongly about him, hon, because you may never have the chance to feel a love like that again."

"Who was he?"

"William."

"Where's he now?"

Rhonda paused before she spoke. "Like I said, Sheridan, we can't change the past, so it's best we just leave it there."

Maggie walked up to the table and sat back down. "You still haven't read the message that came with the flowers, huh?"

Rhonda laughed. "It's just killing you, isn't it?"

Maggie grinned. "Guilty, now read the damn card."

"Fine, but I'm not reading it out loud," Sheridan warned then pulled the note from the card holder and read silently to herself.

You've been selfless in giving your time to the kids, so I wanted to show you how much you're appreciated. Don't be mad. I know you never expected anything for your time, but I hired a local cleaning and painting crew in Carter County to get your mom's house ready before she arrives at Lyle. Now that you have one less thing to worry about, enjoy your lunch, which by the way, is also on me. See you tonight. Derek.

Sheridan placed her right palm over her chest and held in a long breath. Derek's thoughtfulness had moved her so much, that in that moment her heart beat only for him.

"Well, are you going to tell us what it said?" Maggie asked.

"It said our lunch is on him, and he'd see me tonight."

"Well, that was nice of him," Maggie acknowledged, just as the waiter approached the table and served them their entrées.

"Will there be anything else?"

Maggie answered. "No, everything looks wonderful. Thank you." The waiter excused himself.

Sheridan shifted in her chair. "Before we eat, there's something I want to give you, Mamma." She reached into her purse and pulled out the deed, which was rolled up and tied with a thick red velvet bow, and handed it to Rhonda.

"I know you don't like to be fussed over, but it's really important to me that you accept this gift. I know how much you loved your child-hood home and also know you only left Lyle to give me a better life. You've put my happiness before your own, but now it's your turn to be happy. Like you said, we need to embrace all life has to offer, because life's too short. It's your time, Mamma," she said, then nodded toward the deed, gesturing for Rhonda to open her gift.

Rhonda untied the bow, unrolled the deed, and studied it long and hard before she looked up at Sheridan with tears in her eyes. "Is this what I think it is?"

"Yes, it's the deed to your house. Both mortgages are paid off. You own the house and property free and clear."

"I-I don't understand. How did you do this?"

"I used part of the down payment Dr. Riley paid for the angel collection to pay everything off. That's why Rodney and I went to Lyle."

"Oh, hon, I can't let you do this. It's too much. That's your money."

"It's already done, Mamma. Please, it would mean so much to me if you'd accept it without a fight."

Maggie chimed in. "Good luck, sweetie. I've been offering to pay off that house for years, and she's shot me down every time. Just breaks your heart, doesn't it?" Maggie knew Rhonda would never intentionally break Sheridan's heart, so she set her up, leaving Rhonda no choice but to graciously accept the deed.

"I-I just don't know what to say, Sheridan," Rhonda said.

"You don't have to say anything." Sheridan reached back into her purse, pulled an envelope out, and handed it to Rhonda. "It's a plane ticket to fly in to Tennessee on Sunday." Sheridan picked the note card up from the table, held it up, and smiled. "And, I was just informed by Derek he's hired a cleaning and painting crew to get the house ready for your arrival. I'm guessing now the white roses were meant to symbolize new beginnings. And that's exactly what you deserve, Mamma, your own new beginning."

"Why would he do that? He doesn't even know me. Accepting your gift is one thing, Sheridan, but I can't let him do that."

"He knew how important it was to me. Don't worry, I'll find a way to pay him back."

Rhonda rose from her chair and walked over to where Sheridan was sitting. She leaned down and kissed the top of Sheridan's head and looked into her eyes. "It's a beautiful gift, sweetheart. Thank you," Rhonda surrendered.

Chapter Twenty-Eight

The Plaza elevators stopped on several floors before making their way back down to Derek in the lobby. Just as one of the elevator's rich golden doors finally opened, his cell rang. He was late picking Sheridan up, so he contemplated ignoring the call until he saw it was Brody.

"Hey, what's up?"

"Paternity test...he's in New York...Sheridan."

"I can't hear you, what?...Hold on, let me walk outside." He headed toward the front entrance and noticed a man arguing with the clerk at the front desk. *What the hell are you doing here?* he thought, recognizing one of the men. "I'll have to call you back, Brody," he said in a punchy stupor and ended the call.

"MAMMA, YOU LOOK STUNNING," Sheridan complimented when Rhonda joined her on their suite's terrace wearing a sheer black, knee length, cap sleeve cocktail dress. Her makeup was light and flawless, and her soft blonde layered hair fell just below her shoulders.

"It's not too much?"

"No, not at all."

"Rodney picked it out. Said jeans and a T-shirt weren't going to cut it at Jean-Georges for dinner tonight. He's so damn pushy."

Sheridan laughed. "He's pouting right now because I'm wearing leggings and a T-shirt on my date with Derek tonight."

"Lucky you. I can barely breathe in this dress. Speaking of Derek, wasn't he supposed to be here at six-thirty?"

"Yeah, but it's fine. It's a casual date with no reservations. Just me, him, and a hot dog stand."

"So, are you going to introduce him to me when he gets here, or should I hide?" Rhonda teased.

"Of course I am," she said then looked inside when she heard someone knocking.

Rhonda was amused by Sheridan's first-date jitters. "Do you want me to answer the door?"

"No, wait here. I'll bring him out to the terrace," she said, then walked inside. She pulled her fingers through her hair to calm any free strays then smiled as she opened the door. Her smile turned to confusion. "Sheriff Lloyd? What are you doing here?" she asked, immediately regretting the rudeness in her tone. "Sorry, I was just expecting Derek is all."

"He's downstairs in the lobby."

"The lobby? Why?"

"To give me some privacy with you and your mamma."

Sheridan walked out into the hallway and partially closed the door behind her to prevent Rhonda from overhearing their conversation. "I'm assuming your visit has something to do with Hank?" she asked in a whisper.

"Partially."

"What do you mean, partially?" She threw her hands up dismissing his last statement. "You know what, it doesn't matter. She doesn't know what that son of a bitch did to her, and I'm not going to tell her anything until we get the paternity results."

Sheriff Lloyd pulled a folded piece of paper from his shirt pocket. "They're right here, Sheridan."

"Please don't do this. Hasn't she suffered enough? This will kill her."

"The last thing I wanna do is hurt either one of you."

Rhonda opened the door and saw them standing in the hall. "You okay?" she asked then glanced over at Sheriff Lloyd. An unexpected fervid ache brushed across her skin and her knees became feeble. "William?"

Sheridan looked at Sheriff Lloyd, then back to her mom astounded. "Is this the William you—" she started to ask before Rhonda gave her a pleading look not to finish her question.

"Yes, his name's Franklin William Lloyd" she offered. Rhonda addressed Sheriff Lloyd again. "Why are you here?"

"I need to talk to you and Sheridan. Mind if I come in?"

"Sorry, we're on our way out," Sheridan said between her teeth.

"What the hell's gotten into you?" Rhonda scolded then addressed Sheriff Lloyd. "Come in."

RHONDA WALKED over to the wet bar in the corner of the suite's living room and poured herself a bourbon. She held her glass up. "Anybody else?" she offered.

Sheriff Lloyd sat down in the plush armchair sitting opposite of the couch. "No, thanks, I'm good."

"Sheridan?" Rhonda asked.

"No."

Rhonda walked over to the couch and sat down next to Sheridan. "So, what brings you to New York?"

"There's no easy way to tell you this, Rhonda, but you deserve to know the truth."

"The truth about what?"

"About who hurt you twenty-two years ago," he confessed.

Rhonda looked over at Sheridan then back to Sheriff Lloyd with worried eyes. "Sheridan was right, you should go."

"She knows, Rhonda. We both do."

Rhonda shot Sheridan a staggered look. "How?"

Sheridan swallowed hard before she spoke. "I-I came across your file at the center. I'm so sorry. I should've never invaded your privacy."

Rhonda tried holding back the pungent tears now lacing her eyes. "So you know how you were conceived?"

Sheridan looked down to the ground. "Yes, and I'm sorry I've been a constant reminder of what Hank did to you," she let slip. Sheridan's head shot back up expecting to see her mom falling apart, but she wasn't. "I didn't mean for you to find out that way."

Rhonda turned to Sheridan and held her chin between her thumb and index finger. Her tone remained strong. "Don't you ever apologize for your existence, Sheridan Parker Hayes. Ever. It's never mattered to me how you were conceived. I love you and always have. You know that, right?"

"I know you do."

Rhonda released Sheridan's chin and looked over to Sheriff Lloyd. "If your reason for coming here was to tell me Hank is the one who assaulted me, you've wasted your time, because I already knew." Rhonda looked to the floor to hide the shame settling on her face. "Hank called me collect several times after he went to prison, but I never accepted. I knew his goal was to torment me from behind bars because having control over me fueled him. I managed to deprive him of having the upper hand for fifteen years, so when he finally got out, he was pissed and looking for revenge.

"Shortly after he was released, I was taking the garbage out one night at the diner and heard a noise by the dumpster. When I went to see what it was, I found Hank standing behind it waiting to pounce on me. He was drunk and pinned me between the dumpster and the back of the building. That's when he confessed what he'd done to me. Bragged about how he'd fooled me for six years after, and admitted he'd purposely got me pregnant." She paused and looked at Sheriff Lloyd.

"Told me I deserved what I got for sleeping with another boy. He kept taunting me by holding his hand up in the air like he was going to slap me. I didn't flinch, and he became even more enraged. When he balled his fist up, I knew he was going to follow through, so I just closed my eyes and stood my ground. Before he could make contact, I heard another voice say, 'Don't'. When I opened my eyes, I saw a man with a revolver held to the back of Hank's head. It was dark, so I couldn't really make out his features, but his eyes were familiar to me.

"Anyway, when he cocked the gun, Hank let me go and started begging for his life. Said he'd never come near me again if he'd just let him go. The man asked me if there was anything I wanted to say to Hank before he put a bullet in his head. I knew somehow the man was bluffing and wasn't really going to kill him, so I walked up to Hank, called him a coward, then spit in his face. I should have left it at that, but I couldn't resist the opportunity to punch him in the face, so I did. I told the man to let him go, because if he ever came near me again, I'd kill him myself. He uncocked the gun, told Hank to consider himself warned, then shoved him away. Hank ran for his life, and I haven't heard from him since. I tried thanking the man for saving my life, but he walked away without saying a word. I never told anyone."

Rhonda turned her attention back to Sheridan. "Hank may have given you life, Sheridan, but that's all he ever did."

Sheriff Lloyd pulled the folded piece of paper from his front pocket again and opened it. "Sheridan had a run in with Hank herself up on Lyle. Because he implied she was his daughter, we did a paternity test and—"

"Jesus, tell me he didn't hurt you," Rhonda said, growing panicked.

"He didn't hurt me. I'm fine, but I can't say the same for Hank. Derek beat him pretty badly and put him in the hospital."

Sheriff Lloyd leaned forward in his chair and looked Rhonda in the eyes. "Hank's not Sheridan's daddy, Rhonda."

Rhonda's face turned perplexed. "But the only other person I had sex—" she started then stopped because of the awkwardness she felt with Sheridan in the room. "The only other person I was ever with back then was you, and we used protection."

"I reckon the protection we used was defective, 'cause I'm Sheridan's daddy," he informed, then handed Rhonda the paternity results. "When I found out what really happened to you, a lot of things that didn't make sense back then started to. I suspected you'd lied to me about me not being your first, so I submitted my own blood to be tested with Hank's."

Rhonda's face turned guilty, and she allowed several tears to fall freely from her eyes. "I never meant to hurt you, William. It was because I loved you, I pushed you away and lied that day in Doc's office. I know it's hard to understand, but I couldn't bear the thought of you or anyone else I loved finding out. Even if I'd known Sheridan was yours, I don't know that I would've done anything different. I was so ashamed and didn't feel worthy of your love. I'm so sorry."

Sheriff Lloyd got up from the chair and walked over to the couch. He knelt down on one knee in front of Rhonda and brushed away the tears from her cheeks. "How could you ever think you're not worthy? I never stopped loving you, Rhonda," he confessed then held her hand in his. "No other woman's held my heart the way you do, and that's the truth."

He looked over at Sheridan, whose eyes were vacant and hard to read. "I can't imagine how hard this is for you. And I know you don't know me all that well, but I'd like to change that if you're willing."

When Sheridan didn't answer, Rhonda became concerned. "Darlin', you okay?"

Sheridan's mouth formed a faint knowing smile. "I'm more than overwhelmed, but I know everything's going to be okay."

Rhonda grew more concerned by Sheridan's easy calmness. "Darlin, you're scaring me."

"I'm fine," she answered, still in deep thought. "A little bird told me this morning we're both worthy of love. I didn't know what that meant, but it makes sense now." She then addressed Sheriff Lloyd. "May I see your badge?"

"My badge?"

"Yes."

Sheriff Lloyd pulled his wallet from his back pocket, opened it, and handed it to her. Sheridan's smile grew as she traced the edges of his badge with the tip of her index finger. She looked deeply into Sheriff Lloyd's eyes. "The same little bird told me the man in the star would make me happy, and I believe you will. So, to answer your question, yes, I'm willing to get to know you."

Sheriff Lloyd returned his own knowing smile. "Tell Derek I said thanks for seeing things so clearly."

"It wasn't Derek but someone like him."

Rhonda was completely lost. "What the hell are you two talking about?"

"I promise I'll explain later, but right now I need to find Derek," she said then got up from the couch and started walking to the door.

"Sheridan," Rhonda called out.

Sheriff Lloyd squeezed Rhonda's hand. "Let her go. Derek will take care of her."

"How do you know that? She's acting strange."

"Because he gave me his word," he assured then watched Sheridan hang the Do Not Disturb sign on the handle outside of the door before she left.

Chapter Twenty-Nine

Sheriff Lloyd had shared the paternity results with Derek before he'd gone upstairs to deliver the news. Derek had insisted on staying down in the lobby in case Sheridan broke down again and needed him. When he saw her storming toward him with an abstruse fire in her eyes, he stood from the chair he was occupying. The severe look on her face made him question whether he'd made a mistake in giving Sheriff Lloyd her room number after the front desk clerk had refused. He stood tall and was prepared to accept what he guessed was her wrath and his certain doomed fate.

Six feet away and still moving hastily toward him, she yelled out, "I'm worthy of your goddamn love." Before he could respond and without hesitation, she wrapped her determined arms around his neck, pulled his lips to hers, then devoured his rapacious mouth. Derek held the back of her head with one hand while moving over her curves with the other. When he reached her hips, he pulled her quivering body closer to his, causing a seductive and eager moan to escape her swollen lips.

Breathless, she pulled her face slightly from his. "No more games. I want you," she demanded.

Sheridan's abrupt erotic display of affection had Derek spinning. When he saw several curious guests taking in their erogenous production, he knew he had to get her out of there. He lifted her into his arms and carried her outside to his car where his chauffeur was waiting.

The driver wasn't fazed by the lusty scene he saw coming toward him and opened the door. "Where to, sir?"

"My place."

"Right away, sir."

DEREK'S MOUTH continued exploring Sheridan's as he fumbled with the keys to unlock his condo's door. Sheridan's untamed desire was relentless. He feared if he didn't get her inside, she'd convince him to take her where they stood. When the lock finally gave, so did the door they were leaning against. He tried finding the light switch, but their carnal movements prevented it. The Manhattan city lights coming in from the living room's scenic window was all he had to guide them.

Sheridan's arms cradled his neck when he lifted her, and her legs wrapped around his waist. He spun her back to the right wall, braced her against it, then kicked the door closed with his right foot. When he shifted her body up to better support her, he heard a faint biting gasp escape her lips and felt her body twitch from the sudden jerk of her ribs. He broke away from her intoxicating mouth when he realized he'd hurt her.

"Did I do something wrong?" she asked breathless, unlocking herself from his embrace and letting her feet slide to the floor.

He pulled his face a whisper from hers and met her eyes. "No, I did. I hurt you. You deserve better than this, Sheridan."

She evened her breaths before she spoke. "I'm not sure how or why we found each other, but my heart has somehow always belonged to you."

"There are things I need to tell you first, Sheridan. I should've never let it go this far before I told you—"

"Nothing else matters to me, Derek. If you can look me in the eyes and tell me you don't love me, I'll walk away."

"Never in my life have I loved or wanted anyone more than you."

His words melted into her, somehow diluting the mental anguish she'd suffered her entire existence. Sublime lucidity rushed the depths of her core. "Then make love to me, Derek."

Derek lifted her body into his arms and carried her up the stairs to the master bedroom. A silhouette of his bed was all he saw when they entered. He set her feet on the floor next to it and brushed a light kiss across her lips before walking across the room to ignite the gas fireplace then returned to the bed and stood before her. His eyes were intense but never left hers as he removed her clothes, and she his. The lustrous golden light danced across her flawless bare skin; her thick chestnut hair spilled over her full supple breasts; her almond eyes were seductive and glazed over with raw passion. She was an exquisite untouched woman who'd preserved her innocence for this unequivocal moment.

Everything about her is perfect, he thought. "It's you I'm not worthy of, Sheridan Hayes," he whispered as his hands became lost in her hair and he pulled her mouth to his. An aching moan escaped her parted lips, as his tongue seduced her slender neck then moved to her delicate shoulders. The taste of her glorious flesh and sighs of pleasure ripped through his veins, challenging his willpower to not ravish her. He buried his own explosive cravings, mindful it was all for her. He lowered her to the bed and braced himself above her with one palm, then caressed the length of her voluptuous body with the other. Sheridan's breaths became ragged beneath him. Her fervent body arched to his every splendid touch.

Derek searched her eyes. "Are you sure you want to do this?" he asked through his own uneven breaths.

"Take me," was all she could manage.

He caressed the side of her face. "I love you, Sheridan," he whispered.

They kissed passionately as he eased himself into her and broke through her innocence. She clenched the sheets with her fists when she felt a slight pinch but then began gliding her blissful body beneath him as though they were one.

Their immediate world spun into a celestial sphere that felt both tranquil and erotic. Beautiful colors collided into one another within the sacred space of their destined souls. Each time they found each other throughout the euphoric night, time stood still and ecstasy thrust them into eternal climax.

Chapter Thirty

T*hursday, May 2, 2013*

DEREK TRACED the soft mid-morning sun resting on Sheridan's angelic face as she slept. He took in her superlative beauty. His soft lips brushed across hers, stirring her awake.

She smiled dreamily as her eyes opened and found him admiring her. "Hey, you," she whispered.

"Good morning, beautiful."

She grinned. "Do I need to find my cell phone?" she warned teasingly.

"Speaking of war wounds, how are you feeling?"

"I'm fine. In fact..." she said confidently then kissed her way from his neck to his chest, pressing her bare body against his.

"Before you leave me no choice but to ravish you again, you should know your cousin is on his way here."

Sheridan sat up. "Rodney's coming here? Why?"

"He's been blowing up both our phones this morning. Apparently you had a video bio appointment at ten."

"Oh no, what time is it?"

Derek laughed. "Ten-thirty. Don't worry, he rescheduled it for eleven-thirty and is bringing you a change of clothes."

"So he knows I stayed the night?"

"Yep."

"I'm calling him and telling him to cancel all my appointments today."

"He thought you'd say that and threatened my life if I didn't have you up and ready to go by the time he got here."

"He's relentless."

"He's looking out for you. The reveal's tomorrow, so it should be your only focus. As much as I want you to stay in this bed with me today, I won't let you throw everything you've worked for away."

"He has my schedule crammed. I won't see you until after I'm revealed tomorrow night."

He held her chin between his thumb and index finger. "It's okay. Trust me, after tomorrow I won't be sharing you with anyone."

Sheridan's heart fluttered. "Is that right? And do I have any say so about that?"

Derek looked deep into her eyes and answered. "No."

Sheridan's tone was playful. "I'm never going to get that first date, am I?"

Derek got up from the bed, picked Sheridan up into his arms, and carried her toward the bathroom.

"Where are you taking me, Mr. Young?"

"On our first date, Ms. Hayes."

"And where might that be?"

"The shower."

Sheridan's body burned vivaciously at the thought of making love to him again, knowing now she fully belonged to him and he to her.

DEREK WALKED Sheridan out to the car and kissed her before the driver opened the door. "I'll see you tomorrow."

"Are you sure you don't want me to stay?"

Rodney poked his head out the door. "If you don't get in this car right now, I'm going to thrash you, Sheridan Parker Hayes."

Derck chuckled. "For both our sakes, you should probably get in the car."

"Fine." She kissed Derek one last time before she got in.

As the car pulled away, Derek's cell phone rang. When he saw Dr. Riley's name on his phone's caller ID, he quickly answered. "Dr. Riley?"

"No, Derek. It's Lexus."

"Aunt Lexus? Why are you calling from Dr. Riley's phone?"

"That's not important right now, sweetie. Brody told me you were going to Baker's today. Please tell me you haven't gone yet?" she asked, stressed and rushed.

"No. Why?"

"We need you to come to Dr. Riley's house, sweetie."

"We, who?"

"You-your Uncle Quentin and I."

"I was told Dr. Riley wouldn't be back in town until tomorrow. Does Brody know you're there?"

"No, and it's important he doesn't. I need you to come alone. Please, Derek, no more questions, just come."

"I'm on my way."

Chapter Thirty-One

R odney was the first to break the uncomfortable silence between him and Sheridan on the drive to the video bio appointment. "You'll need to change before we get there." He handed her the outfit he'd brought and asked the driver to put up the privacy window so she could change.

"Thanks."

"My mom and I talked to your mom and dad—I mean, Sheriff Lloyd this morning. They told us everything."

Sheridan couldn't help but smile. "He was still at the hotel this morning?"

Rodney relaxed when Sheridan's mood lifted. "Yes, he was. Oh my God, you should've seen it. Your mom thought we were room service and answered the door in her robe. Sheriff Lloyd didn't know my mom and I were there and walked out of the bedroom wearing only a towel around his waist."

"Good for them."

"So, are you going to tell me about your night with Derek, or am I out of line for asking?"

"It's because of my night and morning with Derek I'm mad at you, you know? I didn't want to leave him."

"Night and morning? My God, you really are a brazen hussy," he teased.

"Yeah, but I'm a happy one," she played along.

"In all seriousness, are you okay?"

"For the first time in my life, Rodney, yes, I am. I know this is going to sound cliché, but do you believe in fate?"

"Honey, everyone believes in fate after their first time, especially if it was done right."

Sheridan blushed. "I see."

Sheridan hadn't told Rodney about the dreams Derek had of her as a little girl, how he'd saved her and her mom's life when he was ten, or about his gifts. She knew it would be hard for him or anyone else to accept. She had fought and questioned her feelings for Derek until her eyes were opened to the transcendent truth at Vista. "That's it," she blurted out.

"Okay, that was random. What's it?"

"I need to go to Vista after the video shoot."

"Sheridan, we don't have any spare time. Your schedule's already tight, and being late for our first appointment didn't help."

"Who's our luncheon with this afternoon?"

"Johnson and Wilcox. Why?"

"I need you to cancel."

"Sheridan, they're two of the most prestigious art collectors coming to your ball tomorrow night."

"You told me back on Lyle you wanted me to experience the same happiness as you. Was that true?"

"Shame on you, you know it is."

She took his hand tenderly into hers. "I know how hard you've worked to put my exhibition together, and I promise I'm yours after you take me there. Please, cancel the luncheon."

"You said you'd made plans to go back to Vista Monday. Why the sudden rush to go back there today?"

"Did my mom tell you about Derek making arrangements to get her house ready before she arrives Sunday?"

"Yeah, but she didn't understand why he'd gone through such great lengths when he doesn't even know her."

"She doesn't understand because, with the exception of you, the men in our lives haven't gone out of their way to put our happiness before their own. Derek did what he did because he knew it was important to me, and now I want to do something for him."

"So your happiness is riding on us going to Vista today?"

Sheridan grinned. "Yes."

"And you promise to stay on your schedule afterward?"

"Yes, I promise."

"Fine, but I'm holding you to it, missy. If we're going though, we're going now. The luncheon with Johnson and Wilcox is more important than the video shoot," he said then knocked on the privacy window. "Change of plans, we're going to Vista first."

"Yes, sir," the driver said then turned the limo around.

Sheridan's face beamed. "You truly are the best cousin a girl could ever ask for, you know that, right?"

"Oh, I know I am, honey. I'm a little hurt you forgot to mention I'm the most handsome too."

Sheridan laughed. "I only didn't mention it, because it's a given. I've always sworn you have access to the fountain of youth. I mean look at you. Perfection."

"Well, if you mean the fountain of handsomeness, then I suppose we can move on with our day."

Chapter Thirty-Two

R honda and Sheriff Lloyd had picked back up from the last intimate moment they'd shared on Lyle all those years ago. After he'd been caught coming out of the bedroom wearing only a towel, they'd both agreed it would be best to get their own private room. Rhonda asked him to stay for Sheridan's exhibition and fly back to Tennessee with her on Sunday. He'd agreed and made arrangements for someone to cover him at the department, changed his flight, and went downstairs to book their room while Rhonda stayed behind and packed her things.

Just as he stepped on the elevator to go back upstairs, his cell rang, so he stepped off and answered. "Sheriff Lloyd."

"It's Nancy."

"Everything okay?"

"I did what you asked, and Walt's ready to talk."

"Is he sober?"

"Sober and cranky. Listen, there's somethin' I have to tell you before you talk to him."

"What is it?"

"The night Brody got in the bar fight, I told him Walt would mumble, the 'doll is key' anytime he was tying one on at Dottie's. I swear that was before you told me about the missin' evidence cover-up. But then I slipped up and mentioned it again. When he called to check in with us last night, he started askin' questions about Walt's doll comments. He knows somethin'. I'm sure of it. I'm so sorry," she said in a cracked voice.

"You don't have anything to be sorry about. I told you if the doll turned out to be relevant to their investigation, I planned on tellin' them anyway. And from the sound of it, it must be or Brody wouldn't be askin' questions."

"Walt swears someone framed him and planted the stolen evidence at his house. Said he knew it wouldn't be admissible in court once it was discovered missin'. The only reason he burned the pictures was because he knew he was set up and didn't want to be caught with them, and I believe him."

"What about the doll?"

"He wouldn't tell me. Said he didn't want me gettin' any more involved than I already was but agreed to talk to you."

"Where's he at?"

"Inside, I'll get him, but I have to warn you, he's in an ornery mood."

❧

SHERIFF LLOYD HEARD Walt grumbling as he took the phone from Nancy. "Walt? You there?"

"Why the hell are you gettin' Nancy involved in this mess?" Walt snapped.

"I'm runnin' out of ways to help Derek and Brody. Didn't have a choice. How ya feelin'?"

"I ain't had a drink in four damn days. How the hell do you think I'm feelin'? Let's get on with it. What do you want to know?" he said short-tempered.

"All right, well, let's start with you claiming someone planted Meredith Young's missin' evidence at your house. If that's true, who planted it and why?"

"Can't prove it but think it was Agent Kelly. He wanted Meredith's and Charles Young's cases closed mighty bad. Like everyone else, I thought it was because he was a publicity hound lookin' to be the hero. Didn't take long for me to figure out his reasons were much bigger than that."

"What makes you think it was more than him bein' a media whore?"

"I couldn't let Meredith's case go. Like a fool, I went to Kelly cause he had more resources and connections than we did. Figured if I could convince him we'd accused the wrong man, he'd be willin' to help, but our conversation got heated pretty quick. He insisted Charles Young murdered his wife and that we had more than enough evidence to close her case. Told me I needed to back off and let him put the case to bed."

"We all thought the same thing, Walt."

"Yeah, but he was the only one who threatened me. Said no one would miss an old backwoods Sheriff if I happened to turn up missin'. Suggested I should walk away before someone got hurt. His threats were enough to convince me he was hidin' somethin'. Don't bother askin' me what it was, 'cause I ain't got a clue."

"Did you tell anyone he threatened you?"

"I didn't have a chance. The mornin' after we talked, I found the doll and pictures that son of a bitch planted in my desk here at the house. As soon as I saw an unmarked car pullin' up the driveway, I knew I was bein' framed. I reckon Kelly figured if I wasn't around to stir the pot, he'd be able to play the DA's office like puppets. What that bastard didn't see comin' was that I was willin' to take the fall for the missin' evidence and leak it to the media if they didn't agree to leave the case open.

"Kelly was already in the limelight, so me goin' to the media would've stripped him of all his glory and opened up the can of worms my gut told me he was hidin'. Guess that's when he decided to leave well enough alone. You know the rest."

"And what about the doll? Did you burn it too?"

"No. I'd thrown it in some bushes out back the day I was brought in for questionin'. Lucky for me the DA's goons missed it when they searched my house. Idiots never thought to look outside, I guess."

"You should've told me Kelly threatened you."

"You would've gone after him if I did, and that wouldn't have done me any good. I was searchin' for the truth and knew I'd never find it with Kelly or the DA's office in my way. Hell, even you didn't believe me back then. I only agreed to resign so I could start my own investigation. Kelly hasn't shown his face around these parts since I went out on my own. Odd he shows up after them boys came here lookin' for answers, don't you think?"

"I agree, which is why we need your help. Nancy said she's heard you mention the doll a few times at Dottie's. What's that about?"

"For cryin' out loud, did you or them boys even read my notes? It's all there in the file."

"I ain't gonna lie, Walt, your handwritin' is worse than chicken scratch. Brody and Derek asked me to work with you to figure out what we might be missin'."

"First of all, I never said the doll is the key. I said the doll has the key. In Nancy's defense I was usually three sheets to the wind. She must have heard me wrong is all."

"What do you mean the doll has the key?"

"It means exactly what I just said. Looky here. If you want me to walk you through my notes, you're gonna have to stay with me, son."

"I'm listenin'."

"Believe me when I tell you I'd looked that doll over more times than I can count. I tried to find somethin', anything out of the ordinary, but there was nothin', so I hid it in my attic, and that's where it stayed up until six months ago."

"And where is it now?"

"Be patient, son. I'm gettin' there. One night I crawled up in the attic and had every intention of destroyin' the same creepy doll I'd seen in my dreams every night laying there in Meredith Young's lifeless arms. I ain't gonna lie, I went mad. I started shakin' that damn thing like it was real. And that's when it happened."

"What the hell happened, Walt?"

"The old skeleton key sewn into the doll's dress fell off and landed right at my feet. Now, I'd seen it there before but had always assumed it was just an accessory and part of the doll's fancy dress."

"How do you know it wasn't?"

"'Cause I may be a drunk, but I sure as hell ain't a dumb one. I'd spent a lot of time in New York durin' my investigation and met a few folks along the way, one bein' an antiques dealer. He researched the doll and key for me. Took him a week to get back to me, but what he found was worth the wait. He said the skeleton key belonged to an antique case that held a Masonic dagger from the late 1800s, which was used by the Knights Templar."

"The Knights Templar?"

"They were Knights of God and responsible for protectin' their church and its people. This specific Masonic dagger symbolized strength, honor, and justice."

"And what about the doll?"

"The doll wasn't an antique, but we uncovered an interestin' connection with the dagger."

"What?"

"The dagger was purchased at an auction in 1971, so there were records of it along with the purchaser's name, which was Edward Chancellor."

"Meredith Young's adoptive dad."

"Yes, sir. My dealer said the stamp on the back of the doll's head was the Chancellor Toy Company's mark. Said the numbers right below it didn't make any sense though."

"How so?"

"Said the numbers on all their dolls were identifyin' patent or mold numbers. Our doll was marked with the date 05-03-2013, which is tomorrow. Told me he couldn't find one record that identified the doll or that it was ever manufactured, so he guessed it was custom-made."

"By who, her daddy?"

"No. By Meredith Hope Young."

"How do you know it was her?"

"I took the doll to the owners who bought Chancellor Toys from Meredith in '87. The owners said they were close friends with Meredith growin' up. Said they felt guilty for payin' as little as they did for her parents' company. After she sold them Chancellor Toys, they didn't see her again until 1991. She offered them a million dollars to stop their toy production so they could make her doll. They didn't take her money but agreed to make it.

"Meredith gave them a sketch of what she wanted the doll to look like, insisted on specific manufacturer's marks, and asked them to sew on the skeleton key to make it look like part of the dress. They admitted they thought her requests were odd but did it because she'd stressed how important it was that the doll be perfect."

"Did she tell them what or who she had the doll made for?"

"No. In fact, when she picked up the doll two days later, she made them destroy the mold and shred any and all paper trails, which is why I handwrote the notes. My guess is she had the doll made to conceal the key. I also suspect the true motive behind her murder has something to do with the dagger and its case."

"So you never found it?"

"Edward Chancellor was the last owner, so I went to see him at Baker's. I took the doll and key with me hopin' I'd find the dagger and case there. I ain't gonna lie. I was nowhere near prepared for what I saw. He was...."

"Walt, you there?"

"I'm here."

"What did you see?"

"That place was creepy as hell and just didn't sit right with me at all. The site of them folks wanderin' around the halls all drugged up and oblivious to the world outside of Baker's sent chills up my spine. When I got to Edward's room, I saw a skeleton of a man with deep wrinkles sittin' in a wheelchair colorin' on the wall with his own feces. The orderly said he was seventy-six, but I swear he looked to be a hundred and already six feet under.

"Now, I remembered we'd found out about his eyes and tongue bein' cut out the night his wife was murdered. But, son, nothin' prepares you to see that in person. I just about lost my lunch when he tried talkin' and nothin' came out but desperate moans. I know he couldn't see me, but he'd written the name 'Sheridan' on the wall with feces then started rockin' himself in his wheelchair. I swear it felt like he was tryin' to tell me somethin', but the orderly said he'd been writin' that name on his wall for twenty-six years."

Sheriff Lloyd's stomach turned. "Jesus," was all he could manage.

"Jesus is exactly what that poor man needed, son, 'cause if there was a hell on earth, he was in it. I reckon seein' him like that is what made me lose my own damn mind. That's when I brought you my file a few months back. I feared if I kept searchin' for answers that weren't meant to be found, I'd wind up like Edward Chancellor, alone and crazy."

"Where's the doll, Walt?"

"Edward's room had no trace of ever havin' had a family. I still don't know why, but that doll was important to his daughter. Seemed only right it should stay with him, so I tucked the key in the doll's bloomers and put it under his bed. When I left Baker's that day and brought my file to you, I never expected to see it again. My plan was to drink myself into oblivion, so I could finally find peace."

"I have to tell Derek about the doll."

"I wouldn't expect you not to. You've protected me long enough, son. Do what you need to do."

"You don't understand. Edward Chancellor wrote the name Sheridan on his wall. Sheridan Hayes is my daughter. I never had the sight like my mamma, but my gut is tellin' me Sheridan's connected to Meredith's murder somehow now. I think she's in danger, and I have to protect her."

"Rhonda Hayes' youngin?"

"I don't have time to explain right now, Walt. I've got to call Derek. I'll call you after."

"I ain't goin nowhere. I'll be here," Walt said then hung up.

Sheriff Lloyd's hand was shaky as he found Derek's number and dialed. "Answer your goddamn phone," he said impatiently. When someone answered, all he could hear was what sounded like somebody walking for a few seconds. He heard Derek ask, "Where are they?" in a stringent tone. Another man's voice said, "They're in Dr. Riley's study."

Chapter Thirty-Three

As Sheridan knocked on Vista's door, Rodney realized he'd left his cell in the limo, so he walked back down to the car to get it. When no one answered, Sheridan rang the doorbell.

Vanessa answered and smiled when she saw Sheridan. "I didn't think we were going to see you until Monday. Kids are pretty addicting, huh?"

"Addicting is an understatement, but I'm actually here to talk to you about the art room project Lexus is working on."

"Lexus isn't here. She called earlier this morning and said she was sick and wouldn't be coming in today. She must have caught something from Rebecca because she's got the sniffles too."

"I'm so sorry to hear that. It's perfect she's not here, though."

"Is everything okay?"

"Everything's fine. I wanted to see if you could help me make arrangements to have the arts and crafts room upstairs completed. Derek wanted to take over the project to give Lexus a break and was asking my advice about it yesterday. I wanted to surprise Derek and Lexus and take on the completion myself. I'd pay for everything, of course."

"You do know Derek has the funds and resources to complete the room himself though, right?"

Sheridan laughed. "It's because he was so generous in using his resources for me and my mom that I want to do this for him and Lexus."

"That is an amazing gift. My sister's in town and a creative genius. This project's right up her alley, so I know she'd be willing to help too."

"That would be great. I'll leave a blank check to pay for whatever we need and then come back Saturday myself to help."

Vanessa smiled. "Derek will be so touched. He's used to giving, not receiving, so this will mean a lot to him."

"That's the idea. So, I know Rebecca's got the sniffles, but can I see her?"

"Of course. Blake and Anderson took the kids to the park, but Rebecca's upstairs in her and Tamika's room with my sister. Sarah got a wild hair this morning when she got here and started painting Rebecca's side of the room. Can't say I understand what she's painting exactly, but Rebecca seems to like it."

Vanessa became distracted when she saw Rodney walking up the steps. Her brows came together from confusion. "What the hell," she said faintly under her breath as he walked up and stood next to Sheridan.

"Sorry. Got a call and had to take it, then my phone died."

Sheridan had seen the perplexed look form on Vanessa's face. "Have you two met?"

Vanessa's glare and silence made Rodney uncomfortable, but he forced a smile and extended his hand to her. "No, I can't say we have. My name's Rodney."

"Vanessa, are you okay?" Sheridan asked.

"Yeah, sorry. I'm Vanessa." She shook Rodney's hand. "Listen, I'm not sure what's going on, but you two need to see something."

It was obvious to Sheridan that whatever had spooked Vanessa was paranormal related. She hadn't told Rodney about Derek or the kids having psychic gifts yet and had planned to ease him into it. "Rodney's not familiar with why Vista is so unique, Vanessa."

"Well, he's about to get a crash course."

§&

SARAH WAS STANDING on a wooden step ladder with her back to the door painting a mural on the wall. Rebecca sat cross-legged on Tamika's bed and watched.

"Hey half-pint, can you hand me the other brush?" They both turned and looked toward the door when they heard Vanessa, Sheridan, and Rodney walk in.

Sarah scanned the three of them, but it was Rodney her eyes locked in on in disbelief. She looked at her painting and then back at Rodney. "Holy shit," softly escaped her lips.

Rodney had dismissed the coarse welcome Vanessa had displayed at the front door but having his ego tapped a second time pushed him over the edge. "Name's not 'what the hell' or 'holy shit'. It's Rodney Allen Thurston," he snipped.

Vanessa looked up at her sister. "Sarah, come down from the ladder." Sarah climbed down.

When Rodney caught a glimpse of the mural, he walked closer to the wall to be sure his eyes weren't playing tricks on him. "Holy shit," he whispered, realizing the portrait before him was of his father and himself as a boy.

"Exactly," Sarah said.

Rodney's father sat in an antique Victorian library chair smiling, his cheeks vibrant with healthy color. There was no trace of the cancer that had ripped him away from those who adored him. Rodney was captured as a young boy kneeling beside his father's chair. His hands were crossed, resting on the arm, and he was looking up at his hero.

Rodney swallowed the tears welling up in his throat before he spoke. "It's beautiful."

Sheridan took Rodney's hand into hers but addressed Sarah. "Sarah, right?"

"That's me," she confirmed.

"Derek told me you were a healer, not clairvoyant. How and why did you paint this?" When Sheridan saw Sarah glance over at Rebecca, she had her answer.

"Healer? Clairvoyant? What are you talking about, Sheridan?" Rodney asked.

"I know this is going to sound crazy, but Sarah only painted what Rebecca wanted her to. I should've told you before I brought you here, but Vista is a foster home for kids with psychic abilities."

Rodney looked over at Rebecca and then at Sheridan in awe. "She looks like your—" he said short, seeing the resemblance of Sheridan's first canvas painting of her doll and Rebecca. He looked back to Rebecca and smiled. "And you must be Rebecca." Rebecca slid off the bed, walked to where Rodney was standing and lifted her arms, gesturing for him to pick her up. Rodney complied. When Rebecca was eye level with him, she caressed the side of his face.

Still holding Rebecca, Rodney stared back up at the portrait. "My father passed away nineteen years ago when he lost his battle with cancer. I was only four when he was diagnosed and started chemo and radiation treatments. They kept him alive for three more years, but, the cancer finally won. We lost him when I was seven. Losing him was the most horrible thing that's ever happened to me in my life."

"That makes you twenty-six. Jesus, you must have good genes. Your face hasn't changed," Sarah said.

Sarah's compliment brought a slight smile back to Rodney's face. "Thank you. And yes, the genes in our family rock."

Sarah's tone became apologetic. "Our gifts sometimes throw punches no one sees coming, not even us."

"I'd sat at my father's bedside and watched him wither away into someone I didn't recognize. It was the last days of his life that imprinted in my head and how I'd remembered him until this moment. Supernatural or not, I'll be forever grateful to both of you for helping me remember the strong courageous man he always was."

Vanessa spoke. "I have to admit I'm pretty impressed by how you and Sheridan have accepted the paranormal. Some people do come around but most are petrified of the unknown. My sister and I were separated at birth, so without Vista, we would've never found each other or survived."

"Well, I'm for anything that helps kids, and from what I've seen so far, I'd be an idiot not to believe," Rodney said.

Sarah walked to Rodney and Rebecca. "Hey, sweetie. Why don't you and I take Rodney here for a tour of the house," she suggested then looked at Rodney. "If you want a tour, that is."

"Absolutely. I'll need to cancel our luncheon first." He turned to Sheridan and smiled. "We will be keeping our six-thirty dinner reservation with the Board tonight though, right?"

Sheridan returned his smile. "Yes, I promise."

Still holding Rebecca, Rodney followed Sarah out of the room, leaving Vanessa and Sheridan alone to talk.

Vanessa spoke first. "Rebecca's gifts are more advanced than any of us thought. I don't know what happened during your session with the kids yesterday, but she hadn't drawn a single thing while Derek was gone. But now she's using Tamika as her voice and has Tamika and Sarah illustrating what she's seeing. Rebecca saw that Rodney was coming to Vista today. I only wish we understood what she's trying to tell us."

"Why do you think she saw him as a young boy instead of an adult?"

"Rodney said losing his father was the most difficult thing he's ever experienced. His physical body appears twenty-six, but his inner essence is holding on to the pain he felt watching his father die as a child. The inner spirit produces more energy than the physical self. Rebecca honed in on the boy who's still mourning his father's death."

Vanessa's explanation made it clear that Derek had seen her as a little girl because she still feared her childhood monsters. She had to find a way to confront her past and tell Derek, so she could move on with her life. *After the reveal*, she thought.

Chapter Thirty-Four

Derek's cell rang and displayed Sheriff Lloyd's name on the caller ID. He declined the call when he saw his aunt's car parked in Dr. Riley's circular driveway. Pulse racing, he got out of his vehicle and walked up to her driver's side window to see if anything looked out of sorts. When nothing did, he continued to the front door and barged in without knocking.

Dr. Riley's butler tried to greet him, but Derek cut him off. "Where are they?" he demanded.

"They-they're in Dr. Riley's study." He pointed to the room down the hall. "They're expecting you, Mr. Young."

The study's door was locked, causing Derek's imagination to run wild about his aunt's safety, so he kicked it open. He was relieved to see Lexus and Quentin were sitting on the couch unharmed, and Dr. Riley at his desk.

Quentin rose from the couch when he saw Derek enter. "Derek, we're fine."

"What the hell's going on?" He addressed Dr. Riley. "I was told you would be out of town until tomorrow."

Dr. Riley rose from his chair, expecting to have to protect himself by the accusing look on Derek's face. "I never left New York. I always ask my staff to tell everyone I'm out of town when I take a few days off, otherwise, I don't get any real downtime. If you would've called me directly like you usually do, I would've told you that."

Quentin chimed in. "He's not lying, Derek. We actually had dinner with him last night. Your aunt started feeling a little under the weather during dinner. Dr. Riley suspected it was a sinus infection, so he told us to swing by this morning to pick up a prescription for her."

Derek addressed Lexus. "Why did you ask me to come here before going to Baker's then? You sounded upset."

"Sweetie, look at me," she said. "No matter what happens, I need you to know how much your Uncle Quentin and I love you. I swear we didn't know about any of it until this morning."

"Find out what? What's going on?"

Quentin took Lexus' hand into his. "You're sick, honey. We need to get you home and in bed."

Lexus sneezed, and then spoke. "We should stay in case he—"

Quentin cut Lexus off to prevent her from saying too much. "We agreed it would be best if Dr. Riley talked to Derek alone. Let's give them some privacy. Like I said, we need to get you in bed." He led her out of the room before she could argue with him.

"WHAT THE HELL'S GOING ON?" Derek demanded.

"There's something you need to see," Dr. Riley said, then picked up the VHS tape sitting on his desk. He walked over to the entertainment center behind his desk, placed the tape into the VCR, and turned the TV on.

"Before I show you what's on the tape, I should explain a few things. The night your mother was killed, you had an episode we thought was a seizure. I performed an electroencephalogram and set up EEG video monitoring to record your movements. Both tests came back negative for epilepsy, but the video monitoring suggested possible signs of PNES."

"PNES?"

"Psychogenetic non-epileptic seizure episodes. PNES usually

develops in children who were sexually or physically abused or suffered the loss of a loved one. Because I was close to you and your family, the diagnosis made no sense to me. The day after your mother died, there was a fire that broke out at Providence House. We had droves of victims being brought in by ambulance, so I was at the hospital later than usual helping.

"By midnight, I was exhausted and stayed in one of the on-call rooms. I couldn't sleep, so I went upstairs to check on you. When I got off the elevator, I saw your dad going down just before the other elevator's doors closed."

"Did you talk to him?"

"Yes. I'd seen him earlier that night. I had no idea he'd been shot, was running from the law, or that he'd driven nonstop from Lyle Mountain to St. Vincent to see you. Before he'd gone up to see you that night, I'd found him sitting in the recovery room with one of the burn victims who'd come out of surgery. Charles said his name was Fisher and he and your mom knew him. The vascular surgeon told your dad they had to amputate his right arm and leg, but weren't hopeful Fisher was going to make it. Your dad told me he didn't have any family, so he was going to sit with him awhile."

"I remember Fisher. He volunteered at Providence. He used to play cards with my dad and had gifts like my mom. But, what does he have to do with any of this?"

"More than you know, but I'll get to that."

"My patience is running thin. What's on the goddamn tape?"

Dr. Riley pointed the controller at the VCR and hit play. Derek stared intensely at the screen as he watched Quentin and Lexus sleeping at his bedside, Charles walking into his hospital room, Lexus leaving them alone to talk. He heard Charles and Quentin's entire conversation about the night his mother was killed, why Charles felt he needed to leave Derek with Quentin and Lexus, his mother's letter, the chalet, Fisher, all of it.

The video painted a vivid picture of the raw devastation his father had experienced back then. It was Charles sitting at his bedside saying goodbye to him that almost broke Derek. The last thing he saw after Charles left his room was Dr. Riley walking into the room, checking his vitals, then shutting off the camera recording his movements.

Derek locked in on Dr. Riley, lunged, and punched him in the jaw. "Why'd you keep this from me, you son of a bitch? Why didn't you want me to go to Baker's?" he roared. When Dr. Riley didn't answer, he drew his fist back and prepared to strike him again.

"That's enough, son," Charles demanded.

Derek turned to the familiar voice behind him and released Dr. Riley from his grip. "You're alive."

Chapter Thirty-Five

"Leave us, Riley. I want to talk to my son alone."

Dr. Riley looked over at Derek and rubbed his sore jaw as he left the room. Derek stood quiet examining Charles, dumbfounded by the vision of the man he'd thought dead for sixteen years. Charles' heart stung from the tangled confusion and pain he saw in Derek's disbelieving eyes.

Derek walked over to Charles and threw his arms around his dad. He pulled away and looked Charles over to be sure he was real. Derek found his voice. "How's it possible you're alive? The explosion? The ballistics evidence? Human bone fragments recovered at the scene?"

Charles leaned against Dr. Riley's desk and went back in time. "Two hours after I'd left you at the hospital, I saw 911 and an unfamiliar phone number come across my pager. I thought it was Quentin. When I reached the chalet, I called the number back. I was surprised to hear Riley's voice on the other end. He assured me you were fine, then confessed he'd seen the tape and knew everything, which is how he knew to use the 911 code Quentin and I had agreed on. He told me he had a plan to fake my death and to sit tight at the chalet and wait for him. I woke up the next morning to the sound of Riley setting up surgical supplies on the nightstand."

"He removed the bullet from your arm, planted it in the chalet, and made sure it was found, didn't he?"

"Yes."

"It was reported that human bone fragments were recovered from inside. Somebody was in that chalet when it blew up." He remembered Dr. Riley saying Fisher's right arm and leg had been amputated. "Jesus, it was Fisher's body, wasn't it?"

"I know it sounds morbid, but I can explain," Charles assured. "I'd updated Riley on Fisher's progress when he'd found us in the recovery room that night, so he already knew about Fisher's surgery and amputations. Riley put two and two together and found the limbs before they were burned in the hospital's incinerator."

"So his limbs would've been burned anyway?"

"Yes. Even though it was protocol, we still wanted to pay our respects to him. Fisher had no known next of kin, so Riley claimed his body from the hospital and gave him a proper burial. We'd done everything we could to save him, but in the end, it was Fisher who saved me, and to this day, we all still visit his grave."

All, Derek thought to himself. "You said when Riley called you that night, he told you to sit tight and wait for 'them' to get to the chalet. Someone else came with him."

"Yes, Ronald Fuller."

"Fuller. Why does that name sound familiar?"

"He was Greene County's Fire Chief back then and Jada's adoptive father. You knew her parents as Mr. and Mrs. Fuller. You were only five when your mom and I helped them get approved to adopt Jada and only saw them once a year at our annual barbecues."

"I remember, but I also remember reading his name in one of Carter County's newspaper articles I'd researched. The article said his engine was first on scene, and he was the fire chief who'd investigated the explosion. Greene County DA's office ruled your death a suicide based on his assessment that the fire was started from inside the chalet."

"What the DA's office didn't know was that it was Ronald who started it. He also made sure the explosion was powerful enough to leave no solid DNA evidence."

"Thus the bone fragments. Let me guess, he was also the one who found the bullet at the scene and turned it in for ballistics testing?"

"Yes."

There was a long pause between them before Derek spoke again. "Understand that words can't begin to express how grateful I am you're alive. But, I still have questions. Like who killed mom, and why did she think she had to sacrifice her own life the night she was killed?"

"I know you need answers, son, and you deserve them. But, there are other things that happened before your mom was killed you need to know. They won't be easy to hear."

"Mom was murdered, and I thought you were dead. What could be worse than that?"

Charles' voice cracked when he spoke. "I need you to believe that it's because I love you that you've not seen me for sixteen years, Derek. To keep you, Sheridan, and the natural pattern safe, I had no choice but to watch you both grow up from a distance. I couldn't put either of your lives in danger or let your mother's death be in vain."

"So Sheridan is a part of all this?"

"Yes."

"Then you have to know she's in danger?"

"Unfortunately, I do."

"Why didn't Lexus want me to go to Baker's today?"

"Because your mom knew you'd go and told me I was to stop you."

"Why?"

"She knew you'd possess the gift to see. I think she wanted to protect you from seeing what she saw the night her mom was murdered and her father was mutilated."

"I can't imagine what seeing that must've done to her."

"It almost destroyed her. I tried to help her through it, but like everyone else, she pushed me away. She became withdrawn. It was like her heart shut down. Everything changed when she became pregnant with you. It was like an instant light rekindled within her and pulled her from the futile darkness she'd fallen into. I loved your mother more than my own life and knew what she believed was real, but I didn't know how to help her.

"It was rumored at Providence that Fisher had the gift to see. I confided in him. Like everyone else, he adored your mom and tried to guide her. Those like her were referred to as The Knowing. Even with Fisher's guidance, her nightmares became too much for her to handle. The guilt she felt knowing her parents' assailant would strike again consumed her. Against Fisher's advice, she went to the authorities and told them about her visions."

Derek met his father's eyes when sudden clarity hit him. "It was Agent Kelly she confided in, wasn't it?"

"Yes. He dismissed her."

Derek remembered another entry from his mother's letter, *I was threatened to be institutionalized just as the woman before me had.* Derek realized the other woman from his visions talking to Agent Kelly must've been the woman he'd had committed.

"Did she tell anyone else?" Derek asked.

"No. She never went back to the authorities for help. When I found out Kelly threatened to have your mom committed, I caught up with him in a dark alley one night and beat him to a pulp. Kelly was on probation with the NBI back then for insubordination, so I assume that's why he never brought me in. Nine and a half months after your mom confided in Kelly, the first victim she'd told him about was reported murdered on the news. Kelly never said a word to anyone. After the chalet explosion, I found out he was the agent assigned to your mom's murder investigation. I couldn't believe it was a coincidence, so I had Riley hire a private investigator."

"You thought Kelly had something to do with mom's murder?"

"I did. It was common knowledge that Kelly's colleagues at the TBI couldn't stand him, so it wasn't hard for our PI to find someone willing to talk. Unfortunately, he came up empty-handed. One of the agents he questioned confirmed he saw Kelly's car leaving the TBI's parking garage around your mom's estimated time of death."

"Did the agent physically see Kelly get into his car and drive away that night?"

"No, and because he didn't, we've never ruled Kelly out as a suspect. The facts we have are too sloppy, unfortunately. I know first-hand how someone's theories can lead an investigation down the wrong path away from the truth. Your mom's and my cases were high profile, which is why Kelly wanted both cases closed before a more thorough investigation was conducted."

"He was afraid someone would uncover that he could've prevented the deaths of the victims mom warned him about?"

"Yes," Charles confirmed.

"I was told Kelly almost convinced Carter County DA's office to close mom's case, but it wasn't because of Walter Reed."

"So you know about the missing evidence cover-up?" Charles asked.

"Missing evidence?" Derek asked. "Brody and I were told Walter Reed was asked to step down as Sheriff after he retracted his suspicion of you being their prime suspect. To avoid a recall election, he agreed to resign, but only if they left mom's case open."

"There was more to it than that. An informant from Carter County DA's office told our PI that Walter Reed was accused of stealing and destroying evidence recovered from your mom's crime scene. The DA's office didn't want bad press, so they covered it up. Reed threatened to tell the media he'd stolen the evidence if they didn't leave your mom's case open."

Derek became livid. "I knew Sheriff Lloyd was protecting someone."

"Before you go for Sheriff Lloyd's or Walter Reed's jugglers, you should also know it was believed the evidence was planted at Reed's house."

"By who?"

"Kelly, and I believe it. Walter Reed devoted sixteen years of his life to find your mom's killer. Why would he have stolen and destroyed evidence that could've helped the case?"

"What evidence was destroyed?"

"A doll and pictures of it in her arms taken at the crime scene. I know for a fact the doll was there, because I saw Sheridan leave it in your mom's arms before she ran from the hunters."

"Jesus, Sheridan was there?"

"Yes, she was, but it wasn't the first time I'd seen her or the doll," Charles admitted.

"I've had dreams of mom rocking me and a doll since I was ten, but yesterday, I realized it was Sheridan she was rocking, not me. She was born at Providence, wasn't she?"

"Yes, and I delivered her. Eight hours after she was born, her mom abandoned her. It wasn't uncommon for newborns to be left there. It was the same back when it was an orphanage too. When babies were left, our policy was to contact ACF, but your mom refused to let me call them. In fact, we'd argued about it. Your mom volunteered in the nursery, and like some of the other children she'd held over the years, had seen pieces of Sheridan's future. Because of the unspoken law, good or bad, she never interfered with any of the children's written paths.

"Because I was so adamant to call ACF, she told me Sheridan would play a role in saving millions of lives one day, but she didn't say how. She assured me her mom was coming back for her in four days' time, and if she didn't, she'd call ACF herself.

"She cared about every child who came through Providence but was extra protective of Sheridan. So much so that over the next four days, she only left her side twice. And when she did, I was the only one she trusted to watch over her. The last time I saw Sheridan and the doll at Providence was right before her mom came back for her. I was on my way to a delivery that night and saw your mom cradling her and the doll in the nursery.

"When I saw them on Lyle six years later, they were both nestled in your mom's lifeless arms. That visual has haunted me every day since, and I've spent the last sixteen years trying to understand how and why your mom's life ended the way it did."

"So after all this time, you still don't know who killed her or why?"

"No, and I'm not sure I was ever meant to, son." Charles pulled the weathered letter Meredith had written him from his back pocket. "I'm sure you caught that your mother left me a letter when I was talking to Quentin on the tape. No one has ever read or touched this letter except me. But, I think I'm supposed to read it to you."

"Why?"

"One of your mom's entries said her letter was meant to guide you one day. There were messages written for me, but I believe there were others meant for you. My hope is we can figure out what she's trying to say."

Charles slowly unfolded the letter and began reading it out loud. Derek's heart ached as Charles read, but he heard his mother's angelic voice. As Charles read, the painful memory and guilt of leaving Derek all those years ago was more than he could handle, and he had to stop reading before reaching the end.

Derek looked at his father through forgiving eyes. "How did you find the will to do it?"

"Do what?" Charles asked.

"Carry her last words with you for sixteen years then sacrifice your own life to fulfill her chosen path?"

"I never stopped loving her, son." He then looked down at the letter and paused before he spoke again. "There's more," he said.

"It's okay. I can finish it."

Charles was reluctant to hand Derek the letter but did. The moment Derek touched it, a jolt of burning energy ripped through his veins and visions of the past began flooding his mind.

Chapter Thirty-Six

Derek was pulled into a whirlwind of visions coming at the velocity of his own rapid pulse. His mother's written words to his father, to him, and displaced visions he'd already seen blended together. He tried to focus, to understand, to piece it all together, but his distorted frustration held him captive.

The tangled visions began to fade as an entry from his mother's letter made its way to the forefront of his mind. *Only God is omniscient, which is why we're only given small pieces of much larger puzzles. Acceptance of your own purpose will lead you to the answers you seek.* His mother was saying he was never meant to see all, nor was she. In that moment, he understood it was his own bitterness restricting what God permitted him to see.

He'd thought his gifts resurfacing was a curse and had ignored the blessings they were meant to be. He'd denied his path, his purpose, and built protective walls around his own broken heart, while trying to mend others. *Hypocrite,* he thought.

Sheridan coming to him as a child within their ambiguous world also made sense now. Like him, she'd allowed her childhood demons to obstruct her passage to love, trust, and her own divine purpose. Without question, fate had brought them together, and their guarded walls were crumbling. Within the seclusion of his conscious mind, he welcomed his written path, which he'd always known was to love, guide, and protect the little girl from his dreams. His acceptance permitted him to beckon both familiar and unfamiliar visions into his immediate world.

Visible now was his mother's adoptive mom holding two newborns. A boy and girl, fraternal twins. He felt Edward Chancellor's suffocating guilt as he left both babies on the front steps of Providence. He saw a woman, a nurse maybe, stumble upon them, take the baby bundled in pink, then vanish with her into the darkness of the night.

His mom's adoption papers flashed before him. He saw her as a child walking down a long vacant hallway holding her new parents' hands. An angry boy holding a dagger watched from a distance as they walked through the front doors of Providence. The happy family faded as they stepped into their new life.

A still picture of the unknown woman Derek had seen talking to Agent Kelly appeared and began whirling out of control. The image came alive as she stumbled dizzily into a faceless man's arms with only his back exposed. Despair replaced the woman's haziness when the man rejected her words and loving arms. The vision of the pair melted into the sound of "Pop Goes the Weasel" playing in the background.

The conversation he'd seen between the unknown woman and Agent Kelly in the small room slowly resurfaced. Revulsion rose to his chest as heinous visions began fading in of the hostile attack on his mother's parents. The images fluttered between strobes of sporadic light as the creepy music played on.

The unknown woman reappeared, and like before, was being removed from what Derek now guessed was an interrogation room. Her words were desperate but clearly ignored. She was shoved into isolated darkness. When the unknown woman returned to the light, she was in a white padded room. She thrashed against the walls, constrained and screaming within the confinement of her bloodstained straitjacket. Derek's heart thumped hard when the creepy music hushed and a masked jester with rotten fangs sprung out of its box. And then abrupt darkness. He heard her heart rapidly beating, then slowing, then nothing.

A languid light crept back into his world and revealed his mother standing at the unknown woman's bedside. He knew the woman had passed but saw her spirit trying to communicate with his mother.

His mother was weeping and trying to comfort the desperate apparition before her. She rose from the floor and started whirling in the air like a beautiful angel. He heard her scream, 'Allumer la lumière. Je vais les protéger'. A surge of energy rippled through the air, glass shattered, and his parents were thrown back across the room.

The sound of bloodcurdling screams from women and babies could be heard. Indicative images and active visions began playing within each shard of glass cascading in slow motion to the floor. He felt his chest tighten as he tried to absorb each reflection he saw of the past. He saw a framed picture of Thomas, Vanessa, Sarah, and Ian hanging on the wall of Vista.

Rebecca's mother shooting up heroin then succumbing to the euphoric bliss that replaced her deep-rooted pain. IV lines running from his mother's left hand as she wrote Sheridan's name next to his in a weathered journal with her right. A red rose.

Derek's pulse began rising when a new vision surfaced of Sheridan as a child. The obscure man he saw carrying Sheridan through the unlit woods, he knew without question, was the infamous evil shadow. He saw the man's relentless gloved hands plunge her head under water until her last innocent breath was taken. Her little body began floating down the river as the same red rose drifted alongside her.

The shards of glass falling spun into his mother, pulling Sheridan from the same murky water. She was trying to resuscitate her. He felt his mother's panic when Sheridan wouldn't respond. Desperate, she looked up at the sky and whispered, 'Help me save her, please,' as she sobbed.

The unknown woman appeared at the river's edge and was floating above her now wearing the wings of a luminous angel. His mother gasped as the angel entered her frail body. Her panic turned to calm and an illuminating glow outlined his mother's beautiful silhouette.

She began working on Sheridan again, only this time she was guided by both her and Sheridan's guardian angel. Sheridan coughed up several mouthfuls of water then took in a lively breath. His mother cradled her for a while and placed the necklace he'd found by the river around Sheridan's neck.

The sharp shards of glass with multiple images merged into a single vision of his mother battling the evil shadow. He saw her lunge at the distorted masked man with the golden dagger he'd seen in his childhood dreams. Rage tore through Derek as he saw him punch his mother to the ground.

When the vision became stagnant, he knew it was his own fury making him lose control. He subconsciously steadied his breathing and accepted what he already knew was coming. His mother was going to die.

When the vision began moving again, he saw the shadow straddle his mother and force her to meet his stare. Derek couldn't see what she saw within the shadow's eyes but sensed she felt both fury and sorrow. Peace draped his mother before she spit up into the shadow's face. The last words he heard her say were, 'Too bad you're not psychic. You would've seen it coming.' He felt the man's wrath as he strangled his mother and saw her take her last breath.

The evil shadow emerged as the young boy he'd seen at Providence holding the dagger. With the dagger in hand, he smiled and walked away from his mother's still body, bearing no remorse for what he'd done.

The menacing vision faded and spun into an image of Sheridan and the doll nestled up in his mother's lifeless arms. He heard Sheridan say, 'I love you too,' as she caressed his mother's cold face and fell asleep. When he turned his attention to the doll's exposed face, he understood why Sheridan had been so frightened when she'd first met Rebecca at Vista. Their resemblance was haunting. The explosion of a gun firing prompted a new vision of Sheridan darting up from his mother's arms with the doll, then pausing. He saw Sheridan speak to the doll then place it back within his mother's arms before she fled.

Outside Derek's subconscious mind, he heard two men arguing. He fought to remain in the telling space he was in but made himself let go when he heard his father say, "Riley, put the gun down."

❧

WHEN DEREK OPENED HIS EYES, his vision was slightly out of focus, but he saw Riley had a gun pressed in Sheriff Lloyd's back. "Riley, what the hell are you doing?"

"Don't come any closer, Derek," Riley warned.

Derek was worried Riley's nerves would cause him to discharge the gun, so he complied. "Okay," he said, then took a step back.

Riley looked over at Charles. "What am I supposed to do here? Sheridan's reveal is tomorrow, and we can't protect her if we're in jail."

Charles held his composure. "I'm okay with getting arrested, Riley.

Meredith sacrificed her life so others could live. If you hurt him, her death will have been in vain."

Even with a gun nestled in his back, Sheriff Lloyd remained cool. "If anyone's interested, I ain't here to arrest anyone. I'm only here to help ya'll protect my daughter, Sheridan."

"Sheridan's your daughter?"

"Yes, she is."

"He's telling the truth," Derek offered. "I saw the paternity test. He's been helping me and Brody with our investigation. We can trust him."

"You didn't come here with Derek. How'd you find us?"

"I called Derek earlier. He answered but don't reckon he realized he had."

Derek pulled his cell from the back pocket of his jeans. "He's right, my cell's still connected."

"I heard your doorman say everyone was in Dr. Riley's study. I put my phone on speaker and texted my Deputy back home. Asked him to do a statewide search in New York for all Dr. Riley's. Took him less than a minute to find and text me your home address."

"Also the truth," Derek said. "I searched your name myself and you are the only Dr. Riley listed in New York."

Charles spoke up. "Derek wouldn't lie and risk putting me in danger."

Riley was hesitant but took the gun off Sheriff Lloyd's back and tucked it in the waist of his pants. He walked around Sheriff Lloyd and faced him. "I saw you on my surveillance monitor walking up the driveway. You're one of the deputies involved in Meredith's initial investigation. What was I supposed to think?"

"We've never met. How'd you know who I was?"

Charles answered. "From a picture our PI took of you. We hired him right after Meredith was murdered. Everyone involved in her investigation was under surveillance."

"So everyone was a suspect?"

"Unlike your department, we didn't single out one man," Riley pointed out in Charles' defense.

"You said you heard the doorman tell Derek where everyone was. What else did you hear, Sheriff?" Charles asked.

"Everything," Sheriff Lloyd disclosed. "I know you didn't kill your wife, Mr. Young. I can't change what happened, but I would like the chance to make it right."

"You said you heard everything," Charles said.

"Wasn't my intention when I called Derek, but, yes, I did."

"Then you know Meredith tried to warn me not to come after her that night. I didn't listen and went to Lyle anyway. That isolated mistake is the reason I lost my son and was accused of murder, Sheriff. I blame no one, including you, for the choice I made."

"I appreciate what you're tryin' to do, Mr. Young. If it's all the same, I'd still like to help and know I can."

Sheriff Lloyd addressed Derek. "I was callin' you earlier to tell you about the conversation I had with Walt today."

Riley became irritated by the mention of Walt's name. "You mean the man who started the initial witch hunt?"

"That's enough, Riley," Charles ordered. "We're wasting valuable time. We still have a chance to figure this out."

"How?" Riley asked.

"I don't know. Maybe combining old and new information we've all accumulated over the years will help us see what we're missing."

Charles' mention of old and new information reminded Riley of his meeting with their PI. "Shit. I'm going to be late for my appointment with Leo. We're reviewing Kelly's recent activity."

"Go. We need that information."

"Don't forget my dinner with Sheridan and the Board at six-thirty tonight," Riley reminded. "I probably won't get to the hotel until after nine. You sure you want me to go?"

"I'll be fine. We can start compiling and comparing our individual findings here while you're gone, and then I'll meet you at The Plaza."

"Fine. Call me if you need me," Riley said before leaving.

"The Plaza. That's where Sheridan and Rhonda are staying. Don't reckon it's a coincidence y'all are meeting there tonight," Sheriff Lloyd said.

"No, not a coincidence." Charles walked toward the door. "Follow me."

"Where to?" Derek asked.

"A few years back we turned one of Riley's guest rooms into a space we could work our investigation. Everything related to your mom's case and Sheridan is in there."

❧

"HAVE A SEAT," Charles offered when they walked into the dimly lit case room. He walked over to the picture window and pulled back the plush ivory drapes and allowed the late afternoon sunlight in.

Intimidating masses of organized pictures, articles, and written notes were displayed on an enormous evidence board against the west wall. Hanging center on the south khaki-colored wall was a sixty-inch flat screen TV. Just beneath it was a small oak entertainment stand holding a DVD/VHS player. Against the north wall there was an embossed leather sofa with a tall iron floor lamp that sat to the left of it. Four leather office chairs sat around a medium oak conference table in the middle of the room that held two laptops, a pile of disheveled papers, and several empty coffee cups. The remainder of the room's space was occupied with three stacked file cabinets and an oak bookshelf that sat left of the window.

A photo of Rhonda's Diner on the evidence board immediately caught Sheriff Lloyd's attention. Something Rhonda had said about being attacked by Hank at her diner put him in deep thought. When he came out of it, he looked across the conference table and stared intently at Charles. "It was you. You were the man who saved Rhonda's life the night Hank attacked her at the diner."

"Was it you?" Derek asked when Charles didn't answer.

"Yes."

Sheriff Lloyd extended his hand to Charles. "I was wrong about you, Mr. Young. Seems I've been wrong about a lot of things. Reckon I owe you more than a thank you and apology."

Charles accepted his hand and shook it. "You said you could help. That's enough for me."

Derek addressed Sheriff Lloyd. "You talked to Walt today. What did he say?"

"His chicken scratch was worth its weight in gold, but there's somethin' else you need to know. Do you remember the first day you came to my office, and I told you my mamma claimed to have the gift to see like you?"

"Yeah. You said she had a hard time distinguishing what was real and what wasn't, which ultimately got her locked up in a padded room. She died there."

"That's right. There were other details I didn't mention because they weren't relevant, at least, I didn't think they were at the time. After hearin' what I heard today, especially your mamma's letter, I understand a lot of things now."

"I'm listening," Derek probed.

"Mamma was only sixteen when she had me, so we lived with Granny. Other than strugglin' to make ends meet, we were as normal as any other family in Carter County. Mamma and Granny had always been close, but when mamma was twenty-two, things got tense between them. That's when mamma started seein' and hearin' things no one else could. She'd confided in Granny she'd become a seer.

"Granny had been a nurse in New York for a short time before moving back to Carter County. Because she didn't believe in psychics or anything paranormal, she suspected mamma was schizophrenic and told her so. She tried convincin' her that her mind was playin' tricks on her. Warned her she could lose me and find herself in a crazy house if she didn't keep quiet. After Granny put the fear of God in mamma, she didn't talk about her visions again for seven years.

"A couple months before she was institutionalized, she'd started havin' nightmares somethin' awful. We'd hear her screamin' and cryin' in the middle of the night, but she'd carry on the next day like nothin' was wrong. Granny didn't confront her at first, but the night she did, all hell broke loose.

"I woke up hearin' mamma screamin' and thought she was havin' another nightmare. Didn't take long for me to realize it was her and Granny arguin'. Their voices were muffled, so I only heard bits and pieces of what they were sayin'. None of it made a lick of sense until today.

"She was ramblin' on about a vision she had of her brother and sensed he was somewhere in New York. Granny started sobbin' somethin' fierce. Told her she was imaginin' things, that she was an only child and never had a brother. Mamma got even more fired up and told Granny to quit lyin' to her. Said she saw what Granny did when they were babies and knew the secret she was keepin'.

"Mamma said she saw the evil in her brother, just like their real daddy had before he threw them away. Told Granny she had to go to New York to save his soul and her unborn grandbaby. Said she chose the path of The Knowin' and millions of lives depended on it. Granny begged her not to go, but she didn't listen. Mamma told her she loved me more than life, and because she did, she didn't have a choice. Those were the last words I ever heard her say.

"I was only thirteen, so Granny never shared a lot of the details about mamma's death, includin' the name of the institution she was in. I was told she was paranoid schizophrenic, was institutionalized, and the monsters in her head convinced her to take her own life. I knew she was never comin' home, and that's pretty much all I thought or cared about back then. After everything that's happened, I reckon that's changed.

"Your mamma's letter said, his identity and truth weren't meant to be disclosed within hers or the woman from Baker's lifetime. Baker's is in New York."

"So, you think the woman from Baker's my wife was referring to was your mom?" Charles asked.

"I'll be the first to admit it sounds crazy. Walt told me he went to see Edward Chancellor at Baker's a few months back. Said he saw Edward write the name 'Sheridan' on the wall, and the orderly told him he'd been writin' the same name for twenty-six years."

"Okay, but Sheridan's twenty-two," Charles pointed out. "She wasn't even born when Edward started writing that name on the wall. He must have known someone else with that name."

Sheriff Lloyd sat forward in his chair and spoke with conviction. "I ain't goin' to tell you I understand how, but my mamma, Sheridan, your wife, and her daddy are connected. I'm sure of it," he said then began spouting out facts.

"Think about it. Both mamma and your wife claimin' to take the path of The Knowin'. Mamma tryin' to save her unborn grandbaby because millions of lives depended on it. Your wife sayin' Sheridan's existence would help save millions of lives. Both Edward and mamma at Baker's. Edward writin' Sheridan's name on the wall. And finally, your wife goin' to Lyle to save Sheridan knowin' full well she was goin' to die that night. I'm tellin' you, my mamma's the woman from Baker's."

"I've had visions of the woman from Baker's. What did your mom look like?" Derek asked.

Sheriff Lloyd pulled his wallet from his back pocket and took out a picture of his mother and himself as a boy. "Like this," he said then handed the picture to Derek. "Her name was Rose."

Derek looked down at the old weathered picture then closed his eyes. He beckoned previous dreams and visions he'd had to resurface. He studied every image before tucking them back in the depth of his subconscious mind. Derek had been under for several minutes, and although he was in no apparent distress, Charles was concerned. "Derek? Son, are you okay?"

Derek slowly opened his eyes then looked up from the picture at Charles. "It's her," he confirmed.

"You checked out for a bit. Did you see somethin'?" Sheriff Lloyd asked.

"There are a few things I'm not clear on, but I think I know what happened." Derek turned his attention to Charles. "Unfortunately, nothing in this room is going to help us identify mom's killer before Sheridan's exhibition. I know that now. The man we're looking for is a psychopath. He's taken great measures to ensure no one would be able to identify him. Not even a psychic. The only way we're going to catch him is in the act, which means Sheridan's still in danger."

Charles looked defeated. "So what now?"

"We need to talk about the letter mom wrote me. Quentin gave it to me when I was in Carter County. I didn't know you were alive, so I destroyed it but not before memorizing every word."

"You have to be careful what you share, Derek," Charles warned. "Her letter to you was meant for your eyes. She was clear about me not even reading it, and I didn't."

Derek ignored Charles' warning and started quoting his letter. "'My letter is meant to guide those you trust when the time comes. Your true journey will begin when the secrets of the stars are revealed and you accept the blessings of five thousand, two hundred, and thirteen angels,'" Derek quoted. "Maybe you weren't supposed to know what she wrote back then, but she gave me her blessing to share with both you and Sheriff Lloyd now."

"Me?" Sheriff Lloyd asked.

Charles was confused. "Secrets of the stars revealed? Blessings of five thousand, two hundred, and thirteen angels?"

"I just got it myself," Derek said. He addressed Sheriff Lloyd. "Do you know about Vista?"

"I remember Vista from your mamma's investigation. It was a foster home, right?"

"Yes, Vista was and is a foster home for gifted children with psychic abilities."

"Don't reckon I knew that."

Derek pulled his cell from his back pocket and brought up the picture he'd taken of Tamika's and Rebecca's painting the day before, and then continued. "Sheridan was painting with the kids at Vista yesterday. Two of the girls painted the exact same picture. When I asked Tamika what their paintings were of, she told me it was the good man and the bad boy." He pointed to the day side of the picture.

"She told me the stick figure man in the big yellow star was Sheridan's daddy, and he would make her happy. The shape of your badge makes you the man in the star. Your mom was gifted. The purple third eye represents her watching over you."

"I'll be," Sheriff Lloyd said in awe.

Charles contributed to the explanation. "One of the secrets was Sheridan finding out you were her father." He then addressed Derek. "What about the blessings of five thousand, two hundred, and thirteen angels?"

Derek answered. "Mom must've known we'd all come together. She wanted me to know I had her blessing to share her letter with those I trusted, but not until it was time, which is today, five, two, thirteen. Her killer changed natural patterns by becoming privy to knowledge he wasn't meant to have. She didn't want me to make the same mistake by revealing what I knew prematurely."

Sheriff Lloyd scowled and pointed to Derek's phone. "I reckon the feller on the night side of their paintin' is our bad guy then."

"It would make sense he is," Derek said. "Since I was ten, I've had dreams about a dagger with a purple stone in its hilt. Both of mom's letters mention the deranged boy holding her father's antique dagger. In her letter to you, she states, find the dagger, reveal the monster And then you have the girls painting a man inside the purple stone of a dagger."

Sheriff Lloyd jumped in. "One of the things Walt talked to me about today was a Masonic dagger and its case. You know about Agent Kelly framin' Walt with the missin' evidence. What you don't know is he has the doll, or at least he did have it.

"About six months ago, Walt was fiddlin' with the doll and an antique key fell off the doll's dress. He found out from an antiques dealer the key opens the case of an antique Masonic dagger Edward Chancellor purchased at an auction in 1971. He also found out your mamma had the doll custom-made to not only hide the key but to stress the date May 3, 2013, just like she did in your daddy's letter."

"The dagger was her high school graduation gift from Edward," Charles informed. "I tried to locate it but never could." Charles addressed Sheriff Lloyd. "You said Walt had the doll, or at least used to. Where is it now?"

"Walt said he left it at Baker's with Edward. Said he put the key in the doll's bloomers and hid it under his bed."

Derek got up from the conference table and walked over to the board. "We're still missing something. We need to reorganize new and old evidence," he said as he erased all the handwritten notes and removed pictures and articles from the evidence board. We need to get in this guy's head and figure out his next move. Our best chance is to try and fill in the gaps with the new information we have, mom's letters to us, and the visions I've had."

Sheriff Lloyd spoke, "I can fetch Walt's notes from my rental car."

"The rest of his file is out in my Escalade. I'll have Brody email the pictures he took of the DA's file too," Derek said.

Charles contributed. "Everything Riley and I have is in this room."

"I reckon my only concern in goin' through all this right now, is every minute we're in this room is another minute Sheridan isn't bein' protected," Sheriff Lloyd said.

"Brody's had protection on her since her and Rodney got to New York. No one's getting near her," Derek assured.

Charles also tried to reassure Sheriff Lloyd. "Our PI told us Sheridan and Rodney booked two suites at The Plaza, so I've been there since they arrived Monday."

"Reckon that explains why Riley's meetin' you there later then. I got a private room for me and Rhonda earlier but am goin' to suggest we stay with Sheridan again tonight."

"That's smart. I'll book a room tonight too," Derek informed.

Charles spoke up. "Meredith was trying to warn us something big is happening tomorrow. Whether it's good or bad, I couldn't tell you. What I do know is she saw Sheridan at MoMA and sacrificed her life to ensure she'd be there. That's why I'm more worried about Sheridan's safety tomorrow than I am tonight."

"He's right," Derek agreed. "Right now we're walking into the Unmasked Charity Ball blind. We need to use this time to understand this guy's psyche. We'll also need things followed up on outside of this room too, so I think we need to get Brody involved. We can trust him. He'll be able to follow up on the leads I need him to check out."

"I agree," Charles said. "He also has resources at the Bureau we can use, especially with the new information we have. We need Brody focused, so I think we should hold off on telling him I'm alive."

"I'll call him before we get started to catch him up to speed on what needs to be done," he said and then addressed Sheriff Lloyd. "Are you okay with all this?"

"I reckon all I can do is trust ya'll know what you're doin', but if anything happens to my daughter, I'll—"

"I gave you my word I wouldn't let anything happen to her before we knew she was your daughter. You still have my word, Sheriff."

"I'm holdin' you to it," Sheriff Lloyd warned.

❧

DEREK WANTED Brody to take the jet to Tennessee and pay Agent Kelly a visit at the TBI. Derek wanted confirmation about where Kelly was the night of Meredith's murder. He also wanted to know what Rose and Meredith confided in him about and what transpired after. If he refused to cooperate, Brody was told to threaten he'd provide the authorities and the media with everything they had on Kelly.

When Brody flew back the next day, he was to go to Baker's so that Derek could stay close to Sheridan. Brody was to check on Edward, get the doll, and ask around about any visitors Edward may have had over the years.

During their conversation, Brody had heard the uneasiness in Derek's voice. "Nothing's going to happen to her, Derek. Now that I know what's going on, I'll have Roger put more guys on her tonight and tomorrow."

"Sheriff Lloyd called Rhonda and told her to cancel their private room at the hotel tonight. He told her he wanted to spend more time with Sheridan, so he'll be with her tonight. He's also going to MoMA before the exhibition tomorrow to help finish setting up the staging areas."

"Perfect, so he'll have his eyes on her too."

"As will I. I'm booking a room at the hotel tonight. I'm heading over as soon as we're done here. If I hadn't insisted she put her focus on the exhibition, she'd be with me right now."

"Yeah, but she'd be suspicious if you asked her to stay with you now."

"I know. I need you to be sure not to tell anyone about Rebecca or that she looks exactly like Sheridan's childhood doll."

"Why?"

"Sheriff Lloyd confirmed my mom had the doll custom-made at her father's old toy company. He thinks she had it made to hide the antique key that unlocks the Masonic dagger case I told you about. He doesn't know she also had it made so Sheridan would recognize Rebecca one day."

"Have you figured out why yet?"

"No, and I can't risk that information getting into the wrong hands. We'd be putting Rebecca in danger if that information slipped."

"The jet is pulling up."

"All right. Call me when you get to Knoxville and lockdown Kelly."

"Will do."

§⚭

DEREK, Charles, and Sheriff Lloyd spent the next few hours filtering and reviewing records from Meredith's case. Derek bulleted visions he'd had in Riley's study on the evidence board in chronological order.

"Your granny, what was her name?" Derek asked Sheriff Lloyd.

"Ruby."

"Do you have a picture of her?"

Sheriff Lloyd pulled her picture from his wallet and gave it to Derek. Derek examined the photo then handed it back to Sheriff Lloyd.

Charles addressed Derek. "We've reviewed both letters from your mom and filtered through everything again. All that's left is your analysis based on the facts we have and your visions."

Derek heard the anticipation in Charles' voice. The last thing he wanted was to hurt his dad. Charles caught Derek's hesitation and tried to reassure him. "It's okay, son. I can handle it."

Derek believed Charles but still had concerns about Sheriff Lloyd. "A lot of what I'm about to share is based on paranormal accounts."

"Son, I'd be a damn fool not to be open after everything that's happened," Sheriff Lloyd said.

Derek threw a report on the table in front of Charles and Sheriff Lloyd.

Sheriff Lloyd's brows met. "I don't understand. What does Edward Chancellor and his wife's babies being kidnapped have to do with your mamma's murder?"

"Everything," Derek turned the evidence board around so Sheriff

323

Lloyd and Charles could see the bullets he'd written. "These are the visions I had in Riley's study earlier that played out, and in this order. After you've read them, we'll get started."

☙

Bulleted Visions

- Edward's wife holding fraternal twins, a boy and girl.
- Edward leaves twins at Providence.
- Woman takes girl twin off steps of Providence.
- Mom's adopted by Chancellors. Boy with dagger watches them leave.
- Rose goes to New York and is rejected by brother.
- Rose goes to Kelly for help. Shares premonition of tragedy at toy factory.
- Rose is Baker Acted and put in padded room. Jester with fangs appears. Rose's heart stops.
- Mom talks to spirit at Baker's. Becomes Knowing. Agrees to protect the children. Hears women's screams.
- Picture of Thomas, Vanessa, Sarah, and Ian at Vista.
- Mom having chemo. She writes Sheridan's and my name in journal with red rose.
- Evil shadow drowns Sheridan. Red rose floating. Mom gives Sheridan necklace.
- Evil shadow and mom fighting. Her killer's not psychic. Mom is murdered by boy with dagger.
- Sheridan in Mom's arms as baby. Sheridan whispers, "love you too." Gunshot heard. Sheridan leaves doll and runs.

☙

SEVERAL MINUTES PASSED before Charles and Sheriff Lloyd took their eyes from the evidence board. Both men's faces were flushed with anger but neither said a word. Derek took Sheriff Lloyd's and Charles' silent nods as a sign they were ready to start.

"In 1957, Edward's wife gave birth to twins. It was reported their twins were kidnapped right after they were born and never found. What I know now based on my recent visions is that the twins were never kidnapped. They were left on the front steps of Providence by Edward Chancellor the day after they were born. The babies were Rose and her brother, who I believe is our killer."

"Edward left his twins at Providence because he'd seen the evil in his son, just as Rose had. My letter said Edward was blessed with the use of his own third eye. I think Edward predicted his son would kill Rose if Edward abandoned him but kept his sister.

"Edward saw that Rose would be taken off the steps that night and cared for, so he left her. He knew giving her up was the only way to protect her from his son's vengeance. Rose couldn't die. If she did, Sheriff Lloyd and Sheridan would've never been born. Edward must've also seen the importance of Sheridan's existence, which is why he's been writing her name on the wall all these years."

"Who was the woman that took Rose that night?" Charles asked.

"Ruby. She'd been a nurse in New York the same year the twins went missing, and Rose said she knew about the secrets Ruby was keeping," he said then addressed Sheriff Lloyd. "Your picture confirmed it. Had two baby twins been found at Providence, it would've raised a red flag, but Ruby took the girl. There was only one baby found that night, and it wasn't uncommon for babies to be left there." Derek paused when he saw the disappointment in Sheriff Lloyd's eyes. "I'm sorry."

"I'm fine, go on," Sheriff Lloyd insisted.

"Edward and his wife tried having another baby. After fourteen years of trying, they gave up and adopted mom. According to mom's letter, Edward saw the light of The Knowing within her, which is likely why he chose her. I saw the boy with the dagger watching my mom and Edward and his wife leaving Providence the day they adopted her. The boy watching them leave was Edward's son."

Charles spoke up. "It would've been impossible for him to have the dagger back then. Based on the auction records, Edward bought the dagger in 1971 before he adopted your mom and then gave it to her in 1983."

"Mom's letter also said her first vision of the boy with the dagger was in 1987, which meant she'd had the dagger in her possession. Because she did, I was thrown off too. And then I remembered my premonition of Sheridan's recent attack on Lyle. She came to me as a little girl, even though she was a grown woman.

"Mom saw Edward's son as a boy being held captive by his childhood rage and mental anguish, but she also saw his brutal acts of violence as a man. Her confusion of seeing two identities and her tumor was what inspired her to start writing in journals.

"Understanding mom's confusion helped me see that my visions of him are also interlaced with both his past and future. My guess is that his rage materialized as an adult after he realized his parents were the ones who adopted mom and left Providence with her that day."

"How'd he find out who his real parents were?" Charles asked.

"Rose. She told Ruby she was going to New York to save her brother's soul and her unborn grandchild. She'd seen the hell he'd been through at Providence. She thought showing him he was loved and not alone anymore would heal him, but he rejected her. Unfortunately, it was her presence and what she revealed to him that evoked the evil her and Edward saw in him."

Charles contributed. "A couple years after Meredith was adopted, Providence was shut down after an undercover investigation revealed the heinous abuse taking place there. Meredith told me the things that happened to some of the older kids were inconceivable. She'd always stressed being grateful for being one of the lucky ones who got out."

"Edward's son would've been around fourteen if he was still at Providence when your wife was adopted. If he was, he could've been one of the older kids being abused." Sheriff Lloyd paused and tried to process what Edward's son must've gone through. "Edward left his son to the wolves fourteen years earlier then came back to the same place he abandoned him and adopted someone else's youngin'. Reckon that would fire anyone up."

Derek agreed. "Exactly. Rose's intentions were good in telling her brother about their parents and what she'd seen in her visions. She must've realized her plan to save his soul backfired. After she'd made him privy to all that happened, he became enraged, and his psychopathic tendencies surfaced. I also believe she saw her brother's future vengeance on those he thought hurt him."

"So you think Rose saw her parents being attacked at the factory before it happened?" Charles asked.

"Yes. I also think she saw that Sheridan, her unborn grandchild, was still in danger. She went to the NBI thinking they could prevent the attack from happening. When Rose told Kelly what she'd predicted, he labeled her crazy and Baker Acted her."

Sheriff Lloyd's tone turned suspicious. "Maybe you saw her with Kelly because he's Edward's son."

"He could be. That's why I sent Brody to Tennessee to talk to him. Whether he's our guy or not, we still need to know what your mom said to Kelly in that room. Knowing what she predicted could help."

Sheriff Lloyd pointed to the evidence board. "Says you saw a jester with fangs before my mamma's heart quit beatin'. What's that about?"

"I think the jester symbolizes the moment Edward's son snapped."

"Do you think he killed her?" Sheriff Lloyd asked.

"I didn't see how she died," Derek said.

Charles pointed to the evidence board and read a portion of the next bullet. "'Talks to spirit at Baker's.' I was there the day this happened. That's when your mom accepted the light of The Knowing."

"Mamma was the spirit your wife was talkin' to in that room that day wasn't she?" Sheriff Lloyd asked.

Charles answered. "Yes. And like your mom, Meredith had also gone to Kelly about her own visions, and he threatened to have her committed too but didn't."

"Why do you reckon that is?"

"I can only think of two reasons. One, he realized Rose's predictions were right and didn't want anyone to find out he could've prevented the attack. Or two, he's our twisted killer and wanted Meredith to see the predictions she'd had of his future victims play out."

Derek moved on to the next bullet. "Both of you already know her purpose in life became guiding and protecting those born with gifts. Thomas, Vanessa, Sarah, and Ian were a few of the gifted kids at Vista, so my vision of them in a picture makes sense."

Derek had not included the vision about Rebecca's mom Abigail shooting up heroin to avoid raising questions that might lead to Rebecca's and Sheridan's connection. He found his place and continued on.

"I've had recurring dreams of Sheridan floating face down in the river and a single red rose drifting alongside her. When I was on Lyle, I had a vision of the same red rose lying above Sheridan's and my name, which mom had written in an old journal. Today, like before, I saw the rose and our names being written in the journal again, only this time, I saw mom hooked up to a chemo machine."

Derek spoke directly to Sheriff Lloyd. "I never understood what the red rose symbolized until today. It represents your mom, Rose, who even in death, has watched over both Sheridan and me, just as my mom has."

Sheriff Lloyd's face softened. "Don't reckon any other explanation would make much sense now, would it?"

"'Evil shadow drowns Sheridan,'" Charles read out loud and then addressed Derek. "If Sheridan drowned that night, how is she alive?"

"She's alive because mom and Rose saved her," Derek answered.

"Reckon I'm a little lost now myself. Mamma had already been deceased for eleven years. How's it possible she helped save Sheridan that night?"

"A miracle," Derek said, convinced it was. "I had a vision of Edward's son carrying Sheridan to the river and drowning her. He was plunging her head in and out of the water and didn't stop until she took her last breath. That's when I saw her body floating face down.

"The next thing I saw was mom pulling Sheridan's body out of the water. She was giving her CPR but started panicking when Sheridan wouldn't respond. She looked up to the stars like she was praying and asked for help.

"When your mom appeared to me again, it wasn't in the form of a human or an apparition, but as a beautiful angel. She was hovering above Sheridan, looking down at her lovingly. When she heard my mom's cry for help, she gravitated down and embraced them within her ethereal wings. I witnessed her beautiful essence melt into my mom's physical body. A radiating light encircled her silhouette, and within seconds, Sheridan was coughing up water and breathing again."

Sheriff Lloyd's eyes were glassy. He nodded to show his gratitude to Derek for helping him see his mom in a different light.

Charles grinned. "She tricked him. Jesus, he had no idea your mom was there when he drowned Sheridan."

"Not a clue. Mom wrote false predictions in the journals she intended him to see. He thought he'd outwitted her by going to kill Sheridan earlier than she'd falsely predicted he would. It was she who showed up earlier than him."

"According to your letter, she also saved his future victims by making him believe he'd be caught if his violence didn't stop," Charles said.

"That's true, but he knows Sheridan's alive now and that mom deceived him. He isn't going to stop until he finishes what he started. We have to figure out when he's going to make his move."

Charles saw affliction rising in Derek's eyes but needed him to stay focused. "What happened after Rose and your mom saved Sheridan?"

"Mom was sitting at the edge of the river cradling Sheridan. There was light surrounding mom's body, so Rose was still with them. Mom put a necklace around Sheridan's neck that held an amethyst stone. Sheridan still has it."

"What about your mom, Derek. What happened to her that night?" Charles asked.

"I didn't see water anywhere, so I knew her and Edward's son were in a different location on Lyle. It was dark, but I could tell he was wearing a ski mask when he walked out of the shadows. When mom saw him, she lunged at him with the dagger. The second time she lunged at him, he hit her, and she fell to the ground. He was straddling her and made her look into his eyes. He needed her to know who he was and what had been done to him. I think she figured it out because I felt her emotions were all over the place. I saw her spit up into his face and taunt him. That's when he killed her. When he walked away, I saw him transform into the boy and take the dagger with him."

Charles had another revelation. "In my letter, your mom indicated the boy was holding the dagger like a trophy. You said her visions of the boy with the dagger were premonitions. She saw her own murder before it ever happened."

"Yes. She also knew he'd take the dagger with him after he killed her that night."

Derek pointed to the last bullet on the board. "The morning after mom died, I saw Sheridan and the doll lying in her arms. I heard Sheridan say 'I love you too' and saw her fall asleep in mom's arms. A loud gunshot woke her up. I saw her jump up with the doll in hand, ready to run, but she didn't. She said something to the doll, tucked it back in mom's arms, and then ran. That's the last thing I saw."

Sheriff Lloyd got up and walked over to the evidence board where Derek was standing. "Do you mind?" He reached for the black marker Derek was holding. Derek gave him the marker then walked to the conference table and sat next to Charles.

Sheriff Lloyd drew a straight line down the center of the board and turned back around to address them. "With Derek's visions and what we've reviewed, I reckon we've got a good hold on what happened. Like Derek said, it ain't likely we're gonna identify Edward's son before Sheridan's reveal. I imagine we should start focusin' on the questions we still have at this point. Findin' those answers might help us understand this fella's way of thinkin' so we can figure out his next move."

"I agree," Charles said then addressed Derek. "You said you've had a recurring dream since you were ten. Besides what you've already told us, is there anything else you've seen in the dream?"

"Yeah. I see Sheridan as a little girl being suffocated with a pillow and everything goes dark. A door appears, and she walks through a protective earthquake into freedom."

Sheriff Lloyd spoke. "Sheridan and Rhonda escapin' Hank."

"Anything else?" Charles asked.

"The only other vision I see in the dream is a still image of mom as an angel. She's protecting several infants within her wings, but one of them is just outside her reach. This is the only vision I'm not clear about yet."

"That's all right. We'll put it on the back burner and come back to it. Findin' some of the answers to the remainin' questions we have might make somethin' click for ya. After everything we put together today, what questions are still out there? I have my own, but we'll start with y'alls."

1. Who's Edward's son?
2. How has he hidden his identity?
3. Why Sheridan's exhibition?
4. Where is dagger and case?
5. His psyche—Why did he:

- kill his mother?
- mutilate Edward?
- not kill Meredith at factory?

1. What does, "In the end, they'll follow her tranquil path to the harrowing bloodstone" mean?
2. Help family protect the chosen one, millions will be saved?

- What family members of Sheridan's help?
- Who's the chosen one?
- How will millions be saved and from what?

1. What's his next move?

AFTER SHERIFF LLOYD wrote their questions on the board, they searched for plausible answers. At the end of an hour, exhaustion and discouragement were all they'd unlocked. Charles and Sheriff Lloyd were discussing the plan for Sheridan's protection at the ball, while Derek stared at the cryptic data on the board. The taunting shadow played hide-and-seek within the obscurity of his mind. He rested his elbows on his knees and held his head in his hands to try and steady his thoughts.

Sheriff Lloyd looked at his watch. "Nearly six-twenty. Reckon I ought to head over to the hotel before Sheridan and Rodney wander back."

Derek lifted his head from his hands. "We'll head back with you."

Charles addressed Derek. "Before we leave, can I talk to you? Alone?"

"Yeah," Derek agreed then looked over at Sheriff Lloyd. "We won't be far behind. I'll call you when we get to the hotel."

"All right then." Sheriff Lloyd closed the door behind him when he left.

❧

"WHAT'S UP?" Derek asked.

"You accomplished a lot today, more today than all of us have in the last sixteen years."

"That's what's paying rent in my head. Why have I been able to hone in on so much but not on what I need to protect Sheridan? It's like he's blocking me somehow. The asshole was in my hands the night Sheridan was attacked. Why didn't I pick anything up?"

"Maybe your mom was wrong. Maybe he is psychic. That would explain how he blocked her too."

"He's not psychic. Mom was sure of it before he killed her that night."

"The night your mom was killed, Quentin told me you lost consciousness in his den. When he found you, you were levitating, and he thought he heard you say, 'Sheridan's scared again'. Quentin and Lexus rushed you to the hospital. You stopped breathing. After a few minutes of giving you CPR, he said you spit up a mouthful of water. I assumed your condition was a result of your gifts surfacing. I thought you'd experienced what your mom did the night she died. I also think you were experiencing everything Sheridan was."

"Lexus told me my abilities surfaced the night Mom was murdered, but then I lost them shortly after. I don't remember any of it. I do remember Sheridan being in my dreams. It's hard to explain, but it always felt like she was a part of me."

Charles smiled. "The morning after your mom was murdered, Lexus and the nurse at the hospital heard you mumble, 'I love you' in your sleep. You heard Sheridan whisper, 'I love you too'."

"So you think she..." Derek started to ask then paused, lost in his own thoughts.

"That you loved each other even then? You already know the answer."

"I do, which is why I can't let anything happen to her. Am I crazy for letting her go to MoMA?"

"I don't know why Sheridan is meant to be there tomorrow, but your mom did, and I was to ensure she was. It wasn't easy making everything fall into place, but it did."

"How?"

"Years of patience and planning. I knew Sheridan was the little girl your mom wanted me to protect, that 5.3.13 was a significant date in her life, and that she'd be a gifted artist one day. Because MoMA was your mom's and my favorite museum, I knew Sheridan's work was supposed to be exhibited there, so Riley and I came up with a plan to make it happen.

"We went to Kensington several times a year to check in on Sheridan and her mom. Riley would go to the diner alone and report back to me. When Sheridan was fourteen, Rhonda started hanging Sheridan's work up at the diner. Riley recognized her talent and started watching the progression of her work when we'd visit."

"When Sheridan told me Riley was the one who purchased her paintings, I got suspicious. My gut told me their connection wasn't a coincidence. Guess I let my imagination run wild. That's why I was so hard on Riley when I got here."

"He's been a loyal friend. He's never questioned what I've needed. He just jumps in and does it." Charles chuckled. "He's waited years for my blessing to plan Sheridan's art debut."

Derek became distracted when he heard a text come through on his phone.

"Everything all right?"

"Roger sent me a text. Said his guy just got to Eleven Madison Park with Sheridan and Rodney. They're heading back to the hotel after dinner. That will give me time to stop by my place and grab my tux and a change of clothes."

"Riley's at dinner with them and should get back to the hotel around nine. I'm surprised he hasn't called me with an update on his and Leo's meeting. I'm curious if Leo knows where Kelly was the night you said Sheridan was attacked."

"Yeah, me too. If your guy doesn't know, Brody will get it out of Kelly."

"We've done all we can here, let's head over to The Plaza." Charles encouraged when he saw Derek look down at his watch. He saw the worry rising in Derek's eyes again. "She's going to be fine, Derek."

"I hope you're right."

Derek needs you, Meredith. We all need you, Charles thought as he followed Derek out of the room.

Chapter Thirty-Seven

Derek was told the rooms surrounding Sheridan's were reserved for a wedding party. The suite immediately to the left of hers was the bride and groom's. Derek offered to upgrade the couple to the Royal Plaza Suite in exchange for their own, and they'd accepted. Derek had settled in around eight. He'd showered, shaved, and unpacked the few things he'd picked up from his place. It was a little after nine. Brody hadn't called with any updates on Kelly, Roger hadn't called to confirm Sheridan had left the restaurant, and Sheriff Lloyd, who was in the room next door, hadn't called with any updates either.

Derek was restless. The walls felt like they were closing in on him, so he went out to the terrace for air. The view of the Manhattan Skyline and the night's cool breeze was calming, but his placid temperament was short-lived when Charles called his cell.

"Hey, any word from Riley?"

"He just got here."

Derek was distracted by a text coming in from Roger. "Hold on a sec." There was a brief pause before he spoke again. "I guess Roger tried to call me, but my phone went straight to voicemail. Sheridan left the restaurant about fifteen minutes ago and is on her way back to the hotel."

"Phone reception in the hotel is hit or miss."

"So how'd Riley's meeting go with your PI?"

"Leo never showed up for their meeting today. Riley said he waited over an hour for him, but he never showed. Drove to his office too, but his receptionist said she hadn't heard from him all day either."

"Has he ever not shown up before?"

"No, and he's been with us since the beginning. How about you? Have you heard from Brody?"

"He texted me when he landed in Knoxville. Said he had his tech analyst at the bureau send Roger a blueprint of MoMA so he could set up security tomorrow. That's the last I heard from him."

"Sounds like everything's falling in place. Make sure you get some rest tonight, Derek. We all need to be alert and ready."

"I'll rest easier when Sheridan gets here." Derek saw Brody's name come up on call waiting. "Speak of the devil, Brody's calling on the other line. I'll merge the calls, but you need to mute your phone."

"Muting."

"Hey," Derek answered.

Brody's tone was pressing. "Kelly's heading to New York tomorrow."

"Really?"

"I went to the TBI to question him and was told he'd taken a few days off. Had my tech give me his cell and home address. He didn't answer his cell and wasn't at his apartment either. My tech is tracking his credit card activity to try and pinpoint his location. That's how I found out he'd booked a flight to New York. His flight departs Knoxville at four twenty-five and arrives in New York at six-thirty tomorrow night."

"There's a good chance he'll come back to his apartment tonight then."

"I'm sitting in front of his building as we speak. If he doesn't come back tonight, I'll corner his ass at the airport tomorrow before his flight takes off."

"I'm having trouble with calls coming through, so text me when you find him. I'm telling Sheriff Lloyd and Roger to group text moving forward."

"Got it. Ball starts at seven, right?"

"Yeah."

"I'll try to make it on time. It's going to depend on what goes down with Kelly and how long I'm held up at Baker's tomorrow. If anything comes up, I'll text you," he said then hung up.

"Dad? You there?"

Charles unmuted the phone. "I'm here, we're on speaker."

"Did you get all that?"

"We did," Charles confirmed.

"It's not a coincidence Kelly's flying in to New York the day of Sheridan's exhibition."

"I agree. Until today, you, Riley, the killer, and myself were the only ones who knew about your mom's and Sheridan's connection. How could Kelly know too unless he's our guy or someone tipped him off?"

"Who could've tipped him off?" Derek asked.

Riley chimed in. "I know what you're thinking Derek, and it wasn't me."

"What about your PI? Did he know?"

Charles replied. "No. Most of his work for us consisted of surveillance and running background checks. He's always worked with little information and knew not to ask questions."

"We better hope Brody finds Kelly then."

"It wouldn't hurt to get a picture of Kelly over to Roger and his guys just in case he doesn't," Charles suggested. Derek heard someone walk out on Sheridan's terrace through the thin privacy wall. "Derek?"

Derek stepped back inside his room to prevent whoever was on Sheridan's terrace from hearing him. He spoke in a low voice. "I think Sheridan's back. I'll text Roger a picture of Kelly. I'll forward you any updates I get from Roger and Sheriff Lloyd."

"All right. Remember, get some sleep tonight," Charles warned again then ended the call.

Derek put his phone on vibrate and left it on the dresser before he walked back outside. He walked over to the wall separating his and Sheridan's terraces and pressed his palm against it. Euphoric energy rushed his veins when Sheridan, who'd also been drawn to the wall, placed her palm opposite his. Aware she was there made it difficult to not free her name from his lips. Derek, seconds away from making Sheridan aware of his own presence, was grateful when Maggie joined Sheridan on the terrace.

❧

MAGGIE SAW Sheridan staring at the wall and brushing it with the tips of her fingers. "Sheridan, sweetie, you okay?"

The sound of Maggie's voice pulled Sheridan from her lulling state. "What happened?" she asked, not having remembered walking out to the terrace.

"You look exhausted."

"I'm fine. I got behind schedule today, so I'm feeling a little over-whelmed is all."

"I'm surprised Rodney let that happen. He's a fanatic when it comes to staying on schedule."

"Fanatic is an understatement. It was my fault we fell behind, but it was worth it."

"What happened?"

"I convinced Rodney to cancel some of my appointments so I could stop by Vista. I needed help pulling off a surprise for Derek and his aunt, so I wanted to run my idea by Vanessa. One surprise actually turned into two, then the kids came home, and before I knew it, three hours had passed."

"I love surprises. Do tell."

"I invited Lexus, Vanessa, and the others to the ball tomorrow night."

"Others?"

"Sorry. Sarah, Vanessa's twin, also an artist; Anderson, Vista's house counselor; and Thomas, Anderson's son. Vanessa was telling me about Derek, herself, Sarah, Thomas, and Ian being almost inseparable when they were kids."

"Who's Ian?"

"Ian is one of Derek's surprises. He lives in Chicago, but I asked

Vanessa to call and invite him to the ball anyway. He's flying in tomorrow afternoon, which means Derek's closest childhood friends will be at the reveal."

"That's so thoughtful, Sheridan. He'll love that. And the other surprise?"

"I'm going to take over and pay for getting the art room completed."

"It's been nineteen years since losing your Uncle James to cancer. I love him as much today as I did when he first swept me off my feet. When you talk about Derek, I see that same timeless light in your eyes that once lived in mine. You found the person you were meant to share and create your life story with. I'm not telling you anything you don't already know though, am I?"

Sheridan's smile was telling. "No."

Maggie softly patted Sheridan's hand. "He's going to love your surprises."

Rodney walked out on the terrace. "There you are. Just wanted to make sure you weren't scaling down the wall to go see Derek."

Maggie kissed Rodney's forehead. "Meet you back at the room." She then kissed Sheridan's forehead. "Night, sweetie. Get some sleep," she said then walked back inside.

Everyone was working hard on Sheridan's behalf, especially Rodney. She needed him to know she cared, so she began rambling off her own plans to him. "I ran a few last-minute ideas by Mrs. Hershkowitz for the angel collection's reveal at dinner and she loved them. I'm having additional props brought in. I'll be at the museum all day tomorrow staging it. The critics will love it. You're going to love it," she assured.

"I know you're only here because I pushed you so hard. I'm not going to nag you about pursuing a career in art anymore, at least not full time. After everything that happened at Vista today and seeing how happy you are, it's clear where your heart is."

Sheridan wrapped her arms around Rodney. "You really are the best cousin ever," she whispered.

"I know," he agreed then returned her loving hug. When he pulled away he looked through strained eyes. "We still have to get through the Unmasked Ball. So, until it's over, you're mine."

"Can I at least call Derek and say goodnight?"

"Absolutely not. In fact, I'm holding your phone hostage until after tomorrow." Rodney placed his palm on the small of her back and pushed her toward the terrace doors. "You know I love you, but you look like shit, honey, so its beddy bye for you."

When Derek heard Sheridan's terrace doors close, he walked back into his own suite. A twinge of guilt rested on his conscience for having listened in on Sheridan and Maggie's intimate conversation. Knowing Sheridan was safe and hearing the sound of her soothing voice helped put him at ease. So much so, he surrendered to the sleep Charles warned he'd need to protect Sheridan.

Chapter Thirty-Eight

F riday, May 3, 2013

BRODY STAKED out Agent Kelly's apartment all night, but he never showed, so he drove to Knoxville International to corner Kelly before he had a chance to board his flight. Without probable cause, Brody couldn't detain Kelly or prevent him from leaving Tennessee. There were no laws against buying a seat next to Kelly on the plane. If Kelly didn't cooperate, his two-hour flight to New York was going to be hell.

It was 4:10 p.m. and Brody was sitting in the terminal directly across from Kelly's. The heavy Friday KIA passenger traffic was helping him blend into the crowd. He glanced down at his phone when a group text came in from Roger addressed to Derek, Sheriff Lloyd, and himself.

Roger's text: *Update. Sheridan's still at MoMA. She told driver she's getting ready there, so not going back to hotel. 3 men undercover inside, 6 surrounding MoMA outside, and 2 more inside when ball starts.*

Sheriff Lloyd's text: *She's been in my sight all day. Rhonda's coming early tonight to bring Sheridan's dress and my tux, so I'm staying too.*

Derek's text: *I'm across the street from museum watching the entrance. I'll be there at 7:00.*

Brody's text: *No sign of Kelly. If he's a no-show, heading back to NY. His plane's starting to board, got to go.*

Brody's eyes were exposed from behind the *Knoxville Times* he was holding. He carefully watched each passenger board at the gate. When the last person stepped on the loading bridge and the doors closed, he knew Kelly wasn't going to show. Just as he got up to leave, he received another text from a familiar number.

He's going to kill her. Meet me, Starlet hotel Chinatown #215 at exactly 7:35 p.m. tonight. Come in the back entrance. Tell no one and come alone or she dies.

Brody hastily reached in the front pocket of his jeans and pulled out a receipt he'd written Kelly's information on. The number on the receipt and the number from the text was a match. Kelly had given him no choice but to go alone. He replied, *I'll be there.*

❦

CHARLES HAD TAKEN over Derek's watch across the street from the museum so he could go to the hotel and change. Derek was dressed and on his way back but stuck in traffic when a call came in from Charles. "Everything okay?"

Charles' tone was steady. "Something came up, Derek. I had to leave."

"Where are you going?"

"The entrance is covered. Riley had Roger send one of his guys across the street after I left." The call started breaking up. "My PI... here, have to go—"

"What about your PI? Dad?" The line went dead. "Damn it!" Derek slammed his palm into the steering wheel. He glanced at the time on his GPS. It was 7:24 p.m. and he was still twenty minutes from the museum. He knew Sheridan was heavily guarded, but that knowledge didn't prevent trepidation from settling in his chest. He called Sheriff Lloyd who answered on the fourth ring.

"Hello?"

"Is she okay?" Derek asked.

"Just fine."

"My dad's gone AWOL. I think it has something to do with his PI, but I'm not sure."

Rodney pulled the phone from Sheriff Lloyd's hand. "Derek? Is that you?"

"Uh, yeah."

"It's Rodney. Where the hell are you? Everyone you know has arrived, and I can't get Sheridan to finish getting ready for the reveal. She thinks she has to entertain everyone and said she's not budging until you get here."

"I'm twenty minutes away."

"Her reveal is at eight fifteen; she doesn't have twenty minutes. Here, maybe she'll listen to you." He shoved the phone in Sheridan's hands.

"Rodney, no—"

"Derek?" Sheridan called out.

Derek cleared his throat and tried to mask the worry in his voice. "Hey, yeah, it's me. I would've called you sooner, but Rodney's holding your phone hostage, so—"

"How'd you know Rodney had my phone?"

Derek attempted to make a joke of it, but his words came out bland. "I'm psychic. Remember?"

"It's okay if you can't make it, Derek. Really."

"You said you wouldn't see me until after you're unmasked tonight. It's been thirty-two hours, six minutes, and twenty-four seconds since I've kissed your provocative lips. If you don't finish getting ready, the reveal will be delayed, as will us being able to resume where we left off yesterday morning."

Derek sensed she was blushing and smiling. "You do make a good point, Mr. Young."

"So, you'll finish getting ready then?"

"I suppose I could let Rodney finish. I mean, I wouldn't want to be the person responsible for delaying anything."

Rodney jerked the phone from Sheridan's hand and gave it back to Sheriff Lloyd. "Yes, you could, missy. You're not the only one creating masterpieces around here you know," Rodney snipped.

Sheriff Lloyd shook his head as he watched Rodney take Sheridan by the hand and drag her away. "Anyway, we're all good here. Rhonda's standin' here next to me. Said she's lookin' forward to meetin' you."

"You can't talk, can you?"

"Don't reckon I can."

"I'm trying to get there as fast as I can. Keep an eye on her."

"Reckon we'll see ya shortly then."

An arcane but paramount energy began rushing Derek that felt neither good nor bad. He felt its presence building as he drew closer to the museum.

BRODY PULLED his gun from his shoulder holster as he climbed the stairs of the nearly desolate hotel. When he opened the second floor stairwell door, he became uneasy. He scanned the long shoddy hall painted tacky blue. With the exception of a baby crying in the distance, it was quiet. Just before he approached room 215, he caught an elderly Asian woman peeking at him through the crack of her door. Brody pulled his index finger to his mouth to hush her then gestured for her to close her door.

The door to Kelly's room was ajar. He gripped the handle of his Glock 23 with both hands and extended it out in front of him. He pushed the door open with the side of his boot then turned and entered the room. Upon entering, he saw the back of a brawny man kneeling on the floor over another man's dead body.

"Make one move and I'll put a bullet in the back of your head," Brody warned. With the gun still on his target, he walked up behind the suspect. "Slowly stand up and put your hands behind your back."

When the man complied, Brody freed one hand from the gun and cuffed him. Brody's eyes grew wide and his mouth fell open in disbelief when he turned the man around and saw his face. He was looking into the eyes of a ghost. "Un-Uncle Charles?"

Charles saw the uncertainty rising in his nephew's eyes. "Brody, listen to me." He looked at the lifeless man lying on the floor then back to Brody. "I know him, but I didn't do this. I was set up...again."

Brody was trying to rein in his composure. He didn't take his gun off Charles. "Who is he?"

"His name's Leo. He was my hired PI."

"For what?"

"His latest job was conducting surveillance on Agent Kelly, which is likely how he wound up here."

Brody walked around Charles, knelt to the floor to examine Leo's body, and then looked up at Charles. "Don't move," Brody warned then set his gun next to him. The man had been strangled. Brody turned Leo to his side and pulled up his shirt. A purplish red discoloration stained the length of his side. "Livor mortis. He's been dead for more than twelve hours." He picked up his gun and stood but didn't point it at Charles this time.

"Why would I still be here if I killed him?"

"You wouldn't, and I don't think you did. I'm struggling with how it's possible you're standing here in front of me at all."

"I'm standing here because Leo texted me and asked me to meet him here at seven-thirty. Said he found important information on Kelly. My phone's in my back pocket. Take a look for yourself."

Brody took the phone from Charles' pocket and read the text then looked up at Charles. "I got a text too, but mine was from Kelly. Leo must've followed Kelly here. Kelly killed him then used his phone to trick you into coming. Kelly set us both up. That son of a bitch timed it so I'd find you here."

They both paused when they heard sirens in the distance coming towards them. Brody placed his gun back in his holster, then started uncuffing Charles.

"The doll, did you get it from Baker's?" Charles asked.

Brody was unlocking the first cuff and paused. "How'd you know I was supposed to go to Baker's?" Charles didn't say a word. He didn't have to. His silence told Brody what he needed to know. "Your son's an asshole," he said then finished unlocking the second cuff. "We have to get you out of here. You can catch me up on the way to Baker's."

Chapter Thirty-Nine

The tires of the Escalade squealed when Derek sped into valet parking and slammed on the brakes. He grabbed his tux jacket, bolted out the driver's side door, and rushed into the museum.

His patience was now being tested by a pretentious elderly doorman standing at the hostess podium outside the Grand Ballroom's entrance.

"Name?"

"Derek Young."

The man turned several pages of the guest list until he got to the last names starting with Y. He leisurely scrolled down each name with his arthritic fingers. "Derek Young, correct?"

Derek looked down at his watch. It was seven-fifty. His jaw clenched. "Yes."

"My apologies Mr. Young, but your name doesn't appear to be on the list."

"I don't have time for this." He took a determined step toward the man but stopped when he heard Quentin call his name.

Quentin approached the podium. "He's on the VIP list."

The man flipped back to the first page. "Ah, yes, here you are, Mr.

Young. The last course of this evening's meal is being served. Panna cotta drizzled in raspberry sauce. You're assigned seating is table one. Enjoy your evening, gentlemen," he called out to both men's backs as they walked away from him.

Derek walked to the second floor's balcony and looked over the engraved mahogany railing. He scanned the lively room beneath him filled with three hundred plus dining guests. The orchestra was playing at the far end of the ballroom and several couples had already taken to the dance floor. The opposite side of the room was staged for the silent auction, guest speakers, and raffles. In the center of the ballroom was a white circular stage. Six Roman columns held Sheridan's angel collection, which were veiled beneath six silk shawl scarves. The columns were sized and arranged on stage to create a star shape.

Derek spotted Lexus, Anderson, Thomas, Vanessa, Sarah, and Ian mingling at the table, but Sheridan was nowhere in sight. "Where is she?"

Quentin heard the panic in Derek's tone. "She's fine. Riley and Sheriff Lloyd filled your aunt and me in on what's going on. They knew you'd be worried, so they sent me to find you before you joined everyone."

"Where is she?" he asked again.

"With Rodney and Rhonda getting ready for the reveal. Sheriff Lloyd's outside her door, and Roger has three of his guys positioned on her floor."

He continued scanning the ballroom. "Where are Riley and Sheridan's aunt?"

Quentin looked down at his watch and then back to Derek. "The aunt's not here yet, and Riley's downstairs. He's announcing Sheridan's reveal in twenty minutes." Quentin cupped Derek's shoulder and spoke in a low relaxed tone. "You need to pull yourself together, Derek. If Edward's son is here, he's going to know something's off if he sees how unsettled you are. Everyone will. The best way to catch him is to let him think no one's on to him."

Quentin followed Derek down the grand staircase. Derek's eyes locked in on Lexus. She was laughing and socializing with everyone, but Derek knew it was an act. She was masking her nerves, and he knew he needed to do the same. Derek paused halfway down the staircase when a text came through from Charles. *Brody knows I'm alive. Don't ask, long story, he's fine. We just got to Baker's. Place is a hell hole. Found out Edward passed away a couple days ago from natural causes. Trying to get access to his room to search for doll. Brody's flirting with nurse to get more info. Check in after we get access to Edward's room.*

"Everything okay?" Quentin asked.

"Brody knows my dad's alive," he said in a placid tone. "They're at Baker's trying to find the doll."

Quentin's eyes turned concerned. "How?"

"Brody's fine," he assured. Derek composed himself and began walking back down the stairs. He forged a smile and spoke beneath his breath. "If Sheridan's not out in twenty, all bets are off."

EVERYONE STOOD to greet Quentin and Derek as they approached. Ian's flame red hair immediately caught Derek's attention. Derek shook Ian's hand, wrapped his left arm around Ian's shoulder, and patted his back twice. "I can't believe you're here. How—?"

"Tonight's exquisite guest of honor."

"Watch it, Romeo, she's taken."

Ian laughed. "Yes. I've been informed of this unfortunate news, you lucky bastard. So, Derek Young in love. Who would've thought?"

"I couldn't believe it either," Sarah said as she walked around Ian and hugged Derek. "It's been too long."

"It has," Derek agreed, then stood back and observed her attire. "You look stunning, Sarah."

"Some things never change I see. Always the charmer."

"Vanessa tells me you're here to work with Ashley?"

"I am. I met her and the kids yesterday. They're incredible. If I were you, I'd keep my eye on that Rebecca. I mean her gifts are seriously off the charts."

"It's been years since the five of us have been together in the same room," Vanessa said as she poured herself a glass of 1998 Dom

Pérignon, raised her glass, and gestured for everyone to raise their own for a toast. "To Sheridan Hayes, for making tonight possible."

"Here, here," Ian agreed then joined everyone in tapping one another's champagne glasses.

"How are you feeling?" Derek asked Lexus.

"Much better," Lexus lied and took her seat with the others.

"She should be at home in bed," Quentin scolded then kissed his wife on her forehead.

"I'm glad you two made it tonight. I know you've both been overextended at Vista lately. I can't stress how much I appreciate the time you've both invested in Vista's reopening," Derek said.

Thomas smiled. "Just paying it forward."

Derek noticed several empty chairs around the table. "Looks like we're missing a few people. Blake not coming?"

Vanessa answered. "He's at home with the kids, also sick," she got out just as Anderson sneezed. "Bless you."

Anderson sneezed a second time, then spoke. "Lucky me. Looks like I'm the newest recipient of the Vista cold."

Lexus fumbled through her purse to find Anderson a tissue. Anderson raised his palm to stop her efforts. "No worries, dear," he said, then slid his chair back from the table and stood. "If you'll excuse me, I'm off to find the one home remedy I know will stop any ailment dead in its tracks."

Thomas chuckled when Anderson walked away from the table. "Home remedy, my ass. He's on the hunt for whiskey."

"Good for him," Derek offered.

"Exactly," Vanessa agreed. "How that man manages to donate his time to so many organizations and still do what he's done at Vista is beyond me."

Everyone turned their attention to Lexus when she rose from her chair in awe. With bated breath, Lexus offered an uneasy, yet warm smile to an old friend approaching their table. "Maggie? I-I can't believe you're here."

"Lexus, is that you? Sheridan told me Derek's aunt was attending tonight, but I had no idea it was you. My God, it's been nineteen years," she said, then embraced Lexus with an elated hug.

Derek caught Lexus' blended emotions the minute she'd laid eyes on Maggie. He sensed their connection wasn't a coincidence. He extended his hand out to Maggie. "I'm Derek. It's nice to finally meet you," he said, struggling to stay composed.

Maggie accepted Derek's hand. "It's so nice to meet you too," she said then pulled away to get a better look at him. "Well, I can certainly see how you've captured my niece's attention. Of course, the women in our family have impeccable taste in men. My James was quite handsome himself."

Derek smiled then looked over at Lexus and back to Maggie. "So, how is it you two know each other?" Lexus' eyes rounded with alarm.

"At Norwalk Cancer Center. My late husband James and Lexus' friend, Olivia, had chemo there together. The circumstances in which we met were unfortunate, but for three years, we helped keep each other positive over several hundred cups of stale cafeteria coffee. Unfortunately, when James passed in '94, we lost touch."

Derek realized Lexus' friend "Olivia" was his mother. Lexus wasn't aware Sheriff Lloyd had made Derek privy to the fact his mom had cancer and the lengths she'd gone through to hide it. He saw the color draining from Lexus' cheeks.

"My aunt's nothing shy of a saint." He turned his attention to Lexus. "Your friend was blessed to have you in her life supporting and protecting her during such a difficult time. In fact, we're all blessed to have you in our lives." He raised his glass to make another toast in Lexus' honor.

Derek's telling words were comforting to Lexus. The softening glow of her eyes told him she understood he already knew about Meredith's cancer, what part she'd played in her care, and his gratitude for her loyalty. When Lexus released the breath she'd been holding, she began introducing everyone to Maggie but was interrupted by Rhonda and Rodney when they approached the table.

Maggie was puzzled by the miffed expression on Rodney's face. "Everything okay?"

Rhonda laughed. "Yes, everything's fine. Rodney's pouting because Sheridan kicked him out of her dressing room."

"I've been involved in every last element of this reveal and held her hand through every tedious step. I mean, seriously, not letting me walk her to the base—"

"It's because of the tireless hours you've put in that she asked you to leave, sweetie. She wants you to relax and enjoy the reveal along with everyone else," Rhonda said.

"Fine. You're right. I'm being petty."

Maggie directed the conversation back to introductions, "Rhonda, this is Derek, Sheridan's Derek."

Rhonda extended her hand to him. "It's a pleasure to meet the man responsible for the smile on my daughter's face these days."

Derek was thrown off by Rhonda's calm beauty. His visions of her had divulged a woman who'd lived a tragic life. The woman before him was radiant, kind, and warm. He had an earnest sense of respect for her strength and perseverance. "The pleasure is all mine, Ms. Hayes, and I can assure you, Sheridan is not the only one smiling these days."

"Please, call me Rhonda," she insisted then paused as she looked around the busy room before speaking again. "I'd like to have lunch with you and Sheridan before I fly out on Sunday."

"Of course."

"William, Frank, I mean, Sheriff Lloyd, will likely be joining us too," Rhonda stumbled then laughed. "He's barely let Sheridan out of his sight since we got back from dinner last night. Suppose he's just trying to spend as much time with her as he can before we head back."

"That makes sense," Derek said.

Everyone's attention turned to Riley's voice being amplified over several loudspeakers throughout the room. Derek's heart thumped hard within his chest, and his anxious eyes scanned the room for anything or anyone remotely out of place.

"LADIES AND GENTLEMEN, art collectors established and new, welcome to MoMA's tenth annual Unmasked Charity Ball," Riley announced. The room exploded with applause.

"For nine consecutive years, MoMA has taken great pride in exposing talented emerging artists to art connoisseurs around the world. This year is no exception." Riley reached into the inner pocket of his tuxedo jacket and pulled out an envelope. "The proceeds from tonight's auction will be evenly distributed between the American Cancer Society, the Breast Cancer Research Foundation, and St. Jude Cancer Center.

"By special request of our guest of honor, all donations will be given in honor and loving memory of her late uncle, James Wesley Thurston III, who lost his battle with cancer nineteen years ago. Many of us knew James as one of the most prestigious art brokers in the business, and some of us knew him for his selfless generosity to worthy causes here and abroad. You could say he was not only a master in art but also in the art of giving."

Riley looked over to Rodney and Maggie. "Tonight, we're graced with the presence of James' widow, Maggie Thurston, and their son, Rodney." He gestured for them to stand. Riley pulled a check from the envelope. "It is with great honor I present the first seventy-five thousand dollar donation on behalf of MoMA, and do so in James' name." Everyone gave the pair a standing ovation. Rodney took his mother's hand and placed it in his. Rodney's eyes were laced with gratitude, while Maggie allowed a single tear to fall in her late husband's praise.

When the roar of the room settled, everyone took their seats, and Riley continued. "I've offered a slight hint as to who our emerging artist of the year is, but don't be mistaken, it's her unprecedented work that will divulge all of who she is and what she offers as a boundless artist."

Lighting from each of the six chandeliers in the ballroom began dimming. Hundreds of candles left burning cast a soft radiating light. Shadows of fog began rolling across the floor of the circular stage in the center of the room. Music by RyanDan played. "Her transcendent eighteenth century style infused in today's modern world arouses a poetic reawakening of the human spirit. You will be inspired, touched, and moved beyond the realms of your own conscious mind. I present to you, 'Tears of an Angel.'"

The stage Riley occupied went dark, and the center stage's lights grew brighter, exposing six veiled paintings arranged in a star-like semblance on Roman columns.

❧

SHERIDAN TRIED REMAINING STILL as Mrs. Hershkowitz fussed over the airy train of her flowing white chiffon, floor-length gown. Sheriff Lloyd had stayed with Sheridan until she was lifted up to the ballroom's center stage for her reveal. Mrs. Hershkowitz was tugging at Sheridan's draped shoulder streamers and adjusting her feathered mask.

"Reckon my daughter looks just about perfect if you ask me," Sheriff Lloyd said.

Mrs. Hershkowitz took a step back to get a better look at Sheridan "Perfection is an understatement, Mr. Lloyd. One last thing, though." She freed the large clip from Sheridan's hair holding up a mass of thick curly locks, allowing them to spill freely over her delicate and partially exposed shoulders. "There, now. You look as beautiful as the angels you paint, my dear."

Sheriff Lloyd's lips formed a polite smile. "If you don't mind, I'd like a minute alone with my daughter."

Mrs. Hershkowitz looked down at her watch. Her tone turned peevish. "While I respect your request, Mr. Lloyd, I must decline. The music has started, and Sheridan is being revealed in less than three minutes."

"I know my cues, Mrs. Hershkowitz. We'll be fine," Sheridan assured with a warm smile.

Mrs. Hershkowitz looked down at her own gown, smoothed it out nervously, and then looked back up at Sheridan. "As you wish, Ms. Hayes," she surrendered then left them alone.

Sheriff Lloyd saw a hint of relief settle in Sheridan's eyes. "She's right, you know. You look like an angel."

Embarrassed by her father's compliment, Sheridan looked down to the floor. "Thank you."

There was an awkward silence between them. Sheriff Lloyd spoke first. "I know we ain't got much time, so I'll just get to it. Reckon I've never been a man of many words where matters of the heart are concerned. I know I wasn't there for ya when you was a youngin', Sheridan, but I'm here for ya now. For your mamma, too."

Before Sheridan could respond, she heard Riley's voice boom over the loudspeakers. "Ladies and gentlemen...."

"That's my cue. I-it's time."

Sheriff Lloyd smiled to try and calm her. "Reckon we ought to get ya up there then." He took her hand and helped her up onto the platform.

"Wish me luck."

"You're gonna be fine, darlin'." His eyes followed her as she began rising toward the ballroom's center stage. A breath caught in her throat when she heard an abrupt thump hit the basement floor beneath her. She fell to her knees to see if she could see Sheriff Lloyd through one of the small gaps surrounding the still-rising platform but to no avail. "Sheriff Lloyd? Are you there? Sheriff Lloyd?" Her heart began racing when he didn't respond. Desperate, she called out to him again. "Dad?"

She heard a man's muffled voice below. She rose back to her feet and permitted a slight sigh of relief to escape her lips. She knew she needed to calm herself, so she closed her eyes to steady her thoughts. She drew in a deep breath then exhaled. She pulled her necklace from beneath her gown and rubbed the amethyst stone. *This is it. It's almost over. Find Derek. Focus on him,* she thought as the stage lift continued rising toward the floor above her.

MUSIC from the unearthly song grew louder. The alluring, dark lyrics rushed Derek's core. The stage twirled like a merry-go-round dancing to the graceful rhythm of an intimate waltz. The elegant scarves masking the six paintings began rising. Derek's eyes were drawn to the familiar angel portrait in the center. It was of his mother and five small infants, four of which were protectively embraced within her heavenly wings, one lying just outside her reach.

Derek had envisioned the nebulous painting a thousand times within his fragmentary dreams as a child and adult. The visual epitomized his mother's purpose in life as one of The Knowing, which was to protect and help guide God's gifted children. The revelation of Sheridan being the artist responsible for capturing and painting his mother's life's purpose should've been shocking, but instead, he felt moved by her flawless and compelling interpretation. Derek's perplexed eyes moved up to the prodigious angel painting towering the others. It was of Rose. She wore the wings of a magnificent guardian angel. Her wings spanned the length of the canvas, her eyes watchful over the other five portraits.

The shock Derek escaped caught up with him as his eyes scanned the remaining four portraits completing the star arrangement. Each of the portraits embodied a different virtuous angel crying while embracing their babies, one of which was coddling twins. Derek recognized the angels as the four victims from the Midtown Butcher cold cases he and Brody were investigating. Derek's thoughts spun as he tried piecing together the connections between Rose, his mother, the victims, and their babies. It was Lexus' hand gripping at his forearm and her shaky low voice whispering his name that pulled his attention from the enigma before him.

Lexus leaned in close to Derek's ear. "D-Derek," It-It's them," she stuttered in a raspy tone.

"Them?"

Lexus glanced over her right shoulder and then back to Derek. "I'm not sure about one of the babies in Sheridan's painting of your mother and the children, but the other four babies in the others are of Vanessa, Sarah, Ian, and Thomas. I'm certain of it."

Before Derek could respond, he felt Vanessa staring at him. Ian, Sarah, and Thomas sat numb and uncertain as they studied the paintings, each questioning whether their eyes were deceiving them. Derek's lips parted to speak but closed when he heard Riley's voice again.

Thick clouds of fog began rolling upon the stage. "Ladies and gentlemen...."

The anticipation of knowing he was only seconds away from seeing Sheridan made Derek's heart thrash hard within his chest. There was nothing anyone could do or say in that moment to pull his eyes or attention from the stage.

MUSIC PLAYED in the distance as Riley addressed the audience. "It is my great honor and privilege to present to you MoMA's 2013 emerging artist of the year, Sheridan Parker Hayes."

The music grew louder as Sheridan ascended to center stage. A thunderous explosion of applause filled the room, and the audience rose to their feet. The unveiling of Sheridan's name was her cue to remove her mask, but she couldn't move. She stood before the crowd petrified and battling the unrelenting urge within her to collapse. Sheridan's eyes followed the faces of the calming crowd. Her eyes found Derek's. His presence inspired her to find the fortitude she needed to remain grounded and focused on the task at hand.

The crowd remained standing as Sheridan slid the mask from her face. Her unveiling encouraged another roaring outburst of applause from the audience. A forced confidence contoured Sheridan's face. Her determination to see the reveal through to the end became evanescent when a blinding luminous light enveloped her. An obscure howling breeze crept into the hall, extinguishing the vast display of candles providing supplementary light.

Sheridan became still, and the mask she'd been holding glided from her hand into the thick clouds of cascading fog rolling on the floor. Sheridan's eyes pulled away from Derek's stare and rolled to the back of her mind as though they had become possessed. Her hair and gown began flowing from the enigmatic breeze that found Sheridan, now making its home where she stood in a trancelike state. Sheridan's head fell back, and her body became limp as an unforgiving wind spiraled around her and lifted her from the floor. Incoherent murmurs from the oblivious audience distended the room as Sheridan levitated and began spinning languidly within the air.

Rodney's eyes grew wide. "What the hell?"

"What do you mean, what the hell?"

Before Rodney could answer, Derek heard Sheridan begin faintly chanting, "*Allumer la lumièire. Je vais les protéger.*"

Derek shot up from his chair ready to rush the stage and pull her from what he now knew was Sheridan accepting the ignited light of The Knowing within her. As Derek took a bold step forward to get to Sheridan, the illuminating light holding her hostage released her. The room became immersed in darkness. Derek began feeling his way through the obscure room, screaming Sheridan's name over the naive crowd's boisterous cheering.

Derek was only a few feet away from where Sheridan had been levitating when the chandeliers filled the hall with soft radiating light again. Derek panicked when he saw that Sheridan was no longer on stage. He ran to the hydraulic stage lift. It had been lowered back down to the basement, and there was no trace of Sheridan. It was as though Sheridan had vanished into thin air. His eyes fixated on a man sprawled out on the basement's floor. A high-pitched distortion blared from the speaker resting on the silent auction stage when Mrs. Hershkowitz spoke, pulling the audience's attention from center stage over to where she stood.

"Ladies and gentlemen," she began as steady as she could manage, trying to keep the audience engaged and unaware of what had just transpired.

"Where the hell's Riley?" Derek seethed beneath his breath as he sprinted toward the basement.

Chapter Forty

Both Brody and Charles thought Frances, the head night shift nurse, was a mental patient at Baker's based on her appearance and hygiene. She wore a classic white 1950s nursing uniform. Her greasy gray hair was formed into a disheveled bun tucked beneath a starched nurse's cap. Her sheer white pantyhose revealed veiny legs through the two slight runs traveling down to the base of her white classic nursing shoes. To both their surprise, her credentials were neatly pinned and exposed on a dried blood-stained pinafore apron she wore over her dress.

When they'd first approached Frances, she came off guarded and defensive when Brody showed her his badge, leading Brody to believe she had something to hide. Brody's gut told him she wasn't particularly fond of the patients she cared for. He lied about their reason for being there and fabricated a clumsy story to put her at ease, so she'd talk openly. Brody informed her they were investigating a murder-for-hire crime that occurred twenty-six years earlier, and Edward Chancellor was the prime suspect.

Brody played her like a violin. Her satisfied eyes were more than telling, they were chilling. She began rambling on about how she and others at Baker's had always suspected he'd hired someone to kill his wife and then got caught in the crossfire and how Edward deserved every isolated day he was forced to spend at Baker's behind locked doors. Charles was disgusted by Frances' matter-of-fact tone and was struggling to find the strength to stay on script. Knowing losing his cool would prevent them from getting to the doll, he played his part.

Brody found flirting with the unkempt nurse nauseating, yet his charismatic charm had worked its magic. Frances had not only retrieved Edward Chancellor's mental records for them but also offered to escort them to the room Edward had occupied for twenty-six years prior to his recent passing.

Unbeknownst to Brody, Charles was struggling with more than the mission at hand. As they walked down the corridor to Edward's room, the sounds of episodic screams coming from one of the patients peeking out the small glass pane brought Charles back to the most harrowing time in Meredith's life. He knew her first and last visit to see Edward at Baker's had been the inception of her demise, so he detested being there.

"We'll have to keep quiet in Ed's old room. Trust me, you don't want to wake up the newest resident in there. She's a wild one," Frances advised as she placed the key in the door and unlocked it.

They hadn't been informed that someone had already been moved into Edward's old room, so Charles threw Brody a troubled look. Remembering Walt had last left the doll underneath Edward's bed, Brody immediately understood their dilemma. They hoped the doll hadn't been moved, but keeping Frances' attention from the doll if they found it would prove to be challenging with a patient occupying the bed.

Brody pushed down the relentless queasiness rising in his stomach before he softly stroked Frances' leathery hand to stop her from opening the door. "How about you and me grabbing a cup of coffee at the nurse's station?" He glanced down at Edward's mental records in her hands. "I'd love to pick your brain about Edward," he managed and then gave her a sly suggestive wink.

Frances' thin eyelids fluttered at Brody's suggestion. "Of course. Anything I can do to help, Agent Young." She then addressed Charles. "The patient's sedated, so you'll be fine." Brody shot Charles a swift eye-roll letting him know he wasn't happy to be taking one for the team and then led her from the room.

☙

THE OVERPOWERING HEAVINESS within the dark room inspired Charles to leave the door cracked open behind him. Scattered streaks of moonlight crept in from the meager barred window on the far side of the room, providing little light for him to find his way to the bed.

When his eyes adjusted to the room's natural light, he was able to make out a shadowy silhouette of a petite figure lying within the bed. He felt his way to the bed's frame then searched beneath the bed to feel for the doll. "Got it," he said in a muffled tone when he felt the doll. Just as he began pulling the doll toward him, the woman began speaking in a soft intoxicated tone.

"Don't leave me. Please, I'm sorry. I'm so sorry."

Charles remained still as the woman continued calling out to what he surmised was a loved one haunting her dreams, something he was all too familiar with. Within each vivid dream of his wife, he too had called out to Meredith and pleaded a million times for her to return to him.

Damn it. Focus, he thought then finished easing the doll back toward him again. Charles allowed the uneasy breath he'd been holding to escape and turned to leave.

He heard the woman whisper, "Please, help me." Charles knew he should keep moving toward the door, but his conscience wouldn't allow it. He wasn't sure if she was still dreaming, so he pulled a lighter from his pocket and ignited it above her. When their eyes met, she was shivering and frightened. Portions of her face were bruised and her bottom lip sliced.

"Please, h-help me," she whispered again.

Charles moved the flickering light over the rest of her body and saw that both her ligature marked wrists were strapped to one side of the bed. Just as Charles reached down to free the first wrist, the woman caught a glimpse of the doll and began screaming, "No! She's mine. Give her to me. She's mine! I'm sorry! Please! She's mine!"

"It's okay. You're okay," he said soothing, attempting to calm her. "I'll help you, but you have to quit screaming."

The woman's reckless eyes remained focused on the doll. Her body began thrashing within the confinement of the bed, trying to break free. Her piercing screams echoed through the halls, triggering other mental patients to follow her lead. Charles saw her eyes locked in on the doll, so he took a chance and placed it next to her to hush her screams. To his surprise, it worked. She was no longer screaming, merely weeping and tenderly speaking to the doll. "I'm sorry, please don't leave me."

He bent down to her level and removed one of the leather straps from the bed frame. "Listen to me. I'm going to remove this one too, but you can't make a sound. Just let me help—" he got out before Brody and Frances rushed into the room.

"What in the hell is going on in here?" Frances demanded as she turned on the lights.

The frail woman's eyes grew wide with fear when she saw Frances coming toward her with a needle. Her eyes began fluttering upon initial injection. When Charles realized Frances was trying to sedate the woman, he grabbed the needle from her hand before the full dose was given. "What did you do to her?" he roared.

Frances was taken aback by Charles' thunderous tone and scowl. "I- I was trying to calm her down."

"And the bruises on her face, her wrists? Were you trying to calm her down then too?" he accused through clenched teeth. Charles unbuckled the remaining leather strap from the bed frame. Brody walked around him to better examine the woman's injuries. When he brushed several strands of hair away from her face to get a better look, he was stunned.

"What is it?" Charles asked.

"What the fuck? It can't be. Jesus, Charles, I know this woman. And the doll—" Brody tore Edward's file from Frances' hand. When he found what he was looking for, Brody shot Charles a panicked look. "We have to call Derek."

"Who is she?"

Brody dismissed Charles' question. "Now!" Brody demanded as he scooped the woman and doll up within his arms and bolted out of the room with Charles fast on his heels.

🐌

DEREK STORMED the basement's staircase, taking three steps at a time. When he rounded the corner, he saw Sheriff Lloyd unconscious on the floor. His eyes searched the room for Sheridan but to no avail. He knelt to the floor to check on Sheriff Lloyd, who was coming to.

"S-Sheridan," Sheriff Lloyd muttered.

"Where is she? Where's Sheridan?"

Sheriff Lloyd tried pulling himself up off the floor. "We have to find her."

"Tell me what happened?"

"I-I saw Sheridan rising up to the stage, and then," he paused, closed his eyes, trying to remember. "I-I felt something crack over my head. There was a blinding light."

"So you didn't see her come back down the stage lift?"

"No."

Derek turned his head to the door when he heard several footsteps coming down the basement stairs. Rhonda was the first to enter the room. "William," she cried out when she saw Sheriff Lloyd. "What happened? Where's Sheridan?"

"I don't know, Rhonda, but I'm going to find her," Derek said.

Quentin and Vanessa entered the room with uneasy eyes. "The paintings, Derek. How did Sheridan know? And the women in the paintings, are they our—" she managed, before Derek interrupted her, trying to prevent her from saying too much in front of Rhonda.

"Vanessa, you deserve answers," then addressed everyone in the room. "As do all of you, but we don't have time to sort this out right now. Sheridan's in danger."

"In danger? I don't understand. Somebody, please, tell me what's going on. Where's my baby?" Rhonda cried out.

Sheriff Lloyd managed to pull himself up off the floor. He took Rhonda's frightened face into his hands. "Rhonda, look at me. Do you trust me?"

"Yes, but—"

"I'm going to find our daughter, darlin', but I need you to stay calm." She took in a deep breath and nodded.

Derek addressed Quentin. "Where's everyone else?"

"Still in the main hall," he replied then looked up the basement's trap door. "Everyone thought what happened up there was just part of the reveal's theatrics. I'm not going to lie. I did too until I saw you run."

A tall, bald, brawny man wearing an earpiece entered the basement. "So did we," Roger said in an authoritative tone, then walked over to Derek and extended his hand. "We haven't been formally introduced. I'm Roger."

Derek pulled his fist back and slammed it into Roger's jaw, making him stumble back into the wall. "You son of a bitch. You lost her," Derek accused then started walking toward Roger again to take another swing.

Quentin intercepted. "Derek, stop! You can't do this right now. You know that. We have to focus."

Derek stopped in his tracks. "You're right."

Roger rubbed his jaw between his thumb and index finger then explained, "I had two men placed outside that door, one man outside the basement's emergency exit, and Sheriff Lloyd was in here with Sheridan before she went up. My men were instructed to go up to the main hall and stand guard with the others already positioned throughout the room.

"The program indicated Sheridan was supposed to remain in the main hall after her reveal, not go back down on the stage lift. That's why I'd put more coverage up there. We weren't informed there'd be a thirty-second black out either. If I'd known, I would've had men positioned closer to the stage."

Derek knew no one had anticipated what transpired during Sheridan's reveal. He felt a twinge of guilt rise to his chest for thinking Roger or his men should've known. "I shouldn't have taken my frustrations out on you. I'm sorry."

"I'm fine," Roger offered.

Derek addressed Quentin. "I need you to get everybody from our group together to help search for Sheridan. Have everybody meet in the main lobby so we can divide and conquer every last inch of this building. Every room, every closet, every corner of it," Derek instructed.

"I'll have my men set up parameters around all entrances and exits," Roger advised then stepped out of the room to radio his men.

Everyone began heading back upstairs when Derek saw a call coming in from Brody. He was reluctant to answer but hoped Brody and his dad had something to offer that might help him find Sheridan.

"Brody?"

"We have...doll. Found...at Baker's."

"Brody? You're breaking up. I can't make out what you're saying."

"...doll at Baker's. We found...know who...killer is." The call dropped.

Derek guessed the concrete walls were responsible for hindering his cell from getting a good signal, so he bolted from the basement's emergency exit and flew up the steps leading out to the busy streets of Manhattan. When he reached the last step, he saw a text come through from Brody.

Derek's eyes became wild with every sickening word he read in Brody's text. "No! It can't be!" he begged in a raw rugged scream. "I'll fucking kill you," he seethed savagely between his teeth as relentless adrenaline rushed his scorching veins.

"Mr. Young? Are you okay?" a man asked from the half-cracked driver's side window of the running SUV. "Roger sent me to guard this emergency exit."

Without pause, Derek opened the driver's side door, jerked the man out, threw him onto the ground, then vaulted up into the SUV and sped off to meet Brody and Charles.

Chapter Forty-One

Brody dimmed his lights just before turning down the long winding driveway. The path was engulfed by a thicket of lush woods leading to a three-story mansion. He slowed his vehicle then stopped when Charles spotted an SUV parked behind a cluster of brushy oaks.

Charles got out and walked over to the passenger side window. He found the SUV empty but saw Derek's tux jacket in the passenger seat. Just as he started walking back toward the Escalade, he heard Brody trying to calm the woman they'd saved from Baker's.

"Shit, stop her," Brody yelled when the woman broke free from the backseat and bolted into the woods.

"Go, Derek's here. I'll find her," Charles ordered.

Brody proceeded toward the house, fearing for Sheridan's and his cousin's lives.

SHERIDAN'S heavy lids fluttered as she came to. Her drug-induced vision was blurred, making it difficult to distinguish her surroundings.

Her groggy eyes followed the damp, partitioned brick walls of what appeared to be a renovated wine cellar. She became entranced with paralyzed fear, breaths panicked and labored, understanding now she was no longer at MoMA. Sickening reality struck her core when she saw her wrists were bound, each wrapped in duct tape around the arms of a vintage fauteuil chair. She searched for something she could use to cut herself free.

My necklace, she thought, then tried manipulating the necklace between her tongue and teeth to pull the rugged amethyst up to her mouth. When it became stable, she clenched down hard, cutting at the tape. "Ahh," she cried out, slicing her forearm in her hasty attempts to break free.

"Yes," she panted beneath her breath, as the last of the tape tore away. She freed her left wrist, sprung up from the chair, and darted to the cumbersome steel door holding her hostage. "No!" she bellowed, seeing an electric keypad next to the knob-less door and knowing it wouldn't open without a code. She pounded her fists against the cold steel. "Please, somebody, help me. My name is Sheridan Parker Hayes. Please, let me out!"

A glaring white light bouncing off the back wall within the second section of the cellar caught her off guard. "H-Hello? Is anyone there?" she called out when she heard what sounded like a woman's voice coming from the same direction. She crept over to the jagged partition and peeked around it. She discovered the flickering light and voice were being projected from a flat-screen television resting upon the middle cupboard of an antique bookshelf. Masses of video tapes labeled with Vista kids' names lined the remaining shelves. She read the names familiar to her. *Derek, Ian, Vanessa, Sarah, Thomas.*

Sheridan's eyes lifted to the screen, drawn to the familiar woman's face lying on a couch, eyes closed, and speaking to a man asking her questions just outside the video camera's focus.

'Who is your mother's killer, Meredith?'

'I-I don't know. He's faceless. There will be more victims if Derek doesn't find her.'

'Find who, Meredith?'

'Sheridan. She'll reveal the monster's identity and guide the little girl. Millions will be saved. All will be revealed.'

'How will she accomplish such a big task?'

'Derek's love will guide her, open her mind to the unknown. The light within her will ignite.'

'Your son, Derek?'

'Yes, my son.'

'Where is Sheridan now, Meredith?'

'I-I don't know. The cancer prevents me from seeing all. The journals. The journals will help me find her.'

'Tell me about the journals, Meredith.'

'They're hidden. They help organize my visions. I'll save her.'

'Where do you hide them, Meredith?'

'My office safe.'

'Does anyone know about them?'

'No one except Charles. He won't read them.'

'Tell me, Meredith. Why won't he read them?'

'The natural order and destined paths of those gifted could change, lives would be lost.'

'Can you tell me the code to your safe, Meredith?'

'I-I can't.'

'I've helped you overcome the tragedy that fell upon your parents since the beginning, Meredith. I've been here for you. Always. You can trust me.'

'Five, three, one, three.'

'That's a good girl, Meredith. That's really good. When I count back to one, you'll open your eyes. You'll remember nothing we've discussed today or any of our previous sessions. Do you understand, Meredith?'

'Yes, I understand.'

'Three, two, one.'

§

SHERIDAN GENTLY PLACED her right hand on the screen as the image of Meredith faded into static snow. Tears stained her face, understanding now it had been Derek's mother who'd saved her life. Her shaking hands covered her face. "I'm so sorry, Derek. My God, I'm so sorry," she sobbed.

She turned from the bookshelf, determined to find another way out. A crystalline shadow box displayed on a pedestal in the middle of the room caught her attention. Exposed within it was a gold dagger and dried rose sitting on a worn leather journal. She studied the chipped amethyst placed within the hilt of the dagger then pulled the amethyst up from her chain again. "Find the dagger, reveal the monster," she whispered beneath her breath. Her fingertips traced the outline of the beautiful dagger. *The light. I accepted the light. I remember.*

A luminous lavender glow filled the room as trenchant and chaotic visions began rushing her. Her eyes swayed beneath her lids as merciless pictures from the past and foretelling future exposed themselves to her. Her eyes flew open as the last telling vision broke, falling back into the light within her. "I am The Knowing."

"You're nothing," a voice hissed from behind her. Sheridan jumped and turned toward the voice of the masked man. "You continue to present as the same pathetic little girl I encountered all those years ago," he affronted, then stepped out from the shadows.

"I-I'm not pathetic," she shot back.

"Oh, but you are. Do you really think your new shiny gift means anything to me? Let me ask you this, Sheridan, how well did this gift work out for your savior, Meredith, or my pathetic sister, Rose? And we mustn't forget my covetous father, gifted with a third eye, who started it all. Each one of them was blessed with gifts, yet I'm the last man standing and possess more knowledge than all of you combined."

Sheridan glanced over his shoulder and saw a silhouette of the steel door he'd left open. Her mind scrambled to find a way to buy herself time.

"You know nothing," she challenged.

"Oh, but I do Sheridan, and I didn't even need to inherit ol' daddy boy's gift to gain third eye knowledge. Of course, if it hadn't been for my sister trying to save my soul, I would have never known my father tossed me away like mere garbage because he saw that I'd be evil. In hindsight, he was right. But that's neither here nor there."

"Your father made a horrible mistake. God knows you made him suffer, but your mother was innocent in all of this. She didn't know he left you on those steps, and you slaughtered her. Why?"

His tone became frigid. "So, you're familiar with my mommy and daddy, are you? Both narcissistic simpletons, I might add. But, you couldn't be more correct, Sheridan. That bitch didn't know anything, not even her own son," he seethed between clenched teeth. "My delinquent mother wasn't there to save me from the years of unimaginable torture I suffered. And then, fourteen years later, mommy and daddy walk back into Providence and adopt a sparkly child who possessed the light.

"I saw them walking out of hell's doors and into their new life with Meredith. Do you know, my mother walked past me, looked into my beaten eyes, smiled, and never looked back?"

"She didn't know it was you."

"I was her blood son! She should have fucking known!" he shouted, regretting he'd lost control. He balanced his breathing, smoothed the front of his tuxedo jacket, and tilted his neck to the right and cracked it, his tone now composed.

"You punished your parents for neglecting you, but you also raped numerous women, four of whom you murdered. They did nothing. Why did they deserve to be punished?" she shot back.

"Because, that's exactly what Rose, Meredith, and my father predicted I would do, and it was precisely why I allowed my father to live. Killing him would have served me no purpose. I may have cut his tongue and eyes out, but I wanted his third eye to see the evil prophecy of his son's wrath come to full fruition. Admitting him into Baker's and letting him sit in his own shit for twenty-six years was merely a bonus.

"And then there was my naive sister Rose who thought love could save me. I was living a semi-normal life interning at Baker's when she found me. Told me she was a seer and saw darkness would one day ignite within me. I would assault women and murder four of my victims. She foresaw those I murdered would bear my bastard children and would somehow find me before I took their lives. I contemplated Baker Acting her on the spot, but she intrigued me and knew of my past, so I let her go."

"But in the end, you did kill her."

"She left me no choice. When she realized exposing my future was precisely what ignited the darkness within me, she went to the NBI with hopes of stopping me. Lucky for me, she fell into the lap of an egotistical moron with a badge. She warned him of my future wrath, but he dismissed her as being insane.

"Instead of following up on Rose's predictions, Agent Kelly called me to come pick up my nutjob sister, his words, not mine. He strongly suggested I have her locked up." He chuckled. "It was quite perfect, really. He threw her right back into my hands, and I can assure you, that's the last time she ever tattled on me. Of course, one wouldn't be capable of tattling six feet under, would they? At least her family gave her a proper burial.

"I can't say the same for the incompetent agent, however." His tone turned spirited. "The Hudson River's really quite beautiful this time of year, you know. I'm not sure Kelly would agree, being at the bottom of it and all," he said, his words dripping with sarcasm.

"So, you killed him too?"

"It really is becoming quite exhausting filling in the blanks for you, Sheridan. Shouldn't it be the other way around, with you being gifted and all?" he jabbed. "When Kelly realized Rose's predictions had come to pass, he worried he would lose his badge, and more importantly, stain his flawless reputation. He could have prevented it all or at least followed up after I attacked my parents. But he never said a word until Meredith also paid him a visit, that is."

Sheridan's heart stung at the mention of her name. "Meredith?"

"Yes, your careless savior. Kelly was told not to touch a hair on her head. If he did, I would reveal all his misgivings and take him down with me, so he didn't. In a sense, he was my silent ally, I suppose. When Meredith's body was found on Lyle, he went as far as setting Providence on fire."

"Jesus, why?"

"To destroy any possible evidence that could lead back to her or my other victims' deaths."

"You said he's at the bottom of the Hudson River. Why kill him if he was such an asset to you?"

"Because the moron got sloppy. I wanted to meet my implicit ally in person. In fact, we met just today at his request. I realized what a liability he was when a private investigator showed up at his hotel asking questions. Kelly took care of the PI, and I took care of Kelly. Our meeting did turn out to be quite productive, however. The PI's cell phone held a wealth of interesting information, like the fact Derek's daddy is still alive."

"Derek's father," she whispered beneath her breath.

"Don't get too excited, my dear. I manipulated a surprise meeting between Charles and his nephew Brody, also an agent with the Bureau," he smirked then looked down at his watch. "If my calculations are correct, Charles is already behind bars," he gloated.

"You're insane," she hissed.

"Insane I may be, yet here I stand, thanks to our dear sweet Meredith, the saint and agile savior of all."

"Why not kill Meredith when you attacked her parents at their factory?" she provoked. When he cracked his neck again, she knew she'd struck a nerve.

"You mean my parents, Sheridan. Because they were mine," he stressed. "My father saw the light within Meredith, which is why he chose her over me. And because she took my life from me, I thought it only fair I make her gift my own. Embedding my life into her world before annihilating my parents took a little planning on my part, but in the end, I prevailed."

"How could she possibly allow someone like you in her life?"

"Providence Orphanage was renovated and reopened as Providence House. Meredith had history at Providence and wanted to give back to society. She became a volunteer in the neonatal ward, brought the bastard babies born there toys, and over time, became a member of the Board.

"All I had to do was play to her weakness, which was helping abused women and children. I simply presented myself as someone who wanted to give back. It was Meredith who graciously welcomed me into her nauseating world and did so with open arms. Over time, I became her confidant, friend, and after witnessing her mommy and daddy being slaughtered, her psychologist."

Fire rose to Sheridan's eyes. "She'd seen her parents massacred. You planned it so you'd be there to help her pick up the pieces. You knew she would become one of The Knowing. You put her on heavy doses of anti-anxiety medications and blocked her from seeing you in the future with hypnotherapy before she ignited the light. But you didn't stop there, did you, Anderson?"

Anderson's eyes grew wild behind his mask. "How? How do you know?"

"Because I am The Knowing. You think you're untouchable because you've managed to manipulate others' gifts to serve your own purpose."

Anderson pulled the mask from his face and threw it to the floor. "Feel free to enlighten me. I'd get to it before I finish what I started on Lyle, though. Of course, you don't even remember our last encounter, do you?" he asked, dropping the English accent he used to fool his victims and attempting to regain control.

"You planned to rape me just like you did your other victims," she said disgusted.

"Just like you, those bitches never saw it coming. And just like Rose predicted, four of my victims who bore my bastards found me. Do you know, not one of them had a clue it was me who'd taken them when I counseled them at Providence? Luring them away two weeks before they were ready to give birth was easy. Now, delivering their babies, on the other hand, was a bloodbath."

"My God, you butchered those women and then left their babies at Providence to fend for themselves!"

"Like father like son." Sheridan glanced down at the dagger in the shadow box and then back up to him.

"Now, now, Sheridan, you really must take me for a fool. Do you honestly think I haven't noticed you looking over my shoulder at the door? And now the dagger. What will you do with it? Kill me? Go ahead, the box isn't locked. Maybe you'll have better luck than your savior," he encouraged.

Sheridan knocked the case off the pedestal, grabbed the dagger, and held it in front of her chest with trembling hands.

"That's it, now we're ready to play," he taunted. "If nothing else, you've become feistier since we last met. Good for you," he mocked. He spread his arms out like wings. "Well, come on then. I'm all yours," he provoked.

"And what of your children, Anderson?"

"I left them at Providence to fend for themselves, and I never looked back."

Sheridan's mouth formed a cunning smile. "But, they did fend for themselves, and they did so gracefully, Anderson."

"How do you know this?"

She pointed to the labeled video tapes on the shelves. "Unlike Meredith, Derek, and the other children at Vista, I never went under hypnosis with you. You never used hypnotherapy to help any of them. Instead, you used it to lock away their memories of you and pull information from their gifts to make it appear you were gifted yourself."

Anderson began leisurely clapping. "So, the woodchuck from Lyle Mountain thinks she's figured it all out. I happen to know that even those gifted with the light of The Knowing are limited in what they are permitted to see. You couldn't possibly know my bastards didn't suffer," he accused.

"Oh, but I do, Anderson. With the exception of one child, Meredith found them all. Because each were gifted descendants of your father, Vista was born to give them a home, a chance."

Anderson's eyes grew wide. "No!"

Sheridan took a confident step toward Anderson with knowing eyes. "You killed your mother because she didn't recognize you at Providence. You're a hypocrite, Anderson. Your children were under the same roof at Vista with you for six years. Six years, and you didn't have a clue. Jesus, you even adopted Thomas, your own biological son," she berated.

"You're lying! You fucking bitch," he exploded then crashed his fist into Sheridan's face, no longer in control. The dagger fell from her hands, and she crumbled to the floor.

Sheridan whimpered then reached for the dagger teasing her trembling fingertips. Anderson scrambled for the dagger and thrust it just outside the door. "I'm done playing with you," he blared then picked her limp body up and thrust it back down onto the shadow box on the floor, shattering it to pieces. Her bloodcurdling screams echoed.

Anderson pounced on Sheridan, mangled and defenseless beneath him. "Tell me their names," he demanded with scowling eyes. Sheridan moaned.

"I said tell me," he charged again, pulling his fist back to strike her again.

"I'll fucking kill you!" Derek roared as he plunged into Anderson to knock him away from Sheridan.

They battled on the damp blood-stained floor, both exchanging wild blows. Derek found leverage and crushed Anderson's mortified face twice. As Derek pulled his fist back to strike him again, Anderson rolled over and pulled a revolver from his tuxedo jacket and pointed it at Sheridan. "Back up or I'll blow her fucking head off!"

Derek put his hands out in front of his chest and stood up. Anderson followed Derek's lead and pulled himself up from the floor. He glared into Derek's distressed eyes and turned the revolver to Derek's forehead. "You fucking people couldn't just let it go," he seethed.

"Derek," Sheridan sobbed.

"I'm fine, Sheridan. We're all fine," Derek assured.

"I beg to differ," Anderson debated, composed again now that he had the upper hand. He addressed Sheridan. "You will both die in this room, just as my bastards' mothers did, but not before you both tell me what I want to know." He shoved the revolver into Derek's head. "Understand that your cooperation will determine who goes first and the mercy I show you, or lack thereof."

"P-Please, don't hurt him. I'll tell you everything."

"That you will, but we'll start with you, Mr. Young," he said, now twisting the barrel into Derek's skull. "Your gifts, they came back, didn't they?"

"Yes."

"When?"

"Fully, three months ago. Before that, only recurring dreams."

"I guess my time counseling and consoling you after your mommy and daddy died didn't quite do the trick, did it?"

Derek pressed his head hard to the barrel with turbulent eyes. "I'm going to destroy you," he challenged.

"Careful now, Derek," he warned. "Who else knows about my identity?"

"No one," Derek lied. "I only figured it out when Sheridan went missing."

"How?"

"I had a vision of your house from one of the annual Vista barbecues we held here years ago," he continued to lie. "I came here for your help. I didn't know it was you until I heard Sheridan screaming."

"That's good," he said, convinced his identity was still protected. He looked over to Sheridan using the wall as a brace to drag herself up from the floor. "Stay where you are," Anderson ordered when Sheridan took a step toward them.

"O-Okay," she complied.

"Were you lying about my bastards living at Vista?"

"No."

"Besides Thomas, which of the other useless derelicts were mine?"

"I-I'm your great niece, Rose's granddaughter."

"What the hell are you talking about?"

"Rose had a son, William, my father, your nephew. Edward, your father, is my grandfather."

"So you're also a descendant of that infamous son of a bitch. That won't earn you any brownie points from me, bitch." Derek's eyes turned rabid.

"I don't think Derek here likes it when I call you naughty names," he taunted then spun Derek around to face Sheridan, whose cheek was swollen and forehead bleeding. "Tell me their names!"

"You don't see the light, do you, Anderson?" Sheridan asked in a soothing tone.

Anderson examined the room, but he couldn't see the soft lavender glow enveloping around her again.

"You must want him to die."

Trancelike, Sheridan walked toward Derek and Anderson and began naming the spirits now surrounding her. "They're here with us.

Your mother and father, Rose, Meredith, Clara, Gale, Julia, and Amanda, all victims of your hideous wrath."

Anderson's gun began shaking within his hand. "You're lying!" He walked backward toward the door, pulling Derek back with him, still holding him at gunpoint.

"They've forgiven your heinous crimes, Anderson, and bestow you the fortuity to rewrite your destined path. Take accountability for your venomous destruction and live, or allow your prewritten fate to diffuse the immoral light that burns within your malicious soul."

"I-I'll kill him, I swear."

Sheridan's tranquil eyes met Derek's uncertain stare. "You failed, Anderson," she chided. "Your children survived and overcame the pain and abuse you hoped they'd always suffer. The child Meredith couldn't save will also use her life for the prosperity of mankind."

Anderson pulled back the hammer of the revolver. Derek closed his defeated eyes and took in what he believed to be his last breath. "I love you, Sheridan," he whispered, not fearing death but mourning the life he'd never share with her.

Sheridan's confident eyes beamed at Anderson, her voice now thunderous. "Your children's names are VISTA: Vanessa, Ian, Sarah, Thomas, and A—" she managed before Anderson gasped.

Anderson's body stiffened, and his eyes bulged from their sockets as he stared into the cryptic abyss of the unknown. The revolver slid from his hand. His quivering lips parted as though he wanted to speak. The warm blood gagging him spilled from the corner of his mouth. His lifeless body fell forward, crashing hard to the concrete floor, exposing the beautiful Masonic dagger Abigail had planted firmly within his back.

"And your daughter Abigail," Sheridan finished, gazing at Abigail standing numb in the doorway, clutching the hand of the dangling doll Charles had given her at Baker's before saving her. Sirens could be heard in the distance as Brody and Charles burst into the room winded, both taken aback by the grisly scene before them.

Abigail stood silent as she glared down at her father's lifeless corpse. Her body jerked hard when Brody wrapped his jacket around her shuddering shoulders. "You're okay, Abigail. It's going to be okay," he coddled then walked her out of the disheveled room.

Charles addressed Derek. "You two okay?"

Derek looked down at Sheridan, now shaking, her battered face buried deep within his chest. "Yeah, we're fine," he replied, then kissed the top of Sheridan's head. "We're all going to be fine."

Chapter Forty-Two

*S*aturday, May 25, 2013

A CONTAGIOUS SYMPHONY of spirited laughter bustled outside Sheridan's childhood bedroom window. The harmony of everyone's vigorous moods inspired her to draw back the Victorian lace curtains to peek out at Rebecca's seventh birthday festivities. She laughed aloud at the animated commotion of Sheriff Lloyd chasing after Rhonda's high-jacked tractor mower and trailer. Andrew and Luke took turns fighting over the steering wheel while Charlie, Tamika, and Rebecca held on for dear life, all giggling as the trailer fishtailed.

Rodney, in true Rodney fashion, was wearing a flame red chef's hat and matching apron that read, 'Grill Master! The Man...The Myth... The Legend.' Charles, Walter, Quentin, Ian, and Blake hovered around the grill, advising Rodney on how not to burn the hamburgers or undercook the chicken. Vanessa, Lexus, Sarah, and Ashley were setting up the picnic tables. Rhonda and Maggie were bringing out platters of corn on the cob and southern style dishes of baked beans, potato salad, and coleslaw.

Brody doted over Nancy, pushing her on the old rustic rope swing hanging from a towering leafy white oak, stealing a kiss after every other thrust. Derek walked up behind Sheridan and wrapped his arms around her waist, kissed her cheek, then rested his chin upon her head.

"It's hard to believe this place was engrossed with such heavy despair, a breeding ground for unbalanced monsters."

"And now?"

Sheridan's eyes glazed over with blissful tears. "A home filled with love, laughter, new beginnings, and extended family." She grinned.

Derek brushed her cheek with a kiss. "It was you who created all of this, Sheridan," he whispered.

"I wish Thomas were here with us."

Derek caressed the side of her arms to comfort her. "His emotions are blended over the man who raised him and the man he now knows was a monster."

Sheridan tilted her chin up to Derek. "I just want him to know that none of this was his fault. He was a victim in all this too," she said then turned her attention back to the window.

"Vanessa, Ian, and Sarah are still grieving the tragic loss of their biological mothers."

"Thomas lost his mother too."

"But they were adopted by loving parents. Their closure comes a little easier. Thomas feels responsible for not knowing Anderson was a malicious imposter, so it's going to take longer for him to recover from this."

"I want him to know he's a part of this family too, that we're here to support him through this nightmare."

"Again, Sheridan, he just needs time."

"Time." She rubbed the skeleton key now hanging from her chain alongside the amethyst stone between her fingers. "So much of it has been ripped away from us, especially from you, your father—"

"My dad was acquitted. We have plenty of time to pick up where we left off."

"And Walter."

"My dad knew Kelly prevented Walt from retracting my dad's name as their prime suspect. Kelly is dead, and my dad has forgiven Walt."

Derek pointed out the window to Charles and Walt. "Look at them, they're fine. According to Nancy, Walt even went to an AA meeting last week. What about you, Sheridan? You've been put through unimaginable hell yourself."

"I'm fine."

"Exactly, Mona Lisa. I need you to believe we're all going to get through this."

Sheridan saw Abigail and Riley returning from their stroll down by the creek. She was smiling and holding a handful of wild purple irises she'd picked on their stroll. "It was a blessing Brody and your dad discovered her at Baker's."

"Had Anderson not told us Abigail had committed suicide, we would've never known it was Anderson. I could've lost you."

"But they found her. She saved our lives."

"Yeah, she did, and now I owe her my own. She's come a long way from when I first met her and Rebecca at her apartment." They watched Rebecca run up to Abigail and take her mother's hand. Abigail leaned down and placed a loving kiss on Rebecca's cheek.

A devoted smile formed on Sheridan's lips. "Rebecca may not speak, but she's going to be exceptional, quite exceptional, in fact. I'll make sure of it," she vowed. "After lunch, will you take a walk with me?"

"Of course."

"Good. Come on. Let's join the others."

🐍

DEREK ADMIRED Sheridan's glowing mood as they strolled down the familiar path she'd frequented to escape Hank's wrath. Derek's adoring smile turned uneasy as a vision flashed before him of Anderson lifting Sheridan as a child up into his arms. He pulled Sheridan back into the safety of his embrace. "Not another step," he cautioned.

"Derek, it's okay. I'm okay," she said, soothing, knowing what he'd seen.

"I'm taking you back to the house, now," he ordered sternly.

"Your mother's letter to your dad said, 'In the end, they'll follow her tranquil path to the harrowing bloodstone.'"

Sheridan knelt down to the ground and tugged on the unconstrained mountain rock she'd hit her head on sixteen years ago. Derek fell to his knees to help her. When he managed to move the hefty rugged rock to the side, they began digging into the earthy ground. The shallow grave revealed the antique case of Meredith's Masonic dagger. Sheridan brushed away the loose dirt from the case, pulled the skeleton key from her chain, and unlocked the box. Exposed within it was an isolated letter from Meredith, addressed to Derek and Sheridan. Their eyes met then fell to the handwritten letter.

🐲

DEREK AND SHERIDAN,

If you're reading my letter, my endeavors to realign the natural order will have come to full fruition. The destined paths of those chosen to protect the gifted child will have also shifted back to their natural courses. Your journeys, however, have just begun. We all search for our 'happily ever afters', but the truth, my loves, is that happily ever afters don't exist. There will always be monsters, cruel diseases, pain, and unimaginable suffering in the world. It is written, so it shall be.

There are consequences within every action and decision one makes, both good and bad. Karma determines whether one is punished or rewarded in this life or within reincarnation. God's will, and the child's, have unveiled my reward and permitted me to see pieces of my forthcoming journey. My time has come.

Sheridan, my love, there are others like you, whose art inspirations emerge from channeling spirits who communicate during one's sleep. Upon waking, they believe the messages and images revealed are merely dreams. Unknowingly, they pull from their battered subconscious and use art to recreate what they and others presume are figments of their imagination. Guide the child from your own experience. I have come to the end of my journey as The Knowing. While I will always be with you, it's now up to you to embrace the light you've ignited. It burns bright within you, Sheridan, it always has. You will often be challenged by distorted clarity, however, you have the strength and perseverance to guide and protect the child, to help her end so much pain and suffering through her compelling artistic interpretations of 'science'. Millions will be saved.

My final words to you both are filled only with love. Because you are human, you will make mistakes, face new demons, and endure devastating loss. You must accept they exist, confront the challenges, and learn from them.

True happiness derives from seeing the beauty in all things, both good and evil. The horrific tragedies you've both suffered up to this moment are what brought you together. In the end, your infinite love prevailed, and therein lies the beauty.

In truth, we all possess the light of The Knowing. We know the difference between right and wrong, good and evil, and love and hate. We each govern our own destinies. Each path taken is influenced by a conscious choice. In the end, love will prevail.

FOREVER AND ALWAYS,
    Love,
    Mom

P.S. Derek, yes is the answer you seek. Just breathe, my love, and know I am looking upon your engaging hearts, smiling.

A TEAR from Sheridan's cheek fell upon the letter, as she looked into Derek's eyes. "I will honor her, Derek. I will not fail."

Derek brushed the remaining tears that stained her face and fell to one knee. "I was going to wait until we walked back to the party, but this moment, this place, they're symbolic of how our hearts came to beat as one." Derek pulled an engagement ring case from his jean pocket, opened it, and displayed it before her.

"Derek," she said beneath her breath.

"You are my smile, my world, my forever. Your beautiful soul has opened my eyes to the possibility of all things. I've searched for you my whole life, and now that I've found you, Sheridan Parker Hayes, I ask you for the honor of being my wife. Will you marry me?"

"Yes, Derek," she sobbed. "I will marry you."

Derek rose to his feet and took a telling step toward her. His hands found her hips and pulled her into his arms. He leaned in closer and rested his forehead upon hers. "I love you, Sheridan," he said in a low and husky tone.

Sheridan met his amorous stare, leaned in closer, and began exploring the sweet taste of his inviting lips. "I love you too, Mr. Young," she moaned, surrendering to the illuminating bliss of their souls colliding.

They felt knowing eyes fall upon them. They turned to face the sound of rustling foliage behind them. It was Rebecca, looking upon them and smiling.

Epilogue

Kelly's beaten face slammed against the thick glass stained with spatters of his own drool. His crazed mental outbreaks within the padded room had been ignored for weeks, just as Rose's had. "Help me! I don't belong in here. It was him. He's the one who killed them all!" His arms were constrained within a blood-stained straitjacket, so he crashed his head against the narrow window to get someone's attention. "He's crazy! Let me out of here, please," he begged.

When Frances approached the door, Kelly became quiet and began shuddering, fearing he'd be sedated again. His silence was short-lived when he saw a man wearing a hoodie approach. "Hey, you. I-I need help. You have to help me. Please. I-I'm Agent K-Kelly," he slurred, his drug-induced words difficult to understand.

Frances handed the hooded man the key to Kelly's isolation room then walked away. Kelly pressed his face hard to the narrow window pane again, his anxious eyes bulging in desperation. "I don't belong here. He put me here—"

"Shut up. I know exactly who you are and what you've done, or should I say, failed to do," he said in a rigid tone. "If you'd listened to Rose and Meredith, none of this would've happened."

"You don't understand. I-I thought they were crazy fortunetellers, I didn't know. I swear."

"But, you knew they weren't crazy when what they predicted actually happened, didn't you?" he snapped.

"Y-Yes," Kelly sputtered.

"Your honesty holds no weight with me. You see, Kelly, I'm also what you call a crazy fortuneteller, so I have seen your deception. You knew who their killer was but said nothing to save your own ass. You could've prevented so many things from happening, helped him get the help he needed before he lost his mind."

"I-I'm sorry," Kelly pleaded, now sobbing.

"I said shut the hell up!" the man roared, then paused to gain his composure before he spoke again. He dangled the isolation room key in front of the window. "You have two options, Kelly. One, I throw this key away and let you rot in this hell hole. Or two, let everyone continue believing your body is at the bottom of the Hudson River and help me avenge him."

"A-Anything. I'll do anything," he agreed.

"I suspected you would," he said as he unlocked the door.

"Thank you," he sniffled when the man removed the straitjacket from him.

The man leaned in close to Kelly's face and glared at him through sinister eyes. "Try anything stupid or deceive me, and I'll destroy you. Do I make myself clear?"

"Y-Yes," Kelly agreed, his frightened eyes searching for any sign of who the man was. "Who are you?"

The man slid the hoodie away from his face and exposed his identity. "My name is Thomas, the son of the man you protected."

About the Author

As a freelance writer since 2001, Sarah Elmore, a Trigeminal Neuralgia survivor, has been published as a guest newspaper columnist featuring various humanitarian pieces. In her successful sixteen-year marketing career, she received numerous prestigious achievement awards.

Sarah was raised in North Port, Florida, where she currently resides with her two extraordinary children and husband, who's a dedicated firefighter. She has and continues to use her artistic talents and creativity to help support abuse and rape victims, cancer foundations, underprivileged children, and disabled veterans, all causes close to her heart.

She pulls from her own boundless life experience as it relates to love, devastating loss, disability and survival to illustrate that each path one takes in life is influenced by a conscious decision, and that in the end, we each govern our own destinies.

Visit my website here.

 facebook.com/BellamoreBooks

twitter.com/BellamoreBooks

Made in the USA
Columbia, SC
23 April 2019